BILL FREE

and the Twin Prime Sieve

J. W. Helkenberg

Helkenberg Publishing

Dedicated to all those who dare to dream.

CONTENTS

Title Page

Dedication

Bill Free And The Twin Prime Sieve   1

CHAPTER 1   2

CHAPTER 2   21

CHAPTER 3   36

CHAPTER 4   62

CHAPTER 5   85

CHAPTER 6   116

CHAPTER 7   134

CHAPTER 8   154

CHAPTER 9   179

CHAPTER 10   202

CHAPTER 11   227

CHAPTER 12   251

CHAPTER 13   270

CHAPTER 14   300

CHAPTER 15   341

Books By This Author   351

BILL FREE AND THE TWIN PRIME SIEVE

A scientific novel
by J. W. Helkenberg

CHAPTER 1

High above the clouds glistening in early morning sunlight a dirigible drifted with the prevailing winds. Resembling an upside-down Stingray, its long retractable tail was picking up electric charge as it dragged through the atmosphere. At an altitude of over 100,000 feet the large airship was effectively invisible to any observer located in the Gulf of Aden below. It was not, however, invisible to military-grade radar systems.

Located on the belly of the airship was a substantial command center with 360 degree windows and a large see-through augmented-reality floor. Next to the glass floor and starkly out of character with the overall minimalist design of the space was a 4-post brass bed. Beneath the covers slept a young adult.

A red light started rotating above the front wall of windows. An alarm bell sounded and a robotic female voice warned, "Attack detected. Four surface-to-air missiles inbound. Defensive measures engaged."

The sleepy teenager rolled over and looked down on the world through the glass floor. He saw four faintly glowing balls of fire steadily approaching him from below. He watched as the automated defense system released numerous hawk-shaped glide bombs. These fell from bays located beneath the ship and accelerated on an intercept course toward the blobs of light. He watched as the glide bombs exploded, sending a spray of shrapnel into the missiles, disabling them.

"They wouldn't have made it this high anyway," he said aloud in a groggy voice. He then rolled over and went back to sleep.

######## ERIC JOHNSON ########

Eric Johnson exuded confidence. As a successful writer living a wonderful life he perceived no threats to his well-being. So when he walked into Green Man Coffee he did so without a care in the world. He ordered a drink and seated himself at a high table in the back of the room. He was excited to begin.

-

So. Here I sit. Writing by hand for the first time in over a month. It is hard to hold a thought. Too many electronic distractions. We definitely live in a distracted time. I can SPEAK clearly, but writing is harder. Less forgiving.

-

Eric looked up from his notebook and observed the people around him. He decided to eavesdrop on a conversation between a young man and woman seated at a nearby table. The woman was looking down at her coffee while the man appeared unsure of himself. Finally he got the courage to say, "Been a while, hasn't it?"

She looked up from her coffee. "Yeah, it has been a minute."

"Where have you been?"

She responded, "In the middle of nowhere completing my residency requirements at a small county hospital. Some place where dreams go to die, apparently. Once upon a time I thought I knew where I was going and what the world was supposed to be like 'when I grew up.' Now I see how foolish that was. What I thought I knew got run over by what I learned."

The man laughed and responded, "You know what they say, if you want to make God laugh make a plan."

"Yeah," she laughed sarcastically, pointing a finger gun at him. Pulling the trigger and winking she continued, "You can say that again."

He became more serious, "So where to now?"

She thought for a moment and replied, "Well, unlike before, where my time was consumed by school and work commitments, I am now free to explore. I have no idea where I will go or what I will do aside from the fact I will eventually need to get a job and go do that 'adult life' stuff again."

He looked a bit jealous and said, "Not the worst place to be."

She agreed. "Yeah, well, I also have some baggage to shed. Some of my 'commitments' must come to an ignominious end. It won't be easy and yet it will be."

In a somewhat snarky tone the man replied, "Good luck with that. Or should I say, break a leg?"

Betraying no offense she replied, "It will be a performance. That much I can promise you."

Eric turned back to his thoughts. He felt good knowing he had achieved some material success. But he was not 'known' as a writer. Not like the famous authors of his time. His work 'Modern Processes' was purchased by a movie studio and used as the basis for a hit series. The farmer from his story was replaced with a teacher and the setting went from a farm to a desert. Other changes were made.

After his success he started to receive invitations to speak with emerging writers about marketing and what to look for in media contracts. It was widely reported in the trade press that his decision to select a royalty payment versus a one time payout had proven to be an intelligent move and was a model for other writers looking to sell their ideas. He didn't want to admit that luck was the primary factor in his success so he never mentioned the details surrounding his agent. At any rate, his lectures were not well attended and the invitations stopped coming. He seemed to lack some vital spark that would attract audiences to his ideas.

"The 'Odd Couple' was a hugely popular play and movie and it earned the author practically nothing," he warned aspiring writers. His publisher had given him a $250,000 advance and this was automatically paid off as part of his licensing agreement with the studio. Due to his association with the show his book achieved moderately good sales, but the title did not achieve sustainable best-seller status and the publisher had a few chargebacks from unsold books. Despite these shortcomings his book sales were sufficient to sustain his lifestyle until the royalty revenue began to flow. He knew if he wanted to be taken seriously by his contemporaries and the public at large he would need to write more novel-length works. *"I need more than one success to my name,"* he warned himself.

Eric, having more money in his bank account than most people would see in a lifetime, was languishing. Words wouldn't flow onto the paper. There was no soul in his pen. No amount of money could fix that. Or, so he thought.

######## MARSHALL HAMMOND ########

Marshall Hammond woke up in a hospital bed. He had no idea how long he had been unconscious. Memory flooded into his mind. He returned to the city to visit his mother. By doing so he was fulfilling his promise to her that he would come home again before his 18th birthday. He remembered a man punching him while his mom looked on from the kitchen doorway.

He glanced around the hospital room and realized he had a heart monitor attached to his finger. "How long have I been here?" he whispered to himself while looking around. He had a groggy memory of someone interviewing him, offering him some kind of experimental treatment, but he was unsure if it was a dream or a real experience. At the end of his bed was a clipboard. He reached over and grabbed it. Gripping it tighter as he read he growled, "Motherfuckers. Not. Yet. An. Adult? Hold for treatment. That is bullshit!" His vision blurred with rage. "Adult in all the important ways," he exhaled with a hiss. His protests were useless; being only 17 years of age he had no legal authority over himself.

"Fuck that," he said aloud, tossing the clipboard onto the bed. Marshall decided to escape the hospital. In the bed adjacent to his was an older man who was unconscious and appeared to be on life support. Marshall attached his heart monitor to one of the man's free fingers. He then went to his dresser at the end of the room. His clothes were gone, but he did find his shoes. He searched through the adjacent dresser and found the man's clothes. "You won't be needing these any time soon," he said as he grabbed a pair of pants and a collared shirt. He took an oversized coat from a chair beside the comatose man. Inside the coat he found a pair of sunglasses. Overdressed for the weather, wearing sunglasses at dawn, he exited the building via the front door. He walked several miles to a location deep in the woods near the Missouri river.

Before visiting his mother he hid a tote containing a backpack, cash, debit cards, a fake ID, clothes, shoes, and freeze dried food. His stash was located beneath a majestic Black Oak tree. *"The monitoring systems are really good,"* he thought to himself after he changed into his own clothes. *"No way I won't be found on the highways if they have a good image of me and do a runaway alert. I've got to adapt."*

He went to a thrift store and bought two dresses and a large sun hat. He made his way to an industrial warehouse where large piles of clothes were mixed up with old shoes and handbags. Everything was sold by weight. He found an ID badge and a social security card hidden in the bottom panel of a purse.

"Marcia," she said into a mirror as she looked at herself in a sundress and a large hat.

She left and went to a moped dealership.

The men at the lot were all thirsty and she was a petite glass of water.

"Marcia Martinez?" the man asked her skeptically.

"My dad is from Mexico, but I am adopted. So my name is Martinez," she lied.

"Ahh!" the man winked. He did not believe the story that her car and wallet were stolen and her only identifying documents were a very old looking work badge and social security card. But he also wanted to make a sale and she was offering to pay the full amount in cash. The dealership also sold moped insurance, so she purchased that as well. She would immediately receive a 60-day temporary tag.

"So... you want the full year of insurance?" the man asked.

"Nope. Just the six month policy. And I have the cash right here." Marshall pushed a stack of bills to the man. "You can keep the change as a tip if you can help speed this along."

"Cash is King," the salesman replied, smiling. "We'll get you your 60 day tag and insurance paperwork. You'll be on the road in under 30 minutes!"

"Thanks," she replied.

She drove away on her 350cc scooter. Her full face carbon fiber helmet was dark gray. She disappeared.

"*I can't be seen,*" Marshall thought while changing out of the dress and back into his jeans and t-shirt. He was in a bathroom in a public park. "*I need a disguise... and a plan.*" The park was a familiar place for Marshall. Whenever he wanted to be alone with his thoughts he would walk the grounds of the multi-acre rose garden. As he contemplated his next move he noticed a group of people playing drums beneath a canopy of large Evergreen trees.

"*Hippies,*" he calculated as he approached.

He sat down among the group and listened to their conversations.

"We need gas money to get there!" he overheard a young female hippie lament to her male entourage. "We don't have enough cash to make it to the gathering!"

"We can get cash on the road..." one of her male friends began pleading.

"No! We tried that last time and got stranded in Arkansas. Remember? I am not driving again without knowing I have enough to get there and back again. My dad will disown me if he has to bail me out. He won't accept me trying to 'spange' my way to another Gathering!" she yelled with exasperation and disappointment in her voice.

Whispering obscenities beneath their breath the male

hippies got up and left. Marshall scooted closer to the young woman.

"Kinda jerks," Marshall said about the departed men, pointing at them with his thumb.

"Yeah. They want to go to the Rainbow Gathering, but they don't have any cash and so they want me to be their mommy and I refuse to go through that again!" Making a sign of a rainbow over her head with flair she said in the direction of the men, "Magical thinking is bullshit."

"So..." Marshall began cautiously. "How much cash would it take to go there and back again?"

"At least $600," she replied in a huff. "I want to go, but obviously I can't afford it."

"I see." Marshall said with a hint of curiosity. "So what exactly is a Rainbow Gathering?"

The girl went into great detail about how the festival was started as a prayer for global peace. "Thousands of people from all over America and the world attend to join hands in a great circle and 'Om' together on the 4th of July." She explained how all the food would be provided free of charge by a large network of makeshift kitchens spread throughout the forest. Meanwhile everyone lives together in a communal setting. "Welcome home!" she said with a dreamy, far-away look in her eyes. "That is what we say to each other as a greeting because we are all at home together, all as one people living in peace and harmony."

Marshall was surprised. "Sounds like an interesting place for sure," he said with encouraging eyes.

"Oh it is! Magical! Truly magical!" she exclaimed like an addict recollecting her last fix. "But traveling with a bunch of broke dudes who need you to take care of them makes it lame. Literal Drainbows."

Marshall laughed. "Drainbows?"

"Yeah. Loser hippies who are a drag."

"I want to go," Marshall said. "I have gas money. What say just you and I take off and do this thing?"

"Seriously?" the girl asked, getting excited.

"Yeah I am 100% serious," Marshall replied. "How soon do you think we can leave?"

The girl looked around for the guys, but they were off hunting for a ride. "How about right now? I mean, I am staying at my dad's house and so I don't have rent or anything. I just did my laundry and I have clean clothes in my van."

"Let's do it!" Marshall said.

"You really have the cash?"

"Here," Marshall said, taking out his wallet. He removed $600. "Go ahead. Take this. It is $600. That way you know ahead of time that you have the money and I am not holding power over you."

She was ecstatic when she saw the funds. "No," she said happily, looking around to make sure none of the other people had seen Marshall opening his wallet. "You keep it. Just pay for gas and maybe some food on the way. We won't need money once we get there."

"Really!?" Marshall was surprised. She had mentioned the free food and the kitchens that have what you need 24 hours per day, but was having a difficult time imagining not needing money at a festival.

"Yeah. Money is forbidden as a means of exchange. It is barter only. But if we take stuff with us we can barter on Shakedown Street or The Row. So we will definitely want to buy some cigarettes. For trade. People get really desperate for tobacco and will offer you almost anything for that nicotine fix."

"Noted," Marshall said, making some mental calculations. He then handed her $100 on the sly. "For you, to show thanks." They got up and started walking toward the parking lot.

Marshall looked at the van. "This is like a box truck," he said excitedly. "Do you think I can park my moped inside it and take it with us?"

"I don't see why not. It has this ramp that drops down. My dad buys old rental moving vans for his construction business and so I got this one. It runs really well and I can put a lot of stuff in it and lock it up. It just expensive to drive."

Marshall was shocked at his luck. He was going to leave the scooter at an industrial property owned by his friend Milton Stern. He had planned to drop it off on the way out of town, but now that he could load it into her van he was excited to depart.

"I am Jenny, by the way. But everyone calls me Hippie Girl," she said as they climbed into her van.

"Yeah we haven't even formally introduced ourselves to each other! Everyone calls me Marshmellow," Marshall lied. "Pleasure to meet you!"

######## MILTON STERN ########

Milton Stern woke up in a cave near Cerro Pinaculo Mountain in southern Argentina. On his computer he watched video footage of men raiding his farm. He watched them break into his house and start tearing things apart. He marked the timestamp when he started emptying his tanks of oxygen and hydrogen; rapidly the fuel tanks for his zeppelins poured into the atmosphere creating a fuel-air bomb. He watched on the video screen as a mushroom cloud rose up from the land, flattening everything.

Milton was angry, but also a little afraid. Someone with significant resources clearly wanted him dead. He could no longer rely on the shield of his American citizenship because he had enemies in Washington, DC. To get his mind off the destruction of his home and custom airships he set up a camp stove and boiled water. He made instant coffee. "Sure do wish I'd thought of having creamer," he muttered to himself as he stared at his reflection in the cup.

Meanwhile his partner Jebediah was running vulnerability scans on their infrastructure. He wrote a geolocation program to associate probing attack IP addresses with physical locations on Earth. He saw a large concentration of sophisticated access attempts coming from North Africa.

"*Odd,*" he thought to himself as he researched the locations.

Additional high elevation drones were launched after the explosion and were scanning near their critical infrastructure in Brazil. Jebediah was confident the attack was in response to their international drug sales. They had certainly been taking huge sums of money from someone. It was for this reason he was busy testing an alternative.

He discovered a drug delivery system that employed O2 nuclear spin manipulation to alter consciousness. For an untrained person it would appear as literal magic. The ability to generate an authentic drug experience using only light, a sample of the drug, and spin-entangled water molecules made the drugs untraceable, invisible, non-existent until activated.

His beta testing process began with violently microwaving one liter of water. He then split the microwaved water into two equal parts. One part was sent out to a consumer and the remaining part was stored on a shelf in a warehouse. The consumer logs into a gaming website and chooses from an array of magic potions. Once the potion is selected the user drinks the water. Within 30 minutes of a verified transaction the user begins to experience the full effects of the chosen substance(s).

Jebediah was close to realizing his finished product when Milton's home was raided by mercenaries.

######## WAITRESS ########

Sometimes people lose momentum in one area of life and gain it in another. This is true of writing. Sometimes writers struggle to come up with good ideas and would therefore prefer distractions. Other times nothing can distract them from their focus.

This behavior has a tendency to make the writer at times seem increasingly unapproachable as they disappear into their work or frustration. This personality change resembles the operation of an ON/OFF switch. Most people can't handle the night and day changes to personality and end up abandoning writers. It is a healthy self-defense mechanism.

The Waitress could handle it, though. In her days of serving she had encountered myriad personality types. She had precognition; she could hear the demands of the people seated at her tables before they spoke. Based on subtle cues and hat-trick hand movements she manipulated even the most hardened customers into having a good time.

When she briefly dated Maxwell Pragmatic it was the only time in her life she felt as if she was detecting pure... chaos. Her interest in him stemmed from her inability to pin down exactly *what* he was. Despite her curiosity she rarely thought about him. It was Eric she cared about now. She was willing to do anything in her power to help him. The two of them were tumbling together through space while Maxwell was more like a comet that is rarely seen and only around for a blink.

The Waitress studied people and wanted to learn how to modify their emotions and desires. She felt life could be explained as an experience of patterns and that with sufficient wisdom people can see patterns before they emerge. "We have power over our lives insofar as we can see and modify our habits."

It was a slow day at the restaurant when the Waitress struck up a conversation with the new hostess. They started talking about men, how simple they are and how much they love the attention of beautiful women. They conversed about how to manage and manipulate them via flirting and sex. "Most men are just levers and switches and knowing how to give them what they want translates into an easy life. If you can handle all that attention and money," the young hostess remarked. The waitress was surprised to hear someone so young speak authoritatively about the subject.

"I am a sugar baby," the young woman admitted in a secretive tone. "I work in places like this to meet successful men who are stuck in bad relationships. I can recognize the frustration on their faces and I know how to relieve their boredom and anxiety. I don't consider it being a whore, more like I am a therapist who is helping these guys get better at what they do. I help them renew their spirit of youth and vitality. I don't plan on doing this forever, because I won't be this hot forever and I know it. I plan to do this just long enough to finish paying off my car and condo and maybe, if things go well, enough money to be able to live off interest and travel."

The Waitress was amazed. "How did you find out about this lifestyle?" she asked, truly curious.

The young woman explained that she had a friend who was an online sex worker. "Carrie would meet these guys who would pay her for private cam shows and offered her a lot of money to meet up with them. That is when I realized I needed to look at this more closely. My mom was hot when she was young and she ended up working her life away at a meatpacking plant. What a waste of a life. If everyone is going to look at me as a sex object I might as well make that bread. But I didn't want to be online, so I am doing it more discreetly. I am all about the connections."

It dawned on the Waitress that Eric was missing the thrill of conquest. "So these men are unhappily married and you help them find what they are missing in life?" she asked.

"Not all of them are unhappy. They just need a break from the monotony of monogamy. Imagine being with the same person for the rest of your life. Like wearing the same clothes or eating the same food every day. It doesn't matter how awesome it is, the need for a change becomes the dominant force. And that is where I come in. These guys fall head over heels for me. Most of them end up being happier at home and it actually restores their relationships. That is why I feel good about what I do. It is actually helping these guys, not hurting them. I have seen grown ass men cry and tell me that I have saved their life. Not playing."

In the deep recesses of her brain the Waitress began formulating a plan.

As a result of several years spent working at high end

restaurants the Waitress encountered and befriended a large number of very wealthy men. She usually flirted with them because that ensured much higher tips. She overheard their conversations about investments and used that information to make strategic purchases of stock and other financial instruments. Because Eric allowed her to live bill free she was able to bet all of her earnings on a few highly speculative investments. Some of her picks skyrocketed in value and she became obscenely rich. A whale. All because of Eric.

She wanted to help him. But part of her sensed that she could do more than just help one man. She could help both women and men make the most of their lives. By weaving them together to form a new pattern.

She met young hostesses who worked at several area restaurants. She inquired about their willingness to work with men, to provide them with experiences, for money. "It is a bit like acting class," she explained to a young woman at a coffee shop. "I will help you manage your future success so you can retire early and live the rest of your best life."

Most women accept they are regarded as sex objects by the majority of straight men they encounter. Women are an obsession for many men. "Why not capitalize on that?" she asked the young blonde she met at an elite restaurant. "You are unbelievably gorgeous. I see it. You bend space-time. Use that to launch yourself."

The money was orders of magnitude better than any other job opportunity and would make her richer than her parents in a few short years. But it involved sex, intimacy. "I AM interested," the young woman replied. "But I am also a bit intimidated. This is so new to me. It is astonishing."

The Waitress wanted to learn everything there was to know about the business of selling this form of therapy. So she curated important relationships and connections; she met beautiful and intelligent girls who were desperate for an escape from the rat race. "I have an idea for an ice breaker, an assignment that will be relatively simple and you can use that to determine if you want to continue or not."

The young woman was excited to escape the mind-numbing ordinariness of her life. "Okay. I am in. Let's do it."

######## MAXWELL PRAGMATIC ########

Maxwell Pragmatic was a man on the run. Wanted by the US government on espionage charges, it was best for him to disappear. He took his old name, William Free, and a special arrangement allowed him to get a Canadian passport. He escaped the United States on a cargo ship that set sail from Los Angeles and disembarked in Faro de Manta, Ecuador. He was admitted to the country as a tourist. His destination was Rio Branco, Brazil. On his way there he made a point to stop in Peru to see the ruins of Machu Picchu.

When he arrived he expected to find the usual historical information he had come to expect from American national parks. But this was different from anything he had ever experienced. He made his way to the top of Machu Picchu and found that many of the stone relics were impossibly large or impossibly precisely cut. Crudely stacked stones were added on top of these massive blocks. They stood out in his mind as out-of-place artifacts, things that do not belong where they have been found. Things whose explanations are not convincing.

Maxwell tried to imagine malnourished people moving the massive stones and thought, "*The idea that a people who had not yet discovered the wheel were somehow capable of moving 50-ton stones... stone age people cutting granite blocks with laser precision and then setting them into three-dimensional interlocking patterns. Huh?*" It was simply too much for Maxwell to accept; he felt confident the artifacts implied the existence of a forgotten technology. "*Is the whole story a lie?*" he wondered as he read the information pamphlet.

"*The big chunks of stone in the debris field are the relics, the artifacts!*" Maxwell exclaimed inwardly. "*The people who discovered this recognized the magnificence of the previous culture. This is a sanctuary that honors the broken stones scattered throughout the complex. They knew something absolutely massive existed here in the past. Ancient past."* Scorch marks on some of the stones implied intense heat had been applied.

He wanted to know if there was any similar stonework in the nearby town. He found walls with impossible masonry. *"There is a history that has been hidden from the world. I can feel it, deep inside, like some part of my mind has decided it will not let go of the sensation. This is an eyes-wide-shut type conspiracy."*

Maxwell located a tourist-trap coffee shop and began writing in his journal: "The voice that speaks while the tongue remains still. What is that!? We clearly think in a language, the same language we use to speak."

He overheard a man mentioning the impossible quality of the stone work. Maxwell introduced himself and invited the man to have a seat at his table. They spoke about ancient lost civilizations. The man had traveled extensively throughout the world investigating megalithic sites. He introduced himself to Maxwell as Brien Foerster, the operator of Hidden Inca Tours. "It is an impossibility that primitive people made these constructions," Maxwell concurred with Brien. The man stated that such a worldview was likely incompatible with Christianity and that there is surprising resistance to the idea of an ancient culture that predates the flood stories.

Maxwell replied that in the original translation of Genesis it states that 'the world was void' which means 'destroyed' not empty. "A voided check as opposed to the void of space; destructive void not empty void."

Maxwell was glad to know he wasn't the only person to suspect some details might be missing from history books. He knew from research that when President Kennedy was assassinated there were American bases in Canada that were attacked. "The CIA knows its stuff I guess?" Maxwell offered. The man laughed and gave him a list of important megalithic sites. "This is just the beginning," the man said as he exited the coffee shop.

Maxwell spent several days exploring nearby sites from the man's list. He drove to Sayacmarca, Chachabamba, Torontoy Ruins, Inka Watana, Inka Misana, Qelloraqay, Ollantaytambo, Pinkuylluna, Capilla Cruz Xroax, Monty Xroax, Tambomachay, Cueva Tambomachay, Puka Pukara, Zona X, Qhalispuqyo, Q'enqo Chico, Qapaq Nam, K'allachaka, Saqsaywaman.

It was in Saqsaywaman where all doubt was ablated. He walked in stunned silence. "OK. This is really something," he said aloud as he looked up at the towering walls of stone.

######## MILTON ########

Following the destruction of his home Milton chose to spend a few days at his small underground bunker in the mountains. He had enough food to last several months. Freeze dried and capable of lasting 25 years. He received more video of the explosion, saw the helicopter that flew in and surveyed the destruction. It had civilian markings, but the resolution was insufficient to make a reading of call letters. He would analyze it when he joined Jebediah and could get access to the source file. He was currently working with highly compressed versions.

Very powerful people wanted to kill Jebediah and Milton. But, they were proving hard to hit.

Milton was supposed to be the easiest target, but things had not gone according to plan. No one realized Milton had a self-destruct platform that would wipe away all traces of their mercenaries. Milton reviewed his plan to get to Brazil. He thought, *"I don't want to appear anywhere for as long as possible. I can claim I was in the forest and the hydrogen leak monitor failed. So if I can get into Brazil unnoticed I can get picked up by Jebediah without making any waves. But a rescue effort now would be too obvious and expose too many people to risk."*

He had a hiking path plotted and packed enough freeze dried food to last up to two weeks. As a last resort he also carried a satellite phone that he could activate. *"Depending on who is trying to kill me, if I use this I might instantly appear as a target,"* he thought to himself.

Milton was hiking Southeast on an unmarked trail that followed a mountain stream. He reviewed his waypoints on his wristwatch.

50°46'41.1"S 72°14'12.4"W : 37X96QC7+Q7
50°48'03.9"S 72°10'38.2"W : 37X95RXF+H3
50°47'58.0"S 72°09'03.0"W : 37X96R2X+6M
50°48'07.7"S 72°07'55.0"W : 37X95VX9+46
50°48'19.1"S 72°06'05.6"W : 37X95VVX+V9
50°49'07.8"S 72°04'02.3"W : 37X95WJM+F3
50°50'32.4"S 71°57'00.3"W : 37XC525X+3X
50°52'00.0"S 71°56'09.5"W : 37XC43M7+8J
50°52'13.4"S 71°49'34.3"W : 37XC45HF+RG
51°02'49.9"S 71°48'01.7"W : X53X+4RC

On the second day of hiking he made it to the main road that he planned to follow North. After about 45 minutes of walking on Road 7 he heard a car in front of him. There was nowhere he could hide. He reached into his vest pocket and released the safety on his handgun. He was prepared to use lethal force should the need arise.

He could hear music emanating from the approaching white 1982 Mercedes 240d, "… I need to fuck more and bitch less…. I need to fuck more and bitch less…. I need to fuck more and bitch less…"

Maxwell pulled up alongside Milton and turned down the music. "Hello! I am looking for a gentleman named Milton Stern and he matches your description."

Milton's heart skipped he beat. He gripped the gun in his vest pocket. "Why are you looking for him?" he asked Maxwell.

"I am friends with Jebediah Northcutt and I was given a pin to a nearby location and so I was driving down to meet you, I mean him, when I saw his house explode. I am Maxwell. Maxwell Pragmatic." Maxwell extended a hand out of the window to shake hands. "Well, technically I am William

Free as that is what my ID and passport say. But I am your information broker! The guy who gets you all the scientific journal articles for the airships and hydrogen gas systems and whatnot."

Milton knew Maxwell only in the abstract. His anxiety was not alleviated. He became more suspicious. "Why didn't Jebediah tell me you were on the way here?" he growled.

"Um..." Maxwell hesitated. He realized Milton was extremely stressed. "Hey, I am not sure why he didn't tell you, other than the fact it was stated in passing and he dropped this 50°53'36.3"S 72°12'57.4"W

pin to me without an afterthought. I am on my way to a mine at the Perito Moreno Glacier. To meet Dr. Jaz Kastas. I saw your place explode from the turnoff on Highway 40. It was amazing and terrible. Hydrogen, right? Did your tanks leak? I saw a helicopter come in after the explosion. So anyway I stayed with Jebediah, in his place outside Piramide2, Brazil.

4°46'19.4"S 65°38'36.0W

He flew me out there. Look," Maxwell grabbed a sweetgrass braid from the dashboard of his car. "He told me to give this to you IF I saw you."

Milton saw the sweetgrass braid and knew it was a sign. All of his tension went away. Milton sighed with relief. "Well, I need to go North, so unfortunately we are heading in opposite directions," he said.

"Hey, if you don't mind a few detours along the way I can delay my trip south. There are some things I need to go check out. Some things that don't make sense to me. I know you are a brilliant dude and so I want to get your opinion on some megalithic ruins. They are pretty much on our way to Rio Branco. I assume that is where you are headed?"

Milton got into the car. "Yep. That is the place."

"The future must be able to influence the past if parts of the future are inevitable," Maxwell proposed to Milton. "It was inevitable we would meet at this exact moment. So, forces beyond our control regulate certain or maybe all of the communications infrastructure. So we probably need to disappear. I propose we are just some tourists from Canada!" Maxwell spun the Canadian Maple Leaf air freshener that was hanging from his rear-view mirror.

Milton wondered how he achieved a state of calm having only moments before been close to shooting someone. Maxwell hit a red button on his dashboard that activated his stereo to select a song based on a variety of environmental factors, including recent voice stress analysis.

The radio began playing a vaporwave version of Howard Jones – "Things Can Only Get Better."
Maxwell smiled inwardly. They would arrive soon enough in Brazil. Maxwell thought back on his time with Jebediah deep in the Brazilian rainforest. How it reminded him of his time with the Sundancers of Crow Dog's Paradise.

"Wait until you see the artifacts I am going to show you!" Maxwell said with excitement in his voice. "You will either feel as confused as I do or you will have a way to explain it to me that answers all my questions!"

Milton nodded with pursed lips and slightly squinted eyes. Maxwell understood this to be an expression of doubt. "*A healthy and appropriate response when presented with any evidence-free conspiracy theory,*" he thought to himself. Yet, seeing Milton's skepticism excited him even more.

"*His mind will be blown,*" Maxwell thought as he drove North.

CHAPTER 2

Indecorous truth: She was an unexpected breath of fresh air in an otherwise stale room. Walking in she could feel the eyes of the men upon her. Like lions stalking a gazelle, she knew she was the prey.

She reveled in it.

Feeling the teeth bite down on her neck. Feeling the powerful hands grasp her and force her onto the bed, the table, the floor. She could sense when the transformation occurred. She could detect when reason left and was replaced by pure animal lust.

It was a power she knew how to use. For as long as it lasts.

The first time it hit her she was alone in a classroom working on a poster. She was an exceptional student; one who possessed the rare talent of being able to speak and act with wisdom beyond her years. Her fingers found themselves probing the wetness between her legs as an image of her father appeared in her mind's eye. She saw him, muscles bulging, hairy and strong, watching over her. She plunged her fingers deeper and faster into herself as she imagined him unzipping his pants revealing his thick, throbbing cock. She imagined him climbing on top of her, pressing his full weight against her as he forced his way into her.

"Ohhhh....." she whimpered. "It is so big..."

She could sense his excitement build with every thrust into her. She spread her legs as far as she could, her small body taking the full pressure of a strong man.

Fingers exploring. Rapidly in and out. She wanted her father to fill her with cum. "Daddy," she whispered into his ear.

"I want you to cum in me so bad."

He was sweating as his thrusts increased in speed and ferocity. "Fuck me daddy. Fuck my tight little pussy as hard as you can. You are sooo biiiig...." she moaned as her body quaked with the force of an orgasm.

It all started when she was a young child. At the age of 4 her father was arrested and jailed. When he walked back into his daughter's life she was not yet 14. When she saw him walk through the door she immediately felt herself get warm inside. He lifted weights and grew bigger and stronger while in jail. She wanted to please him, this father-stranger, and give him joy. His strong arms wrapped themselves around her slender body; she felt protected and loved. She felt like she wanted to meld with him and become a single entity. If all her skin could touch him at the same time it would fulfill a dream.

Some obsessions are healthy. Or, at least, not completely harmful. However, some can take on a character of destruction.

Because life isn't simple.

It was never simple for her. She yearned for sex. Her libido could easily rival any teenage boy. She acted upon it.

Having only bad male role models from ages 5 to 13 she grew up experiencing the devastating impact the absence of a strong father has on a family. She saw a connection between herself, her father, and the happiness she had known when she was a small child. When he returned to his family his budding daughter could recall only fond memories of him. She was excited to have him back in her life.

Her mother and older sister had different memories. They knew him to be a mean and at times dangerous felon. She only remembered his strong arms picking her up when she fell. She remembered him cuddling with her when she was scared. When he left there was no one to protect her from things in the night. There was no one to comfort her when she fell. No one there to stop her first sexual encounter before it happened.

For her, the sudden arrival of a strong male stranger

turbocharged her recently-emerged primal desire for love and protection. She hung on his every word. Her mother and older sister seemed to tolerate, but not love, her father.

"A woman needs to keep her man satisfied," her dad explained to her. "A woman should give a man a blow job every damn day. Not pleasing your man sexually is a crime. It's bullshit."

She took mental notes. She encoded every word. These were things he could never say to his wife or step-daughter, but she was in love with him and she agreed with everything he said.

"*I would suck your cock every day*," she thought to herself. "*I would let you fuck me any time you wanted.*" She hoped he could hear her thoughts, but he betrayed no awareness.

As weeks became months she could sense his mounting sexual frustration. Her mother was clearly a poor lover and never offered herself to him. She started to see how it was making him angrier and it made her fear she might lose him again.

The thought of her father disappearing a second time because her mother refused to offer him sexual gratification made her extremely angry. "Dad," she asked him one day, "Have you ever thought about meeting someone just to have sex with?"

He grew tense. "Yeah. But I just got out of jail and I have you and your sister to take care of," he replied, honestly. "You mom at least cooks and does some cleaning. I don't trust her not to try to divorce me and ruin my life. I need to play it straight."

She wanted so badly to tell him that she would suck his cock, that he could have her any time he wanted. She knew she could please him, was confident that all the things men enjoy she could provide. She WANTED to do it. Her pants grew wet as she thought about making him feel good. Providing that for him. Hearing him make that sound men make when they explode.

######## MAXWELL ########

Maxwell drive toward Lake Titicaca in Peru. The first site they visited was Puma Punku. "Some of the stones that are sticking out of the ground around here appear to be precisely cut, but they are randomly scattered. Like maybe this place was hit by some kind of disaster?"

Milton looked at finely cut H-block shaped stones. They had internal high precision cuts on their faces which made them appear to be machined using a pattern, but each stone possessed unique dimensions. The surfaces were absolutely flat. They were not particularly large blocks, but they were incredibly smooth and regular. He then noticed humongous stones in the ground. Each large stone had a few small knob-shaped protrusions jutting out from different locations on their surfaces.

"How did they move these?" Maxwell asked.

"Yeah, I have no idea," Milton replied. "How did they get these high-precision cuts? I mean, look around us. This stuff was buried in the ground? What covered it up? How did the dirt and sand get on top of it to begin with? It isn't like there is a lot growing up here." He paced around. "Perfect right angle cuts for several feet in length? No way. No way! All the later examples are crude stacked stones! And some of these pieces that are still in the ground are even larger than the stuff that's standing! I read that the largest block is 131 tons!"

"Yeah, that is not a small ask for people with no wheels," Maxwell stated in response.

As they walked through the site they studied the stones, the H-Block pieces truly had perfect cuts, were perfectly flat across large surface area. Untold numbers of stones were still buried in the ground. "These stones represent superior engineering. It cannot be primitive tools that produce this quality of stone work. But it feels old. Tens of thousands of years old. The weathering. And a lot of it remains beneath the dirt. I want to see what is beneath the dirt." Milton had been shaken by the artifacts.

"Yeah, those H-blocks and drill holes... This is representative of a large-scale cataclysm. Or, it is so old that the civilization died out from other causes and then over the course of eons the artifacts got caught up in cataclysms. I don't know that these artifacts being scattered indicates anything other than ancient things end up buried in dirt. But these stones aren't trivial to produce using modern human labor. You need advanced machinery to get this level of precision."

Milton, pacing, offered, "Imagine a house that got hit by a tsunami. The heavier an object is the less distance it will travel in the blackwater. I also feel that if there was a group of people who found something made of these blocks they might take it apart and leave the smaller stones scattered around. They might want to deconstruct it to see if it contained anything hidden. And then over the course of tens of thousands of years it gets swallowed up by the sands of time. Then some farmer hits a piece of it with a plow and you get archaeology. But some of these rocks feel old. Really, really old. But maybe these lichens and mosses that are growing here are only 12,000 years old? Or two thousand? I am not a patina expert. But it feels ancient."

They found an example of an 'I' bolt juncture that linked two very large blocks. "Think about moving blocks this size and then joining them with relatively small metal bars. Was there something piezo-electric happening in the material? Was there an electric current being generated?" Maxwell asked.

Milton thought about it. "There are a lot of missing pieces. We don't know what we are looking at. We are trying to paint these relics in the context of what we are familiar with. I no longer feel certain that the laws of physics are entirely fixed. They may be habits. And so materials might have very different behaviors based on the gravity and atmosphere and other variables over time. I mean, the concentration of atmospheric oxygen is a sine wave that oscillates between 16% and 24%, give or take a few percent. And consequences are catastrophic if you get to, say, 28% atmospheric oxygen, because everything would burst into flame. So if we think about how far technology has taken us in the last 200 years, especially the last 80 years, and we think about extending that for another two thousand years, how advanced can our civilization become? Is there is a terminal velocity for the acceleration of a culture via advancing technology? Or, can we skip ahead and get to the end point of technology if we are given the correct clues? Can we look at these artifacts and skip directly to the technology that produced them? Can we perceive a technology if it exceeds our current level of understanding? Can we skip a bunch of trial and error and end up at the correct conclusion?"

Maxwell thought about Milton's questions. He replied, "These stones are markers in the game of life that point to a property of reality itself. I mean, we don't need to know the name on the gravestone to know we are looking at a grave. And we can know from a single bone that we are looking at some kind of body. A stack of stones indicates human presence in the land, like with the cairns we see when we're out hiking. These artifacts to me indicate a pointer to an allowable state for the player evolution within the game of life; a high-water mark for a civilization long ago destroyed. In the past some intelligent life manufactured these stones. They did so with the kind of precision we've come to expect of the hyper-modern world. These aren't the relics of stone age tribes. The stone age tribes of the world discovered this library of relics and starting mimicking them, using them as a foundation to evolve. These H-blocks and some of these drill holes imply a culture that possessed advanced tools."

Milton responded, "So we can state with a fairly high degree of confidence that these artifacts necessarily are coupled to machine tools and all the infrastructure and manufacturing that is implied by that. I mean, it takes a huge global supply chain to manufacture a power tool."

Maxwell saw his point. "Yeah, that is right. The highway systems or skyway systems, there will still be some form of manufacturing and transportation of goods related to supporting a technologically advanced civilization. I mean, so long as we are restricting that civilization to the limits of our own. Which is a tough thing to certify with any confidence."

Milton pondered his next words and said, "So the level of destruction it would take to erase all evidence of the supply chain associated with supporting the power tools that manufactured these stones would need to be cataclysmic AND located in the very distant past. Only the artifacts made by the tools remain, but there are clearly drill holes that are machine-grade. And there are also these massive stone blocks. If these stones were part of a construction then we should be able to reverse-engineer the structure by discovering enough of the parts. Our problem is we don't know if the parts belong together or if they are all mixed up as you would expect from a tsunami-like disaster."

Maxwell replied, "From the aerial view I feel like we are looking at a giant mansion. I think a lot of animals try to build impressive structures as a way of representing wealth and achievement. Simultaneously, it might be a religious building or a purely functional building. But these stones were part of something that was constructed with some discernible purpose. It seems to me there is also scorching on the surfaces, or they look like they may have been subjected to intense heat. I can almost see a time when the builders were impacted by some terrible solar blast then thousands of years later an earthquake and tsunami. But we are at 12,500 feet above sea level. One of the things Brien Foerster points out is that Lake Titicaca has freshwater seahorses. Only place on Earth that does. That one datapoint supports the conjecture that the land we are currently standing on has been thrust up 12,000 plus feet by the past cataclysm."

"Well, okay. In the case of an earthquake of that magnitude

the acoustics of the roar could turn the soil into a sort of foam and buildings that would have already been destroyed would be swallowed as the density of the ground changes. Big gas vents in the oceans can cause a bubble or swarm of bubbles big enough to swallow ships and sink them. So if something like that occurred rapidly then everything could get really scrambled."

Next they drove to Tiwanaku. Similar to Puma Punku the area was littered with precisely cut stones including some examples of very large cut stones still embedded in the ground. "This is a disaster zone. Plainly." Milton advocated.

From there they traveled to Sillustani, an ancient graveyard containing several megalithic stone towers. The site presents large stacked-stone tombs resembling small grain silos. Milton immediately noticed the fine quality of the stone work on one of the towers. "The stones are perfectly cut and perfectly curved. The surface defects are minimal. It is definitely an enigma that some of these blocks are heavily worked while everything on top of them is just stacked rough-hewn stones. The oldest stones seem the most expertly worked while the newer towers are crude copies."

Maxwell was overtaken by a sense of deep foreboding. A type of nightmare realization that 'history' has been 'happening' for a very, very long time on planet Earth. That life has been around much longer than anyone would believe. He sensed thousands, perhaps millions, of years of history in the stacking of the stones around him. An altar that had witnessed more than one cataclysm.

Milton walked toward one of the towers. "I am not sure how they were able to do this. But it does not seem utterly impossible and perhaps I am missing some vital knowledge that would make sense of all this."

Blown apart. Maxwell noted the stones 100 feet away from the tower. More stones that contained the unique protruding 'knobs'. Maxwell saw the debris field as evidence of a massive cataclysm.

"Vitrification on the stone. Appears to be melted on one side," Milton pointed out in the ruins of one of the towers. It was only two courses of stone tall and one side was the color of burnt toast.

They stayed at a hotel. Maxwell and Milton headed down to have breakfast. "Okay. So up until now we have seen some impressive stuff. Definitely we are missing some pieces on how they were able to do some of the work. But today I want to take you somewhere that will truly challenge us to come up with an explanation for what we are seeing."

Maxwell removed a pamphlet from his back pocket and handed it to Milton. The cover simply contained the word: SASQUAHAYAMAN

Maxwell drove Milton into the ruins. Milton paced in front of the stones, his mind running on overdrive as he attempted to make sense of what he was seeing. The stones were carved into extremely complex shapes and also fit perfectly together with no mortar. They were massive. Hundreds of tons. "In order to build this, the stones would need to come together simultaneously," Maxwell said. "They are not like bricks, flat on six sides. Not a single surface is flat. You cannot set them one at a time; they need to come together like a 4 dimensional puzzle, or at the very least in a precise sequence. And each one is unique so if you were cutting them you would need the entire pattern prior to beginning so you could understand the full shape. So the only way to do this is to lay it out in a design program and then tool each stone and then organize them for laying them in the correct sequence." Milton considered his dirigibles to be extremely advanced. He was using ultrasonic motors for propulsion and was channeling sunlight via fiber optic cables into solar furnaces that drove turbine generators which ran his hydrogen electrolysis systems. But these stone artifacts reflected a technology that he felt must have been almost immeasurably beyond that of the current age. "Our age is a mechanical one, where stones are set sequentially, but this implies that all the stones converge simultaneously and are held in place as a unit before finally being set in place. Not like a mason who muds the stones from the base to the top using equal sized bricks. The base and the top meet in the middle and the assembly is placed onto the ground. My conjecture is that this was a solid object held together by possibly sound before it was a stationary object held in place by gravity. But we need to generate a pressure to oppose gravity which is not a feasible operation from a phonon pressure field, from sound mechanics. It must be that we identify the source of gravitational momentum and cancel that. But we cannot pretend that we can just 'decouple' from the Earth's gravitational field without presenting an anti-frequency that is proportional to the gravitational field strength. We would maintain our momentum w.r.t Earth moving relative to the Sun and other planets. But the Earth is generating gravitational curvature. To neutralize that curvature you must increase the curvature above the object. By doing this it implies that the area above the stone(s) reference frame has shifted such that photons incumbent on the upper surface are blue shifted by the same amount they would be if they were absorbed near the bottom of the rock. It is the red and blue shift that determine gravitational acceleration relative to a non-homogeneous mass-generated gravitational field. So if you can mimic the relative gravitational attraction of the Earth directly above the rocks you should have no acceleration due to gravity and then the object is accelerated from above and below with the same pressure. In such a theoretical lift machine you would need to be able to compress matter in order to curve space which itself will end up weighing more than the rock you are trying to lift." Milton kicked a pile of dirt in frustration. "I am missing some ingredient for dealing with the gravitational blueshift."

Maxwell was suddenly overcome by a desire to comment. "Zero-point energy," he said. "They must have been able to cancel gravity. You know..." he stopped to think. "So the acceleration due to gravity drops to zero at the top of a parabola or an elliptic curve associated with a thrown object. So, if I toss this rock," Maxwell picked up a rock and tossed it into the air, "At the top of its height the velocity drops to zero and it is NOT being accelerated and it has no 'tension' from the gravitational field, no internal stresses on coupling to the accelerative force. It is weightless. So it might be they knew a way to cancel the acceleration of gravity thereby allowing them to move these massive stones. If we are saying that they cannot survive the internal tension of being lifted by traditional mechanical means we must eliminate acceleration due to gravity AND momentum due to a change in position. That is the only way I can see them bringing them together simultaneously as seems to be implied by the way the stones fit. To me it seems that way. They don't just need the ability to lift the stones, they need the ability to put them into position without suffering the momentum that comes with moving heavy objects. Even if they are setting one stone at a time they can't just swing these things around. But, since some of these appear to have some kind of metal keys linking them together, imagine that you have a graphite writing pencil attached to a special frequency generator. By touching the stones with this wand you can lift them as if they are cotton candy. The electric frequency transmitted by the wand agglomerates them and allows you to trivially place them. I can see this pen-like object that you can touch to a stone and it becomes weightless relative to the local gravitational field. The key is that we cannot get something for nothing. There must be a way that we absorb out of the stone the energy it would ordinarily require for us to lift it and move it. We oppose gravity by lifting things from a lower energy to a higher energy state. They want to fall back to a lower energy state. Gravity wants to flatten everything. Imagine a baseball flying at your face at high speed. If you can catch it you might bruise your hand because the momentum must be transferred in order for it to stop moving. A heavy stone that we are moving around normally has momentum. A heavy rock on the side of a mountain is being constantly accelerated. All it wants to do is fall. How do we cancel that acceleration while retaining the ability to move the object around?"

They continued walking through the site and came upon an area that appeared to contain polished and grooved stones of tremendous size. The Rodadero. They dwarfed the size of the largest wall stones. "Maxwell," Milton began, "What if these giant slide rocks were part of a structure? These walls are just industrial grade retaining berms to hold a massive object and keep the ground underneath it from slipping. Look at the stone, it appears polished. Kids sliding down the grooves? That is not ordinary rock; I feel like it was part of some huge structure. We may not be thinking in large enough terms. It might be the case that these wall rocks which we think of as 'big' are actually relatively small compared with the things they supported. And these perfect cuts made in some of the surfaces. That looks like where pieces fit together. Like this was a massive sculpture."

"If that is true then the scale of destruction is also a lot larger," Maxwell returned.

"The overall area where we are visiting these artifacts is far too large for these to be isolated centers. I feel there was a mega city here that spanned hundreds of miles and the only pieces left are industrial grade walls and some scattered fragments of buildings. I have no idea what was originally here, but I know it was a lot larger than these walls. I just feel it. We think the walls survived because they were large, but in fact they survived because, relative to the other structures, they were small. These are the small pieces."

Maxwell drove on to Naupa Iglesia. "I missed this one on the way down to you."

They hiked up the trail and into a cave opening where there was a niche carved out of the mountain. Milton looked closely at the perfectly flat surfaces. "No way this was done by stone age people. This is similar to that debris field in Sasquahayaman," he remarked to Maxwell. "This is not in its original place. This is a piece of some larger structure that somehow got lodged here during a catastrophe. I can imagine rushing water being capable of doing something like this. Water flowing at hundreds of miles per hour. Or, if the land rose from sea level to over 12,000 feet then the turbulence may have embedded large chunks of the sculptures or whatever these were part of into the mountains. Imagine what we are looking at is a part of a join, the way an artist attaches different pieces of a sculpture. These look like locking points for joining materials. Like the lock-joints they use in concrete parking garages. But if that is correct, then what we are looking at is a huge piece of a building that was smashed into giant chunks, one of which got itself embedded into this mountain. The destruction was so thorough that the details of what this was have been completely erased. But I have now seen these trapezoidal cuts in the stones in the debris fields and I think that these are the real remnants. Half of this mountain was once a statue or some crazy shit."

Maxwell ran his hand along the stone niche in the side of the mountain. It was perfectly smooth, as if cut by a laser. "Milton," he began, "there is no way this was done with stone tools." Milton was examining the site, the strange 'pedestal' carved out of the rock in front of the strange 'doorway.'

"Absolutely not possible," Milton agreed. "But this is obviously an incomplete picture. We might be looking at... the equivalent of a foundation... that housed something else. This could be tens or hundreds of thousands of years old. Anything 'technological' which might have been superimposed on this would have been lost long ago." He and Maxwell watched the people burning sage, chanting at the wall. "They might be worshiping the equivalent of an empty picture frame. Also, we might be looking at this the wrong way."

Maxwell saw a tattered book on a stone ledge inside the cave. It was bookmarked to a particular passage. Maxwell read the highlighted parts to Milton:

"Archaeological historians Jean-Pierre and Stella Nair

conclude: "[...]to obtain the smooth finishes, the perfectly planar faces and exact interior and exterior right angles on the finely dressed stones, they resorted to techniques unknown to the Incas and to us at this time [...] The sharp and precise 90 degree interior angles observed on various decorative motifs most likely were not made with hammerstones. No matter how fine the hammerstone's point, it could never produce the crisp right interior angles seen on Tiahuanaco stonework. Comparable cuts in Inca masonry all have rounded interior angles typical of the pounding technique [...] The construction tools of the Tiahuanacans, with perhaps the possible exception of hammerstones, remain essentially unknown and have yet to be discovered. Noticeable features at Puma Punku are I-shaped architectural 'cramps' which are used to join the stones. The metal used is a copper-arsenic-nickel bronze alloy. The 'cramp' technique can also be found at buildings of Ancient Egypt (Temple of Khnum) and Ancient Greece (Erechtheion). According to Stubel and Uhle the cramp sockets of Olympia and the Erechtheum in Athens are of the same shape as the ones of Tiwanaku."

######### WAITRESS #########

The Waitress recognized the dilemma; Eric was transparent. His writing was suffering because his life was too routine. She was reading his notebooks. Deciphering his handwriting was challenging, but she had taken a course in medical school to learn to read 'doctor handwriting.' In that class she discovered she had a talent for understanding rapidly scribbled notes.

A lot of Eric's writing involved attempts at developing stories or characters. But occasionally he would write letters about how he felt about life and his current state of mind. The waitress found Eric's most recent entry included a 'letter to self':

-

I am able to focus and concentrate on my work. Since my

story was made into a streaming hit show I continue to earn a nice royalty and can afford to relax a bit. I guess this is the definition of success?

Okay. I feel a little depressed. A little down. Which feels like a perverse lack of appreciation for my setup.

I am not sure how to evolve myself into a better state of mind. Perhaps I need to feel this way to achieve a new perspective? Part of me is restless and angry and feels like I should push everyone away and reset my life. But I have no clear cut path forward. I am just floating around without a definite writing objective. Or, my default objective is to survive and maintain my current level of comfort which has little or nothing to do with making good writing. Worse, writing about an inability to write is not a good use of time. I am not learning anything interesting about the world if I just retreat into the comfort of a home and a savings account.

I normally enjoy my life and find my daily routine to be a source of inspiration. I admit that I am selfish and self-centered and it makes it hard for me to form friendships. I am manifesting the characteristics of physical exhaustion that normally accompanies psychological distress / unhappiness and yet all aspects of my life are good to awesome. I should be in great physical and emotional condition. What do I fear?

-

The Waitress saw Eric beginning to decay into The Stale Man. For her this was a fight or flight moment. Millions of years of evolutionary pressure helped her invent a solution to his problems. Because his problems were her problems.

CHAPTER 3

######## ERIC and LYDIA ########

He held her small hands in his own, larger hands. She giggled, lowering her gaze when he looked at her. "I want your cock," she whispered, standing on her tip-toes momentarily.

Millions of years of evolution helped shape Eric's reaction.

She reached over and started massaging the crotch of his pants. "I want you to fuck me."

Floored, taken aback, caught off guard, he grabbed her by the back of the neck and kissed her passionately. "You want to fuck my little pussy, don't you? Pleeeeeaase...." she begged him as they disengaged.

"Ye...ye...yes," was all he could say, dazed and shaking. He was at a writing conference in Salt Lake City, Utah, staying in a hotel without the Waitress.

The bed was beside them. They were standing in front of a large full-length mirror mounted on the wall. "Here, let me get your cock ready," she said in an excited voice. She knelt before him and unbuttoned his pants. As she slid his pants down his penis came out of the front of his boxer shorts and hit her lightly on the chin.

"Oh, daddy!" she exclaimed, looking him in the eyes with a mischievous smile. She then positioned herself beneath his erect penis, so that it was laying on her face. The tip of his penis rested on her forehead. She smiled up at him from beneath the shaft.

"Look in the mirror," she said, reaching up and grabbing his cock while licking his testicles.

He looked over and saw a relatively ordinary man with a gorgeous angel of a girl kneeling before him. She looked at him looking at her in the mirror and then took his cock and swallowed it. He watched as she grabbed his testicles and pushed him further down her throat. He could feel her throat tightening and releasing as she sucked on him and swallowed.

Instinctively he grabbed her head and began thrusting into her. She choked a little. She pulled off him and giggled.

"I am so wet for your cock," she said, wiping away a few tears. She stood up and bent over the bed, pulling her skirt up while doing so.

"Will you fuck my little pussy daddy?"

A primal instinct to smash overwhelmed him. Never in his wildest dreams did he expect to be confronted by such a scene. He had no preparation, no training for such a test.

She reached back with both hands and pulled her ass cheeks apart a little bit. "I am dripping wet for you," she said as she used her fingers to open herself for him.

He dove his face into her and licked. He stuck his tongue as far into her as it would reach tasting the delicious nectar of her.

"Oh my God I want you to fuck me!" she whisper-commanded.

He stood up behind her and wiped his face off with his hand. He used the slick juices on his hand to lubricate himself as he grabbed her and thrust himself into her. It felt amazing. Like a deliverance. The warmth and wetness of her grip on him.

"You're such a bad girl," he said, feeling his commitment to the role overtake him. Pushing her down on the bed he started moving like an animal. She was suddenly tiny beneath him, an instrument of pleasure and fulfillment being pleasured and fulfilled.

"Will you cum in my mouth daddy?" she asked, sensing his impending release. "Will you fuck my little mouth again?"

He pulled out of her and she quickly flipped over. She slid

off the end of the bed and took him into her mouth and down her throat. She grabbed him and sucked on his cock. Grabbing the sides of her head he pressed himself against her face until he exploded down her throat. She worked to swallow it all, eventually pulling away. "Thank you," she said in an obedient tone.

He moved her onto the bed and laid down beside her. He instinctively began using his fingers to trace invisible lines upon her body. She, looking into his eyes and studying his face, manifested adoration, sweetness and relaxation.

"That feels incredible," she said as she touched his face.

"You are..." he looked for words. "Amazing. An angel sent from God."

She laughed. "Now, now, don't go getting 'creative' on me," she teased.

But he meant it. He was a thrall for her.

"You said some dirty things back there," she remarked with a wry smile. "Were you surprised by how you felt?"

He struggled to find words. "I... I... I've always been such a prude," he stuttered. "I've never been with anyone..."

"So forward?" she helped him.

"Ha! Yeah!" he laughed somewhat uncomfortably. "That is a diplomatic way of describing it."

"I am attracted to language and people who know how to use it. It also helps that I love sex. I mean, I want it. And there is nothing wrong with that."

She paused, then continued.

"I don't meet many people who are comfortable with my fetish," she said while starting to stroke his cock. "Your dick is getting so hard again!" she said in a tiny voice.

"It's wrong for daddy to want to fill your pussy," he said in a serious tone, pulling her closer to himself.

"I try to say no, but daddy doesn't listen," she whimpered as she squeezed his testicles in one hand and pulled on his cock with the other.

"That is daddy's pussy," he said to her, spreading her ass far enough to touch her labia. He began to tap on her clitoris.

"What are you going to do to me?" she asked, twitching.

"You are such a bad, bad girl to get me all hard and then think daddy isn't going to fuck your tight little pussy," he scolded as he moved on top of her, the full weight of his adult male body smothering her. Using his knees he forced open her legs.

"That's daddy's pussy," he said into her left ear while grabbing his cock and sliding himself into her.

"Yes, daddy. Please be nice to me, daddy, okay?" she begged. Wrapping her legs around him she exclaimed, "You are going to make me cum. You are a bad, bad daddy. Soooo baaaad...."

"You are such a dirty little princess," he moaned as he reached back to grab her ass, thrusting into her harder and faster, pressing down on her more and more, squeezing her. "That... is... MY... PUSSY."

It was the release he didn't know he had been praying for. She shivered beneath him in orgasm and soon thereafter he pulled out of her and ejaculated upon her breasts.

"Oh my fucking God," he panted. "Fucking Goddess!" he went on, collapsing next to her on the bed. "You are amazing to me. I want to say a million things and hear all your stories. I want to experience every delicious essence excreted by your pores and kiss your pretty forehead..."

She interrupted him. "It's been a while since you've fucked like that, huh?" she asked, laughing.

Her pedestrian attitude toward the emotions she had unlocked in him was in one part exciting and in the other part terrifying. "You are the most unique person I have ever met. You might come from some planet where people of your emotional intelligence are common. However, in my world, you are a sapphire embedded in a diamond resting atop a mountain of gravel." He meant it.

######## JEBEDIAH ########

Suspension of disbelief. Bad policy in a world dominated by math.

Mind Pixels were a method for explaining consciousness on the quantum level. Pixels, expressed as molecules of specific elements, can simultaneously orient themselves as pointers to external data by varying the direction of nuclear magnetic spin relative to a universal background space, which is experienced by consciousness as a 'Sign of the Object.' Universal Signifiers (in this case mind pixels) generate consciousness by collapsing into pointer states that manufacture the experience of reality. The nuclear spin states form the REPRESENTAMEN in the mind. The triadic relationship between the background memory, the nuclear pointers, and the microtubules that detect the changes in spin must all be simultaneously present for what we call 'consciousness' to emerge; to instantiate the experience of a SIGN matter must be implicated. The weakly bipolar elements in the brain orient their magnetic poles and this 'points' to memory or experience generally. Neurons pick up and amplify the signals generated by the nuclear spin states of atoms, resulting with consciousness.

Jebediah had made a small fortune selling drugs on the black market. Part of what he worked on and developed for Maxwell Pragmatic was the Information Brokerage Institute. They used the Institute to distribute scientific literature. It was a success and generated a lot of income in its own right.

As such, Jebediah had seen a large number of scientific papers come through the portal. Maxwell, too, until his sabbatical in South America, had been witnessing huge volumes of scientific information. One thing they both saw was an experiment involving non-local information transfer in human consciousness, mediated by lasers and microwaves. Jebediah opened a line of investigation and was soon on his way to beta testing a new product.

Water, subjected to 'entanglement force' and then

separated, can be used to transmit information across arbitrary space.

It was a simple setup. The end user drinks one half of an entangled liquid while Jebediah laser-irradiates the other half; laser light is shot through crystallized or liquefied drug samples into a mirrored chamber containing the water. For example, liquid morphine was placed into a semi-silvered tube and then lowered into a transparent cup of water. This was lowered into a laser irradiation chamber which incorporated 14 unique frequencies of lasers. The lasers could be pulsed in and out of unison and trained at different locations on the sample. The entire apparatus was then contained in a mirrored box.

Lasers shoot into the sample and then exit the sample and enter the water. The light which is radiated into the water has the information signature associated with the morphine molecules. The photons carrying the morphine data then strike an $H2O$ molecule and imprint a frequency upon it that is measured both in unit h (Planck's constant) and also ORIENTATION. The nuclear spin state of the $H2O$ molecule then aligns with the information pointer carried in by the morphine-encoded photon, and due to the enhanced entanglement generated by violently microwaving the water molecules this information-pointer-alignment occurs instantly across entanglement space. The human brain whose $H2O$ molecules are orienting themselves with nuclear spin pointers correlating to the shape of morphine can then experience morphine-adjacent reality because the intoxication due to morphine is entirely due to the detection of spin states at the micro-tubule boundary. The CONSCIOUS AWARENESS of morphine is information-theoretic in terms of its agency at the micro-tubule boundary.

The person who drank the water felt the effects of morphine due to $h2o$ spin interfering with and influencing $O2$ spin. Once Jebediah added Postassium into the water the entanglement amplitude went up substantially. A new product was born.

Milton was only somewhat aware of the project as he was spending his engineering time focused on a new possibility: using his dirigibles to shuttle lunar helium 3 and other minerals off the moon and back to Earth.

Once he discovered Mind Pixels Jebediah realized they no longer needed to involve themselves in any kind of 'actual' drug trafficking. 'Intentional Water' was the name he decided to give the product. Word on the street was that it "contains good vibes as quantified in the nuclear magnetic spins states associated with H2O and Ozonated water." The vast majority of people had no idea what any of that meant.

The mechanics of the product were as follows: A user would purchase the Intentional Water within an online game or discussion forum. Once the water arrived the user would scan a code on the label and then be taken to an online platform that would allow the user to select from a list of drugs. Back at the lab a water was moved from a storage area into a laser irradiation chamber along with the drug samples correlating with the customer's choice. The water was then irradiated with several frequencies of laser light creating a large number of possible 'drug cocktails.'

Users would feel the influence of the substance "as an information theoretic object resonating via the entanglement bridge that exists between two or more water molecules that were subjected to heavy microwave radiation" and the mind will interpret the spin-signature as 'liquid morphine', but the body will in no way be exposed to actual morphine.

What began as an incidental observation from a research paper was now set to profoundly reshape global consciousness.

######## ERIC ########

Eric the Writer was shaking with excitement. The girl he met at the convention, the one who had taken him to her room and made crazy love to him, had texted him asking to meet some time in the week. And telling him if he wanted to chat before then she would be available.

"I am going to go out for a bit," he told the Waitress. It was unusual for him to mention coming or going. It was 'suspicious.' It was 'unlike him.'

"Okay," she replied, revealing no trace of curiosity.

Eric loved the woman living in his apartment. He loved her to the very ends of the Earth. And he wanted to protect her from any harm. He felt at times the moral conflict of a man lacking credible sociopathic abilities, but she was ALWAYS ready with a funny quip, or would tell him to go on a 'writing trip.' She always had a way of erasing his guilty conscience.

He used his writing trips to be productive. His beautiful mistress would soon begin volunteering to go along. She was going to evolve into a willing lover. But there would be times, especially 'moon times', where she would not available. She would be protecting him from herself.

The Waitress served him in the most practical and perfect ways. Any bills in the mail or other issues that might arise would be magically resolved without his involvement. It was as if he was being loved and cared for by people who truly wanted to help him perfect his life.

In Colorado, in a mountain town, they went shopping. His lovely companion pretended to be his daughter. She enjoyed playing that role. She would always push him, gently, to the edge of his comfort zone, then fall back into perfect form. Her voice was so sweet and innocent and yet the things she said and asked him to do were hard for him to repeat or write down.

His life had been transmuted by this amazing gift from God, this beautiful woman skilled in the art of lovemaking. And yet, he felt she was *not* in love with him. It was something else. It was something that made it more intense. It was like she was in love with her job; like she loved some aspect of giving him tremendous pleasure.

"I love feeling your cock throb in my pussy when you cum

in me," she whispered in his ear. He had just been on top of her thrusting into her fiercely. He ravaged her. She wanted him to lose himself. "When you lay on top of me after you fuck me and hold me down and its kinda hard for me to breathe and I feel your cock slide out of me.... That is the best feeling! I love it when you, you know, SUFFOCATE me."

He was extremely turned on by her.

"I see you when you get up sometimes in the night, when you do your writing. I know you look at me and want me. I've seen you in your robe walk into the bathroom. You know if you want to fuck me you can. You can fuck me when you feel horny. Just open up my little pussy, make it yours. It belongs to you."

He was instantly aroused.

"You are telling me that if it is the middle of the night and I want you I can just come over and take you?"

"Yes. And please, actually. Nothing excites me more than waking up to you using me for your pleasure."

That night he worked on his story.

And he was very productive.

But when it got late he remembered her offer. He always felt lustful when he wrote well. He felt confident. And when a man feels good it is likely he feels sexual.

He stood over her, beside the bed, massaging his cock. He was engorged. He pulled the sheet off; she was lying face down. He got on the bed such that he was straddling her legs. He spit on his cock and slid himself into her. He held her head down against the pillow.

She woke up and lifted herself a little bit to allow him to have more access to her. "Are you going to use me? You gonna use that little pussy daddy?"

He was pounding her and came quickly. It felt amazing. Her beautiful body was art to him. He saw his cum leaking out of her.

He collapsed on the bed next to her. She got up and wiped herself off. She got a glass of water and offered him the first drink.

"I love feeling your cum drip down my legs," she whispered in his ear.

######## JEBEDIAH ########

Jebediah had locked in on the mind pixel as the key to sustaining profitability. The technology to induce a drug state non-locally via O2 spin was a game changer. The product was being tested in Miami. At first, people were extremely skeptical.

"What do you mean, we can get high on water?" an acquaintance asked him in an online game.

"Just scan the bar code image on the back and choose what you want to do. Then pay the fee and feel it."

Jebediah had discovered the white paper on teleporting drug information across entangled water particles when scanning Maxwell's article database. Since he helped Maxwell set up the site and was hosting it in one of his datacenters he had access to the backend and could see all the requests and all the submissions. He found it was not only O2 and Potassium, but also Phosphorus which could modify human consciousness. He was able to transmit the effects of psilocibin, LSD, heroin, opium, cocaine, methamphetamine, and numerous pharmaceutical compounds. The brain could be 'tricked' into experiencing the effects. He made a video for Milton regarding progress on the new project.

"Turns out neurons are not really the seat of human experience and consciousness. Rather neurons and dendrites host microtubules which work more or less like sensitive microphones. They are designed to detect changes in the magnetic spin of molecules in the brain. In fact, many emotional pointer states for O2 can be 'pre-conditioned' by interactions with the external magnetic field generated by us humans. As air enters the mouth it passes through the external magnetic field and is thereby altered, magnetically modified at the quantum object scale to have a specific orientation. The mystics believed that control of breath could lead to control over emotions, and this is qualitatively true. Quantitatively it is far more involved than just breath."

"The magnetic field around the body works like a polarizing filter in the sense it can adjust the orientation of the particles entering the body. This adjustment modifies the particle spin which is picked up by the neurons and microtubules and decoded as human emotional data/experience. The spins works as 'memory pointers' and also 'emotional context generators' depending on which side of the operation you are on. In such a system it appears that the universe is the hard drive, the brain is RAM, and the molecules allow the brain to point to memory. The memory then MIGHT BE stored externally, in the 'Universal Cloud of Signs', and the nuclear spin connects to Signs by pointing at them."

"New memories or new concepts are then associated with magnetic orientation of the individual atoms relative to the 'Universal Memory Map.' Sort of like we have a lot of webservers pointed at the same storage area network (SAN) and they can serve up the same data to different users without needing to make duplicates on the SAN or storage side. Thus molecules serve as a form of multi-mode transistor whose spectrum of possible states include pointing at any unique position possible on the interior surface of a sphere. A transistor with the same number of states as there are unique points on the surface of a sphere."

"The brain-body dychotomy now includes the 'external' Universe as a memory structure," Jebediah observed.

"Now, I talked with Maxwell about this when he was here and he has an interesting way of looking at it. He thinks the human isn't a self-contained machine that is doing work, like a computer isolated from a network. The work of consciousness is also happening outside the human being and the body is a listener that is awaiting an update from an outside process. The processing that occurs outside the human brain is transmitted TO the mind pixels as a change in their orientation. Our brain then renders the mind pixels into a format we can comprehend using Object Language. We can't then download our soul onto a machine because we aren't actually doing all the processing locally, we are an instance that receives communications from outside processes we are currently unwittingly entangled with."

The video ended.

######## ERIC and LYDIA ########

A beautiful young woman and an older man tend to attract attention. But she knew how to handle herself so as not to draw unwelcome eyes. "You are famous enough that someone might recognize you," she said, inflating his ego. Beneath the table she took off one of her shoes and put her foot against his crotch. She began arousing him with her toes. "But don't you just love how fine dining establishments have such long tablecloths?" she said with a sultry undertone. He was hard, throbbing. He looked down and saw her cute toes working on him through the black nylon stockings. She sensed a waiter approaching and withdrew her foot.

"Just water for me," she told the waiter. "I'm not old enough to drink yet." The way she said the last sentence made her sound so innocent. So uncorrupted.

They had a wonderful dinner and returned to the hotel room. "So!" she said, clasping her hands together. "I have been working on my book."

He finally felt useful, valuable. She was so delightful, so charming and beautiful. But more than that, she was a Goddess of Sex. She understood him and how to make him feel amazing. He had never experienced an orgasm as powerful as she could extract. He wanted to do anything, absolutely anything, to repay her. She always had her own money, would invite him to fancy hotels and restaurants and pay for it all. But she was also a writer and he desperately wanted to give something back to her.

He listened, took mental notes. She went over numerous scenarios for the main character, his motivations, why he desired change. Eric pointed some things out. "There is too much tension for something like that to happen so early in the journey," he observed. "You are setting a furious pace if he has to deal with such a threat at the outset. I could see if that were his REASON for going; but giving him an existential crisis as soon as he ventures out will make it challenging for other obstacles to seem as important."

"I see," she said. She understood his point of view. She saw herself in her character, saw herself as at the beginning of her journey. She had taken an extremely unlikely path and was mapping her experience into her work.

"Less autobiographical!" she thought. She experienced a moment of anger with herself for not seeing it. It made her feel juvenile in a bad way.

He noticed the emotion on her face. "Hey, this is a great idea and I think it needs to be part of the story. I just think the intensity won't be fully appreciated unless you can sustain it. Pacing. To keep the wanderer encountering such intense scenes also risks becoming monotonous. Wait; allow momentum to build. One second." He grabbed his computer. "Something I want to show you."

He opened a video of a lecture titled, 'Kurt Vonnegut, Shape of Stories.'

A voice vibrated from the computer.

"Stories have very simple shapes, ones that computers can understand."

"The G,I axis (good, ill fortune) vertical axis and the B,E axis (Beginning, End/Entropy) horizontal axis."

```
Good
|
|
|
B-------------------------End
```

|
|
|
Bad

"Death, disease, poverty at the bottom, good fortune, good health, etc., up here at the top."

"People who can afford books don't want to read about diseased sick people. So start your story up here, in a good place."

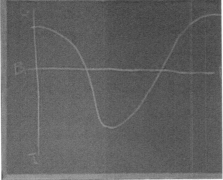

"This is a story that can be retold infinitely many times, and apparently they are trying. I call it 'MAN IN A HOLE.' Somebody got into trouble, and then gets out of it again. You end up a little higher than you started because the reader, you know, they're human and they want that kind of ending for themselves."

"Another story type is 'BOY MEETS GIRL.' But it needn't be about a boy or a girl. Starts on a day like any other day. Comes across something wonderful. 'Oh boy! This is my lucky day! Shit!' Things go bad. Then he gets it all back again."

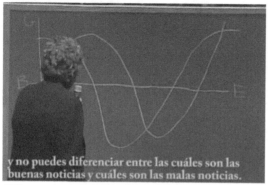

"I have a masters in anthropology, but it was a big mistake. I can't stand primitive people. They're just so stupid! Anyway, proof of their stupidity was I, you know, went to the library and dug up stories they told. Boy these stories stunk. They were just dead-level like that B-E axis there. 'We came to a river. We came to a mountain. Little Beaver died.' You can't tell what the good news is and what the bad news is."

"You look at the wonderful rise and fall of our stories and, you know, they deserve to lose."

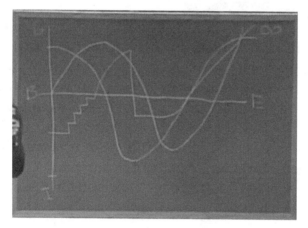

"Another very popular story, and it breaks my rule, starts down low. Young girl, teenager, I guess 19 or 18. Why is she so low? Well, her mother has died. Reason enough, right? And her father has remarried almost immediately to a terrible old battle ax with two mean daughters. And there is a party at the palace that night. You've heard it? Alright, so she has to help her new mother and her new sisters get dressed for this party. And she doesn't get to go. Not good enough to go, but they are. So, does she get even sadder? No, she is a stout-hearted little girl whose maximum grief was death of her mother. So everybody leaves for the party and the fairy godmother shows up and gives her panty hose, mascara, perfume, means of transportation, carriage with horses. Everything you need to go to a party and have a good time. So, she goes, and the prince falls in love with her. You must realize she is so heavily made up even her own relatives don't recognize her. But, come midnight she loses it all. Doesn't take long for the clock to strike 12, so she crashes. Does she drop down to the same level? No, for the rest of her life she will get to remember when she was the Belle of the Ball. So she poops along at this considerably improved level. Until the Prince comes, and the shoe fits, and she becomes off-scale happy."

"Does this have any use in criticizing literature? I think perhaps it does. I think this rise and fall is in fact artificial. It pretends we know more about life than we really do. And what is a true masterpiece cannot be criticized on a cross of this design. Alright, let's try Hamlet, Okay."

"This is the same chart as Cinderella, except the sexes are reversed and he is a little older. His father has died. And his mother has remarried his uncle. So he is as depressed as Cinderella. He is depressed, unhappy. Then his friend Horatio comes in and says, 'Hey, Hamlet. There is this thing upon the parapet I think you better go talk to it. He says its your father.' And so Hamlet goes up there and this thing, whatever it is, we don't know, as any of you who've horsed around with Quija Boards or any sort of seances or anything, you know there are malicious spirits around. Looking for saps like you who are trying to hurt you. Give you bad advice. So to this day we do not know if that thing was his father and if it was telling the truth. The whole story remains ambiguous up until the end when Hamlet dies in a duel. This is as bad of story telling as could come from any Arapahoe, and yet I have just told you how it is a respected masterpiece. WE ARE SO SELDOM TOLD THE TRUTH."

"And in Hamlet Shakespeare tells us we don't know enough about life to know what the good news is and what the bad news is. And we respond to that: 'Thank you Bill.'"

"If you think about it, we pretend to know what the good news is and what the bad news is. And you think about our training in this matter and all we do is echo the feelings of people around us."

"Imagine a little kid. Three years old. Maybe four. And the parents are SO excited. They have the most wonderful piece of news for this kid. Little kid looks around wondering, 'What can it be?' The terrible news: 'Its your birthday!' What could be a more empty piece of information?"

Kurt Vonnegut then appealed to the audience to say the name of the teacher who had most profoundly influenced their life. She whispered in Eric's ear, "Eric. Johnson."

She absorbed it all. The story of Cinderella when explained this way made total sense to her. It was the best lesson on the mechanics of story writing she had ever received. She straddled him and began kissing him, first on the neck, then the chest. She was unbuttoning his shirt. "I think I can see the shape of your story," she said in a seductive voice. She slid down between his legs and undid his pants. She pulled him out and began to suck on him.

######## MAXWELL and MILTON ########

Milton made some calculations on a notepad. "There is simply no conceivable means by which these stones could have been moved by 'primitive people,'" he told Maxwell. "Even IF there was some means by which they could carve stone with such precision, they could not move it. So we have been fed a lie, or an incomplete truth."

Maxwell had never seriously considered the proposition that the ancient world contained a civilization more advanced than the current age. But that was before he was confronted by the artifacts. "What would need to happen to so thoroughly erase the history of such a people?" he asked.

Milton thought about it. "Maybe there are a few options? A massive solar flare? A meteor strike? Some kind of incurable disease? If their world was as interconnected as our own it might not take much of a shock to thrust them into a new 'dark age.' Knowledge is a bit like tree rings in how one layer adds upon the previous one. If the tree dies, one must start over again from the beginning. Seeded from mythological stories about the past."

Maxwell could see how that would be so. "Well, given that, is it possible the world has seem more than one advanced civilization? Could we be seeing artifacts from multiple civilizations or epochs? Like the tides come in and go out, do civilizations reach a zenith and then recede, with all or most of the information being lost?"

"It seems possible," Milton mused. "It cannot be ruled out. But the extent of the apparent destruction leads me to conclude it was not a gradual abandonment. Something catastrophic happened. Also the nubs and other irregularities on the large stones are consistent across all the sites so far, so it leads me to suspect we are observing a single cultural collapse. Or, primarily a single culture."

######## ERIC and LYDIA ########

Eric enjoyed working alongside his young mistress as she developed herself as a writer. He was reading the notes he took from a recent lecture to her. "According to Glen Gers, telling a story is somewhat like Newtonian mechanics. A character has a trajectory. A body in motion stays in motion until acted upon by an external force. The main character, or characters, are the bodies in motion. The story is the sum total of forces acting upon the characters to create a change in trajectory. Every character acts as if they are the main character of their story, though not all characters are exposed enough for the audience to see that. Dramatic action is what defines the flow of time in a story. Every story is about a character trying to accomplish something and the obstacles or assisting elements they encounter along the way. The actions engaged by the character is the story itself. Obstacles can be external or mental/internal."

"Go on," she encouraged Eric, meaning it. She was excited to learn with him.

He read, "Writing is a process of asking and answering questions. Think in scenes. You start with a, let's say, general aim. 'I want to write about aliens.' Then you start asking questions. 'How will I tell my story? Is the point of view omniscient, or is it first person?' Every question represents a choice. Who, what, when, where and why.

According to Glen there are six fundamental questions:

1) Who is it about?
2) What do they want?
3) Why can't they get it?
4) What do they do about it?
5) Why doesn't that work?
6) How does it end?

These six questions will help you write anything. And it always works. Just keep asking questions. Also, there is no 'best' way to write. The key is to not keep trying if you are getting diminishing returns. So do not destroy your best work trying too hard once the momentum is lost. Starting a story is a bit like noodling." Eric finished.

"Noodling?" she asked, puzzled.

"Yeah," Eric replied. "People swim along the banks of a river and reach into mud holes to try and find catfish. Every once in a while they find one! However, occasionally they find a turtle instead. And some get their fingers bitten off."

"Get it out of your mind and into the world," she thought to herself.

Eric continued, "In some stories you need decisive moments where people are changed. But in real life such moments are usually not so clearly defined. You need to seed your creativity. So if you want a scene to include someone who is miserable, write that. Literally start off the scene with, 'He is miserable,' then ask the questions, 'How do we know this?' We know this through the actions and possibly inner thoughts of the character. That is, roughly, how Glenn Gers describes his writing process and offers a kind of 'algorithmic basis' for achieving repeatable success."

"The Thirsty Turtle," she thought to herself. *"That is my working title."*

She recalled her work.

-

Life had been good for a good while. Turtle knew because, generally speaking, turtles live a long time.

Water had always been flowing in Little Creek. There had always been enough food.

Turtle outlived the most vulnerable phase of life and now had few predators.

Life was predictable.

But Turtle wanted to know... what lies beyond the edge of the creek? What world was Turtle missing out on by virtue of staying put?

One day Turtle decided to find out.

Slowly, methodically, Turtle plodded up the bank. With a craned neck turning in all directions to spy an easier road, none appeared.

Turtle encountered a lot of dead ends. A lot of slippery slopes and nopes.

Finally, while working along the edge, an inlet into a dry creek intersected the stream and offered a new path of least resistance.

Turtle followed it.

Turtle stopped and thought about leaving behind a familiar, safe world. "And for what?"

Turtle's question was soon answered by the vision of a new world.

A mechanical part of Turtle was driving onward without asking for permission.

Turtle realized it was exactly THIS, going to an unfamiliar place, that began to sate this new thirst. The desperate need was not of Turtle's making.

Turtle left the comfortable puddle with its minnows and frogs. One small increment at a time Turtle moved into the unknown.

-

"I love what you are describing," Eric said in a plaintive tone. "But why won't you let me read it?"

"Its... the shape of stories," she redirected. "I am making something happen and if you see it now you might guess it, so I don't want you to read it until I am ready for you to see it whole. I want you to have a total experience, not just a snippet. That is why I am speaking in such general terms about it."

Eric intuitively grasped the logic of what she was saying.

"*Thirsty Turtle, a Book for Adults and Babies,*" she thought to herself as she amended the working title.

He said, "I can offer you insights into my own process, I can give you unfiltered observations regarding anything you want to share with me." He leaned in close to her, ""I am so excited to read you."

"Don't be!" she reproved, meaning it. "That is way too much pressure coming from you. You have already achieved the success I am only just now aiming at. I am terrified of showing you my work. You overstating its importance makes your desire feel inauthentic."

He looked at her, stunned. Her saw her first vulnerability, the first closed door. "When I look at you I don't see someone who is in any way beneath me. You are... clearly you are an extraordinary person. I've never met anyone like you."

"You've maybe not met that many people?"

He reflected on her face. So young, so beautiful. But him? A man in his 40's. He felt so great, so energized by her. She had never hit the pause button, had never shown any signs of emotional vulnerability. Since the day they met it had been a whirlwind of sex and fun and productivity. In many ways she had allowed large parts of his world to completely dissolve from view. What would he do if she left him?

"*When she leaves you*," he heard his subconscious mind say.

"I didn't mean to scare you," he said, choosing the perfect words by accident. "I am not trying to pry you open or force you to give me anything against your will. I CARE about you. So I am curious because I want to be helpful to you."

Outside of her control she became very wet. Her fantasy, her kick. She was hiding something from him, something he wanted to see. His masculine instinct was to care for her and protect her from harm. He wanted to provide her with security and opportunity. "*Fatherly.*" It made her love him, but not respect him.

As a fiction writer he was capable of authoring himself into the role she wanted him to play. But she never anticipated that he would become an authentic version of the role model she never had.

######## JEBEDIAH and MAXWELL ########

Jebediah's villagers were not the only 'natural' people in the Brazilian forest. Maxwell, for his part, possessed a pre-existing frame of reference for understanding just how far removed he was from established social norms and customs. There was no bridge to a world of law enforcement in the deep jungle; in some important ways it wasn't all that different from life on the Lakota Reservation. His four years of attending the sacred Sundance and the teaching he received from the Elders had inoculated him against culture shock.

The people in Jebediah's village mostly ignored Maxwell. They did not make eye contact.

Jebediah laughed over dinner. "Once upon a time I thought the world was large, then I saw a new world, and it made my previous experience seem smaller than I could have imagined. In some places you can discover a world within a world; there are people whose only connection to the outside is from the internet services we provide with our airships. But where the old model WAS to slash and burn for grain crops, row crops, we now help the Brazilian people sell bio-diverse flora and fauna, mushrooms, all manner of rare things you can only find in a thriving rainforest ecosystem. We harvest from the entire forest in a way that seeks to build and sustain a profitable pro-biodiversity stewardship model for the land. And that system recognizes the food generating power of a natural environment. Combine that with our zero-emission water-based hydrogen gas fueled zeppelins and we now have the ability to ship and receive all over the planet while maintaining carbon neutrality. Better than Carbon Neutral, in fact. So we engage with these kinds of populations at several locations, though mostly we are sourcing raw materials from the Southern Hemisphere and delivering it along the equator. Your research helped make all of this possible. And while you have been traveling we have continued to update our methods, and we have an account which accrues income daily. So you will always have access to capital."

The Australian scientist chimed in, "We have worked out a plan to get you to Australia. My family has 140,000 acres there. Based on what you described it seems like this should meet your requirements."

Maxwell was looking at the location on a map on a massive screen embedded into one of the walls of Jebediah's office. "That looks perfect," he said.

"We can drop you there along with a couple of shipping containers for the additional things you wanted." Milton added.

######## ERIC and LYDIA ########

Eric had her bent over a desk and was pumping against her like a man on a mission. A mission to utterly fill a woman up. She moaned and begged him to cum in her. "I want you to cum in me. Pleeeeeease daaaaaaady!" He exploded. And exploded. And exploded. He pulled away and watched as a semi-translucent white fluid oozed out of her. She turned around and got on her knees in front of him and began licking his still-throbbing cock. "A good girl always cleans up her messes."

She was so seductive and attractive. He could not believe he had been chosen by the Universe to receive such a blessing.

She stood up and guided him onto the bed. He could see where some of his cum had dropped down onto the lacy ruffle top of one of her bobby socks. She placed him on the bed, on his back. She began massaging his feet, then his calf muscles. She was really working on him. She made it up to his knees then told him to turn over. "Lay on your stomach now, okay?" He rolled over and she got on top of him, straddling him just below his tailbone. She began to massage his back. She whispered in his ear, "I hope daddy doesn't mind if I leak cum onto him."

"No," he whimpered.

She lightly bit his ear, then whispered, "I will clean it up. I promise." She massaged his back down to his glutes. "Okay. Turn back over." Where she had been sitting she had been dripping cum onto his testicles.

She worked his legs above the knees. She then started kissing him on his cock, causing it to rise. She started licking his testicles. With cum on her chin she took his cock into her mouth and down her throat. Up and down she went. His toes started to twitch. "Oh... my... God... I'm... gonna... cum... in... you... so... HARD!" He forcefully grabbed her head and started fucking her face. He came down her throat.

"Holy shit... holy shit.... holy shit..."

She climbed up to him. She hugged him around the neck and asked, "Was I a good girl?"

"You ... are a ... very .. bad girl... ." he said, still catching his breath.

She giggled.

After cuddling and drifting off to sleep they got up and showered together. Eric ordered brunch to be delivered to their room. They sat at a table near a window and ate together.

The young woman was driven to learn more about Eric's writing style. "So you have a minimum number of pages per day that you write?" she inquired. "Do you fear that it makes you too mechanical? Do you ever feel like you are forcing the words to come out?"

"It is how Stephen King writes," he explained. She looked back at him, puzzled. "He's a fictional horror expert and is one of the prolific authors of the 20th Century. I always wondered how he managed to write so many books. Then I heard him tell George RR Martin, the fantasy author, that he just made sure to write six SOLID pages per day. If you do that there will be some good things that come out of it. Once I did the math I realized I could write an entire library of books if I can pull that off."

"So that's what you do. Write six pages every day?"

"It has become my new habit, though I hate to admit I don't always hit my target. I am trying, though. It removes all the excuses. You either make the time or shut up. Whining, whinging is F-."

She thought about it. "I choose my words extremely carefully. I write with purpose. I don't move on until I KNOW I've said it exactly perfectly. The idea of hitting a mandatory target of pages every day sounds soul crushing to me."

"I sometimes edit as I write, but not often. It just pours out of me. I write to read, to discover, to see what my brain comes up with. Maybe that is lame a lot of the time? Sometimes though, even if only by accident, something new gets put down. Something good, a gem, reveals itself. It is similar to working out on a treadmill to prepare for a long distance hike. Without the preparation it is unlikely you will do well on a challenging trek. But additionally if you don't practice and work out the trek itself will suck and you will have a bad time. It is about maintaining momentum and making things easier on yourself as time goes by. Habits not goals."

"Maybe I will try that out?" she thought to herself.

CHAPTER 4

######## MILTON ########

Following Maxwell's departure for Australia Milton dove into researching Megalithic sites across the world. He was attempting to make sense of the pattern that was emerging. The stones in South America had startled him. The stones in Egypt presented yet another mystery.

"*A great culture spanned the world,*" he thought to himself. "*And some disaster befell them.*"

The stone surfaces showed signs of intense heat. Almost, or not unlike, a nuclear blast. But also the extent of the destruction. It appeared as if most of civilization had been tumbled or washed away. Subjected to scouring by water.

"You need to go to the base of the ruins of the Temple of Jupiter at Baalbeck in the Eastern Valley of Lebanon," Maxwell told him over video chat. "Some people say that it is the remains of the temple that Cain built when he was trying to make a survival plan for the coming of God's inevitable wrath. Others say it is embedded mathematical ratios that represent an ancient understanding of the laws of the universe. There are 24 400-ton stones stones and three 1000-ton stones on top of them. The placement is intentional. In the Book of Revelation 'The Throne of God' is described as being surrounded by the 24 Elders. The Western flank. Feel it for me!"

Milton did some reading as the airship transported him from Brazil to the Middle East. Milton's airships were able to drop trailers from South America and pick up trailers at the Suez Canal terminals in Egypt. Milton had made large investments in infrastructure that were beginning to pay real dividends. Despite the fact pirates and rebels had attacked his ships with guns and missiles, he had yet to lose any cargo.

He was watching a video by Brien Foester and taking notes. Milton wrote:

-

'Enigmatic Ba'al Bek' by Vincent R. Lee, Architect. Near Heliopolis (City of The Sun). Not until 1900 did formal studies of the site, including excavations, begin. German expeditions supported by...

Why it is doubtful the Romans built/moved the Trilithon stones?

1) Design of the Temple of Augustus suggests they were present earlier.

2) Extreme weathering strongly suggests the 'Maxiliths' have been exposed for longer than the smaller, adjacent blocks that are indisputably of Roman origin.

3) The giant blocks still in the quarry prove that whoever built this had in mind a much larger project - the scale, finish and design of which bear no resemblance to anything remotely Roman.

Most telling of all, however, is the fact the Trilithon and its supporting horseshoe of mega-stones would have been a pathologically un-Roman thing to do.

In one story. Cain is believed to have used giants and Mastadons to build the 'fortress' as a refuge from Yahweh's wrath following the murder of his brother, Abel. Others say Solomon built it to impress Balkis, the Queen of Sheba, whose romantic attention he sought.

Beneath the temple mount in Jurusalem there exists 'the Stone of the West.' Estimated weight is 600 tons. The 'putholes' hypothesized to be for scaffolding are the same for the Trilithon stones as well as the Stone of the West. Chisel marks on the Jurusalem stone are similar to those found at Ba'al Bek.

Ba'al Bek =

24 x 400 ton stones

3 x 900 ton stones

NO TRACE of an elaborate 'haul road' from the quarry to the ruins has ever been found. Also, the mountain of fill material needed to ramp up to the work area as its height increased is entirely absent.

Conventional wisdom attributing this to the Romans is based largely on a lack of alternatives.

These builders placed smaller stones at the base and ended with the largest stones on top. Opposite of most conventional wisdom.

Saw marks in the flooring outside Great Pyramid at Giza. Examinations of the striations caused by apparent saw, which was less than a quarter inch thick, seemed to have a cutting rate of 2 to 3 millimeters per revolution. At least 500 times more efficient than a modern day diamond saw. No way bronze age dynastic Egyptians could have pulled it off.

Granite slabs show flaking from extreme heat being applied.

Conjecture: Approximately 12000 years ago the planet was struck by a massive cataclysm.

'Cataclysm; Compelling Evidence of a Cosmic Catastrophe' by Allan and Delair.

Approximately 9500 BC a comet struck the Earth or came close enough to cause severe disruptions. Crustal shifting, tilting of Earth's axis, mass extinctions, upthrusted mountain ranges, rising and sinking landmasses, volcanic eruptions and earthquakes.

'Catastrophobia: The Truth Behind Earth Changes and The Coming Age of Light" by Barbara Handclow.

Ancient villages beneath the Black Sea. The biblical flood, Atlantis, likely REAL. We are a wounded species, and this unprocessed fear, passed from generation to generation, is responsible for our constant expectation of apocalypse. Insidious global forces have used these collective fears to control humanity for thousands of years.

A very advanced technological civilization preceded the dynastic Egyptians.

The Osiron at Abydos.

There is no way that the dynastic Egyptians created these granite and syenite boxes, period.

The Serapeum is one of the most classic examples where the paradigm of the conventional academics reaches comical proportions.

Tanis. Why is it so guarded? Military base. Noting grows there.

Certainly something happened in the past. A phenomenally advanced civilization existed. At the temple of Jupiter there are 24 400 ton blocks and 3 900+ton stones on top of them. No possible way to move those from the Aswan quarry using logs and soldiers.

The Great Pyramid is composed of an estimated 2,400,000 stone blocks weighing between 2 and 70 tonnes. Margin of error at the base is on order of one centimeter and within one degree of alignment with North. Assuming the Egyptian workers managed to cut, transport and place one block per day, it would have taken exactly (2,400,000 : 365) years to build the Great Pyramid, i.e., 6575 years to finish it. This means that the pyramid, given for completion in about 2500 BC, would have been started in at least 9,000 BC. But according to archaeologists, the great pyramid was built in only 10 years around 2500 BC. What does this statement imply?

To be built in 10 years, calculating that work was only done in daylight hours and thus 10 hours per day, each block of the pyramid must have been cut, transported and placed at the rate of 1 every minute, i.e., one every 60 seconds or so. (1 block x 60 minutes x 10 hours x 365 days x 10 years) = 2,190,000. Can you imagine a group of workers with tools as soft as copper, who do not even have the wheel in that time, cutting blocks from 2 to 70 tonnes, transporting them on logs via ramps and placing one every minute without interruption, every day, every week, every month, every year, for 10 years?

Milton stopped the video and paced around his large room aboard the airship. He spoke to his reflection in the window. "It is like realizing you have been a little baby playing with simple baby technology and you open the door to see the real adult world, the world of advanced ancient machines. I am just a snail trying to make sense of a fragment of a decaying log. Trying to reconstitute an image of the tree from the foamy bones of the rotted and burnt wood. And yet, because the artifact exists and is a relic of intellectual intent, it means there must be a way for me to learn how to reproduce the implied forces. I just need to understand the forces involved."

######## The PDC ########

His grandmother died.

She loved her 'PDC.' Even in his punk/goth phase where he earned his trademark nickname, she thought he was the cat's meow. Even when he dyed his hair green and pretended to be an atheist, she knew Grace comes to the joyful giver. He was always authentic. She knew he would never lie to her.

It was, of course, perceived by all her kin that the PDC, or the Piss Drunk Cock as his uncle had labeled him, was undeserving of inheriting any piece of her estate. With ever-increasing fervor they conjectured about his downfall, about the inevitability of his demise. "Karma's a bitch," an aunt snarled while thinking about him.

Many of PDC's relation speculated 'MeMaw' Silus might be rich. Though she made no outward moves to lead anyone to believe it. Her car was 40 years old with 112,000 miles on the odometer. The house was from her first marriage at age 19. Many times family members would stop by, pretend to be interested in her life and ask her to tell stories. Invariably they would ask her for some money. She would cough and laugh and say, "Aww, darlin', you know you can always lead with the questions. Check in the cookie jar in the kitchen." Always a $20, sometimes a $50. By hanging around with her for a while the family felt like they earned the money. Having 'earned it' they were absolved from the shame of begging.

PDC NEVER went to the cookie jar. Even when she told him to go grab some cookies, he wouldn't do it. He knew what it meant and how his family made a habit of visiting her to get paid. He was legitimately interested in her life, in her struggles and how much different things once were. He earnestly loved his grandma for being his ancestor and his only living link to the past. She appreciated his aura found him radiant. He truly loved her and would ask her to retell him stories from her youth so he could be sure to remember them. He brought high school friends by her house and would have them listen to her stories about the past.

"Before electricity. My grandmother gathered water from a stream. We melted snow on the hearth in our copper pots." Other relatives would roll their eyes. But he clung to every word; loved hearing stories of how his Grandmother lived. Survived. "You are hard-core grandma. I wish more girls were like you." She would laugh and laugh and cough and laugh.

"No really!" PDC's friends would say, ""You were hardcore. Having to boil snow and ice for drinking water. None of the kids at school would even know how to survive in that kind of world. That is insane."

She leaned in to PDC. "Nobody understands what life used to be like," she warned. "They all have hot water on demand, everything under the sun on their grocery shelves. We walked everywhere! Had to save seed to grow plants in the spring. All these people are softies. But you get it, Jeremiah. You remind me so much of my Grandpa. He lived through things that made my life seem easy. But you have his face, his eyes. I see him looking back at me."

PDC honored his ancestors. He lived as a nomad because he knew his Grandmother was correct. Everyone was soft and it was all too easy to fall victim to comfort. "Calorie overdosers," he had once said to his grandma, who chuckled.

"We had sugar in a lockbox. Can you imagine that!" she said to him.

Finally the day came; he got the message from one of his 'cool cousins.' "Hey man. You need to come back to Independence. Grandma died."

PDC got a bus ticket. He was saddened. "I wish I could see her one last time, but now she is gone. Dust. Like Great Great Grandma Silus in the snow. Poof. Gotta keep rolling."

After the funeral PDC decided to go out and have a few drinks with his family. The Last Will and Testament would be read in a few days.

PDC awakened the following morning with a hangover. He was unsure if he could trust his memory of the previous evening. He remembered an argument about politics, two uncles disagreeing. They believed there was a real difference between political parties. He had interjected with the observation that "all political parties have been captured by large financial interests." He offered that "the 'differences' are being maintained by players in both parties as a means of controlling the electorate. By ensuring neither side ever 'solves' the hot-button issues it guarantees the continued success of their 'divide-and-conquer' Uniparty strategy."

A proven method to get people who ordinarily disagree to rally together is to deny the validity of all sides simultaneously.

"Yeah, it isn't perfect. But my side respects individual rights."

"Oh yeah, Mr. Prison-Industrial-Complex over here supporting human rights!"

"It was your guy who made the drug laws."

"It is your guy who runs the war on drugs!"

On and on.

PDC recognized how worthless such conversations were, serving primarily to make the participants feel invigorated while ultimately advancing no change in the status quo.

"Morons," PDC thought to himself. *"The game has grown so stale."*

PDC owned his home outright, much to the chagrin of his family. His friend Maxwell Pragmatic helped him purchase it, in large part because Maxwell wanted a fall back plan should he ever end up homeless. "If you own a house I might have a place to come home to if my life gets fucked up," Maxwell had explained at the tax auction. Owning a home outright allowed PDC to quit his job and instead live on short-term rental income. It was a meager existence, to be sure, but he enjoyed the intellectual freedom that unlocked once he was able to buy back all his time. They met in college when Maxwell worked at a comedy club named The Aqua Vitae. They became best friends over the course of a summer spent doing drugs in an alley behind the club. They were Writers and Thinkers. Maxwell had been successful for a stint and made a bit of money doing information brokerage. He bought the house in PDC's name at a tax auction. It was a bargain like only Maxwell could produce.

During his time with Maxwell they studied the 'ways of the world' and concluded that life could be modeled as a game taking place within a massive multiplayer map. The majority of people spend their lives fulfilling very specific roles. While they are in their roles they become machines. The mechanical duties the players perform ensure the relative stability of 'culture' which is primarily understood to be the continuous re-supplying of goods and services. Consumerism mixed with a few 'meaning of life' pursuits.

They analyzed the motivations of the players. Most seemed to be working on the basis of 'avoiding failure' while a select few seemed to be seeking to 'achieve success.' The 'avoid failure' players were obsessed with compliance. With being perceived as successful inside the context of the 'median.' They took few to no real risks. Also, they did not seem to recognize what the 'real risks' were. He saw these people as being primarily 'reactive' - they seemed to seek a state of 'least action' as a baseline – and they lived to avoid stress by conforming to the status quo.

Together they calculated that those people who were 'striving for success' represented the set of consummate risk-takers. These people set goals whose achievement could not be guaranteed. The path would need to be created or discovered. Few to no road maps. They seemed to thrive when challenged and almost universally rejected the status quo. They were non-conformists.

He sensed as a result of what Maxwell had done he was in some kind of limbo or third state. Rent always kept him motivated to work a straight job because he wasn't interested in taking on the responsibility of managing his own business. Because he had to work he had an excuse to rant about not having time to write. When Maxwell set him up with home ownership his motivations for playing the game changed. He was neither avoiding failure nor striving for success. It was more like he was watching other people play the game. A spectator with nothing at stake, no skin in the game.

People in both camps were envious of his position.

"So you don't have to work?" a friend asked him.

"No. Not really. Not with desperation as my motivation. I do need to keep the house nice for the rentals. My friend got the house at a tax auction for a crazy low price so I don't have a mortgage or anything like that."

"Must be nice," the friend replied, sarcastically.

Being, in a sense, above the fray of the ordinary playthrough had placed him into a category where the only people he related to were 70+ year old retirees. People who, like him, had no real overhead, but were also forced to be somewhat frugal as a result of inflation eroding some of their retirement purchasing power. Everything in PDC's life was paid forward. His morning routine involved hanging out with his retired crowd of friends at a popular coffee shop. He was by far the youngest member of a group whose previous youngest member was 63. But because PDC had spent so much time talking with his grandmother he knew a lot about the times the 70 year old folks had lived through. "How do you know this stuff?" one of the men asked him.

It seemed a bit absurd, the notion that it had become relatively trivial to survive in the modern age. Thanks to scientific advances and the widespread proliferation of technology a person can, with just a little luck, live better than the kings and queens of the old world.

"Having my perspective altered after a life of drudgery and wage cuckery is disorienting," he explained to the group. "It is like seeing some foreign language for the first time. Like reading the code that makes a website work. We usually never have insight into the underlying mechanics that generate the reality we experience. But when you can decouple from the demands of the game for a while you can take time to go deeper, do a more detailed and patient analysis of time and experience and the laws that drive Life, The Game." The old men encouraged him to enjoy his time as much as possible, "Trust me. I fucking worked my ass off in a job and now I can't go out in my boat because I have carpel tunnel. Retire now if you even have a small chance at it. It is TIME you can't get back!"

PDC avoided his family following his night with them at the bar, but he had to meet with them all one last time for the reading of The Will. For the most part everyone was unhappy that he was in attendance.

"I hope she left him nothing," an aunt said under her breath with a glare. "What a freak. Does he even have a job?"

The group of gloomy people went into the conference room where an attorney was seated. "Thank you all for coming. We have a few things to go over regarding the estate of Wilma Silus."

PDC leaned against a wall in the back of the room. One by one the family learned of their inheritance. "To Jane I leave my Buick LeSabre and the contents of my garage. To John I leave my Jade china set. To Kristin I leave the contents of my third floor guest bedroom. To Amanda I leave all my kitchen appliances." On and on the lawyer droned. PDC wondered if his name would be called at all. Finally the lawyer looked up and around the room. "Is Jeremiah here? Jeremiah Silus?"

"Present," Jeremiah said.

"Your grandmother has left you her stocks, bonds and current bank balance, which today stands at a total value of $14.4 million dollars."

His entire family turned to look at him. "What?" one of them said. "You cannot be serious. She was a millionaire!?"

"That stingy bitch!" another squealed. "You have got to be fucking kidding me! I would listen to her dumb stories about riding those stupid fucking horses for hours!"

PDC was in a state of shock. The lawyer went on to explain that the $2.3 million dollars in her bank account would be immediately transferred into his name while it would take longer to migrate the stocks and bonds. After the angry family left the room accepting they were excluded from the payout, but promising to get a second opinion on the matter, the lawyer approached PDC.

"I worked with your grandmother on this. She wanted me to make sure you understand that she really loved you, that of all her relation you are the one she feels has the greatest shot at doing something meaningful with your life. She appreciated your toughness and stamina. And she loved the idea of your relatives getting stung at the end. She laughed and laughed thinking about how mad they would get once they found out you were going to inherit all her money."

PDC left the lawyers office in a state of shock. He went to his new bank. "I am Jeremiah Silus," he said, removing his ID from his wallet. In his best British accent he stated, "Mr. Harry Potter needs to make withdrawal."

######## MARSHALL ########

Marshall and Hippie Girl were on the road. His initial

strategy involved dissolving into a crowd of dirty hippies and remaining hidden until after he turned 18. After that he would worry about getting back to Argentina. He now understood that the Rainbow Family was a loose-knit global community that had people who could assist in arranging transportation to and from a wide variety of places on the planet. If this 'family' was connected it might be possible for him to assume a new identity and get back into South America with their help.

"*I need to be prepared,*" he thought. "*There is a time and place for everything.*"

They took a circuitous route to their destination. "If you have never seen the Great Sand Dunes it is worth the trip. Plus my uncle has some acres out in the San Luis Valley so we can camp there for a few days before we hit the gathering. Maybe gather some sage."

"Sage?" Marshall inquired.

"Yeah. Desert Sage. For eliminating bad vibes and driving evil away."

"I can't wait to see it," Marshall replied.

After hours spent in the vast flatness of Western Kansas Marshall offered to rent a hotel room. At 10pm they went to sleep. At 7:00am the next morning they woke up and started driving.

Eastern Colorado gave way to mountains. As he came around a bend in a two lane highway he was confronted by massive 'wall dikes' outside the town of LaVeta, Colorado. Giant walls radiating out from the Spanish Peaks like sun rays. Their geometry made them look engineered, but their scale was beyond human constructions.

Marshall merged into the slow lane as they started the ascent to LaVeta pass. Up and up they went, their ears popping as they climbed. Marshall turned on the hazard lights and carefully monitored the engine temperature and oil pressure gauges. Eventually they crested and started the long descent.

A massive valley emerged into view with Blanca Mountain to their right. They took highway 159 south toward San Luis and about halfway there took a turn down a dirt road into a sea of sagebrush.

Marshall drove down the sandy road. "You have arrived at your destination."

They got out and stretched. Marshall felt like he was the tallest object for possibly hundreds of miles around. They were completely alone, with only a few homes visible in any direction. "This place is insane."

"Oh yeah it is!" Hippie Girl exclaimed, shivering with excitement. "I am so glad we got to come! My uncle owns this spot and I can camp here whenever I want. But I have never been able to afford to come out here in my van!" She grabbed a lawn chair and set it up in the middle of the gravel road. "This is a major UFO hotspot and you will see why once the sun is fully down."

The sunset was purple due to smoke from western wildfires. Marshall was captivated by the beauty. "This really is an amazing place," he said to Hippie Girl. "I have seen some amazing landscapes, but truly this is one of the most surreal."

The sky grew darker. "The moon is only 6% illuminated tonight so we should be able to see the Milky Way." Marshall walked in circles looking at the horizon in all directions. Mountains were changing color and high elevation snow was turning purple and glowing. A wave of deep blue-black flowing from the East was gradually overtaking the azure blue as it retreated into the West. The first starlight penetrated the dome of the heavens with a few twinkling orbs and then dozens more.

The Sangre de Christo mountains changed from blood red to slate gray as the sun disappeared.

"Awesome," Marshall said. "This place... is crazy."

"Snippy the Horse is from here."

"Who?" Marshall asked.

"You don't know much about UFO stuff huh?" Hippie Girl laughed. "Well, a horse was mutilated out here in an impossible way. There was no blood, but there were what looked like laser-cuts to remove certain portions of flesh. It was the first one, then there were a lot of mutilated cows. Sometimes organs would be missing, but there were no cuts. All the blood would be gone, completely gone, but no punctures. Super, super weird things. A two thousand pound cow stuck in the top of a tree. How did it get there? Did it fly up there? That is where we are. Where all sorts of unhinged weird shit has happened in the past. And keeps happening."

"Are there any traces of, like, the government doing that stuff?" Marshall asked.

"Yeah, well, funny you should ask. I guess where there have been the discoveries of the mutilations there are also eye witnesses who say they saw an old-timey helicopter flying around. My grandpa watched a show on his antenna TV called MASH and it was about the Korean War in the 1950's and they say the helicopter in MASH is the same one reported by eyewitnesses. And I have for sure seen old-timey World War Two planes and stuff like that out here. If you look long enough you will definitely see some things."

Hippie Girl looked up Snippy and read the detailed autopsy results to Marshall. She went on to describe similar cow mutilations. While Hippie Girl was talking about Blanca Mountain being hollow Marshall received a vision. He saw a horse being surrounded by an electric globe and part of the surface of the globe got close enough to burn off part of the horse flesh. He saw a blue meshlike lightning-fluid that started to touch the horse at different locations. But he felt certain it was not supposed to do that. He felt it was an engineering issue they were trying to fix long ago. He could hear the horse scream and see its eyes grow wide with terror. "You say it happened with cows also? And the blood would be gone and they would be found in the tops of trees?"

Hippie Girl responded, "Yeah! Crazy stuff. And that is just the beginning. They also say this area is full of vortexes that allow space travel. That this area is some kind of space port for ethereal energy to move between worlds. I mean, it might also be possible that they move stuff that way, but my understanding is that it allows consciousness and information to move between worlds through a kind of electromagnetic gate. They are natural formations, but of course a lot of natural things can be turned into exploitable resources. So they say the government controls most of it now."

Marshall had seen with his mind's eye the failed experiment with Snippy the Horse. He could hear it scream as the 'entanglement field' collapsed. Some parts of the horse arrived at a distant platform while other parts of the horse remained behind.

Marshall felt an intense sense of foreboding, like he could see eyes staring back at his mind's eye. "I think you are right, there is some weird stuff that goes on out here for sure. I can feel it."

######## PDC ########

PDC was shaking. He was not able to focus and instead felt overwhelmed with the number of options that had suddenly presented themselves. He was walking down the street and saw a billboard advertisement for a motorcycle store. Something in him clicked like a light switch and he looked up the address. He went in and bought a new dual sport motorcycle. He paid cash.

"So..." he asked the salesperson, "How do I drive this thing?"

The salesperson was nervous. "Um, here, let me show you." The man got on the bike and demonstrated shifting gears, how to use the brakes, where the turn signals were located. He helped PDC set the clutch and brake levers to fit his hands and helped adjust the foot shifter to fit his boot. PDC then drove around the parking lot, pretending like he didn't know how to ride a motorcycle. He pulled back up to the salesman. "I think I get it now." He paired his phone with the helmet so he could listen to music. He was wearing black full body armor and durable riding boots along with a carbon fiber helmet.

He would have purchased the inflatable airbag add-on for his armor, but they were all sold out.

"If you can come back next week..." the salesperson began.

"Not possible," PDC replied. "But I will see you in the future! Maybe."

PDC drove to a box store and bought camping gear, a waterproof backpack and a tire plug kit. He strapped his gear onto the motorcycle luggage rack and adjusted the suspension to support the added weight. He slammed a cold brew coffee drink and did a final pre-flight check.

He got on the motorcycle and plugged in a location to a mapping app on his phone. He put on his helmet. "Head South," the mapping app instructed. He thumbed through some screens and launched a music app. He put the phone in a holder on his handlebars and drove to the highway entry.

As he turned into an onramp to merge onto I-70 W he hit shuffle on his playlist. As he accelerated the volume increased to compensate.

A sped-up version of Quiet Riot's 'Bang Your Head' bombarded PDC as he accelerated his way into the fast lane. "More power! I'm gonna rock it till it strikes the hour! Bang your head! Metal health will drive you mad! Bang your head! Metal health will drive you mad! All right!"

######## X ########

X was at an outdoor table at a coffee shop in Alamosa, Colorado. She had a camera and a selfie stick and was speaking to the camera:

"The desert is a wonderful, magical place. There is nothing quite like it. And if you want to amplify your desert experience you should come to the San Luis Valley. The average height of the valley floor is 8000 feet. 8000 feet!" She noticed a doe and a fawn grazing on grass across the street from the coffee shop. She turned the camera to show the scene. "This is a magical place to start your day."

She turned the camera back upon herself. "So, I arrived last night. Smoke from California fires had reduced the visibility somewhat based on the online smoke map. But then, after we set up our tent and got settled in, it rained and hailed. The sky totally cleared. It was clear enough to see the Milky Way! So remember, maintain a positive mental attitude and bring some rain when you visit!"

She paused the recording to take a drink. She stretched her arms above her head and opened and clenched her fists. She started up the camera again.

"So I am charging my phone at this coffee shop and waiting on a breakfast sandwich. We are gonna go on a hike with Happy Goku Potter today!" she said as she turned the camera on her dog, a Great Pyrenees-Anatolian-American Akita mix. "To get acclimated to this place I ate some melatonin last night and stood barefoot in the sand. The sand is filled with quartz crystals. And I swear to you I could feel and hear the signals coming from the crystals in the ground. It was out of this world! Happy Goku Potter is with me on this trip because we are going into some 'bear country' and then later we will be going to a Rainbow Gathering, where he will be protecting me from bad people and introducing me to good people. He is THE BEST traveling companion. I love him. I can't believe how good he is being. And remember, he is totally adoptable from the Pet Project!"

"I also want to shout out my appreciation for all the people who are doing all these tasks so this cool dog and I can take this adventure vacation. Everyone is fulfilling their specific economic roles and because they are working I get to experience this awesome place. I am here to buy their stuff and have a good time. Remember to always show some love for our restaurant workers, baristas, gas station attendants. Stop in at some of these small local shops. All the people who make this wonderful life possible want to see your smiling face walk through their doors!"

She looked over at her dog. He was sitting on the ground

next to her monitoring the deer across the street. She looked back into the camera, "I might go find a shower later, after we go for a hike."

A car drove by and she heard the lyrics, 'Out on the road today I saw a dead head sticker on a Cadillac... said don't look back you can never look back...'. She knew she would need to cut that out of her recording. It was always 'so annoying' when cars came by blasting copyrighted music. It made her editing much harder.

She continued, "I haven't been posting much lately because I have been working out like a maniac and I don't want to be one of those people who is recording at the gym. But to update you I am feeling really good. The plan is to hike the Embargo Creek trail today, then Crestone Pass tomorrow. Today up to maybe 13,000 feet and tomorrow we are looking at around 11,800. Should be a good time, provided the pupper can take it. I think he can do it!"

The same car drove by and she heard the lyrics, 'It keeps you running... girl, it keeps you running...'.

She restarted, "Well, this is me, signing off from lovely Alamosa, Colorado."

There was a wreck on the road to her original destination. She looked at a map. "We should go here instead," she said to Happy Goku.

She parked near the Cathedral Campground. She started recording, "This is perhaps the most beautiful place I have ever seen. We are going to climb up Mesa Mountain today!" The camera revealed she was dressed in very lightweight clothes. Business casual attire. She turned off the camera and loaded her backpack with some snacks, a collapsible dog bowl and a gallon of water. She then began hiking up the trail.

Up and up she climbed, stopping in various spots to record some video. She noticed the sky was darkening, but chose to ignore it. "A light rain might actually clear out more of that smoke from California," she said to Happy Goku. But then, as she climbed above 11,000 feet, a hailstorm exploded. She was well above the treeline, but there was a dense thicket of small shrubs near her. She ran and tried to hide beneath one. The hail just kept coming. The sleet and rain were freezing her clothes. She pulled her arms into her shirt and tried to keep the fabric away from her skin, causing her clothes to form a sort of igloo around her. She was afraid. Her fear turned to terror. She began to pray. "Please, God, if you can hear me. Please let me live. Please let me get out of here."

The hail lasted for several minutes before letting up. X got to her feet and started moving as fast as her frozen clothes and limbs would allow. She had been defeated by the mountain. Happy Goku Potter appeared much better equipped to survive such stormy conditions and showed no signs of distress. He led the way.

As she descended the mountain the air rapidly changed from freezing to hot. Her clothes were almost completely dry by the time she arrived at her van.

She glanced at her backpack and realized it was looking pretty rough. She got her camera.

"I could kick myself for not recording what I just went through. I got caught in a hailstorm on top of a mountain wearing this!" She pointed to her clothes. "I am an idiot! I prayed. I mean it. I prayed to God, a heartfelt begging prayer, for the hail to stop. What is insane is that it can go from hail and freezing to hot and dry in what feels like 10 minutes of walking." She paused the camera and packed everything into her van.

On the drive out she noticed the smoke from wildfires had been cleared by the rain. She was presented with mind blowing vistas. She turned on the camera to record her drive. She didn't speak over the image, she just recorded the scene. She shared her media.

Once back on US Hwy 160 she witnessed a complete triple rainbow. Then it started pouring rain. Driving was very slow.

"If this rain had hit us in the mountains, as ice and snow, I would probably be dead right now," she said to the dog. "I will never do that again! That was INSANE!!!"

######## MARSHALL and HIPPIE GIRL ########

The morning air at 8000 feet was brisk and Marshall was up early. Hippie Girl explained to him earlier how to gather sage so harvesting was already well underway. By the time Hippie Girl woke up Marshall had already collected all they would need for the gathering. Despite the fact the sun had only been up for half an hour it was already starting to get oppressively hot.

"Let's go get some grub and some stuff we can use for trade at the gathering," Marshall suggested. He looked for the pawn shop nearest to his location and found one in Alamosa. It was close to a local coffee shop. "Let's go here. Breakfast is on me."

Marshall ordered breakfast for Hippie Girl and ordered a coffee for himself. "I will order food when I get back. I want to go check something out at that pawn shop."

Marshall entered the pawn shop with his coffee and walked up to the counter.

"What can I do ya fer?" a man asked.

"I was wondering if you have gold and silver for sale."

The man looked at Marshall with suspicion. "I do," he replied, slowly.

"I am looking to buy."

Marshall returned to the coffee shop with a heavy box and sat it down in a chair at their table. "Stuff for trade," he said. He ordered two eggs over easy with wheat toast, two slices of bacon, a double order of hash browns and an orange juice. "Oh, and can I get an Americano to go in about 15 minutes?"

"Sure thing," the barista said as she turned to take the order to the kitchen.

Marshall went to a high end outfitting store to get clothes and gear for the gathering while Hippie Girl went to a thrift shop. He spared no expense and wanted to be as comfortable as possible. He bought more than one of everything. The store had a vacuum sealing machine so he was able to compress a lot of his spare clothing into a much smaller space. This made it appear as if he hadn't purchased all that much stuff. He changed into his new clothes and threw his old clothes away.

He asked Hippie Girl if she knew what tobacco hippies preferred. She professed to be an expert. "Okay," he said, handing her a roll of large bills, "Spend 100% of this on the best tobacco strategy."

Hippie Girl was excited to shop. It was a lot of money! She bought a few dozen cartons of the best cigarettes and 40 packs of loose-leaf rolling tobacco. "You let people use the rollies for free if you feel nice, but you only use your prerolls for trade and favors," Hippie Girl explained. "Around the fourth of July people will trade you a house for a pack of these."

They decided to eat a light dinner and then head for the Great Sand Dunes National Park. "I am so excited to hike the dunes at night. I have always wanted to do it, but have never been able to! Finally it is happening!"

They set off from the parking lot through a grove of trees and emerged into a large flat plain of sand. The sun had already set, but the sky was still bright with waning light. Before them stood massive pyramids of sand. Shifting. Formless. Terrifying and harmless.

They marched to the edge of the dunes and started climbing. Marshall lost his footing and fell forward into the soft sand. There was no sound. It was not an experience Marshall could describe in words. As the sunlight disappeared the landscape changed. The valleys between sand dunes were disappearing into shadow. No. It was more like the tops of the dunes were emerging out of a lake of nothingness. The valleys between dunes had no estimable bottom and when you looked at it from an angle the nothingness looked like a sort of watery surface. Beyond darkness. Veiled.

The total absence of sound was crashing into him. Onward and upward he climbed, every step backsliding in dissolving sand. Finally they arrived at the peak of the High Dune. The Eastern Mountains lit up with the pale light of a waning moon and the snow caps glittered like stars through fog. They could see what appeared to be an unending ocean of sand waves to their North. They were at the highest point in the dunes. Marshall was stunned by the view. "You are seeing this, right?" he asked Hippie Girl. "I almost feel the need to pinch myself to make sure I am not dreaming."

"It is incredible. I can't believe how beautiful it is. Thank you for suggesting we keep hiking. I have never seen anything like this before," Hippie Girl professed.

A sound arose from the mountains to their South. Out of the total silence Marshall could discern a whisper. The trees were rustling. "I think there is a ..."

Before Marshall could finish his sentence a powerful burst of wind blew Hippie Girl off the peak of the high dune and she disappeared into the gray-black murkiness of a deep ravine. A gale force wind was bearing down relentlessly upon them, turning sand particles into tiny painful projectiles. Marshall lifted his jacket to protect his face. "Hippie Girl!" he yelled out, stumbling down the deep sand embankment in the direction she had fallen. He could hear her. "Where are you!? Can you hear me?"

"I can see you!" she said as they converged on each other.

"We need to leave. Obviously." Marshall said somewhat apologetically. Once they made it back to the top of the dune they oriented themselves toward the murky black treeline located to their south. They hoped to find the quickest path back to the parking lot. It felt like it took forever, but 55 minutes later they were standing in front of Hippie Girl's van.

"I am going to go use the bathroom and change," Marshall said.

"Will you come into the women's restroom with me? Just while I check to make sure there are no weirdos in there."

"Sure," Marshall said. "I'll stab 'em if they try any funny business," he promised.

There was no one in the restroom, so Marshall went ahead and took an open stall where he changed into fresh clothes.

They left the Sand Dunes in the midst of a severe windstorm. Large tumbleweeds were flying over fences and hitting the van. Miniature sand tornadoes illuminated by their headlights were crossing their path as they exited the park.

Ominous clouds formed over the San Luis Valley south of Fort Garland. A dark, heavy mass of lenticular clouds. It felt like it was hovering directly above their campsite. After they arrived at Hippie Girl's spot Marshall decided to take a walk. They were camping on a five acre rectangle and there were hundreds of similar plots divided into large neighborhoods. Almost all the lots were empty, but a few held the remains of failed lives. A broken down RV. An abandoned trailer. Any signs of life were all located far in the distance. As Marshall walked he witnessed the mass of clouds completely vanish. As if the moon drank them through a straw.

Marshall had never witnessed anything like it.

Making sure to avoid the thorns of the tumbleweed saplings and the spines of cacti he removed his shoes and socks and stood in the middle of the sandy road. He raised his hands above his head and stretched out as if reaching toward the heavens. He then dropped onto the ground in a lotus position. Eyes closed he attempted to make sense of what he was feeling.

Rose quartz sand. Far beneath them was a layer of electrically-conductive blue clay. Hot springs ran through the valley. And Electric Peak near Crestone was being continuously struck by lightning. This mountain was one of several responsible for charging the valley.

Marshall did not see the relationships as one of objects to each other. He felt there was some energy which was binding matter together so that the valley was one thing, a continuous object. He felt that he was inside an entangled space. A place where super-macroscopic forces were constantly at work. A place where if you needed gigajoules of energy you could realistically generate it from the environment itself.

CHAPTER 5

######## ERIC ########

Eric attended a lecture regarding the use of fantasy in the context of science fiction.

The author took the stage. For some audience members with specialized glasses the speech was augmented with the appearance of real time images and props. So when the author pretended to swing a sword users wearing the augmentation glasses observed a ghost-like sword mapped to his hands that slashed through space. The motions would leave a 'vapor trail' in its wake. Eric was not using augmented glasses as he listened and took notes.

-

"Fantasy is generally differentiated from science fiction by how the author explains technology. For example, take the mythological sword which can cut through stone because it has been imbued with magical charms versus the light saber which creates a plasma from an energy/crystal interaction and melts stone. Both are fantasy. But one relies on magical explanations while the other relies on scientific implications. The author masks the un-reality beneath the language or, better yet, obfuscates reality via descriptive language. An amulet of invisibility versus a military uniform that can curve light and project the image of the background. Both are fantasies, in the sense they are invented whole cloth by the author. Yet, one relies on magic and the other, hoodwinking via quasi-scientific reasoning."

"It is rare to see an author combine these disciplines. I

think this is true in part because the audience wants 'constant' suspension of disbelief. Mixing 'fantasy-magic' with 'science-physics' does not seem to work. I suspect audiences will reject it."

"There are, however, counterexamples of this that have been successful. Comic book characters mix magic and science fiction and manage to pull it off. But comic book type narratives that are mostly consumed as pictures or movie experiences are not the same as literary prose consumed in a book. In prose it seems more challenging."

Eric leaned forward as he listened to the lecturer.

"Alien characters and alien worlds are rarely, if ever, fully fleshed out. What I mean by this is, simply, that over half of our cells, the cells in our bodies, are not even human. Are not our DNA. So how does this go for aliens? Clearly their gut biomes have not been taken seriously by most writers. But more and more audiences know what this is. As science fills in the blanks it opens us up to a requirement to make our scenes plausible to an ever-smarter audience. Or, at least, an audience that is being exposed to ideas like quantum computers. Exposed in such a way that it will be hard to talk about them without mentioning q-bits moving forward."

"Science fiction audiences are usually fairly well informed of 'popular science,' so they know generally the concepts of 'dark matter' and 'anti-matter' and 'fusion.' So as we incorporate these scientific hypotheses and eventual technologies into our present-day writing we need to make sure we are treating the audience seriously. They will see right through bullshit."

######## ERIC ########

Eric was writing.

-

Studying the magical world began with the non-magical world.

The Poynting Vector.

They are ancient machines, quantum information machines, and they can be accessed via spells or sounds or specific configurations of your mind or combinations of those. They are entangled with all humans, and by virtue of their existence they facilitate access to an alternate universe of 'power flux outcomes.' 'Wizards' and 'witches' are those who are born possessing awareness of magic. They can both witness and demonstrate 'magic force' as it is now called. But beneath the primitive and artificial exterior of 'magic' lies a technological infrastructure that is a remnant of a civilization that was destroyed long ago.

The oldest texts of the Magic World reference the time when the 'Quantum Machines' were first built. A great civilization penetrated the secrets of molecular impermanence and learned how to re-arrange atomic matter into new stable configurations. By directing and manipulating frequencies they could remake matter. For example, the long mythologized 'philosopher's stone' was stated to be able to transmute lead into gold; obviously taking a lead atom that contains 82 protons and reducing it into a gold atom that contains 79 protons seems on the surface a lot easier than taking 79 individual hydrogen atoms and crushing them into one atom of gold. The technology was created so that the frequencies which were practical and useful would always be available in the background across the entire planet. As an analogy, there are tuning forks embedded within the Earth that are vibrating at all times. The frequency a given tuning fork produces is invisible to us, because literally all objects we can interact with are simultaneously vibrating with that frequency. All the molecules of Earth are vibrating with that frequency. The magician taps into these pre-existing rivers of vibration and adds or subtracts a specific 'key frequency.' This allows him or her to levitate a lead ball or generate a fireball out of otherwise ordinary breathable air. It is because the Oxygen atoms that are vibrating with one of the macro-keys can have the magical micro-key applied and they will all aggregate into the area around a wizard's hand, whereby the wizard can then throw and engulf an adversary in an oxygen cloud and cause their skin to burst into flame. A wizard can drain all the blood from a creature, can remove just the iron from the blood. But these are not trivial micro-keys to unlock. Additionally, most of the keys are lost to time.

Magical Mechanics. When two sources of vibration are positioned close and are of sufficiently high intensity, two new vibrations appear: a vibration lower than either of the two original ones and a vibration which is higher than the original two.

There are now four vibrations where before there were only two. The two new vibrations correlate with the SUM and the DIFFERENCE of the two original frequencies, which we refer to as 'magical vibes.' For example, if you provide a micro-key frequency of 100,000 Hz and combine that with a macro-key frequency of 101,000 Hz, you will produce the sum, 201,000 Hz, and the difference, 1,000 Hz, which is in the range of human hearing. Magical 'combination tones.' By analogy, in music this effect is called a 'Tartini Tone.'

The Magician Gorman Heimholtz (1894-1821 BC) re-ordered thinking on spell mechanics when she reported that she could also detect 'summation vibrations.' Heimholtz demonstrated that the phenomenon had to result from a broken linearity.

Alone, sound waves contain insignificant energy. For instance, if every man, woman, and child in New York City spoke loudly at the same time, the total acoustic energy would barely warm a single cup of tea. It is when the correct micro-key frequency is applied to the already present macro-key vibration that a magician unlocks RESONANCE. Magical resonance allows matter to be reconfigured in ways that appear to violate the laws of classical physics.

The micro-keys can be channeled by anyone on the planet who learns how to generate the constructive or destructive interference required to unlock 'magic harmonics.' But in the scientific parlance of trial and error, there are far more ways to fail than succeed. Exploring new magic is dangerous.

The 'machines' are structures of a specific shape that were embedded in the Earth long ago and whose purpose is to generate frequencies across the entire planet. Everything in the past was once powered by these frequency generators. Energy cannot be created from nothing. So the pressure generated by gravity and also the torque generated by the tides couple to the surfaces of the mega-structures and deform them, twist and stretch them. The deformation and relaxation of the large structures generate frequencies that are useful to the intelligent beings who live on this planet.

Earth; a ruin. But the large machines continue to operate. The magician in a game of chance attempts to add a new complementary frequency to trigger a new magical reaction. A lot of famous wizards and witches possessed a knack for expanding the library of spells. They had a talent for choosing the best frequencies. However, a lot of witches and wizards have been blown up over time by choosing unwisely. And since they perished they could not tell others what to avoid.

It was the remnant who adopted the use of spoken words and wand flourishing to activate 'magical outcomes.' The survivors incorporated a mythology into their rendering of the technological underpinnings of magic because it was the only way to preserve the utility of the machines. They could never hope to rebuild the resonators and so thinking in terms of the actual technology was seen as useless at best or, in the worst case, a threat to social stability. The remnant accepted that no new machines could be built. New magic explored new ways to reconfigure matter which is to say focus different 'intentional frequencies' or 'micro-keys' simultaneously.

Experimenting with magic is dangerous because there is no handbook for developing new spells. There is no science of prediction for new magic. It is trial and error, luck and faith. Like climbing a mountain in the dark, there's no way to rush it without risking tragic consequences.

The existence of the machines passed into legend and into dust. Eventually it was such an un-serious topic that no one talked about it. The prevailing wisdom argued that magic was a property of the human body and the wand and motions were required to manifest the 'aural-charge' which equates with the ability of a spell or potion to generate change in the environment. The 'aural-charge' was the explanation for why some people could see magic and other could not. It was simply a property of a physical human body and magic extends outwardly from the user into the world. The user is the seat of magic; not only the host of power, but also its source.

Layer upon layer of unnecessary complexity had been piled into the magical world until, finally, all practitioners became somewhat paranoid about being discovered. A slow-growing population of magic users hid themselves away as a secret society while the rest of the world kept rocketing forward. Necessarily, the magic users live among non-magic people, but as a general rule do not participate in the affairs of the non-magical world in any meaningful way.

As time advanced so, too, by trial and error, magic. But an obscuring cloud of mysticism was growing stiller and darker over the magical world. Bureaucracy crept into magical society. The politics of the magical world were starting to mirror those of the non-magical world. A death penalty was introduced as punishment for revealing magical reality to any non-magical person. A magical person could have relations with non-magical people, but if those people found out about magic then both could be killed. Also, if they had a magical child it would need to be sent to live with a magical family while the non-magical mother would be told her child was dead. There was a system in place to manage magic users.

-

Eric saw the story forming. He twirled his pen and began writing again.

-

He came to the conclusion that magic works this way because of a conversation he had with the woman who became his wife. She was a physics major. And she believed that the current understanding of the laws of physics were far too limited. She believed matter could be 'recompiled' into new things. That there was a fine structure underlying the classical experience of reality that did not require brute strength to access and modify. It was when she said to him, "It sounds like magical thinking, to say you ought to be able to reconfigure matter with just a thought, with just the power of your mind." It was in that moment that he saw 'magic' light upon her; an aura radiating out from her body. As soon as it was there it was gone. But he knew he had seen it.

"You are correct!" he said. "You have to believe in it!"

-

"But I need to get the introductions correct," Eric thought. *"Why would a magical man meet a non-magical woman? Under what circumstances? Was he working in the non-magical world? Why? It doesn't make sense."* He sat contemplating.

Eric was writing, but was winding down. Noiselessly, invisibly, she had been watching him from her pillow. As he wrote she was touching herself and thinking about him. She earnestly wanted him to succeed.

When she was certain he was finished she slid out of the bed and crawled on the floor toward him. He saw her and looked surprised.

She was naked save for a white v-neck T-shirt. He was in a dress shirt and boxer shorts. The chair was a swivel-type and she gently spun him around to face her.

He rose out of his boxer shorts and she took him into her mouth while maintaining eye contact. He felt wonderful staring into her eyes.

She stood up and turned around. She reached around and grabbed him and slid him into herself. She then worked up and down, moaning.

Her beautiful skin, her lovely body, the whimpering sound

she made as she took all of him . "I want to cum in you," he said in an animal voice, grabbing her waist.

She pulled her shirt off and began moving faster, rising higher then taking him deeper. "I want you to cum in me. Pleeeease..." she pleaded.

Eric stood up and directed her to the back of a couch located near a window overlooking Las Vegas, Nevada. He bent her over and began ramming himself into her as he watched their reflection in the glass. It was amazing. He felt like a wild animal.

"You feel so good inside me," she said, moving herself to give him the best access.

"Oh fuck!" he exclaimed. Thrusting into her as hard as he could he pushed his cum deep inside her. "Oh my God. Oh my God." he panted. They laid down together.

Eric woke up after a few hours of sleep. He was pressed against her, spooning. He got hard. He began to move against her thighs. He then lifted her leg up and put his leg between hers. His pre-cum lubricated him and allowed him to slide into her.

She awoke to him fucking her. "Ooooooh," she moaned. "That is your pussy."

"That's my pussy," he snarled back to her in agreement.

"Own that pussy," she insisted.

And so he did.

######## MAXWELL ########

All the arrangements were finalized. Maxwell's car was loaded onto the dirigible and was being secured for shipment to Australia. It would take a few weeks to get to the location deep in the Australian outback, a compound of 140,000 acres. He would be out there alone, far from the clutches of the US government or any other agency which might have a reason to interrogate him.

Maxwell was impressed with the Zeppelin. "It is fascinating

to me that it generates its own Hydrogen. So the electrolysis is run from the solar furnace that you heat using concentrated solar light. The sunlight is focused by Fresnel lens concentrators and is channeled via fiber optic cables into your furnace. What a brilliant design!" he said to Milton over video chat. "I am so thankful I got to be your information broker. Thank you for transporting me and everything you guys have done for me!"

Milton was all too happy to help, seeing that Maxwell had been the one who clued him in about Megalithic artifacts. "Just let us know when you want pulled out and we will come get you. Barring any unforeseen events that might interfere, of course."

Maxwell's car with him inside was lowered. Once it was on the ground he unhooked the cables. A large shipping container was then dropped. And another. The ship then lifted back up and disappeared heading East.

Maxwell took stock of his situation. The desert. Heat rising off the unending ocean of sand and brush. The accompanying mirage of water always just out of reach. Snakes and lizards and tiny field mice darting around. Maxwell used a portable jack to lift his car onto blocks. It was going to be outside for an unknown amount of time. He wanted to keep the tires at low air pressure and off the ground to preserve them for as long as possible; they were partially filled with nitrogen gas. From the shipping container he unloaded and installed three large solar panels on the roof and hood of his car. He hooked them into a charge controller that was feeding energy into four deep cycle marine batteries located in his trunk. He then powered up a bank of microcomputers and got his laptop connected to set up his network. He went over to the shipping container and removed a one gallon jug of water. He immediately drank it all.

His 1982 Mercedes 240d started broadcasting in FM. He set the program to play songs and also send notifications if anything moved while in range of his cameras. His car was set with a 'sentry' mode of operation and had a 360 degree camera attached to a pole that he mounted on the trunk. There were additional cameras mounted on the car as failovers should the primary cameras fail.

Jebediah had given him several solar powered smart cameras that he mounted on t-posts using a large slender tube of electrical conduit as a sleeve. These could detect animal movement and broadcast text-to-speech messages on an FM channel. The messages were designed to be detected by the computers located in his car. The transmitters in the smart cameras were very low power while the transmitter in Maxwell's car could have a range up to 30 miles. Possibly more.

The laws of probability weigh heavily against the existence of such a car in such a place. However, it is precisely the improbable that contains the emergent.

Maxwell was excited to experience a span of time where he could concentrate without any distractions. He was returning to his work on a problem in mathematics. His recollection had been triggered by a conversation with Milton regarding the configuration of a particular megalithic structure.

"I dated a woman who would add numbers on license plates to get to a single digit. So if you take the number seven hundred and seventy seven (777) and you add (7+7+7) you get 21. Then if you add 2+1 you get 3. Turns out this is called the 'digital root' of a number, but before I found that out it was just part of what I call 'hippie calculus.' Hippie calculus states that any repeated pattern of 3 numbers always adds to 3, 6 or 9. Also any 6 repeated numbers add to 3,6,9 and any 9 repeated numbers. So in hippie calculus there are a lot of rules that determine how the numbers are distributed throughout the 'number universe.' She came at this from the perspective of numerology, the study of spiritual numerical meaning. She would make determinations based on the number she would get after adding. If the wrong thing was there we would literally take a right or left turn. To change the timing."

Milton was unsure he understood. "Huh?"

"Some numbers were good and some were bad. I never paid

much attention to it, but one day while sitting in a coffee shop I started writing out the counting numbers one through nine, then 10 through 18, then 19 through 27." Maxwell started drawing it for Milton in his notebook. "I noticed that the columns preserved the digital root of the descending numbers. I didn't know this was a digital root back then, so it was all new to me. I decided to look at the location of the prime numbers in this setup and noticed that the numbers 2,3,5 and their related composites were a simple ordering." He showed Milton those values on his chart. "See, they are a pattern, a simple pattern. What we are left with are the primes greater than or equal to 7. They are in these 'octets' and are also part of a pattern. I worked on this for a while and discovered that if you take a prime number and divide it by the numbers 1 through 9, the remainder tells you which column to use the number in to cancel composites in that column. A modified Sieve of Eratosthenes that works for isolated digital root 'channels.' So anyway the algebra starts to become difficult to explain in plain language, but it got me thinking about the possibility that there are some kinds of information that might represent a UNIVERSAL SIGN. Like, all sufficiently advanced life must arrive at certain inescapable conclusions, among those are certain mathematical truths. So the 'final solution' to hard problems must be a sign that is universally translatable without needing an intermediary 'language.' Like, the Fibonacci series is evident in all languages as the SAME CURVE. So is it possible that megalithic architecture had certain ways of encoding meaning in their constructions?"

1	2	3	4	5	6	7	8	9
10	11	12	13	14	15	16	17	18
19	20	21	22	23	24	25	26	27
28	29	30	31	32	33	34	35	36

Milton was listening. Maxwell continued.

"Well, this girl claimed that the Great Pyramid in Egypt was actually built around a much older structure. That they built the great pyramid to close off a gateway to another planet or planets. That only by surrounding the structure with all those stone blocks could they squelch the resonance that it generated."

"Why wouldn't they just destroy it?" Milton asked.

"She claimed it was closed with the intent of re-opening it when the time was right. She said that there were these 'people' who came here from another planet and sealed it off on purpose, sort of like a catastrophe-proof mothballing, and that they or someone already here will then remove the stones at an appointed time. By removing the stones they reopen the portal. Crazy, right? She told me that we are just short-lived workers who are placed here to extract things that these much longer lived beings need or want. They live for millions of years whereas we live for maybe 120. And that is by their design, so we cannot rival them intellectually. Well, her most interesting idea was that there are these UNIVERSAL SIGNIFIERS that beings of a certain intelligence must converge upon and that is how intelligence finds itself across the cosmos. That there are portals to these faraway worlds and they are built using universal shapes and 'universal signals.' And so that started me wondering, what can actually be known with total confidence? What can we actually know about a universal truth? As a student of biosemiotics in college I knew that unary numbering systems must be universal. So I decided to study prime number distributions, because the primes might represent a universal signifier. The order of primes cannot be destroyed or modified by analysis. It is both order AND chaos, or pseudo-randomness at the very least. So, could it be that these megalithic artifacts represent not only one different culture, but maybe numerous cultures that have arisen and subsided over hundreds of thousands of years? Or possibly even millions or billions of years? And could it be that they are embedding UNIVERSAL STRUCTURE into their designs. That is what some of these stone artifacts make me think. That there is a universal sign encoded in the structure with the express intent of allowing us to find ourselves over and over again. As ruins. Intellect discovering itself. A type of 'coming full circle' that all sufficiency long-lived cultures get to grapple with. The Earth is designed to be a ticking timebomb and if we are not sufficiently interplanetary we cannot survive as a cohesive world society. Every so often the destruction is so thorough that without being off-world the likelihood of survival is minute."

The conversation with Milton reminded him of his previous work on counting numbers. A file opened in his mind. In Australia his entire mission was to focus his consciousness toward witnessing the Sign of the Primes.

"I am orbiting these questions like a satellite pings a black hole. This is so deep I am not sure I can get a reflection."

Now he was using a compass and a paper map to locate a cave the Australian Scientist had marked for him.

######## ANNIE ########

Annie was out checking the irrigation system for her family farm. An 800 acre estate in West Central Australia.

She and her mother moved to Australia when Annie was 12 years old. Her father had been killed in an attack on their family farm in South Africa. The tensions were so great that her father realized ahead of time they would need to emigrate. So he purchased the farm in Australia to flee the political upheaval in his home country.

Her father was an automation design engineer and he taught Annie how to program and think like a data scientist. He taught her how to make simple the things others make hard.

She loved her father with all her heart. She loved her home also, but was old enough to understand the dangers they were facing. He negotiated with the Australian government to get citizenship for himself and his family. As he was financially successful this was accomplished without much difficulty.

A month before they were set to depart for their new home a group of men attacked their farm. Workers on the farm repelled the attack, but not before her father was fatally shot.

She automated the new farm in Australia. Her mother, devastated by the loss of her second husband, stayed in a condo in Sydney. Annie would visit her from time to time.

The farm was located near a rail spur, and Annie would work to load refrigerated shipping containers with food grown on her farm. Not a lot of shipping containers, but enough to ensure the farm could meet all its expenses. Even though money was no object, she did not want to be a drain on the estate. The cars were scheduled for pickup and the train operator would attach them and take them away.

It was originally designed more as a retirement hobby farm for her farther, but since he did not live to see his vision realized it was up to her to make a new model. It was her vision now.

It took several days, but her candy onion harvest was finally completed. Her automated harvester, which resembled the operation of a 3-d printer running in reverse, gently removed the onions from the sandy soil and placed them in an internal bucket. Once the bucket hit a specific weight the platform zipped to one side and dumped the onions onto a conveyor belt. From there the onions were sent into a cleaning machine which operated like numerous smooth soft fingers massaging the onions as water sprays from above. From there the onions went into a blower cage and then were filtered back onto the line where they were scaled and boxed. She then loaded them onto pallets and used her stickering system to track each package. Once she completed a run of pallets she would load them onto her big truck, stick her forklift on the back, then drive and unload onto the freight cars. In a month a new batch of refrigerator cars would be delivered for her radish harvest.

After the escape from South Africa, Annie decided to run her property with no outdoor lighting. A system was in place, but she did not activate it unless there was an emergency. She did not want her farm to be visible at night. Instead she installed thermal imaging cameras and sensitive microphones. She would be alerted in the event an animal or person entered her land.

Very few people knew anything about Annie and her mom. No one would ever inquire if they were okay. They were truly alone.

Annie knew the closest occupied property was about 50 miles from the farm. A town of less than one hundred people who all lived near the train station. She wondered if any of those people knew she existed.

Her father was a secretive man, and the existence of a rail spur was all he needed to finalize the purchase of the land in Australia. Building materials were delivered by rail and he hired a major building contractor to do most of the site work. Because it was a very remote location it was an expensive undertaking.

Word had spread in the small town that a wealthy foreigner was building something out on the back roads, possibly something big. But no business ever arrived as a result and people soon forgot.

Only a food broker in Sydney knew of Annie's Farm, and it was unlikely he ever told anyone. She was providing him extremely fair wholesale pricing for greenhouse-grown grade-A produce. It was profitable to keep her location a closely-guarded secret.

######## ERIC and the WAITRESS ########

There are no writers without words to unite them. Unless those words are intelligible to an audience there is no story. But it is the STORIES that define the success of a writer. Can a normal person with an ordinary dictionary generate meaningful, believable stories?

He started in the Children's Books genre. 'Chirpy Cheetah' was a book to relate 'sound types' to 'animals.' So a Cheetah doesn't chirp, because chirping is for birds not cats. Cheetah's roar and meow and purr. So 'Time Traveling Tony' takes a trip through seconds, minutes, years, decades, centuries to stop 'The Jumbler' from jumbling up all the animal sounds. He used simple juxtaposition coupled with great visual art to sell his books.

Selling a story about a drug dealer to a movie studio while it was still in the 'pre-printing' stage had been a lucrative choice. His royalty income paid well. But the entire universe of those characters was, to a certain extent, cut off. Warped beyond recovery by what they had been turned into by the studio writers.

It had to be a numbers thing, winning as a writer.

"The mood lighting here is the best, right?" the Waitress said while looking up at him from across the table. She was 'scrunched down' in the opposite seat. It gave her the appearance of being smaller and more vulnerable than she actually was. "Have you been working on any new story ideas?"

He swirled the wine in his glass. He rarely drank it; he would watch 'the legs' of different wines. The restaurants would bring him small amounts from open bottles for him to rate. He was very knowledgeable of wine chemistry and would give the owners his opinions. "I've been working toward something... but it isn't really there yet."

She looked over at him. "You ever think of writing movie pitch ideas? With your success you could get a lot of attention."

She wasn't wrong.

"I have seen some characters in specific places. I know it involves..." he paused, thinking carefully. "Well I am not sure what it involves to tell you the truth."

She laughed. "That isn't writing."

"I write six pages a day now," he lied. "Damn it, sometimes I don't do it. I've been bad about it lately. So I need to focus and be more realistic about achieving specific aims. Right now I am writing letters to no one. I just start writing and instead of something 'narrative' emerging it is more like I am writing to...." He paused again. "Like, letters to God."

"That is a terrible genre for sales purposes," she warned,

laughing.

"Yeah, it is probably not a valid exercise. It is an excuse for writing, a way to fluff up and fill those six pages per day. There are flashes of insight, moments where I forget I am the one doing the thinking."

"Letters to God," she mused. "Better have an Asimov or Phillip K. Dick feel to it if you want to sustain sales with a title like that." She winked at him.

"The story itself takes place in the future," he relented. "It is called 'Our Man' and it is based on the world following a large solar flare and magnetic pole flip. Only those who were prepared really 'survived' and so this story takes place 500 or so years after the solar flare. Cities collapsed, nuke reactors failed. But we don't reminisce about that because we are looking at the world long after all that."

She listened attentively, surprised by how excited he was.

He continued, "I can see this society that compartmentalized its knowledge and allowed a large population to resume a near-hunter-gatherer level of existence. Meanwhile, outlier groups rebuilt a technologically advanced culture. See, about 125 years after the collapse only the most clever and intelligent individuals had the ability to thrive. There was a lot of chaos as resources dwindled. Early attempts to restore services and order were met by hundreds of thousands of starving people who were living in lawless wastelands. Just in America alone."

She didn't speak and implored him to continue with her eyes.

"The catastrophe happened during the height of consumer culture, a time when people had begun robustly experimenting with modifying genomes, especially to make designer pets. One method used fluctuating magnetic fields to induce, in the case of dogs, permanent mega-gigantism. Very, very large dogs. Not 12-hand horse size, but big enough to kill a full grown buffalo on their own. So, the sought benefit had not been an increase in size, rather it was an extension of life.

The large guardian breed dogs don't live very long and people who own them as pets really wanted to change that. So, the experiment facilitated the life extension, but it came at the cost of mega-gigantism. So the dogs in question were causing a firestorm of debate because it was effectively like having your own weapon of mass destruction. Sure, weapons could take them out. You could blast the dog with several shotgun slugs and kill it. And laws were being passed to ban them and there was a movement to have them all exterminated. But, before the issue with the gigantic dogs can be resolved, several huge solar flares strike the planet, wiping out all satellites and seriously damaging a lot of electronic infrastructure. Then, the shock of the solar wind causes the magnetic poles to flip. All hell breaks loose. So our story takes place in a time when the cities of America have been 'reclaimed' and the 'city dwellers' get food and shelter and medicine so long as they are willing to work for 'the Corporation.' The Corporation primarily exists to support a breeding stock of humans and to ensure genetic diversity among the families that control the new world. Due to the lack of education and extreme resource limitations much of these modern cities remain in ruin. The Ruins serve as an option for those people who do not want to be part of the Corporation and who prefer to live in the Wastelands. By having society built on these pillars the result has a lot of durability. If society collapses again you have a somewhat builtin group of humans who are living in similar circumstances already and so are adapted to survive. The lawless wastelands are the disaster recovery platform. So 'Our Man' has a house and has also fenced in two entire city blocks near a former major city. The blocks are abandoned and overgrown and there are remnants of old brick homes, basements, swimming pools. His home is ultra modern."

He was seeing it for the first time because she was pouring yen into the crucible of his Yang. She was projecting psychosexual power into his subconscious mind by paying attention to him. He continued, "So when you meet people in the

'Corporation' their families have been 'working the program' for multiple generations. So people have 'generation numbers' and when the children of the old families reproduce they *might* select a person from the Corporation inside a city to start a new, first generation Newcomer. Many young men of older houses get 'jobs' in the city and work as Directors and Engineers; the Directors exist primarily in situations where they can explore for possible mates. However, many ABSOLUTELY REAL jobs are required and this is the work of Engineers. Engineers need to be aware of the whole history, all the things that happened in the past. It is their job to maintain the imbalance of knowledge that sustains the deficits of power. There are 'levels' to this thing. And the people in the cities are living frozen in what we might think of as today's 1940's. Limited analogue technology with compartmentalized training on how it is made. But outside the cities there is a network of these older families that have technology that is far more advanced. It advances because the children they raise in the outside system are given more information, and then their children's children receive more information then they had. So that by the time you are a child of the 30th generation you are raised to have all knowledge and become a Senior Engineer. This system took over 120 years to design and deploy by the Original Founders. Once it was underway the Founders maintained external control until 10 generations had passed. By that time the knowledge of the Founders was lost, erased, and the people who were currently running things were doing so by a design they had literally nothing to do with creating. And when the Founders died out the knowledge of the true past was completely lost. In this way they considered the world to be truly cleansed with everything set up to run on rails."

"Our Man?" she asked about his working title.

"The Corporation philosophy. Gender roles are brought back in a big way. The power dynamics that emerge are very different from today, but the standards to which people are held are also much, much higher. Your House can be eliminated if your children become Wastelanders. Chaos is attractive to some people. People of talent can descend into the wasteland because the wasteland is a paradise of uncertainty. In this case 'Our Man' is a specific person, from one of the oldest families, who likes four Corporation women. It is expected an Engineer may have several children by several women, but for those children to hold any kind of title to lands they must produce 10 generations of Offspring who follow 'the Code.' The generation number of the child is always determined by the lowest rank of the person mating. So a 4th generation male and a 9th generation female produce a 5th generation offspring. So Our Man will not live to see any of his offspring with city dwellers be allowed to leave the city unless he mates with an 8th or 9th generation corporate female. A child born of a 9th generation female and a Director or Engineer produces a House Wife who moves out of the city and gets a place in the country where she will raise a first generation House Child. You can only have three Corporate Housewives and one Family Wife. He is thinking of mating as a way of projecting his genetics into the future, so he isn't looking for a 9th generation female at this time. Engineers, though, can impregnate as many 1st generation females as they want as there is effectively no limit. So in this story that is who he is courting. Code is a set of rules. They are not based on perfection, they are based on maintaining a rules-based order. As a direct-line descendant of a 'First Family', 'Our Man' is unrestricted in his potential mates. Women have been educated to believe that if they are good mothers in the Corporation their children will advance, and on and on, until at GEN-X a pregnant female gets converted to a House. The houses take the names of the Females. And there are House Females and they only have children with House Males. The 10 Generation rule to establish a House allows a wider pool of female genetics to gradually enter while Houses are 'delisted' when the children fail to uphold the standards set by the

House Rules and Code."

"You seem to have thought about this a great deal!" the Waitress replied excitedly.

"Not really. Just hanging out with you I can see flashes of possibility. Like I kinda have the mechanics of the timeline and some of the social evolutionary policies roughed in, and I have started on one of the courtship stories. But that is were things are really falling apart. The interactions between this serious engineer and a girl from the city is stilted, wrecked. She is desperate to please him, obviously, because she knows he comes from a House and if they have a child she will be elevated in the Corporation as the mate of an Engineer. But here we have this man who must never reveal the reality of how the world actually works, so he can make small talk with this woman, but she cannot even leave the area she lives in because of the rules of the Corporation. So I am going two directions, just writing it so that it is very mechanical OR making it a moral dilemma for him that he has to work through and maybe which ultimately either ends with him in the wasteland or makes him sociopathic. In the latter case he just breeds and forgets these woman and returns to his House Wife and they raise their kids in a robotically gardened paradise somewhere in Northern Arkansas. I don't see him devolving into a Wastelander, though, so that storyline feels kinda dead."

The Waitress was excited for him, but felt his frustration with the story. "I see your problem. They both sound like possibilities. I would think the audience would probably identify more with the Engineer who gives it all up to go explore the vast wastelands. But since he is an Engineer I would think he probably has access to whatever exploration he wants to pursue. I am not sure what his limitations are or if the rules constrain him too much in terms of roaming around and using his imagination. It seems like imagination would be the thing everyone is trying to control. And, yeah, I can see the woman being infatuated and how she would see having this man's kid as a way to achieve her own version of success. And he would have to think that it was sort of pitiful, right? Her desperation and lack of knowledge. It would almost be like having sex with a farm animal rather than a human being. It might be more interesting if he went into the wastelands to find a mate. Are there any rules against that?"

Eric had been frustrated, but hearing the Waitress say these things made him realize that he was maybe the luckiest man on the planet. To have the Waitress as his partner was like winning the lottery. He looked at her, how she was legitimately interested in him and what he was doing. How she enjoyed him even when he was gloomy or self-absorbed. "Hey," he said, surprising her. "I want you to know that I really, really love you. I don't want to make it corny and I am not trying to be diplomatic. I think you are amazing and I want you to know it. I haven't even considered that as an option, but of course it is the correct one. Of course the more interesting story would be his boredom with the women in the Corporation and his discovery of a wild woman that he wants to breed with. His high intellect wants to project itself into the wastelands because he wants to ensure the survival of his genetics in all possible domains. He might already have a child with his House Wife and a few Corporation women. Then he has the realization that he needs to meet a woman in the wasteland. Fuck. That is incredible. I love that idea, it is the whole story. You are a fucking genius! My God I cannot believe you are in my life!"

She smiled and blushed. "You don't have to say that," she said seductively. "You are Eric Johnson and I am in awe of you."

He was almost ready to cry. "*What have I done to be so lucky?*" he asked the universe in his smallest voice.

The waiter arrived. "I want the Rainbow Trout," the Waitress said gleefully while pointing at the menu.

######## MILTON and JEBEDIAH ########

Milton knew the technology required to move massive stones was beyond even the present age, let alone people of the past. But he was struggling to make sense of the missing components. "What am I failing to see?" he said to the image of Jebediah on his screen.

"What was it that Maxwell said?" Jebediah responded. "It was something like someone told him that there are ancient artifacts embedded in the Earth and spread throughout the Universe. And that the Moon is more ancient than Earth and is an artifact. Like an arrowhead."

"Yeah, it was a girl he dated. She said there are dust grains older than our moon, but the Moon is the oldest surviving artifact of intelligent design in the universe. The oldest large scale structure that was built by intelligent life. And that the tides are responsible for much of our consciousness and our awareness of eternity stems from how old the dust on the Earth is relative to the age of the Universe. We feel linked to eternity because of the age of the surrounding matter. Matter has a patina that forms as a result of existing for a very long time."

"I mean, how far back do we go?" Jebediah asked. "I feel a bit haunted right now, like I am looking into an old crypt and some undead corpse is in there. I mean I feel like we are looking for something that isn't dead, but also isn't alive. And it freaks me out a bit, to be honest. I know we have done some dangerous things in our time, that we have taken great risks. But it was terrestrial risk, it was human risk. It was playing the game of life. This feels different, like we are moving beyond normal human experience. Like maybe the answers we find if we keep going will be too terrifying to accept. Additionally, I just feel like the closer we get to this the more I fear we are going to run into a powerful group of people who would prefer to keep all this stuff a secret. Like there is a secret society controlling these artifacts and if they know the secrets of this ancient technology they might want to keep that under wraps. I mean, we have clearly made enemies with our selling activities, but this might be much, much bigger."

Milton thought about it. "I sense it too. It isn't something I can put into words, more like I can see a flash of knowledge and then my brain shuts it down."

"Like a self-defense mechanism?" Jebediah asked.

"Yeah," Milton acceded. "Like something your mind refuses to learn. But it is more like turning away from horror. And I feel it. Just when I think I have an insight, boom, mind shuts down."

"I look at it like a runaway process that consumes all the system memory before it gets killed off. Our brain starts to see something, but it is larger than our available memory and we hard reboot."

Milton nodded in contemplative agreement. "I feel like we can figure this out though. No one knows we are even looking at this. And based on what you are doing with Intentional Water there is going to be plenty of turbulence out there to distract eyes away from anything we may or may not discover."

Jebediah hoped he was correct.

######## MAXWELL ########

Maxwell accepted the possibility his life was badly derailed. He was wanted by the government of the United States and had escaped an FBI station under very foggy circumstances. Then he successfully fled the country. He was traveling with a fake ID and had taken up residence on a 140,000 acre estate owned by a rich and very eccentric Australian scientist/industrialist. Thanks to Jebediah's efforts at automating his Information Brokerage service he was still earning an income and was, technically, still operating the business that was the source of all his legal problems. But it seemed people were helping him for no apparent reason. It was hard to make sense of their motivations. "Fuck it," he said aloud. "I don't need to think about the past right now. I am here, in the situation that emerged, to pursue the Truth. A single kernel of eternal."

Maxwell made a cup of instant coffee. He already missed the smell of roasting beans and the sound of busy sidewalks. He missed the taste of fresh fruit. Alone in the desert he had no distractions. But a life without distractions can be distracting in other ways. "It is challenging to concentrate when there is no voice besides your own to keep you company," he replied to his conscious thoughts.

Maxwell studied the distribution of prime numbers because they represented an immutable aspect of the fabric of reality, a universal sign that should persist throughout all intelligent life. He saw mathematics as a nerds version of a Thunderdome, a battle arena where all outsiders are welcomed to fight to the death. *"Any conjecture enter; only proof leave."* Because the prime numbers form a pseudo-random sequence their structure regulates or models many of the dynamic behaviors observed in the physical universe. Emergence herself may be governed by the same pseudo-randomness that describes the prime number distribution.

In college Maxwell's work on 'Universal Biosemiotics' was greeted with indifference. His study of the use of symbols and schematics in communication - by ALL living systems - was ignored. Not intentionally. Becoming a discernible signal against the roar of background submissions was nigh impossible. Maxwell suspected he lacked the charisma to inspire curiosity for his ideas.

Prime numbers, in his mind, represented the ultimate proving ground. One that would accept all warriors and, with only a few exceptions, grind them all to dust. Maxwell had no formal math training. But this did not dissuade him from walking across the threshold.

"Chaos from Order," he muttered to himself. "Not the other way around. Humans find the unknown to be fertile ground for the mind. The mind roams, seeking a pattern." Maxwell witnessed a pattern. It attached to him like dew on grass. The grass exists, but it has no intent or desire that the dew fulfills. Nature entangles the grass and the moisture by making the environment conducive to condensation. Knowledge works this way. It finds a binding site in a mind and condenses there.

Maxwell, though, was swinging his sword blindly. It was as if knowledge had tapped him on the shoulder and then disappeared. But he believed he saw the next leg of his journey.

"Patterns are capable of being described by an algorithm or an equation. In some ways these are the same thing. But in some important ways they can be very different."

Maxwell converted the patterns into recursive algorithms. He improved by identifying quadratic equations that replaced recursion. The rate of change in the growth of composite numbers became his target. "I can see it!" he exclaimed. "Why is it so hard to express it!?" The work was tedious. Day after day hunched over notebooks, testing numbers for relationships. He felt like a man who, having climbed a dangerous, lonely mountain, looks up to realize he is nowhere near the top. His learning was far from over.

He was seeking a function that was guaranteed to produce only primes. *The true end game,*" he thought to himself as he paced through the hot sand.

######## WAITRESS ########

The Waitress was home alone. She decided to read Eric's journals to catch up on what he had been exploring. She noticed that his handwriting had changed for some pages, as if his hand was moving extremely fast and with passion. It took her several minutes to see the letters correctly, but eventually it clicked.

Eric had written:

-

Thinking of her. Building momentum. Heart skipping with the memory. The contents of her suitcase. Little things.

Watching myself. Tasting her lip gloss. Touching her throat.

Holding her legs.

She kneels and takes. She chokes and laughs. She grabs and swallows.

I haven't explored any of these feelings on paper. Why? Am I terrified of what will come next? Am I worried about what might happen?

When I am alone and I think of her. I think of all the things I want to do to her. All the things things that have been done to her.

I imagine her in class. The way a man can tell she's special. The way she is unique. Imagine impaling sweet, innocent her over my desk. I imagine her performance. I crave to know how he fucked her, trained her. I crave to know what he did to her. The stories she tells of her coming of age, so remote from my own experience.

I love the scent of her; her sweet essence is my fondest memory. I will admit that I want her to be my little slut. "Daddy's little slut." Fuck, I love hearing her say that. Seeing her on the bed in her cute white ankle socks and panties, rewarding me for existing.

I am an older man who nurtures and fucks a young woman. She is so sweet and I love to take her when she is asleep. I love coming into the room where she is sleeping, guiding my hand between her legs, using my fingers to explore her.

It was intense to hear her describe her first relationship. Thinking of her sitting there, no panties, wetness dampening the plastic chair as her pussy swells in anticipation of an old cock using her perfect pussy. Her bending over for him. Spreading her ass cheeks in an offering to him. Him fucking her and her being in complete control. The madness and mania of such a thing! Women are powerful creatures!

-

The waitress smiled. She could see the emotion in his handwriting, how excited he was to explore these new feelings. She was proud of his achievement. She cried a tear of joy for Eric. But she also worried.

She knew an intervention would be required. He was getting too comfortable and eventually he would aim frustration at her.

"Maxwell changed me," she thought to herself. Since her time dating Maxwell she had evolved from being an observer of the external world to being an observer of herself operating on the world. She had gone from playing the game in the first person to playing the game from an omniscient point of view. She saw herself upon the map. She could 'sense' but not exactly 'see' the people she was entangled with.

But she could neither sense nor see Maxwell. Yet she knew he was out there, on the map. She could detect his gravity. Like dark matter curving space, Maxwell was still pulling on her.

######## MAXWELL ########

"Words are fallible tools!" was written in permanent marker on the outside of the action camera case. Maxwell got the camera and attached it to an extensible selfie stick. He powered it on and started speaking to it as he walked through the desert. "Holy hand grenades it is hard to talk about math. I have been attempting to unwind it all. Whoa! Been a minute since I've tried to speak like this. Okay. Stop. THINK. Concentrate. Focus." Maxwell paused his walking for a moment and looked up into the sky. Endless blue with not a cloud to be seen. Turning his eyes back toward the camera he started walking again.

"Numbers can be considered as objects. The counting numbers can be subdivided into distinct classes or assembled into distinct sets. So, for even numbers, we say the numbers share a 'symmetry property' that allows us to categorize them based on some measurable feature or testable condition. The even numbers are symmetrical with respect to all of them ending with last digit 0,2,4,6, or 8. This is their class symmetry." Maxwell saw an interesting rock on the ground. It was deep green. He picked it up and studied it. He showed the rock to the camera and then asked the rock, "What story do you have to tell that I likely have no chance of hearing?" He put the green stone in his pocket.

Maxwell looked into the camera. "I need to explain how I saw it. The function that I dreamed when I was in a 400 year old adobe home. It was just after the January Deer Dance at Taos Pueblo in New Mexico. I had a fire going trying to stay warm against a brutal cold. It was an aboriginal experience; near the ends of the Earth on a dusty road headed toward the start or end of civilization. It was in that adobe where a woman gave me a few cups of tea and I saw the prime number distribution as a large field of Quadratic sequences." Maxwell paused as he thought back on his vision of hundreds of quadratic functions mapped onto a graph. He had seen the quadratic functions as glowing lines upon the x,y plane. He saw it with his mind's eye. "Of course, I had no idea what I was witnessing when it happened. It was just these golden glowing lines in space. Numerous parabolic growth curves. I didn't even think about it again for many years. Only now have I started to understand it."

Maxwell spun around so the sun would be behind him as he walked.

"The composites for Sloane's A201804 are PERFECTLY ORDERED beneath 12 quadratic sequences!" he said to the camera. The sand blowing in the wind reminded him of humans being tossed to-and-fro by chance or by things over which they exercise no control. "Smaller even than a grain of sand is consciousness," he said looking away from the camera. "How can a thing as small as a human mind contain DATA regarding the infinite? As an abstraction! As a sign!"

He turned off the camera.

######## ERIC ########

Eric sat eating tomato bisque in a hotel bar. Writing. An elderly female bartender cleaned glasses and did other sidework. He felt amazing. The dirty things he and his young lover said to each other were unlike anything he had ever experienced. He was intoxicated from the lust he felt for her nineteen year old body.

The improbability of such a thing! He was no famous author. Not really. His story had been adapted to make an extremely popular series. But he was no... George Orwell. He had a long, long way to go before he could feel secure in his own legitimacy.

"I am just a lucky bastard who has no real writing success," he thought to himself as he stirred his soup.

But that didn't matter. When he met his lover his entire world flipped and he knew nothing would ever be the same. He decided to return to his hotel room.

His young lover was there, thinking of him as she worked on her story.

-

Turtle woke up to a new world. A vast expanse of uncertainty extending forever. The Unknown Quantity.

"Will I survive?" asked Turtle. A grasshopper hopped into Turtle's mouth. "Chomp." Breakfast served itself.

Mechanical feet started pulling Turtle forward at an unreasonably fast clip.

-

She heard the lock and looked up to see Eric walking through the door. She wanted to share her work with him, but hesitated. *"Some things need to remain a bit mysterious,"* she thought to herself.

"How is your writing coming along?" he asked when he saw she had a notebook.

She closed the journal and put it into a nearby backpack. "I am working on some ideas. I am wondering if a person can be considered a hero for doing normal things."

"The Hero's Journey is a common theme among writers," he said to her. "Many times the hero is unintentionally pulled into a situation."

"But... what if an act of bravery is really just a 'normal' act undertaken by a person for whom such an act is highly unlikely?" she asked in response.

"Like the school nerd 'accidentally' asking the prettiest cheerleader out on a date?" he asked.

"Um," she thought about it. "Yeah. I could see that. In that vein."

"Bravery, to be real, requires a person to truly understand the risks. For a nerd, the risk is that he will be rejected or, conversely, become a legend. The consequences of his action or inaction will stick to him for the remainder of his school career and possibly his entire life. This is played up by the writer. The writer builds up the tension to the point it feels like a life or death situation. The *pressure* is real despite the fact that when you drill down it is just a guy asking a girl on a date. But when a character does something without knowing the risks that isn't bravery, that is *spontaneity* and possibly a foolish venture. Don Quixote is sort of the pinnacle of taking that story arc to the most absurdist lengths possible. A fool acting brave as an act of insane rebellion."

"Don Quixote," she murmured, thinking of her Turtle. Was it really that simple? Was that the shape of her story? Her Turtle had no trusty assistant and had yet to encounter a beautiful wench. But could her character amount to anything more than the maximum power of a turtle?

She appeared shaken. Like something he said had stolen her self-confidence.

"Look, there are Universals. All stories contain certain inescapable elements. Language itself is a limit."

She got his point, but some part of her stubbornly refused to accept his limitations.

CHAPTER 6

######## ANNIE ########

Robert Plant – "Big Log" was broadcasting from a small computer in the middle of a desert. In the stillness of the sand, in the deepening nowhere, only Maxwell and the animals ranged. His writing setup was a small table beneath a relatively large stone outcropping that led into a cave. Cool air exited the cave behind him as he typed, providing him with a primitive form of air conditioning. He dragged two large solar panels out to the site and drove T-posts to set them facing South. He also carried two large batteries, one at a time, and hooked them up to a charge controller and an inverter. Maxwell's laptop consisted of a 'Raspberry Pi' computer and a low-power e-ink screen with a trackpad and a clickety-clack keyboard for inputs.

A gold pin attached to the motherboard of microcomputer sent signals via a connected wire to an FM transmitter. On station 98.9 his car would broadcast information about the temperature, humidity, condition of the batteries, tire pressure sensor data, and then would play music. Between the hours of 2am and 4am the computer would do text-to-speech conversion of poetry content that had been previously 'scraped' from a large number of websites. It would read out the text using a believable male or female voice to reflect the gender (best guess) for the name of the poet. If it was only initials then it would be an androgynous voice.

Maxwell had significant memory set aside for music. His car contained a large number of micro-computers, though many of them were currently set up to mirror data and were only powered on long enough to run backups. They were distributed throughout the vehicle as disaster recovery nodes. He had enough redundancy to ensure his time would be uninterrupted.

On Maxwell's map there was no Annie's Farm. He had no idea that someone was living 'relatively close' to him.

It took a while for her to discover Maxwell's signal, but when she did she experienced terror unlike any she had known since she fled South Africa. She thought she was alone and that no one was anywhere near her.

She had installed temperature monitors in her greenhouses that contained low-power FM-band radio transmitters. Her device allows a farmer to scan using the truck radio and get the current temperature, humidity and a host of other detectable values from numerous installation locations. Each greenhouse transmitted on a unique frequency that could be set by the user, and this allows farmers to monitor variables without needing an app or any form of internet connectivity. It was something she developed, patented, and licensed to a company for mass production. They were being sold in box stores throughout numerous countries. They doubled as globe chandeliers.

Her transmitters were very low power and so had negligible range. Maxwell, however, had increased his transmission wattage completely ignoring any potential consequences.

It happened one morning when she discovered a dead truck battery. The door was left slightly ajar and the interior light drained the battery. She had to re-add the presets on the truck radio after she jump started it. She decided to use the scan function to pick them up one at a time.

The first scan didn't detect Maxwell's transmission; there may have been too much static. She was driving to the end of her greenhouse rows after reprogramming her presets and for no particular reason decided to use the scan function one last time. One after another the greenhouse monitors were detected by her radio. Playing sound for a moment, then moving on. But then her radio landed on 98.9, a static transmission with music in the background. She turned up the volume and drove toward the end of the rows of greenhouses. The signal got stronger once she was in an open field.

"...the humidity is 14% the charge is 92% the tire pressure is not available, that concludes stats." The signal contained metadata and her truck radio displayed the name of the song. She read 'Refugee by chipmunkson16speed.'

She saved the channel as the 1 slot, displacing her house monitor. She listened to the music fade in and out with the wind. As she drove along the only road the signal grew weaker. She recalled that at the far end of her property was a parcel owned by a single family. Over one hundred thousand acres. As far as she knew there was no public road connecting to the interior. *"Maybe someone flew in and has a radio transmitter?"* she thought to herself as she drove toward the end of her property. She approached a very old barbed-wire fence where the signal was strongest.

She sat back in the truck seat and stared at the property in front of her. The song was haunting.

"... It don't really matter to me baby ... Everyone's had to fight to be free ... So! You don't have to live like a refugee.... Don't have to live like a refugee... "

She got out of the truck and approached the fence. She put her hand on the rusty wire and twisted it to the right. The wire broke. She stared at the horizon. "... don't have to live like a refugee... no, you don't have to live like a refugee..." The song ended and she got back into the truck and turned around.

As she drove toward her home the radio displayed, 'SIMPSONWAVE by FrankJavCee.'

######## PDC ########

"The Key sets the frequency. Or something," the front desk clerk attempted to explain. "Honestly, I am not sure how the electronic room keys work auto-magically with the door locks. Like, how does the door lock know?"

TV on; muted. The PDC lying on a motel room bed with nothing to do.

He got up. He took the hotel-provided notepad and pen from the nightstand next to the bed and walked to a round table at the end of the room.

He sat down and wrote, "I haven't written a letter to myself in a long time. What am I doing? I bought a motorcycle and armor. A vast endless mystery awaits. Thanks for the adventure with words. Strange feelings. Up against a hard mental wall. Been trying to define how to do this thing.... define even WHAT this thing is. All The Gear All The Time." He triple underlined the last sentence.

He looked at the paper. He ripped it off the notepad and crumpled it. Aiming, he threw it into a nearby trash can. He then grabbed the paper and flattened it out on the table. "Start something," he said aloud. "Do something." He slid out of the chair and fell to his knees. The enormity of the change in his life was starting to dawn on him. He experienced foreboding, a sense of danger. He moved to one knee, then stood up. He fell back-first onto the bed. He got up and grabbed the room key. He stopped and put the room key back onto the dresser. He inhaled and exhaled deeply several times. "Go slow. You have already been living frugal. It was like Maxwell knew or some shit. That I would need to be this calm about it." But PDC was not calm. The energy coursing through his wallet was liquid electric, the stuff of neon signs and chrome forever. Enough to always be shiny.

But he was already living in a zone of relative self control. His cravings for trappings had been annihilated by the value of living bill free. "*Why mess with that? Why risk the lovely balance of invisibility?*" Even his hotel room was a bargain type, second least expensive option in the area. His habits were designed to maximize his economic freedom. With the help of Maxwell he was able to buy back almost all of his time.

PDC and Maxwell had a close mutual friend, a woman they met while taking creative writing classes in college. PDC had given her many thousands of dollars in cash so that she could take time off work and meet him in Colorado. They were going to climb some mountains before going to the rainbow gathering.

PDC, though, was hit by a rainstorm on his way and was forced to divert from his original path to avoid hail. He was running a few days behind as a result. "Everything is timing," he said, pacing, excited to see her. "Just chill the fuck out and get some rest." But try as he might to relax he still felt tense.

######## ERIC ########

Eric looked around as the audience gathered in the room. They were waiting on a presentation from an acclaimed author. The conference was scheduled to last six days. Eric arrived alone, but his mistress would be joining him for the last two nights. The author took the stage.

"The secret to science fiction, from my perspective, is to use the relatively small amount of scientific knowledge possessed by ordinary readers as a lever to pry open their imaginations. The writer can take advantage of the information the readers already accept as true and use those pre-installed ideas to reveal inherently possible futures or alternative worlds. Jules Verne really set the bar here. '20,000 Leagues Beneath the Sea' was such a work. An example of a good writing hack is that Jules mentions real people who were famous during the time in which the book was published, such as Commander Matthew Fonataine Maury. He does several more of these shout-outs to famous living people. But while the contemporary references within the novel are meaningless to the modern reader this does not negatively impact the story, because he designed the references to be durable through time. We don't need to know that he was referencing a famous

Commander for us to enjoy the story. It adds something for readers who know, but subtracts nothing for those of us who don't. Since we lose nothing by being unaware this offers an interesting trick; the writer may be able to draft upon the fame and name recognition of his or her contemporaries. Maybe it can help drive sales if famous people are referenced by your work? Never underestimate the power of other people's spotlight to illuminate your name on the marquee. But this is clearly a delicate balancing act. And I am sure it has risks."

"Today's technology is in some ways moving faster than science fiction. Our primary task as authors is to try and keep up with the innovations. What seems far-fetched today might be a consumer product in just a few years. So if you don't want your work to seem horribly dated it is central that you don't adopt the wrong technologies."

"In contrast to Jules Verne we have Kurt Vonnegut's 'Player Piano.' In this work we are presented with a dystopian future where the vast majority of labor jobs have been taken by machines. The author dates this book by indicating that the machines use 'tape memory' for reading the instructions. The author did not know there would be other formats available in the relatively near future and thus his reliance on too much present day description dates his work. It now rings hollow because it is in desperate need of an update. My point is, the story itself is great, prescient as ever, but the decision to write 'tape memory' rather than 'memory' has turned his idea into a joke, a comical attempt at modeling the future. He chose to use the literal technology of his day, tape drives, to describe a distant future. Had he only used 'memory' the work could stand as an eternal warning regarding the dangers of AI. It could stand with the likes of 'Animal Farm' in its timelessness. But he didn't. And now most readers will toss it aside after just a few minutes of reading because it seems hokey rather than forward thinking. The moral of the story is that you need to make sure your work references science, but pick your words such that a reader can impose his or her future technology upon the theme of the work without needing to look up any antiquated terminology. If you rely too heavily on the discrete language associated with the technology of today, as opposed to what the technology does in the more general sense, your work risks becoming stale and irrelevant. And it might do so much sooner than you would dream possible."

Eric left the lecture feeling lucky to have gained an important insight into the durability of stories through time. The next lecture was about using conspiracy theories in stories, and how to adopt them.

The author Jimmy Corsetti entered the lecture hall to applause and began speaking.

"There are a lot of conspiracy theories in the world that have built-in audiences whose reception of your writing can be enhanced or harmed depending on how you treat their subject. The conspiracy we will look at today is the proposed existence of a Great Civilization that existed a long, long time ago. How did we get here? Well, prior to Archaeology becoming a formal science most people in the West thought the world was divided into two periods, pre- and post-diluvial. That is to say, pre-flood and post-flood. Additionally, most world traditions contain a flood story which is important to note when you think about your work being translated into other languages. Most religions mention a great cataclysm that reset the world and they argue we are inevitably going to be confronted by another one. For many archaeologists this is just a curiosity, a novel coincidence or a natural conclusion drawn by primitive people on their march toward enlightenment, but nothing more. History is viewed as a relatively linear progression from the primitive toward the advanced, from unknowing to knowing, with a few retrogrades along the way. A lot like climbing stairs. But the conspiracy theorists argue that there are simply too many unexplained megalithic constructions, outright marvels of human ingenuity, to accept that the general trend of human history has been one of moving from primitive to advanced. It appears to them that the history of technology looks a lot more like a parabola than linear growth. That is to say, the world appears to have *started* with nigh-impossible feats of engineering, collapsed into a stone-age primitivism, and is now slowly crawling out of the pit of relative darkness toward re-enlightenment and then re-industrialization. The incrementalism of the history of science looks like we are climbing stairs because we are recovering from the annihilation of the previous intelligent culture."

"Indeed, the Southern Hemisphere is littered with numerous examples of impossible artifacts. Some of these artifacts bear the scars of intense heat on one side. Like the statues in Egypt, at Luxor. It appears as if they were subjected to a short-duration blast of intense heat. What all this adds up to is that we are missing key episodic knowledge. For the author this opens up an almost unlimited realm of possibility. We don't need to worry about our academic credentials being smeared by radical conjectures regarding the origin of these megalithic wonders. As creators we get to make it up. Now, while I do honestly believe most current historical assessment is just flat-out wrong I am not writing a book to challenge the current orthodoxy. Instead, I want to capitalize on the huge mass of people who suspect we are missing some key information and play to their skepticism with my fiction. I might want to claim that aliens came to Earth and selectively engineered humans to perform mineral extraction work. I mean there are endless possibilities that pivot off a few ACTUAL artifacts. As fantasy writers there is no rule that says we aren't allowed to reference the real world when developing our stories. And few real world objects generate more debate than the stone works of the megalithic builders."

-

Eric took copious notes. He figured he would need to see these artifacts for himself if he wanted to get a real feel for their potential as story elements. *"I need to touch these, feel the weight of these stones, see if they can unlock some kind of understanding inside me."* He began to look for tours of ancient megalithic sites. He found 'Hidden Inca Tours' and sent an email to inquire about upcoming trips.

Eric poured over text and watched videos until early in the morning hours. He then forced himself to go to sleep. There were four more days in the conference and he did not want to be derailed by his passion. *"I need to sleep or I will be trash tomorrow,"* he said to himself. Once he climbed into bed he realized he was exhausted.

He dreamed of an ancient world, an advanced civilization. But he recalled none of it once he heard his alarm.

######### MILTON #########

Milton walked through the debris field at Tannis in Egypt. He marveled at the monumental constructions jutting out of the sands. He struggled to understand how 'primitive' people were able to erect such magnificent structures. "It is almost as if they were magical," he mumbled to himself. He imagined witches and wizards carving the stones with thought alone. The long, laser-precise cuts being made by wands rather than blades. He knew of no modern processes capable of manipulating the huge blocks. *"Ockham's Razor,"* he thought to himself. Then, laughing, he thought, *"Milton you are losing your mind, there MUST be a legitimate method to move these. Just, what is it!?"*

He picked up a handful of sand and poured it out. "Time keeps marching on. The evidence of the past disappears into dust."

Try as he might to avoid it, the idea of magic kept returning to his thoughts. *"What is or is not possible?"* he asked himself. *"Why do I automatically dismiss ideas that are unfamiliar to me? My world is dominated by machines. But not all worlds need to be like my own. The world may have been different in the past. Maybe it was different in barely-imaginable ways? Clearly something happened here which allowed the impossible to become actual. Maybe I need to broaden my view? Take alternative explanations and explore them?"*

He was open to the idea that something he considered a fantasy could, in all actuality, be the correct interpretation. But he suspected his lack of knowledge was the explanation, not some miraculous or magical pseudo-technology. *"I am just missing some pieces of information that will make all this plausible."*

Milton wondered about the variables which might be assumed to change through time. *"Gravitational force on the surface of the Earth might not be constant through time. We really don't know if a change in the magnetic field of Earth could modify the surface characteristics of objects or if there exist large-scale harmonics within the Earth that control the evolution of quantum systems. We model the quasi-steady-state system and we experience the reality we can fit into our minds. We only have access to real events as real is defined by our brains."*

Milton built engines that used ultrasonic motors to drive large propellers. He used electrified piezo-ceramic wafers to cancel load accumulation in the structural elements inside his airships. He knew that sound was a powerful and underutilized technology. But ultrasonic motors were ubiquitous on satellites in the drive units for control moment gyroscopes. They were also used in platter drives in computers to spin disks. He had scaled them up for use in large-scale industrial motor applications, but he doubted the stones could be moved using his current understanding of phonon energy transport.

"Even if I could create a frictionless surface to move the blocks, that still doesn't solve for the fact I need a material that can withstand the initial 1000 ton load. If sound was used its amplitude would need to be so high I would think it would shatter the stone due to harmonic accumulation, essentially the phonon energy dispersal in the defects in the material would result with its destruction. And even if I made a frictionless surface that could handle the load we still need to deal with the incline and lifting it. No, it has to be something else. Some way that gravity is canceled or greatly reduced for the entire object. It cannot experience internal stress while it is being moved. It must be weightless relative to itself. Like the accelerometer that is thrown into the air. At the top of its flight it has a moment where it experiences no gravitational acceleration. It has zero point energy. The blocks must be held in such a state to be manipulated for placing into the walls and structures. It was necessarily a trivial act to move these stones. There was no struggle. The scale and magnificence of the past civilization is beyond our wildest imagination. Only God or Nature could destroy such a civilization. And I mean so thoroughly destroy it that only a few pieces remain. But those which are here point to that past. By measuring a part of it we should be able to reconstruct all of it. Or at least reverse-engineer which technologies would be required to produce these results."

######## ERIC and LYDIA ########

Eric got up early and ran on a treadmill in the hotel spa. He was listening to 'America – You Can Do Magic' as sweat poured off his body. He felt alive. He was inspired. His young mistress was on a train heading toward him.

She was working on her story. Methodical. Focused on the perfect words. Nothing spurious. Not even one page per day. She was writing:

-

The sky darkened. No familiar place to sleep. Turtle made for a bush by the bank of the creek.

Up and up.

Finally! Turtle eclipsed the edge and witnessed, for the first time, the Horizon.

Seeing the Sun set low on the edge of reality Turtle was

overcome with emotions. The banks of the puddle, the reeds and trees, all seemed infinitely small when compared with this scene. The realization of the vastness of space hit Turtle pretty hard. "I must keep going," Turtle said, before withdrawing to sleep in his shell.

-

Eric was sitting in the hotel lounge after his workout, drinking coffee and writing.

-

When I am with her I want to write. I want to see the outline of her body beneath the sheet as I grip my pen and manifest meaning. When I have her I am filled with energy and light. I am illuminated and the work becomes effortless, pure joy. It should be more challenging than it is, living this duel life. A young, savvy, amazing lover that I travel with and also a dedicated woman at my home who loves me and takes care of all the distracting details. When I come back from my conferences she is always there to greet me with a smile. She is so understanding and yet I rarely think about her.

But in the final assessment I truly love her. And deep down I think she knows how much. How much she means to me. I cherish her. And yet I am a man and I am electrified by my young writer-lover.

She won't show me what she is working on. I get hints from her. Things she reveals against her will because sometimes she comes so alive she cannot help herself. The fire she feeds for her writing insists on more fuel, and so I give her anything and everything I can. To feed her. To give her something in return for the amazing gift she has given me. Her youth and vitality are irrepressible forces that work toward my rejuvenation.

I love what she does to me.

-

The train stopped to drop off and pick up passengers. She looked out the window at the faces of the strangers. "*So many stories. So many estate sales,*" she thought to herself. "*So many who disappear forever and whose stories are never told.*" She returned to her writing.

-

The tall grass tortured Turtle, but it felt like the way. Onward he crawled.

-

Eric was writing in his hotel room. His ideas were very disjointed. He was asking questions to scope a new idea.

-

Who are humans? A remnant from the past? What have we forgotten about our origins? Did we evolve from more primitive life, in the relatively recent past, or did we 'devolve' from a much more advanced civilization that existed long ago?

-

He thought about it all. Wondered how the pieces fit together. *"Can we even know? Can the artifact be so thoroughly eroded that there is no possible forensic analysis that can reveal what's missing?"*

######### MARSHALL #########

Marshall was driving the van as his female companion unpacked and then repacked her camping gear. They were only a few hundred miles from their destination in Adams Park, Colorado.

Marshall wasn't certain if he could get back to South America before getting caught as a runaway 'hospital escapee.' He wanted to avoid population centers until after his 18th birthday, but he wasn't sure if being 18 would put him in the clear. He knew from news reports that federal agents were at the 'Rainbow Gathering of Love and Light.' He attempted to do some independent research and was extremely surprised to find almost no reliable information.

"This has been around for how long?" he asked.

"This is the 50th anniversary," she replied.

"How have I not heard of this before now?"

"It isn't well known. A secret among the Lost Tribes of the

World. It will be so nice to go back home."

"Huh?" Marshall asked.

"Welcome home! Remember!? That is what we say when we greet people. Welcome home, because we are all part of the same family."

Marshall looked out at the mountains. The snow-capped peaks encouraged him to continue.

######## ANNIE ########

Annie's father had served in the South African military as a high ranking officer. He trained her in the use of night vision and how to avoid detection. "The most dangerous animal is man, and evading man is not an easy thing to do. The intellect is so great, intuition is part of it also. Never underestimate your gut feelings."

Tracking Maxwell in the desert was the most excitement she had known since moving to Australia. She was fascinated. She brought a long-range microphone and would listen to him talk to himself, talk to God. He wanted to know about numbers. About the oldest artifacts in the universe. About what things are possible to know with certainty.

He talked about Ice1. About chaos ice. And the Moon. He talked TO the Moon.

"The moonlight is polarized except during a full moon!" he yelled at the daylight Moon. "Why!? How!? Such wonderful chaos that you have chosen us to be your witnesses! Such unlikely odds we should be here to notice ourselves noticing you as an illusion on the horizon!"

She kept her distance. Didn't want to be seen. Enjoyed the thrill of hunting.

Maxwell at times felt himself being watched. The longer he spent wandering the desert the more lost he felt. He assumed if he was being observed he would know it on an instinctual level. He believed all living and thinking beings share the same electronic space. Share the same 'now.'

Maxwell drew lines in the sand. "It takes a machine to reveal it," he said. "The patterns in things."

For days at a time she would watch him, only returning home to get more food and check on the greenhouses. It reminded her of time she spent with her father tracking lions.

"Ever since your father died you have been a lost soul," her mother said to her the last time they spoke face to face. "I miss him too, but we have to move on."

"I'm fine, ma," she replied. "This is the path the Universe chose for me."

######### WAITRESS and ERIC #########

The Waitress was a human being. She was made of flesh and flash. She could feel anger toward Eric. On this day she walked into the kitchen and found dirty dishes in the sink. *"He expects me to be his maid,"* she thought to herself as she turned on the water.

"Moontime." She programmed him to rely on her for those things. By volunteering to wash dishes she became the dishwasher. She did it all the time. He had grown accustomed to it. Sometimes she found herself resenting it. *"I am on my period,"* she growled at God.

Washing dishes did not reduce her sense of self-worth. Not really. It was the fact Eric was free to roam the world while living off the spoils of his success. He had entered a place of such liberty that he could be utterly irresponsible. *"Eric never gets cramps. He pees standing up. He has me taking care of life's messy details."* She was thinking of all the reasons she resented him. After a few moments she shook her head and said to herself, *"Quit having negative thoughts!"*

For his part, Eric had given up a lot to become financially secure. He had sold off the rights to his first and possibly best work under an agreement that the characters would not be further developed. The storyline belonged to the movie studio insofar as any derivative material would need to be approved by them.

"I may have sold myself a little short," he said as he swirled coffee in a cup. Turning to look at her, he said, "I don't know if I will ever come up with a good story again." He was searching for words of encouragement. And she knew it.

She turned off the sink. "You don't need to rely on those characters. It would be best if you lock away or burn all your materials related to that project. You must embrace these other stories. You need to dive headlong into that."

Eric knew she was correct. "Yeah, you are right. I need to remove it all, mothball it and don't look back. Thank you. Hey, hold on a second," he got up from the table and walked over to her. "I want you to know that I don't take you for granted. I realize I left dishes there last night and that was rude of me. Here I am sitting at the table reading my phone and there you are cleaning up my mess. Let me do that and you sit down and relax for a minute."

She was shocked and for a moment worried Eric might be clairvoyant. "*Thoughts matter,*" she said to herself as she took a seat at the table. Eric set up the dishes and with military precision cleaned them. He then got sausage, eggs, cheese, milk, butter, onion, garlic, anchovies, capons and horseradish from the refrigerator. He retrieved several knives and a large cutting board. He brought out a mortar and pestle and began grinding the peeled garlic with the capons and a few slivers of horseradish root. "Eggy-In-A-Basket with a twist." He heated a pan and began caramelizing onions. In another pan he cooked sausage patties. Her mouth began to water. "I haven't had much focus in the direction of quality of life lately," he said as he cooked the sausage. "I have been really self-absorbed and haven't been paying you the attention you deserve." He got the toast and cut out from the center of the bread a hole roughly the same diameter as an egg yolk. He removed the sausage patties from the pan and placed them on a plate, covering them with a lid. He then put the bread into the sausage grease and cracked an egg into the hole. As the bread absorbed some of the grease the egg cooked. He then flipped the egg into the pan with the caramelized onions to fry the other side. "Let me dress it." He added the garlic capon paste as a light condiment using a butter knife and placed some anchovies on a small plate as a garnish. He prepared a glass of mango juice spiked with ginger and cayenne and a smaller glass of water. "Bon Apetite!" he said, setting everything before her. She ate the food while he made another. He handed her the next plate.

"I can't eat all this," she said as he sat down at the table.

"Let's split it."

He quickly ate his half and then proceeded to wash the dishes and clean the prep area.

"I got us tickets for 'La Finta Giardinera' tomorrow night at the Lyric Opera," Eric said, surprising the Waitress. "We don't, like, need to go of course. I thought maybe…"

"No that is awesome!" the waitress replied with enthusiasm. "You have amazing timing. I will go look at my outfits and see what I can put together. As a man I am assuming you will go in your tux?"

"You know, I hadn't considered it," he replied, cocking his head to the right as he, for the first time, pondered what clothes he ought to wear.

"You are hilarious. I will lay it out for you," she said as she turned to go back to the master bedroom.

Eric had installed an app on his phone that he could use to track the menstruation of all the women in his life. It also had a setting that allowed him to turn on voice stress analysis to detect the emotional state of the person who is talking. His mistress had shown it to him and explained that it was helpful for her because "hormones are real and they control some percentage of personality. So if you don't take an active role in mastering your emotions you aren't taking life seriously."

Eric learned when the Waitress was on her period and was using this knowledge to craft experiences that were designed to manipulate her into feeling good. As the app learned it would suggest events, like 'dirty dishes resolution,' which were designed to help Eric (the end user) 'build value' in the relationship. Value was described as achieving positive to neutral voice stress in the environment. When he signed up he had to answer questions about who in the household was responsible for which tasks and with what regularity. Once Eric responded that the Waitress did all the tasks the app knew how to build in strategically timed 'load balancing' for Eric. It was shown that by assisting with household chores using the 'optimal minimum energy' the end user can gain a long-lived positive voice outcome. The suggestions were tailor-fit to meet the voice-stress needs of the subscribed user and any 'targets' he defines in the environment. Eric's phone was on the table listening to the Waitress and updating Eric's watch with her voice stress scores.

Since the voice stress monitor allowed him to detect when she was unhappy, he was then able to create good outcomes for her that would reinforce her good feelings toward him. This made his life more enjoyable. The app was then able to monitor millions of individual voice stress events across a pools of hundreds of thousands of users and was creating pattern recognition filters which were able to update the 'tactics library' from which the app could call for suggested behaviors. So the app appeared to rotate in suggestions that scored positively across multiple users experiencing similar voice stress events. For example, the app had already soft-scheduled for Eric to give the Waitress a foot rub at 10:30pm, once they were home from the opera.

As a result of the 'gamification' of human interaction 12,000,000 dish duty hours and 1,000,000 additional unsolicited foot rub hours were worked by users of the app.

She was not aware Eric was using her hormones to hack her fondness vector. He never wrote about it in his journals.

CHAPTER 7

######## PDC ########

PDC wandered the busy streets. He observed the tightly packed humans lining the outdoor barstools. *"No shortage of skin,"* he thought to himself as he studied the bare midriffs and mini-skirted legs that were brightening his night like so many searchlights. An outdoor bar played music and he heard the lyrics, "... and its been you, woman, right down the line..."

Tens of thousands of dollars in cash and also bank cards tied to accounts with significant sums. *"I can have anything I want,"* he thought to himself. *"Crazy."*

He stopped at an expensive steakhouse. The hostess looked at him with skepticism seeing he was quite under-dressed for the Texas Black Angus Club. "Table for one?" she asked in a somewhat hostile tone.

"Yeah," PDC replied while completely missing her attitude.

"Right this way," she stomped.

The hostess put him in a dark corner to minimize his visibility to other patrons. He was clueless and actually preferred being out of sight and out of mind.

"Would you like to begin with an appetizer?" a young female waitress asked. She assumed the tip would be terrible based on PDC's beat up look.

"Yeah... how about your... caviar? Have you ever had caviar?" PDC asked.

In a rare moment of customer-facing honesty the waitress acknowledged, no, she had never experienced that menu item. "It is a bit expensive and they don't offer that with the free shift meal."

"Well," PDC said, "I'll take two, one for me and one for you, for when you get off work."

"That... is over $80 apiece," she warned.

PDC, still suffering from the shock of his vast inheritance, knew on some level it was unwise for him to be in public. He hadn't taken much time to process his new economic circumstances before hitting the road and as a result he was not emotionally prepared to deal with ordinary situations. He motioned for the waitress to move closer. "A little secret," he whispered. Looking around as if hunting for spies, he continued, "I'm rich. Like really, filthy rich." He grabbed his wallet and took out a $100 bill and gave it to her. "Here is an advance on your tip. But promise me you will keep my secret your secret."

Her mood improved dramatically. She winked at PDC and left to get his drink. "Enjoy that caviar!" he said to her as she departed.

He grabbed a tablet computer from his bag and reviewed a map. He estimated it would take about 9 hours to arrive at the Great Sand Dunes. *"I can load up and leave early in the morning and text X to let her know I am on my way. Then we can caravan to the gathering,"* he thought to himself.

The waitress came back with his drink. "So are you passing through?" she asked him.

"I was on my way to Southern Colorado, but I got hit by some crazy storms in western Kansas and Oklahoma, so I drove south as fast as I could to outrun the lightning. Ended up here. I am staying at the motel across the street. This area seems really busy."

"Really sketchy," she said. "But then you also have places like this scattered throughout. This is maybe the most expensive restaurant in this whole town."

"Funny that. I was just walking around looking at things and randomly chose this place. But I am glad I did. I need a big meal before I hit the road."

She realized his pants were motorcycle armor. "Oh, so you are on a bike!" she guessed.

"Yeah. Figure I can eat and go to bed after this so I can get an early start on the day. I am heading up to the Sand Dunes."

"The Sand Dunes? Like up by the UFO Watchtower?"

"The what?"

"You are talking about the Great Sand Dunes National Park, right? There are tons of UFO's up there. All the time. There is a UFO Holiday festival that happens every July. Are you going to that?"

"Uh, no. Though I must admit that sounds fascinating. I am actually going to the Rainbow Gathering up in northern Colorado."

"Oh, is that like a concert?"

"Something like that. It's more like drums and hippies. I've never been, but a friend of mine is going and we are meeting up to hike the dunes. Then we are going to drive to the gathering."

The waitress made a mental note to look up the Rainbow Gathering festival when she got off work.

PDC ate his medium rare steak and most of the massive baked potato. He ordered a piece of cheesecake to go and left the restaurant.

"Keep it shiny side up!" the waitress made the sign to him on his way out.

"Always," he said, making the sign back at her.

PDC looked at himself in the bathroom mirror in his room. "You need to chill the fuck out. You need to quit blowing money like a damn retard. You are going to wreck your life. She knows biker shit. For all you know her one percenter boyfriend is going to come rob your ignorant ass. Just chill the fuck out and lay low."

He went over to the bed and stripped down to his socks, boxer shorts and a t-shirt. He grabbed fresh socks, underwear and a new t-shirt from a bag next to the bed. He took a shower.

"I will see X tomorrow," he said to his reflection, grinning like a Cheshire Cat.

######## ANNIE ########

She was listening to Maxwell's radio. It was 3:42am and she was working on a water leak. She heard a male voice speaking:
-

The Bible must be durable to survive so many bad preachers.
Bible testifies to itself.
Historical preservation.
Evidence of changed lives.
Everything Jesus did. Testimony to the power of God.
Honest intellectual.
Co-exists with God since before eternity.
Witness of the Old Testament.
When on Earth he affirms the Word.
Blazing integrity of Jesus.
Even non-believers.
Respect.
Somewhere He would have said He was there in the beginning.
He never testified that there was inaccuracy.
What is True?
Under temptation there was no debate.
"It is written."
Power. The Word.
Satan does not dispute the power of God's Word.
"They neither believe nor do they tremble."
A bunch of normies asking the loving God to deal with the validation of the stories.
"Not the smallest letter will by any means disappear from the Word."
The fulfillment.
You cannot pick and choose without calling Jesus a liar.
Be simple.
The Word is Itself.
"Thus saith the Lord."

WORDS TAUGHT BY SPIRIT!

Be dominated by the Holy Spirit.

66 different books written over 1500 years.

40 writers.

Doctors, Kings. Shepherds. Tax collectors. Fishermen.

As varied as you will ever find.

A span of 1500 years. And yet that work is Unified.

The convergence of 66 stories and 40 writers over 1500 years.

UNIFIED!

The seeds were sown in the beginning and then the fruit is ripened.

40 writers unified in ONE GOD ONE MIND ONE HAND.

Uncommon accuracy.

Book of Acts. There are so few written documents.

Chronologically the History.

We have a longing in the Heart

surrounded by things

more things than ever

more vacations

and yet people are dissatisfied

miserable

why? Root cause?

Failed to understand, "Little is much when God is in on it."

Politics is no salvation.

Obedience to God is the Secret to Power.

Give to get. Wake up. Listen.

True Blessings.

Verse 8: "Go up to the mountains and bring down timber to build my house."

Put me first. Put obedience to God first.

Prophet cried out. To the death.

Verse 8.

Convicted of the God of Holy Spirit.

So sought to obey.

Haggai spoke to them August 29, 520BC

Do I place God's work ahead of my comfort?
Seven rules for self-examination:
What do I want most?
What do I THINK about most?
How do I use money?
How do I use leisure time?
Whose company do I enjoy?
Whom and what do I admire?
What do I laugh at?
Answer? God.

-

She was surprised and a bit confused. She had never heard spoken word on his radio broadcast. She made a mental note to check her recordings.

######## MAXWELL ########

Maxwell was walking in the desert. He turned on his action camera and began recording himself.

"Messing with prime numbers may have been a bad decision. Most of what passes itself off as progress is just repackaged observations from the past. Just because you don't have a map doesn't mean someone hasn't been there before."

Looking away toward the horizon Maxwell continued, "Eratosthenes! I see you on the shores of the Mediterranean noticing the behavior of prime numbers. I see you carving with a stick in the sand as you map out the steps of your algorithm. Each prime number generates a family of composite numbers. You saw it and described it. The schematic associated with your algorithm is fundamental to all realities and all possible worlds. This algorithm can be modeled precisely because it is deterministic."

Maxwell was unsure of his last statement and his face momentarily displayed pain. "Well, does an equation exist such that only prime number outputs are solutions? To approach this problem is to ask if there exists a universal pattern underlying the prime number distribution."

Maxwell looked down at the ground as he was descending into a small ravine, "Of course the general theme of applied science is to work out the laws that allow us to predict subsequent states of a dynamically evolving system. We seek a method by which we can make accurate predictions about the evolution of any number of possibly 'complex' systems. Prime numbers are no different. We want to take our general understanding of the distribution of primes and transmute it into an exact understanding."

Maxwell slid and then regained his balance, "Upon looking at Sloane's A000040 we find a list of operators one uses to construct a prime number sieve. We might think that this sequence represents the distribution of the primes, however this list of primes must be used as operators to further generate additional primes via the Sieve of Eratosthenes. Therefore what we have is a list of prime operators and not the *characteristic function* that details the location of the primes relative to each other and the composites. The characteristic function represents the ordering of the primes while Sloane's A000040 represents the list of prime operators. This is an important distinction. We do not often think about the numbers that we call composite, with the very important exception of those semiprimes used in encryption. The composites are secondary to the gems known as primes. A statement was made in A000040: 'Reading the primes mod90 (excluding 2,3,5) divides them into 24 classes[.]' We will evaluate the prime distribution from the perspective of one of these 24 classes: A201804."

Maxwell reached up and turned off the camera.

######## Dr. JORDAN KEAL ########

Jebediah was having great success with his new drug delivery platform. People in colleges and universities felt they could ingest the intentional water and have a great time with zero consequences. It was truly an amazing product. However, it was deeply connected to the industry associated with rTMS, or repetitive Transcranial Magnetic Stimulation. Dr. Jordan Keal, a man who had invested his life into making rTMS the dominant mental manipulation technology, was in awe of the reported effects. It was all starting to make sense.

"I didn't see it! The deposition of magnetic field potential in a particular location was affecting the nuclear spin states of the atoms and molecules! Of course! This means we should be able to identify the spin orientations and then induce the pointer to generate the super-state known as conscious awareness. The entanglement is such that if you collapse one node then all or sufficiently many nodes collapse into the correlated pointers. Awareness is the global state, but that state collapses as one of the allowable quantum eigenstates for the mind pixels. The mind pixels are what get modified while the microtubules detect the change in spin orientation!"

Jebediah would have been amazed that Dr. Keal had this much familiarity with his drug delivery process, however he was not aware of the US Military capability for intercepting signals and generating situational awareness. As soon as they became aware of the existence of the product they acquired it and conducted tests. They allowed Jebediah to continue. They even assassinated some of the men responsible for attacking Milton. All because Jebediah was conducting a large-scale test of the properties of mind pixels. Dr. Keal had been granted special access permissions to review the data and ascertain if it could be used for mind control/modification. Dr. Keal realized that they were missing a model for brain pointer states. "I have been reverse-engineering the spin state from liquid morphine and find it to be a universal global pointer. Much like we use the North Star to determine our location on the Earth, these molecules have bipolar spin and they orient their poles to point at locations in 'outer space' if you will suffer that term for a moment. We all align to something external using quantum-scale pointers. Our brains then detect these orientations and that produces conscious awareness. What we need to develop is a targeting system that will allow us to administer spin states to human minds by using rTMS to align the molecules. We can then direct consciousness all the way down into hallucinating the experience of a painkiller in the bloodstream. Or, possibly hearing a private communication as an auditory hallucination induced by spin manipulation."

The Generals were all very excited and almost unable to contain their thrill at having made the discovery.

"What about the people who are currently using it for street drug emulation?" asked one of generals.

"I think we should let them operate as currently situated. Since they haven't made any connections to using a targeting system to induce states this means as their technology eventually leaks out people will be following the trail of using laser and physical interfaces rather than modifying mind pixels using remotely located magnetic pixel targeting systems. So if we let them run away with it our approach will likely remain obscure and overlooked. Also, we could never hope to run tests on human subjects at this volume without generating serious oversight. So we are also getting a lot of valuable data in our overwatch which we could not otherwise gather. Eventually we will use the mind pixel water technique to hydrate our soldiers who we will then be able to modify using a technician on a base located 12000 or 12 billion miles away. But we will need time to develop our dataset and targeting system. Simultaneously, we can monitor the pool of drug users for adverse side effects."

The Generals agreed with Dr. Keal's analysis. They would continue to monitor and allow things to proceed. They would treat Jebediah's operation as an asset not a liability and even go so far as to protect him from hostile foreign powers. Jebediah had been unwittingly conscripted into the Space Force program named "Operation Mind Pixel."

######## WAITRESS and MAXWELL ########

The waitress had a powerful dream. She saw Maxwell for the first time since they separated, lying on his back in a desert. She was floating above him. She began to rise, higher and higher. She then saw trails in the sand. Somehow she knew they were from Maxwell. The tracks began to glow. From where she was it looked as if Maxwell was inside a glowing lotus flower.

It was amazing in its beauty. At the edge of the large lotus there was a figure dressed in a yellow robe with gold highlights. He wore a large pointed gold crown adorned with peacock feathers. He was attempting to walk toward Maxwell, but at the edge of the lotus a shimmering force field was pushing him back.

She understood. It was her decision to open the force field and let the Golden Man approach Maxwell.

"Are you kind?" she asked the man.

"Love is both kind and firm," he replied. "But some things are even beyond love. He has seen something... something that cannot be unseen. And so he has been changed by seeing it."

She waved her hand and the field disappeared. As it dissolved so too did her vision of Maxwell until, once the field was gone, she woke up.

######## ANNIE ########

Annie made the potting soil. She filled the grow bags. She grew the starter plants. She arranged the harvests. She sent the invoices. She hassled people until she got paid. Sometimes she made threats. Never promises.

Her mother had been hit by two bullets on the night her father died, but the wounds were superficial. It was her mother's mind that had been blown away. As a result she and Annie grew apart. They maintained their distance, as if loving people was too dangerous.

Although they lived independent lives, Annie promised herself that her mother would never need to worry about money or any of life's messy details. Despite the fact her father left a substantial inheritance she insisted on running multiple profitable businesses and on building the family wealth while paying for her mother's home and servants in the city.

Watching Maxwell from a distance came naturally to Annie. She would rather observe than interact. From a distance she retained all control. She would snake her way along the ground using a periscope lens and a shotgun microphone. She would watch and listen in on Maxwell. She played his music as a soundtrack. She had witnessed him working at his writing cave for as many as 10 days in a row. He would start in the morning, hunched over his keyboard. Then, at night, he would use a projector and a large sheet to set up images of math functions. Rates of change and parabolas.

It was completely strange.

######## ERIC ########

Eggs Benedict and orange juice. Fruit salad. A tall dirty chai with three shots of ristretto espresso. Eric enjoyed his food. Once the table cleared he ordered another dirty chai and started to write:

-

Magic derives from the presence of ancient artifacts. Pieces of the original explosion of the Universe. The universe started from a state of 'pure possibility.' As possibility collapses into actuality there is the emergence of ORDER-ENFORCING MATTER. The first matter sets the laws which regulate the emergence of classical reality from a foam of quantum fluctuations. Everything that is now real is an artifact of the first matter.

This matter has survived since the very beginning. As the primordial artifact it controls the emergence of new properties in material. The Laws of Emergence overlap with the domain known to the humans as 'Magic.' The power of magic flows from the 'Primordials.' Real world items can be influenced, re-shaped, brought into a new 'state of being' by the force of desire. This power of transmogrification and physical alteration follows from the fact the vast majority of an atom is empty space and the entirety of what we call physicality is actually immaterial energy resisting or attracting other immaterial energy. This is always in the form of vibrations and so classical reality is the ensemble of quantum oscillators vibrating with the same or similar frequencies over some volume of space.

The original wizards (most likely 'witches') may have discovered this property of the universe by chance. Long ago a mind strained to manifest a new outcome and stumbled blindly into the power of intention. A person grabbed a stick and imagined lifting a rock. The rock moved. The mind was allowed to see the 'sign of agency' in the act of pointing a stick at a rock. But it was the THOUGHT FORM that was moving the rock, and it was not 'moving the rock' it was altering the frequency of the rock. The magician alters the frequency of the rock by harmonizing his mental state with one of the frequencies that are currently present in the Earth. The magician lifted the rock by transferring vibration from the rock into the ground. This is mediated by creating destructive interference between the rock and the Earth. You do this by calling upon and directing an always present sub-frequency to generate asymmetry which results with lift. Gravity is a frequency operator upon the rock and the magician can modify it using harmonics and psionics. From these humble beginnings an entire world of magic was born.

In modern times we might say that the meta-Epigenetics triggered by a desire to lift a rock unlocked abilities that were dormant or already present in the human form. All matter and energy are part of the 'same Universe' and can be shaped by willpower. The Human has a pre-installed capacity for magic because the human can generate frequencies on the quantum scale where gravity and information couples to matter. Whether 'spells' and such are 'necessary' is not currently known. So much mythology has grown up alongside the physical manifestation of magic that it is extremely difficult to differentiate between what is necessary and what is sufficient. One thing, however, is certain. The protagonist knows the dangers of discovering magic while living outside the world of magic.

As such, he is desperate to avoid discovery. He lets no one know he is investigating 'The Physics of Magic.' The magical world would be threatened by a person seeking to divine the physical underpinnings of magic. It might be possible to harness the power in new ways. Or, perhaps more menacingly, it might be possible to nullify magic.

The magical world was aware of such threats. For thousands of years magic had been the dominant technology on the planet. Primitive humans were... exactly that, primitive. Magicians were God-like in terms of power scaling.

But slowly technology began its inexorable climb to emerge as a force unto itself. Electrical and nuclear secrets divulged to the humans opened up new possibilities for harnessing a power that could realistically threaten the survival of the magical world. The discovery of a quantum reality underpinning the classical world offered the insight necessary to quantify how magic 'works.' Magic rearranges information on the quantum scale which manifests as new classical states of matter. Levitation is the simplest example, as it is a state that has been achieved not only by magicians, but also by the meditative shamans of the Far East who are tapping into frequency modification using an alternative technique. The origin of magic was the Quantum Fabric, the fact that information determines reality and matter arranges itself and behaves on the basis of frequency. The manipulation of frequency was all that was required to instantiate magical outcomes. Meanwhile all information is frequency sustaining a work function on an invariant length or mass.

In modern parlance, the magician imposes new information upon an apparently-Classical system such that a new state becomes 'Einselected,' or environmentally superselected. The magician imposes an 'Einselection pressure' upon an object and this allows 'magical outcomes' to appear.

Energy is conserved, no 'illegal outcomes' are permissible. Simply, magic IS a subset of the physics which rules the quantum scale. The relationship has been hidden beneath a veil of self-preservationist myth and folklore. To attempt to battle the myth would result in being expelled from the community and possibly killed.

No one wanted to know 'why' or 'how' magic worked. For fear of destroying it.

######## MAXWELL ########

As Maxwell wandered the desert he admitted to himself that sex had always been a major motivating factor in his life. He had spent the better part, the much better part, of his social time pursuing intimate female companionship. In most ways the memories of his lovers involved their feet being up in the air; he remembered their kinks. The things that made them feel good. For some women it was being caressed and gently loved. For others it meant being degraded, slapped, choked, abused. The spectrum of sexual experiences fills itself with a wide range of desires.

The Waitress was the one who now stood out in his mind. Not because of the sex, but for the discussions. She was legitimately interested in him. She would talk to him when he was asleep; he had awakened on several occasions to find himself speaking normally and her listening intently. It was as if he was another person entirely. It freaked him out on more than one occasion.

"What was she asking me? What did I tell her?"

He had a feeling, a sixth sense, that he had told her things about how he observed the world. The way he saw a tall rectangle filled with symbols floating above people's heads. His unawareness of what it all meant.

She had discovered things about Maxwell that not even he knew. His conscious mind was unaware of what the Symbols meant, but his autonomic mind was a separate entity. His unconscious mind, the part the Waitress probed, knew much, much more about how the symbols were generated in the mind and how consciousness arose from pointing at memory.

Maxwell had begun to dream about her. He repeatedly saw her in a penthouse of some kind, alone, reading a book or writing something in a notebook. He wondered if he was seeing real images. They seemed real. He would try to read her notebooks, but he could never make it out. The letters were illegible. *"It's just because she was the last woman I fell in love with that I am having all this recall about her,"* he reasoned to himself.

She learned more than she knew from Maxwell. And she felt a strong connection to him. But she couldn't see him, couldn't find him in the aether of her dreams. She would write his name, write how she wanted to see him, but he never appeared.

They were on opposite sides of the world. He was awake when she was asleep. A part of Maxwell's mind saw her on its map, though. It continuously monitored her. Wanted to know what she was doing with the knowledge it had given her. It was listening.

She was a part of its experiment.

It influenced her actions. It wasn't giving orders, more like it was giving powerful subconscious suggestions. She thought of it as similar to 'intuition' and by listening to it she had earned tens of millions of dollars.

She could not have known. She had been given just enough information to open her mind. It was soon invaded and hacked by a force she could neither understand nor control. She had become part of a mental botnet, a multi-node consciousness that was operating simultaneously across multiple hosts, sustaining itself by using local processes to survive and replicate.

This led to her manifesting some surprising new behaviors; not unlike being infected with a purely electric version of Toxoplasma gondii, the cat parasite that turns humans into risk taking entrepreneurs.

The translocation of information from the unconscious mind to conscious awareness occurs in a part of the brain known as the ANTERIOR INSULAR CORTEX. Neither Maxwell nor the Waitress were consciously aware of this region of their brains.

######## MAXWELL and ANNIE ########

"You are listening to Basil Poledouris, Column of Sadness, Wheel of Pain," her text-to-speech converter spoke the metadata from Maxwell's radio broadcast and converted it to voice output. She heard the music playing through a set of headphones which were simultaneously connected to a shotgun microphone she used while spying on him. Maxwell's car was programmed to keep track of his emotional state. It could detect frustration in voice stress results it received while taking measurements when he was speaking. The measurements would be made by Maxwell's watch and then later transmitted back to the main computer once Maxwell was close enough to the car network to link to it. As such, the analysis was usually running at least a day behind real time. Knowing this, Maxwell wrote his code to use several moving averages in the hopes of achieving better projections.

Maxwell's wristband recorded his biometric state, including his heart rate and blood pressure. He had measurements for air temperature, relative humidity, number of steps taken, respiration events, elevation change, solar gain, quality of sleep. His code analyzed the values for trends and broadcast music designed to reinforce good behaviors. He scored music in a very fuzzy logic using the Greek scales of

Ionian, Dorian, Aeolian, Phrygian, Locrian, Mixolydian, and Lydian as the baselines for his training model. When he needed to rest the music would skew more Lydian, when he needed to move more it would skew more Ionian. Maxwell was able to add weights to certain songs and these were used as patterns in the scoring system. He wore battery-powered headphones that he integrated into a large straw hat. He would listen to the music to gain insights into his physical and emotional evolution.

He spoke down toward the band located on his wrist. "Timestamp now. This song, +1 to weight."

Maxwell thought of the scene from the related movie. A child grows into a man by pushing a giant grist mill. Day after day pushing the column. The crunch of Maxwell's footfalls disappeared as he marched in time to the music. "Mind control..." he muttered, starting to walk-stumble.

She watched through her binoculars as Maxwell moved in sync with the soundtrack. He started his video camera and began speaking.

"The entire world as a game map. Every individual ability is detailed as a list of skills for your avatar. The humans are easily distracted. So, yeah, I struggle a bit with my sense of meaning. Everything I see reduces to mathematical sequences."

Maxwell spun around in a drunken-style pirouette and resumed walking.

"I know the 'impossibility operator' must exist," he said to the ocean of sand surrounding him. "A range of probability exists for transitions between allowed states, but the range of permissible outcomes is bounded by a region of impossible outcomes. A region of forbidden solutions. And that which is utterly and necessarily impossible... can it be known?"

Maxwell moved the camera so it was shooting from a lower view up at him.

"Can a person define with certainty the boundary between the possible and the impossible? Impossible knowledge cannot be cognizable and therefore the sign of the impossible is naught. It cannot be materialized. The unknown is possible. The unlikely is possible. The impossible cannot be known or unknown, likely or unlikely. The path integral formalism defines possible paths for particles and virtual particles. The impossibility operator identifies the existence of impermissible paths, but makes no attempt to give a precise accounting of them. There must be infinitely more impossible paths than possible paths for an electron in a cloud chamber," Maxwell stopped. He tried to understand what he was saying. Was it all nonsense?

Maxwell was frustrated. He imagined a cloud chamber and the room outside the cloud chamber and the planet and solar system. He kept widening his view until it extended beyond the edge of the known universe. No matter where he went, the probability of the electron in the cloud chamber being found there was always greater than zero. *"Where can the electron NOT be found, ever?"* he asked himself. *"Can the existence of such a place be proven or disproven?"*

His sense of purpose dissolved into a mass of malcontent. All his thoughts turned darker. What began as a journey started to feel like a trap. A relentless beat he could not escape; the padding of his shoes on hot sand. Only the shoes get worn out, the sand never changes.

Inside himself he knew the better part of his biosemiotic transactions occurred without his attention, without his involvement. In fact, most of the mechanical processes responsible for his continued physical existence remained completely unknown to him.

"How can so much of my life exist below the surface of consciousness?" he asked, to no answer.

Unsure how to proceed, he laid down and attempted to forget his questions. He desired a sense of emptiness. This was a rare occasion where he covered his face with his large straw hat and fell asleep during the day.

When the Waitress was also sleeping.

Maxwell woke up in his dream and found himself in

an empty world standing on a black floor. Around him on the ground appeared a series of rings that radiated out from his position with increasing spacing between each ring. Eventually the rings disappeared at the horizon. A man in fine robes wearing a golden crown with peacock feathers approached Maxwell. As the man approached he stopped at one of the rings, still standing a good distance away. He began speaking as he walked around, orbiting Maxwell.

"Truth and love conquer all. As you know I cannot be other than aligned with truth. And yet I can love even those who persist in untruth. However, my love cannot save them from an inevitable fate."

Maxwell was confused. He had no frame of reference for this visage. "Why are you here, now?" he asked.

"No mortal mind can help you," the man replied. "No Sage of this world has a map or can show you. Just know that all things are born and then perish, and yet this thing is eternal, timeless, has no beginning and no end. Even the laws of the material universe can be altered by the passage of time; even the very foundation of experience itself, the soul, is ephemeral compared to the permanence of this design."

"It came to me as a vision," Maxwell explained.

"What is a thing that comes to you not as a vision? Did the image you see resemble a lotus flower opening?" the man asked.

"Yes!" Maxwell exclaimed. "Well, sort of. Tracing the curves of a flower petal, unlocking the patterns behind the prime numbers."

"And there are 24?" asked the man.

"Yes, and 576."

"Your lack of self-awareness is holding you back," the man said with a serious tone. "You are wise to seek solitude. But you are not alone. Even now as you sleep you are observed. There is a part of you that knows this, and it is that part which is manifesting me to you at this very moment."

Maxwell was confused. "I am not alone here? I am not the

only person out here?"

"You are not," the man laughed as he jumped one ring closer to Maxwell. "You are being observed and as a result you are vibrating with frequencies that are not of your own making. It is interfering with the signal."

######### ERIC and LYDIA #########

He was writing and the story was moving. He leaned back in the chair, then pushed away from the table. He remembered what she told him: *"Hey, if you are working and you want to fuck me, you just get your cock hard and come use my little pussy for your pleasure. My pussy is yours."*

He looked at her and started to get hard. He pulled his cock from his boxer shorts and began stroking himself.

Her perfect body. He stood and went to the foot of the bed. He could see her, exposed. Her beautiful skin pale in the low light of his writing lamp.

He spit on his cock and rubbed it. He then slid into the bed and into her. He was behind her, on top of her.

She was awake when he got on the bed.

"That's bad," she moaned. "Are you gonna use my little pussy daddy? Are you gonna beat up that pussy again?"

He was furiously thrusting into her, using her for his pleasure. He pumped every last drop of fluid out of himself. He felt drained. But it was an amazing feeling.

He got off of her and rolled onto the blanket beside her. She started kissing his inner thigh and gently licking his cock. "I love daddy's cum," she said before taking him down her throat.

She slid on top of him, making him feel large compared to her. She was so innocent and also not. She was a darling and a total submissive. Yet, she was topping him from the bottom.

And he was loving every second of it.

CHAPTER 8

######## MAXWELL ########

Maxwell started his camera.

-

"The game of primes. What is it? The OG player is a guy named Eratosthenes. He was born in 276BC. His method works every time on any planet. But the model matters. So I have an alternative approach. Bear with me.

Consider being a home insurance salesman or underwriter. You need to write a home insurance policy for every address of the counting numbers, OEIS sequence A000027. You have discovered an algorithm that can tell you ahead of time how profitable your contracts will be, the 'payout ratio' algorithm. The 'Law of Insurance' is that every address has a certain number of factors. For a 'prime number address' only the number itself is a factor so this contract is a 1/1 contract and 100% of the paid premium is retained as profit. For a 'semiprime address' we see the number has two factors. So address 77 has factors 7 and 11 and thus this contract is a ½ payout, or 50% of the gross income will be retained as profit while 50% will be returned as paid claims. There is a pre-existing law which states that an infinite number of 1/1 addresses exist, so in theory if an insurance agency could identify those addresses ahead of time they could write 100% profitable contracts. For small addresses this is an easy task. But as the addresses grow larger solving the calculation can take billions of computation years. There are, however, some addresses that can be arbitrarily large (so long as they are configured in a specific way) that are trivial to factor. For example, any address that starts with an even number followed by all 0's will be trivial to calculate for profitability purposes. A prime-property is disaster proof while 'composites' are disasters-by-degrees. So, semi-prime addresses pay 1/2 gross profit, and addresses of the form a*b*c or a^2*b pay 1/3. The total number of factors for the property represents Big Omega. So the equation of gross profit is 1/[Big Omega].

Since there is no known way to pre-calculate the risk for the vast majority of addresses the insurance agents must rely on the Prime Number Theorem which resolves an 'average risk' or 'average compositeness' for any given range of addresses. Given the state of technology the insurance industry has all but given up finding a better model. The problem is just too challenging.

However, there is a man named John Conway who proposed a rethink of our approach to the composite numbers. He conjectures that there exist two types of composite number, trivial and nontrivial. This means we have the trivial addresses and non-trivial addresses.

We can now go from looking at each number as a distinct individual and start to address the 'neighborhoods' into which these addresses fit."

Maxwell paused and looked away from the camera. He then said, "This is really hard to explain. I can come up with a lot of analogies, but they are not persuasive. I need a model that can be understood by the largest possible number of people. That means it must be visual."

######## LYDIA ########

She looked over at the man sleeping next to her. A flood of emotion washed over her. Memories of her childhood, memories of growing up faster than everyone around her.

"*Men...*" she thought to herself.

Her father had been arrested when she was young. He returned when she was 13. He was a violent, dangerous man. Though he never hurt his family, his cruel self-absorption helped shape her personality.

She was disgusted by her mother. Such a weak woman. At least her father explained the real world to her. How things and men really work. Whether he knew it or not he was programming his daughter.

"See, women like your mom are what's wrong with the world," he explained to her. "I fucking work for my family. She should give me a blow job every day I come home. Understand that. Men want to cum. Plain and simple. It is such fucking bullshit women aren't more aware of that. It is the ultimate form of spousal abuse."

She was afraid of her father, but felt that being afraid of a man was not a bad thing. She remembered the day her mother's ex boyfriend, the father of her half-sister, came by to visit. Her dad beat him up, made him cry and piss himself with fear. She watched in awe of his power. "Your mother should suck my dick for me doing stuff like this," he said to her, slapping the crying man in the face.

Eric was not such a man. He was kind-hearted and generous. He was able to perform, act the role she needed him to play, but he was not an authentically dominant person. He was too childlike to be worthy of her fear.

Some experiences are received as gifts from a loving God. Eric wasn't sure if he believed in a personal God, but he definitely believed in the allure and consequent power of a beautiful woman. The arousal, the loss of language itself, was an experience so hard to explain that he avoided describing it in his work.

She would pay for things, surprise him with a hotel room and dinner. Perhaps both before and after dinner she would get him aroused and have sex with him. Or suck his cock in the parking lot outside the restaurant.

He would watch her sleep as he wrote.

Many times he would get aroused and she would wake up to him having sex with her.

She authentically wanted to make him feel good.

The morning arrived. The conference was officially over. Eric was packed up. His beautiful mistress had her suitcase on the bed and was dressed in pastel light pink capri-style pants matched with a bright white polo shirt.

The shirt had the word 'Obscure' embroidered in a light pink font where a human heart would be.

"I have to leave you," she said to Eric, electrocuting him.

"Wha..." He was in shock. "When? How? Why?"

"Eric," she said, truly feeling sad, truly feeling conflicted. "Eric, a thing has come up, something I cannot discuss right now. But this is how the Universe works."

He was dumbfounded. "I love you so much. I never stopped..." he paused to regain his composure. "Well, to be honest, I saw the inevitability of this moment. Whatever it is, I want you to know I support you; you go for it. I have never given you anything, you've never accepted anything from me. But let me give you this: My promise that should you ever need a friend, need anything at all, you reach out for me. I will be there for you. And if you ever want me to review your writing or provide any kind of reference I am your biggest fan. We don't need to have a physical relationship to sustain an emotional connection." It was perhaps his best performance as an actor.

She grabbed her suitcase and walked out the door. She felt both sadness and... relief. Maybe more like excitement. The next chapter in her life had begun. She put her earphones in and listened to Sandra sing 'Maria Magdalena.'

Lydia, Eric's preposterously attractive mistress, was off to her next affaire. Everything had worked out. She was free from credit card debt and would be making the final payment on her first home within a few months.

She was introduced to a man while she was still with Eric. A man who showed her... things. A man who knew how to use her exactly correctly. He was a successful Founder-CEO at a large military weapons supply company. He was a former Navy Seal in peak physical condition. He was scary intense. The world she explored with him, the ways she used and was used by him, made her time with Eric seem like a vanilla ice cream social following a Sunday school prayer meeting. She accepting the CEO assignment because it was well-suited to her kink and felt more dangerous. It was her best available move in the 'game of life.'

Eric, though, felt that he had entered the gravity well of a black hole. The acceleration was unlike anything he had ever known. It was an out of body experience, but where the body and then the world disappears and leaves the soul alone in a nothingness of void. Alone in an object-less world.

A gruff man with a large beard pulled up in front of Eric. "You mind if I play some music?" he asked as Eric got into the car.

"No. No problem," Eric said, still in a state of disbelief.

As they started the drive toward the airport Lita Ford and Ozzy Osborne 'Close Your Eyes Forever' played on the car stereo.

In the car drop off zone Eric noticed the driver was crying. The man turned the music down a bit and, without making eye contact, explained, "Sorry, man. My girlfriend just broke up with me. She just said it was over. Poof. No warning. I am tore up man. It doesn't make any sense. So I am hurting bad, real real bad. And I hope you have a good flight because I want somebody to be at the opposite end of the spectrum I am on. Okay. So … so… always cherish the time you have, you know? I should probably shave my beard. She always hated it. I really need to change," the man lost track of where he was and started sobbing on his steering wheel. Eric exited the car. He tipped the man large on his phone and backed away from the car toward the automatic doors of the airport, stupefied.

######## PDC ########

The PDC was not known among his friends as a person who could keep a secret. His emotions were always on the surface, barely restrained. He had little difficulty speaking his mind, telling his truth. But things changed with his windfall. It wasn't that his emotions were less on the surface or that he was in more control over his body. No. In fact he was in less control.

Outwardly he exhibited all the hallmarks of a man caught up in a manic episode; close examination would reveal a person who was arguably insane or close to it. But inwardly his voice was squelched. He refused to talk or speak more than a few words. But he couldn't control his grin.

He was smiling so much it was hurting his face. He was shaking so much one might think he was freezing. On a few occasions he felt powerful tingling sensations run up and down his spine. He writhed and was surprised by his own surprise.

He had chosen to go the Rainbow Gathering because he needed to escape familiar people. He was afraid they were going to find out he inherited money and that it was going to change the dynamics of his friendships in a bad way. *"Maybe if I can spend some time with strangers I can get a grip then go back and figure out what to do next."*

He was almost to the Sand Dunes. His ride was slowed by construction on the road. But overall he made good time.

He approached the sand dunes parking lot and searched for X's van. He found it. She wasn't inside.

"I'll wait here I guess," he thought to himself as he peeled off his motorcycle helmet.

######## ANNIE ########

She was up early. Again she caught Maxwell's car with spoken word:

-

God loves the generous CHEERFUL GIVER!

We all crave appreciation. We have some we keep closer.

A friend. A peer. Those we revere.

It matters to us what they think of us.

Heavenly God APPRECIATES human giving.

Not a ritual giving. A cheerful giving!

There is no comparable favor for your ACTIONS to effect God!

Generous? CHEERFUL. Givers.

Must come from the heart.

Not obligation.

Systematic joy. Not begrudgingly.

Determination. Not compulsion.

"I show my appreciation to the cheerful giver!"

As the appearance of ABUNDANCE!

Nobody can love without GIVING!

God uniquely blesses the Cheerful Giver!

God's gracious giving is limitless! Beyond measurement.

When you Give to God the Eyes of Sight.

-You have less.

-No. Not the less.

When I give to God I have MORE not LESS.

You must live in the impossible

instead of the world of Sight.

Counting my blessings I cry.

The non-cheerful giver laments.

$5. $10. What is giving money?

-Uncheerful giver.

Cheerful loves!

Blessings are beyond human description.

-

She made a mental note to clip this out from the recordings she was making of Maxwell's broadcasting.

######## MAXWELL ########

Maxwell was making a video of himself as he walked in the

desert.

"Twin prime distribution. Electric bills. Things that are real independent of your feelings."

The dust hurt Maxwell when it started to pelt him in the face. "Damn. The wind has really kicked it up a notch." He wondered if a storm was blowing in as he felt the energy in the sky.

"These words feel strange," he heard himself say. "These worlds are colliding," he heard his voice echo back.

He was stumbling between Sagebrush. He felt dizzy. Like he might lose consciousness. He still had his Critical Resource bag strapped to his back.

"*I need to find somewhere out of the sun,*" he mumble-thought to himself. But in the recesses of his memory he could not recall how to get back to his cave.

He didn't dare remove his backpack; he could tell he was not in his right state of mind.

"I am not correct," he said to the camera.

He wanted to lie down and go to sleep, but he feared that if he did he might die.

So he kept walking. Stumbling.

Moving away from the Sun, with his back to the Sun. He knew that was the direction he needed to go. He tried to focus on how he got to his present location, retracing the steps in his mind.

Had he been bitten by something? Was he having a neurological breakdown? It came upon him quickly... fading memory.

He kept stumbling forward.

"*Who am I?*" he suddenly wondered.

He sat down in the sand, defeated. He leaned back and rested his upper body in the cradle of a desert shrub. He covered his face with his hat. He fell into a trance.

He woke up standing on a dark floor with rings emanating out from his location. It was similar to a previous dream.

A Man in a golden robe covered in gold and silver chains

and precious gems wearing a large golden crown adorned with gems and peacock feathers approached him. Beside him was another man, dressed in silver wearing a silver crown. Maxwell could see symbols flashing above their heads and knew that the man in gold was named Krishna and the man in silver was named Arjun. Krishna had so many symbols that it was impossible to see anything other than a glowing mass above his head.

They came closer to him until only a few rings separated them. However, a thread ran out of the visage of Arjun and another out of Krishna and these threads twisted together and shot upwards and disappeared into the infinity above. Maxwell then heard a voice.

Arjun: "How is action without desire possible, Krishna? Reward motivates action. Without reward who will act?"

Krishna: "Because life is impossible without action. You will do something. You'll either eat or not. You'll either give away food or not. You'll either wage war or not. You have the option to do something or not. The result, the reward, is not in your hands. The option is the limit of your control. Even if you desire it, victory may not be yours. You could also lose. Your desire to win will make you fear defeat. If you are indifferent to victory and defeat, but fight the war as your duty, then there will be no question of happiness or sorrow. Such a person without desire is unperturbed. Hence, shed any desire for reward. Do what is in your hands. Which means, do your duty. This is KARMA YOGA. Understand it well! You can opt to do or not to do, but that is the end of your right. You cannot control the result. Be steady and firm in your duty because its efficient fulfillment is yoga. Yoga is the fulfillment of duty. Giving up temptation to do one's duty will result with an ability to become imperturbable."

Arjun: "How do I recognize one who is imperturbable? What are the signs? How does one behave? How does one talk?"

Krishna: "It is not difficult to recognize such a person. Like him, you must shed your desires. Free yourself from ambition. Go beyond happiness and sorrow. Neither happiness nor sorrow can move you. The imperturbable man always remains calm and balanced. None can make him lose his balance, when he speaks it is not with sorrow or happiness but from the depths of his soul. He speaks not of attachment, but of action without desire. He is his own fortress. His senses are under his control. Only the one who can control his mind can control his senses."

"The ordinary mortal thinks of objects. This in turn leads to attachment, which further leads to the birth of desire. When desire is unfulfilled it leads to anger. From anger is born greater attachment to the object. With this, the ability to think begins to stray. When this happens, intelligence is destroyed. This in turn leads to the downfall of man. Temptation will destroy your intelligence. How can you get peace without intelligence? How can a person who cannot distinguish between peace and turmoil ever be happy? Like a gust of wind buffets a boat, desire makes intelligence stray. Hence, control your senses. Let not the senses control you. Listen to this with care and understand it: When the world sleeps the perfect man awakes. He only sleeps when the world awakes. The ordinary man is prey to temptation. That is the aim of his awakening. He wants food when he is hungry. He wants water when he is thirsty. He needs a house to save himself from the weather. His thoughts are selfish. The perfect man's thoughts are selfless. He is beyond selfish hunger and thirst. He does not think of the fallen fruit but of the tree. The ordinary man needs fuel for his engine. He will go on cutting trees until the forest is destroyed. The perfect man thinks of the importance of forests, about the balance of nature and the relations of forests and the seasons. The sensual man's day is the perfect man's night. The latter has gone beyond duality. The sensual man's night is the perfect man's day. His sun also rises in the stillness of night. The perfect man is also interested in solutions. That is what separates him from the sensual man. Truth is beyond the senses."

"It is not that the perfect man is not hungry, but he goes beyond hunger and thinks of a solution for hunger. That's why the sensual man's day is his night. The sensual man can make himself perfect. The sensual man is like the river which flows on eagerly without realizing where it is going. It merely knows that it has to flow on, only to squander its water into the sea. Even the sea does not cross the limits of its shore. The river of desire overwhelms the sensual man. The perfect man, however, can absorb it, and still not cross his limits. Become like the sea. The sea is knowledgeable. You, too, be knowledgeable. Knowledge is excellent."

Arjun: "If knowledge is better than action why do you ask me to act and fight this war?"

Krishna: "There are two types of people in this world. The mediators and the doers. The mediators search for God within themselves. This is the path of knowledge. The doers try to attain God through actions. But there is no freedom from action. Searching for God within is also an action. There are only two paths, the path of knowledge and the path of action. Seeking knowledge does not mean giving up on action. Life without action is impossible. The eyes will see and the eyelids blink. The ears will hear. The man who forcibly suppresses his sense and tries to meditate is not a yogi, but a liar. The yogi does not suppress the senses he controls them. He does not live with his eyes closed. The body's journey without action is impossible. So long as man breathes he will experience both a perfume and a stink. If there is a rhythm or a noise around him his ears will not wait for an order to hear it. The perfect man controls his senses and gives them a direction with his awakened mind."

"He realizes his options and knows how to organize them. Doing routine tasks is better than doing nothing. It is true that the eyes see, but the yogi decides what they should see. None of his senses are completely free. This separates the yogi from the sensual man. So, action should be like a ritual offering. Action is a ritual, its aim being the indestructible Godhead. The path of action goes straight to the Godhead. His life becomes valueless if he does not participate in the life cycle. Don't go towards a valueless life. The one who thinks only of himself is a sinner. So, recognize your duty and do it. Desire for the reward is the real obstacle. It is the real millstone around the neck. It does not allow him to rise above himself. This isolates the person from his society, pushing him into the mire of profit and loss. Society is not a part of you, you are a part of it. So, your prime duty is the people's welfare. What is good for society is good for you. Acting for the people's good is your salvation. Selfish action is a sin. It takes you away from the path of salvation. Remember - you are a great man. Other people will walk the path of desire and greed. Great men are always emulated as ideals. Even the sensual man acts, but it is from the selfish point of view. The yogi's acts are selfless, for the world and the welfare of the people."

Arjun: "Why is a man sometimes compelled to sin?"

Krishna: "His lust and his selfishness. His anger and temptation compel him to sin. Recognize these enemies. Like smoke cloaks a fire, dust cloaks the mirror. Desire, anger, lust all cloak knowledge. The fire of temptation and desire destroys knowledge and is its enemy. Cleanse the mirror and purify the fire. Modify the senses and kill this enemy of knowledge."

"The power of the senses is no doubt great but greater than that is the mind. Greater than mind is reason, but the soul is greatest. So, worry about the soul. Take it beyond the senses, mind and reason. 'I desire no reward so my action is not contaminated.' Act without desire and selfish greed. Distinguish between action, inaction and bad action."

Arjun: "What is the difference?"

Krishna: "Action free from desire is inaction. Action not good for society is bad action. Action is superior in inaction, the non-doer is superior to the doer. The non-doer does not desire reward. After the action he does not wait for a reward. He moves to his next action. The fire of his knowledge burns anger, temptation, ambition, gain, sorrow, loss, happiness and purifies his action. Through this the doer becomes the non-doer. Do what is essential for life and all actions are good for society. Though a man, he is not contaminated by sin. His very existence is good for society. Such a life is a ritual offering to God. You, too, make your life such an offering. Burn to ash all desire, greed, anger. There are four types of ritual offerings:

1) DRAVYA YAGNA: Wealth is used for the good of society, for the welfare of the people.

2) TAPO YAGNA: When a person makes his actions a penance his life becomes a Tapo Yagna. Following your religion is a kind of worship. It is not religion-based, but eternal. It benefits a person and also society.

3) YOGA YAGNA: Yoga is studied as part of this. It takes a person to meditation. Life's very breath is the offering.

4) GYAN YOGA: The BEST because knowledge can distinguish between good and bad. The fire of knowledge can purify action. Knowledge is the focus of action. Knowledge frees you from the bonds of temptation. Only knowledge can cross the sea of sin."

"Hey, human, I am telling you. This Earth is your realm of action. You will be judged by your action. Hence, do not run away from action. Action without desire is your duty. Your duty is your religion. If your action is only for yourself then it will take you toward sin. So, become free of yourself and do good for the world, for that is the path of salvation. Other actions are prisoners of temptation, anger, lust. How can such action lead to salvation? If society is unhappy, so is the individual. If society is in tears then so are you. If trees are cut, they cannot give you fruits and shade. It is the trees duty to yield fruit and give shade. You are a part of society. Do not think you are the owner. Your betterment lies in this. This is the best knowledge. The lives of those who know this is a Yagna."

"There is nothing holier or purer than knowledge. He who has neither faith nor knowledge, he who is forever in doubt, is lost for all time. He is neither happy on Earth nor in Heaven. Hence, Arjun, get rid of doubt and awaken the penance and awaken the sage within you. Follow the path of knowledge. Renunciation is the ultimate limit of knowledge."

Arjun: "You praise both renunciation and the path of action."

Krishna: "Are they not contradictory? Both are good. But the path of action is better."

Arjun: "Why? How?"

Krishna: "The one who has truly renounced rises above jealousy and ambition. He is above contradiction and thus frees himself. Only the foolish think the path of action and renunciation are contradictory. The wise do not think so. The path of action is actually known as unselfishness. Renunciation is impossible without the path of action. The one who follows the path of action has full knowledge of the elements. Whether he sees it or not, tastes it or not, wakes or sleeps. Whether he takes it or not. Whether he leaves or not. Whatever he does, his every action, is for the welfare of man."

"The man of action surrenders all rewards and is happy in the castle of NINE GATES of his body. What are the nine gates? Two eyes, two ears, two nostrils, a mouth and two excretory openings. All the senses."

"Man is inebriated because his ignorance covers his wisdom. When the wisdom of the soul destroys ignorance the Supreme can be seen in its radiance. The wise thus obtain God in their mortal life. They do not need to be reborn. They obtain salvation in their mortal life. This mortal life is very important because after it you won't exist though your soul will. Hence, make this mortal life meaningful. Knowledge is light! Obtain it! If you do this, you will not go astray, which in turn will give you peace. Without this war there can be no peace. Running away from truth will not lead to peace. This war is your religion. Follow your religion. Don't think of the result. It is not your problem what lives and what dies. Accept as the path what others call renunciation. Fight without doubt, jealousy, or ambition. None can be perfect without sacrificing them. It is your duty to stay alert and awaken the soul. Arise, O Man! Your soul can be your friend as well as your enemy. He who can control his ego, mind and senses will be his own friend. Those who are controlled by them will become their own enemy. Those who are in whatever they face, be it sorrow or happiness, insult or respect, and stay balanced will find peace and will be totally devoted to God and oneness with God. However, those who eat more or don't eat at all, or those who sleep a lot or don't sleep at all, cannot find fulfillment. Life should be balanced. Those who live a balanced life will find their sorrows disappearing."

"Like a lamp in the steady wind his soul is steady in temptation. Steady the restless mind with your soul. That is the solution to your problems."

Arjun: "But even the perfect mind can go astray."

Krishna: "Of course it can go astray."

Arjun: "How then will this affect achieving Godhead? Is the person who strays destroyed?"

Krishna: "Whether in Heaven or on Earth the person who does good is never destroyed. Set your mind on love. The entire Universe revolves around love."

-

The Waitress was jarred awake by the sound of a ball bearing screeching in the refrigerator compressor. She had been dreaming of Maxwell. In her dream she initially saw him as a miniature person tied up in the center of a dartboard. She woke up inside the dream having already thrown several darts at him. He was trying to get her attention by yelling something in a tiny voice. As she approached him the room folded into itself and she and Maxwell re-materialized sitting next to each other in an empty movie theater. Out of the top of her head projected tiny threads of light which rose up and then moved toward the movie screen. The threads were then absorbed by the screen and it appeared as if the white surface was now made of some kind of liquid light. The screen then played episode 73 from B.R. Chopra's Mahabharat Stories. Maxwell, to her left, was shrunken in his seat with terrible posture that made him look ill or extremely depressed. She tried to reach out and touch him, but her hand passed through him as if he was a ghost. The dream seemed hyper-real, like it wasn't a dream at all.

The refrigerator motor was making a high pitch wailing sound. She walked over to it and out of habit opened the door to look inside. She then slammed it shut, frustrated. The whining stopped. She looked at the refrigerator with skeptical eyes. "Be good," she said to it as she backed away slowly.

The Waitress was not able to go back to sleep. Being jarred awake by the sound of a screaming ball bearing had been enough to dump some adrenaline into her bloodstream. She decided to read from Eric's journals. He had removed one himself and left it on his writing desk before leaving town to attend a conference. A pencil was placed between pages to mark a particular passage. She opened it up and started reading:

-

It isn't easy, making time for writing. Should be trivial for a person in my position, with all this available time. And yet I don't always feel up to it. Such a pathetic excuse.

I must tie certain rewards to being successful at writing. No distractions until I finish my required task. Six pages per day. This is the first day of a new ritual.

Admittedly today I feel terrible. A migraine. And some part of me wants to give up. Doesn't want to do the hard work of writing. Yeah, it doesn't appear hard from the outside. Looks like a guy sitting in a chair scribbling notes on paper. It isn't the physical work that is taxing (though, in its own way, it does deal some damage). It is a mental challenge.

What is the reason for it? Why? I have no real needs anymore, at lease none that I fund by doing this. I am not desperate like I once was. Do I secretly, unwittingly, believe I am capable of becoming a great author? Why would that even be a dream in the first place?

One thing is for sure and that is the fact I have not felt inspired to do the actual work. Do the actual writing that is required to achieve another novel. I have been... working on stuff. Just not with the kind of passion that one should expect from a professional creator.

Again, writing six pages per day is no joke. My body and mind want me to stop and instead watch some funny videos or go for a walk or anything else besides this work. Lazy brain syndrome. I want distractions not destinations. Something I need to work on if I really want to achieve my next goal.

I am definitely forcing it. I could just cap the pen and walk away. No one is going to find out that I failed myself. There is no consequence, no external judgment anyway. Yet here I sit, head pounding belly aching, hunched over writing. Forcing the words to come.

I am not writing toward the end of completing anything. Just writing because I told myself I must. That today is the first day of six pages per day. No matter what I MUST write. And with a goal of achieving a good outcome. Something people will WANT to experience.

There are scenarios where the will to achieve catches you unaware. Like a lightning strike on a clear day. Moments like those you are a mere tool being wielded by a force from beyond. It is effortless and you watch as the words appear on the page. Not premeditated in any real sense the narrative drives itself. Those moments are magnificent. The 'Flow State.'

Then there are moments like these where I must force myself under penalty of self-loathing to do what it takes to achieve the minimum result. And I am trying to find the desire to write. But even if desire fails and I am depressed I will instead rely on ritual to complete my task.

A bit like starting a fire with wet wood. They say where there is smoke there is fire, but in my case it is more like a smoldering mess of mud and twigs. Technically something is burning, but don't expect it to illuminate or provide warmth.

Just a lot of effort for very little gain. One might even argue it is a waste of effort. A sign that someone is desperate and willing to ignore facts so long as they 'feel' like they are being productive. Perhaps another form of distraction? Or, worse, self-delusion.

This is different. This activity leaves an artifact. Maybe a useless artifact? One that ranks among the least significant contributions. Stacked stones. Nonetheless if you are one of the only people stacking stones your paths are the only ones that can be 'discovered.' A fact that is both hilarious and horrifying at the same time.

Page 4 of 6. Almost like a prisoner counting down to his release date. It is effort and sometimes you just want to be lazy. But if I allow that voice to win I am doomed as a writer. I must kill off the voice that asks me to drop the pen. I must fight against the easy road as it leads to ruin and regret. I may not achieve greatness, but at least I won't fail to make an attempt.

And that is the message. You never need to start. You certainly don't need to finish. If you manage to start and keep going and finish there is zero guarantee it will matter to anyone. You must act from a place that does not seek rewards. You must avoid setting yourself up for disappointment.

Build your momentum and keep the pace. Not because you must and not because it is easy. Rarely is it easy. Do the thing because you accept it is your duty to do so. Become one with your duty and all other concerns disappear.

I must acknowledge that sometimes it is easier to write self-help notes than it is to write creatively in the storyline of my characters. The act of seeing the arc of life for these numerous individuals I create and destroy, hearing them speak and sympathizing with them, removes me from other pursuits. I do not know how their stories end. You might expect that the writer knows ahead of time where his characters are going. But I don't actually know. I am on a curvy road and cannot see very far. I have no map, no compass. In many ways I have no clue.

I offer myself to the task of writing and it uses me to see its objectives fulfilled. And so here I am, forcing the words.

The characters are all locked into various situations. They are enduring and slowly evolving. The characters I am writing are, for the most part, under various kinds of pressure. They are simultaneously enamored with and troubled by the objects and pursuits that define their lives. Their goals allow them to transcend the limitations of 'ordinary' experience. Most of my main characters are dealing with issues of life and death, freedom and incarceration. Meanwhile they are chasing impossible dreams. Improbable dreams.

Dreams make for excellent distractions. Can the extraordinary be discovered simply by evading the ordinary? It is by running from tradition that the new emerges? Maybe? Sometimes?

This aspect of my characters is likely a reflection of my own life. I am focused on writing. I feel strongly about it and yet I know it also serves to get my mind off the inevitability of my own mortality. My inevitable end when the pen can no longer write. Chasing a dream attempting to outrun Death.

And what happens if you catch the dream? You have no idea. Not really. You have a bunch of hallucinations regarding possible futures. But that is all they are. Fantasies.

You made your choice and you are walking the path. There is no going back, no changing history. You must focus on the act of writing.

Day 1. I am here now and have made a stand. I will achieve these outputs and it will not be a lack of willpower that determines it. Habits not goals. Create habits for yourself.

Gotta admit, I wanted to quit on page 2. But I forced myself to keep going. Glad I did. I can do this. I shall. I will it into being by doing it.

In 10 days I will have 60 pages. In 100 days I will have 600 pages. If I keep this up I will churn out several novels in the next handful of years.

But these 'Letters to God' have no place in that. I probably shouldn't even count this toward my six page per day goal.

This is more like patient-doctor privilege where I address my insecurities and self-doubts in the context of a private session with a therapist. But I am going to count it anyway. Because I can.

-

The Waitress wondered why Eric marked this passage before leaving to go to the conference. *"Maybe he just wanted to remind himself of where he was when he started writing his six pages per day?"* she hypothesized.

She knew Eric was likely going to arrive some time late in the evening. She was excited to see him and hear about his travels.

######## PDC ########

PDC and X drove into the rainbow gathering. Once they parked he was able to slide his motorcycle into her van. He was legitimately excited. They marched several miles into a large meadow where the fire pit and drum circle were located. They decided to set up their tents very close to the main performance stage. After they finished setting up the campsite PDC noticed the sun was getting ready to drop below the horizon. X wanted to spend some time in her tent to recover from the long drive and subsequent hike into the forest. PDC decided to walk around.

Primitive trails. Recently created channels in the dirt were his highways now. He followed one and soon found himself marching deep into the woods. Alongside the path were occasional pockets of tents where groups of people were camping together. He saw several primitive kitchens where people huddled around the main earthernwork stoves and told stories or just listened to the sounds of crackling firewood. Everyone was dirty. Very few feet wore shoes. No one looked particularly successful based on the standardized metrics people use to measure such things.

The small dirt path eventually looped him back onto the

main trail that headed away from the gathering, but he was not aware that he was headed toward the parking lot.

Marshall drove into the Rainbow Gathering just as the sun was preparing to set. "We need to go fast because we don't want to look for a spot in the dark!" Hippie Girl urged. The trail was several miles with a lot of hills and ravines. It was slow going. In addition to all their gear and supplies they were porting in five gallons of water. Marshall crossed a small stream that cut through the path. He slipped on slick mud and started to fall toward a deep ravine located to his immediate right. Just as he was about to lose control someone grabbed Marshall's backpack and saved him from disaster.

Marshall turned to see the face of the person who saved him and in an instant knew, or had a strong feeling, that this person was important. "Hey, I'm Marshall. Thanks for that."

"No problem. Are you guys heading in to camp?"

"Yeah," Hippie Girl replied.

"Man, I think I am turned around then..." PDC said, looking up at the sky.

"You want to get high?" Marshall asked PDC.

"I thought you'd never ask," he replied.

"We need to set up our tents first," Hippie Girl insisted by stomping one of her feet.

"Hey, to that end. I am set up by the main stage. That is actually where I am headed now. We should go there. It is pretty much the main attraction. You should set up by us. Super convenient. Here, I can take some of that water for you," PDC said as he hooked four gallons into his fingers.

Hippie Girl was skeptical, but Marshall was already thinking past the sale. "Thanks," he said. "Lead the way."

Off they went.

As they walked down the path Marshall saw a couple camped alone who were fighting with each other. The girl looked sad as the guy stomped around looking for something he lost. PDC removed a desert sage smudge stick from the right thigh pocket of his cargo pants and handed it to the girl. He said, "For you. For vibes." The girl immediately looked happy and went to talk with her boyfriend. Marshall continued to glance at them and watched as their attitudes completely transformed.

As they walked further Marshall saw small clearings emerge containing makeshift kitchens with water and tea available. He saw children playing in the mud. PDC was wearing a nice iridescent pearl-white dress shirt with the French cuffs and had the over-sized collar turned up. His cargo pants pockets were loaded with Desert Sage Smudge Sticks. His boots were unfamiliar to Marshall and had large clasps that fastened to lock the boot onto the foot. He wore a tie as a belt.

Marshall continued to scan the environment. They passed a group of 'dirty kids' seated within the numerous nooks and crannies of the exposed root system of a large tree. They were covered in very poorly executed tattoos and called out in guttural tones requesting tobacco and candy as toll for the road. "The very definition of the nihilist look," PDC said to Marshall once they passed out of earshot.

Hippie Girl glared at him. "That isn't nice. Those dirty kids aren't hurting anybody."

PDC agreed with her. "I only meant to remark that they are clearly free from the stigma associated with rejecting social norms." Marshall laughed and winked at Hippie Girl.

They crossed an open glade and headed toward a large, though primitive, covered outdoor stage. PDC and X had set up their tents just outside the audience seating area on the left side facing the stage. They could open the flaps to their tents and watch the audience and the stage acts. "Set up there," PDC pointed to the tents. "Right in the middle of everything."

Hippie Girl immediately noticed that there were no other tents set up out in the open with them. Out of the thousands of people at the gathering, they were by far the most conspicuous.

"I'm not so sure we should set up here..." Hippie Girl warned in protest.

"Nah. C'mon. This is fine. Trust me." Marshall persuaded her.

"Okay."

Marshall was unsure why he felt it was the correct thing to do, but it was a powerful premonition. The smell of wood fires and vegetarian cooking rolled out of the forest and onto them from all directions, transporting them into a simulated experience of neo-primitivism. Most of the campers had been living in the forest for weeks. *"This is not an easy way to live,"* Marshall observed silently. People were showing signs of strain and distress. Tobacco was in short supply. Dog food was in short supply. Chocolate was a luxury.

They set up their tents. "I am going to take off to find some friends," Hippie Girl told Marshall. It was apparent that Hippie Girl was not inviting him to come along.

"Sure. I'm gonna hang out here," Marshall replied, bearing no trace of awareness. Marshall decided to lie down and listen to the acoustic music. It was not amplified; there were no generators, no electrified equipment of any kind. Numerous famous people were in attendance, sitting on chairs or in the dirt. Marshall, though, felt like a VIP. He listened to the voice of Patch Adams as he fell into a deep sleep.

######## WAITRESS and MAXWELL ########

When they were dating the Waitress regularly 'interviewed' Maxwell while he was asleep. She would inquire about all kinds of things and he would tell her what he knew. He described how people had a box of symbols that hovers over their heads and describes everything they know as three-dimensional shapes. He then told her that he believed people were programmable. And that they could be treated as 'NPC's' in 'The Game.'

"It is a map and there are players upon it," he explained. "They have, effectively, 'skill stacks' and you can see these and how they work to complete the individual."

She listened intently even if she wasn't taking anything very seriously. If Maxwell had the ability to see his own symbols he would have recognized she was harvesting data from him. That a part of her mind had awakened from exposure to Maxwell and as a result she was downloading symbols from his libraries.

Hypervisor code. The ability to install a virtual machine that can run concurrently on separate human hardware. Two brains bridged by one process.

The Waitress continued to dream about Maxwell in the desert. She could see him pacing, pounding sand. When she tried to read his notebooks the letters moved on the pages. But she sensed Maxwell was obsessed with something. She had seen graphs and charts that represented mathematical reasoning of some sort. They were glowing when she saw them.

The psychic connection between the Waitress and Maxwell was unknown to them both. It was established in the past and reinforced when Maxwell embedded some of his semen into her. Between the embedded DNA and the information she was given in her interviews she transformed. They were communicating across an 'entanglement VPN' that set up a direct link between their brains. They shared space and they hosted an application that was running simultaneously in both of them irrespective their distance from each other.

Eric returned from his trip a changed man. He seemed to be wincing with some kind of invisible pain. However, he worked to pay attention to the Waitress and wanted to make her happy.

"I know I have been a bit aloof lately and I want you to know I am thankful you can tolerate me when I am in my self-absorbed phase. It isn't easy to be ignored and neglected and so I really want you to know that I am grateful to you. For everything."

She smiled at him. "I love you," she said. "When you love someone you don't want them to be anyone other than who they are. I love you for who you are. Perfection isn't real. I don't live in a fantasy world where you need to be Prince Perfect in order for me to act like a decent person. I want to provide you with the feminine version of environmental management. I want to see you thrive. Maybe I don't even know why I feel that way, and so I choose not to think about it? Like, I chose you and I hope you chose me. And so long as that keeps going then we can find ways to help each other achieve meaning and validation. Maybe?"

A deep sense of guilt hit him. Here was this wonderful woman who loved and adored him and he was feeling lost because the 19 year old lover he was lucky enough to experience had left him; as if he wasn't still an unbelievably blessed soul. His eyes twitched and betrayed his conflicted feelings. She saw it and said, "Also, and I want you to really understand this, I accept that you are a man. I want you to be yourself, to take all that life is giving you and have a great experience. Do not look behind you only look forward. Trust me."

He did.

CHAPTER 9

######## ERIC ########

Eric walked out of his apartment and onto the street. He was thinking about his next novel. He wanted to ensure his work would resonate with a large audience. He felt compelled to write about magic and how it comes to pass that the laws of physics are in fact just habits of materials. Behaviors we have come to rely upon with no basis for doing so aside from an apparent regularity across a relatively large number of experiments.

He entered a coffee shop and ordered a large dirty chai. He sat at a table and began to write.

-

Coffee Shop. Writing.

Gravity is everywhere an attractive force. But why? How? Isn't that a perpetual motion machine?

An ancient civilization existed which harnessed the laws of physics in such a way that the physical world could be modified by thought alone. But that civilization was wiped out by a cataclysm and only the barest essentials of truth survive into the present age. Superstitions involving 'witches' and 'potions' and 'wands' replaced the scientific understanding of the past. Now a loose-knit confederation of magic users are the gatekeepers. They persist in power due to the masses relative lack of knowledge.

The young man whose mother was an initiate in the magical world. His studies of Quantum Mechanics and the nature of human intent as it operates on the physical world.

It is not known if all animals experience jealousy, however it is beyond doubt that humans suffer. When a person perceives they have been unjustly denied access to a basic right or are being unfairly excluded from accessing knowledge they have a tendency to grow resentful. This resentment can fester until it consumes the totality of one's thought.

Upon hearing his mother's description of magic he felt that he had been denied his birthright. She was on her death bed and felt she could not die in peace if he did not learn the truth. The truth that the world was not as it seems.

"Magic?" he asked.

"Not like card tricks and pulling rabbits from a hat," she mumbled. "Real magic. The ability to transform into animals. To fly. To brew potions. Its all real. They live among us. You would never know. They hide access into their world."

He was stunned. It was like he knew what he was hearing was true, but he couldn't believe it.

"Your father was a magic user," she went on. "They came and took him away. But they didn't know about you. He told me your power would be concealed as long as I was alive to keep you wearing your bands. But my time is almost here. I am sorry I didn't tell you sooner. You see, anyone can learn magic. But some people are born with the ability. Long ago they chose to separate themselves and live as a separate class. Your father disagreed with this. And for that, they killed him. But not before he had a chance to create the bands that hide you from them."

He was stunned, couldn't comprehend what she was saying. "Mom ... I ..."

"No. Understand we don't have much time. I didn't ever dream I would be in this kind of state... There are so many things you need to know."

For as long as he could remember his mother instructed him in scientific analysis. By inserting reasoning and the scientific method into his daily life she taught him how to accurately measure bravery. She never hit him. She truly loved him.

So she told him the truth and gave him a key to unlock the trunk in her room. Then she died.

His father had accidentally discovered the relationship between magic and high energy particle accelerators when he was hanging out with a girl he liked. A 'Book Of Magical Names' marked him off the list and then rewrote his name, as if he had died and returned to life. When he was questioned about it the Magical Inquisitors discovered that when a magic user enters the realm of quark mass they are in a place where magic fails. There is some form of 'renormalization' that only allows magic to work in a specific range of gravity intensities. So magic works on Earth because the protons, neutrons and electrons are all experiencing 1g of acceleration force, whereas at the surface of a neutron star the pressure is much greater, for example 1,000,000g. There appears to be a relationship between gravitational field strength and magic that limits the use of magic to Earth-like gravity fields. To achieve the QUARK STATE of matter associated with stable quarks one must generate a field of a certain frequency and magnetic pressure. To generate the interactions necessary to collapse ordinary matter into quark matter states the matter must be accelerated to extremely high frequencies. So, a strange quark star does not permit magic because magic exists in the domain of protons, neutrons and electrons at or near Earth's gravity. So the fields and associated frequencies which generate quark mass are also frequencies where magic has no basis and cannot operate. A magic user in the presence of such a machine is not detectable to other magic users or devices. A magic user in the presence of such a field cannot be influenced by magic and cannot utilize magic. Such a person disappears from all magical sight. This is because magic operates in the quantum scale, but only upon matter stabilized near the 1g 'force regime.' Additionally, matter on Earth can experience magic because the Solar System contains one of the most ancient artifacts in the entire known universe.

Once he discovered the power these frequencies have over magical detection his father and mother developed a bracelet, ring, necklace, and a watch that generate high frequency low amperage fields. This field creates a skin-effect which makes a magician invisible to magic sight. Additionally, it neutralizes the use of magic at the skin boundary. Where the field can be breached (by touching) the 'ward' is of no use. He was able to work with her to create the bands that would shield her from their observation as she became more informed and became able to read magical texts. They had a son. They had their baby in a forest in an RV so that the moment it was born it could have the field applied. It was the frequencies and the cancellations and the out-of-band additions that allowed them to remain hidden.

######## JEBEDIAH ########

Jebediah's progress with Mind Pixels was accelerating. He experimented with numerous drugs and was getting impressive results. They now had 'Intentional Water' selling worldwide. A large warehouse hidden in the Brazilian forest contained a fully automated system that used robotics to move the water and drug samples into laser irradiation chambers. They were able to process many thousands of orders at one time, with new capacity being added daily.

The American scientist and business magnate Dr. Keal was studying how to transmit thoughts, feelings, and emotions using rTMS to induce granular changes in the molecules being tested. His laboratory was far more advanced than Jebediah's. With his significant technology advantage Dr. Keal was able to begin assembling a 'spin map.' He discovered that the same orientation of molecules that contains a neutron produces different pointer results than those without. He also found that mental states could be induced across a broad spectrum of molecular species whose atomic weights vary far less than the mass of a neutron. "Strange Oxygen and Strange Xenon yield entirely different pointers than ordinary versions of those atoms." Even though emotional regulation of soldiers was an excellent achievement it paled in comparison to the ability to send messages directly to front line officers across entangled particles that by their very nature cannot be hacked.

The US Military was working with state and local police to identify users and distributors of the intentional water product, but not because they wanted to arrest people. In fact they were instructed to avoid any behavior that might cause the suppliers to pull back. They wanted the product to flow. They set up special cell phone towers near large events so they could tag individuals who were using the substance. They wanted to conduct an invisible investigation into the potential side-effects.

Jebediah had not explored sending verbal communications through spin modification. He had not considered the technology for anything other than delivering 'images' of physical substances into remote user brains.

Over the years Jebediah adopted dozens of children throughout all the world's inhabited continents. Some of them were becoming adults and were beginning to assist in the operation of the family airship transport business. Having highly educated native born children in other parts of the world allowed the company to grow. Of course, not all children in Jebediah's adoption program were promoted into the family business. Some went on to become poets, some painters. Some failed and lived in relative squalor. The Pareto Principle seemed to apply to his selection of intelligent children.

Under ordinary circumstances Jebediah's drug dealing activities would have resulted with a large investigation and probable issuance of an international warrant. As it stood, he was being protected by the world's largest military. The profit margin on selling the water was nearly infinite. The water bottles had been forward-delivered and were stored in faraway regional distribution warehouses. Intentional Water was projected to have one billion units sold by the end of its second year. There had yet to be any reported side-effects.

######## MAXWELL ########

It was early morning and Maxwell had just mashed the red button on the dashboard of his car before walking away. 'Got Me Under Pressure' by ZZ Top started playing in his headphones as he dance-walked in the general direction of his writing cave.

Focused on his challenge. He was leaping through the desert thinking to himself about numbers. He wanted to understand the primes. In his way. The autodidact way. He spent months estimating the correct values to model curves he had witnessed in his dreams. Curves that represented the distribution of composite numbers. It was his belief that he could discover the complement to that vision. The prime generating function.

He needed to express his algorithm in the language of The Mathematician. He wanted to present equations in lieu of recursions. So he crunched numbers and built large tables of data and did calculations by hand. Equations replaced recursive functions. Where once he had to call into memory he now generated output. The circuit was complete and had no bottlenecks.

Maxwell, isolated and ignorant, had no idea if he was reinventing the wheel. He had only himself. And the numbers.

He saw the numbers as objects, as distinct individuals. They had properties and traits. They lived at addresses and had children. The children had traits they inherited from the parents. The Mathematician employs a tool named 'modulus' (%) that can be used to reveal inherited 'genetic' characteristics associated with prime number operators. Maxwell used modulus to describe family trees.

Maxwell danced without speaking. He was praying to receive a Sign of the Primes. He pulled his action camera out from his back pocket and extended it on its pole. He started recording himself as he resumed walking. "If primes have order there is a Sign of that order. The 'sign of order' communicates on behalf of itself. One discovers it as a property of reality. We don't invent such laws. We observe laws in action. The Sieve of Eratosthenes is the observation of just such a law. It is not an artifice or a highly accurate guess. It operates precisely because it is a natural law. Incontrovertible and infallible. Imagine our dear Eratosthenes diagramming algorithms in the sand. Primes represented mythical objects to the ancients. They were recognized as being important players with powers over their child numbers."

######### PDC and MARSHALL #########

The drums never cease. All night long feet stamping around the fire. The pressure waves radiating off the drums filled the open spaces and crashed against the wall of trees. The trees absorb the acoustic waves and this stimulates the growth of beneficial fungi in their root systems. The trees awaken with the sounds of the people and are responsive to their prayers.

Marshall woke up feeling great. For the first time in a long while he felt he could let his guard down.

Marshall unzipped his tent and found PDC seated in a lotus position facing East. He was holding his hands in a prayer fold in front of his body. Without opening his eyes he said in a quiet voice. "We should probably get high now."

Marshall grabbed his marijuana and exited the tent.

"Oh, I see," PDC said, looking down at the tray. "Let me add something to that."

PDC put down a shot glass full of what looked like green hash keef. "Mix that with your weed."

"This is nice," Marshall said, breaking up a chunk.

"I came here with nothing," PDC said. "Well, that isn't technically true. I have about 100 smudge sticks and a bunch of tobacco. So last night when I disappeared I walked through some camps talking with people and trading them cigarettes.

When they see I have the best premades they start to offer me things. I initially protest, say things like 'this is my last pack.' Make it worth more to me so it becomes worth more to them. Then I trade a pack of cigarettes for a brick of hash. Hate the player AND the game, am I right!?"

Marshall tapped his nose with his left index finger and replied in an British accent, "Not too hasty." PDC laughed, getting the attention of some people walking by. Marshall rolled several hog leg marijuana cigarettes.

"You keep those," PDC said to Marshall.

"Here ya go then," he said, extending a joint to PDC.

PDC lit it. Inhaled. Exhaling he said, "Oh yeaaaaah. I am going down to The Row today to try and trade for some, well, whatever comes our way. If you want to tag along I could use someone to watch stuff while I maybe run away and conduct some sidequest transactions. And vice-versa. If you find stuff you want you can take some of my tobacco to trade for it."

"The Row?" Marshall reflexively asked.

"Yeah. There is part of the main trail where we can set up a blanket and barter and trade for goods with other people. I have cigarettes, but literally if there is anything you want to trade for and you can use my tobacco to get it I am totally down for that. I have plenty. Probably more than anyone here."

Marshall laughed. "I have 15 cartons in my tent."

PDC was surprised. "The odds of us running into each other indicates one of two possibilities. The 'Set of People' who brought that much tobacco here contains only 2 people, or more than 2 people. My bet, based on my read of the situation last night, is that it contains two people. Me and you. So the chances we would meet are pretty epic against."

Hippie Girl had yet not returned to camp.

Marshall left a note on her sleeping bag stating he had gone to The Row to conduct trades. He packed 9 cartons of cigarettes and a small box into his backpack. He then went to PDC's tent. "Okay," PDC said after emerging with a large backpack and a black tote. "I have the blankets and the stuff I plan to use for trade. You good?"

"Yeah."

"Kick ass. Let's do this thing."

######## MAXWELL's CAR ########

Radio signals transmitted into the void. A military flight on overwatch detected the signals emanating from Maxwell's car. "Looks like just another noise emitter running above the legal wattage." The transmission was sent forward to a data fusion center. "All predicted nodes accounted for. New node not authorized for monitored zone." Image capture was automatically scheduled for a satellite. "An automobile. Likely 1980's model Mercedes 240d with mounted solar panels near some shipping containers. Map updated to reflect a recent sweep. Image updated."

A spreadsheet containing a list of names and unique identifiers. *"Humans never truly disappear until they are dead. Else they are making waves and leaving trails."* Maxwell was one degree of separation from Jebediah Northcutt. Jebediah was under the protection of the US Government and, by extension, so was Maxwell Pragmatic. As a result of his involvement with Project Mind Pixel he had been placed on a list of US_VIP's who were not to be stopped when traveling through international ports. Were not to be stopped for any reason ever, period. Only if Maxwell was attempting to assassinate a world leader could any military or police service generate a stop order. And even then it might be denied.

The overwatch flight captured a spoken word transmission. A program performed speech to text and compared to known values. It was a strong match for Dr. Michael Youssef.

-

Ecclesiastes.

Not vanity.

Emptiness. Emptiness. Searching. Always searching.

Seeking what is missing.

Life without meaning.

Solomon wrote Ecclesiastes. Wrote during a midlife crisis with 100 wives.

No doubt.

In your 40's and 50's you question and wonder what you have missed.

What you cannot possibly live long enough to experience.

Life's activity. Make things happen while you can.

We are concerned with cleaning, work, etc.

Solomon says as he approaches it. Let me warn you. At the end of life. Emptyness. Emptyness.

Creation itself.

Mountains, oceans.

They seem constant.

While people are more finite. Shorter lived.

Nature should come and go, but humans should live forever. Living under the Sun.

Do not forsake God. He who is living UNDER THE SUN.

Do not live under the Sun. Live ABOVE it.

No pursuit can bring you happiness.

Connection to the divine and divine action done are fulfilling.

Know your limit.

All the distractions. On and on. Repeat. They convince you to remain distracted and engaged.

The eyes and ears are never sated. Never satisfied.

Materialism. What we want. Then we need.

Process. Easy to forget our purpose for living.

Verse 18: Ecclesiastes, "With an increase in knowledge comes an increase in sorrow."

Issac Newton: "I have been paddling in the shallows of a great ocean of knowledge."

Honest people acknowledge the vastness of the unknown.

Living above the Sun. Living connected to that.

Seeking perfect knowledge. Perfect yourself. Know who you are. Have a PURPOSE for living.

######### ERIC #########

Eric was in a coffee shop sitting at a high-top table looking out a large window at the street outside. He had a dirty chai and a large slice of carrot cake. He was mining the carrot cake with a spoon as he stared at the blank page. He took a sip of his coffee and began to write.

-

We all start with the same amount of time every day. Irretrievable time. Writing is doing a thing. The writer must be dedicated to the doing. The artifact is a book.

I am trying to write in the Fantasy genre. Why? What was my motivation when I began? And now, why sit in a coffee shop and write with a pen about imaginary worlds?

'Because.'

I also work out. To do a routine. To pick up a rhythm. To become. What exactly do I become? A voice? An expression laid out on paper.

And, again, for what? Is not staring at the sunset equally valid, equally monumental? Maybe so. Maybe not. But for the works of others there would be no collective memory! Each of us wills the self into becoming something. A transmission to create a transmission.

Picking it up and putting it down, the pen. Six pages per day. And it can't all be letters to God.

I benefit from focus. I benefit from stability. I benefit from money. Money is currently the only thing I am good at making. It is stable like a wave eroding a shore. I must be like diamond, must be unyielding to the corrosive effects of the RIP tides.

The relative utility of time. A theme for me. Something I have chosen to revisit. As if there can be an answer!? Who can possibly measure it objectively!?

-

A Korean War Memorial was located directly across the street from the coffee shop. Eric stopped his writing and watched as a woman started marching to and fro in front of the wall of missing soldiers, swinging her arms and legs with exaggerated motions. She was dressed in a black skirt and oversized jean jacket with the letters 'KC' embroidered on the back. A grizzled man approached and began to chastise her. He, with even greater exaggeration, began to march back and forth in front of the memorial. After several passes in front of the list of names he collapsed on the ground next to a large flagpole. The man was now lying motionless on the ground. Eric returned to writing.

-

These are my times. This is my era. The whole world devolving into a ruined low-trust prison. I am to blame. My bad behaviors, my selfish choices.

I was given the universe. It cannot be undone. The finality and truth of that. All the vices and the fall. My legacy. The sound of waves lapping at the shore of my undying.

-

Eric stopped writing. The scene outside had bent him nihilist. *"I am a product of my environment,"* Eric said to himself as he packed up his things to leave. *"I don't need public spaces to write. I can generate the distractions I need at home."*

As Eric exited the coffee shop an ambulance arrived to treat the collapsed man. Eric looked up and noticed the flag was tattered, but still there.

######## MILTON ########

Milton was in North Africa visiting megalithic sites. He was also working on several modifications for his airships that he hoped would allow them to access low-Earth orbit. *"From 120,000 feet to 6,000,000 feet is no small feat,"* he chewed to himself.

Milton studied the diagram of his orbital accelerator. He manufactured a laser that was designed to pulse with a specific frequency onto a small surface area. In his childhood he had owned a 'capgun.' It was a toy pistol that had a 'receipt-ticket' style of feed action that advanced a strip of paper under a firing pin. Each time he pulled the trigger it fed a new strip of the paper under the 'hammer' and the falling hammer would then cause the gunpowder in the paper to explode and some smoke to be released.

Milton developed similar rolls of 'tape' that contained micro-particle sized lead mixed with trace amounts of zirconium. He trained his pulse laser onto the lead-zirconium alloy and it would violently explode. The energy density of the lead fuel was very high while the volatility was extremely low, making it an inherently safe fuel. He was using the explosion to ignite his fuel-air mixture of hydrogen and oxygen which he injected from the gas used to float his airships. The goal was to get thousands of small nozzels with independent orientation control and be able to create micro-adjustments or macro-adjustments based on the number and orientation of firing nozzles. The energy density and stability of the fuel made lead the best option for space travel. He was using a Pulse Detonation Engine design, but was scaling it over hundreds of smaller nozzles.

Milton's space dirigibles were 'rigid' with very strong 'ribs' upon which he had attached large piezo-ceramic strips. By changing the current through the piezoceramic material he could cancel stresses in the frame elements. He could also create small deflections to generate torque and cause the ship to begin rotating. Since internal stress in a metal support is equivalent to the accumulation of excess phonons (registering as a load failure) an engineer can cancel it with destructive interference, resulting with far less stress accumulating in the matrix of the material. He recalled reading the article 'Active Control of Buckling Using Piezo-Ceramic Actuators' by Andrew A. Berlin from Xerox Palo Alto Research Center. American Institute of Advanced Aeronautics Paper A95-38493. It was from those observations he was able to reduce the weight of his zeppelin frames by a factor of five with no loss of strength.

He began to experiment with loading reels of his lead-zirconium paper onto the bottom of his ships. By feeding the sheet then irradiating it and causing it to explode he was able to use pulse detonation to lift his airships out of the Earth's atmosphere. "Or, so it looks on paper. I honestly don't know the mechanics of space flight so I am going to be monitoring sensors to try to get a better understanding of setting up a geosynchronous orbit. As I understand it the higher we go the faster we are moving in order to maintain geosynchronicity. By descending we aren't losing that forward velocity so it gets transferred as heat upon re-entry. But that is where I have a few ideas."

Milton spoke directly to the computer camera, "By injecting hydrogen and oxygen as part of the fuel I am simultaneously dropping mass as I enter into low-Earth orbit. Once in space I can deploy my frame-dragging cables and pick up enough charge to run systems and purify water and return oxygen and hydrogen into storage. Upon re-entry I should be able to use the thrusters to generate a cloud of water vapor that should surround the bottom of the ship. In theory a cloud of water vapor will help us offset some heat accumulation during re-entry. Maybe. Re-entry mechanics are something I still haven't fully modeled. But I have a few ideas. I feel like I can get a payload of fuel high enough in the atmosphere that I can use pulse detonation motors to achieve low Earth orbit. But really the forward velocity will need to be sufficient to sustain orbit, there is a minimum velocity."

"On the business side we could work with several of our partners here in South America to provide communications backhaul and disaster recovery services. I bet we would have a lot of takers depending on what we can do with our shots, if we can stabilize the channels. And maybe we could start looking at mining the moon?" Jebediah proposed.

"I need to figure out the Van Allen radiation first," Milton replied. "We would need to protect our equipment from intense radiation, which currently stands a bit outside my area of expertise. I think we could launch from either the north or south pole, though. We might be able to fly over the belts and down to the moon. Landing on the moon, honestly, I have no clue. Less gravity than Earth so I won't be able to use known constants for burn rate upon deceleration. I have been working up some pseudo-code to use visual data to make burn off decisions, more like a cybernetic response system that can make autonomous decisions, but we are talking about landing a zeppelin on the surface of a moon. So, really, I can't say I can promise anything. Honestly, setting up geo-synchronous low-Earth orbit under the pretense of providing telecommunications services seems more achievable. I am planning on probably losing at least a few of our first flights so our testing area needs to take that into account. Where is it safest to crash?"

Milton felt he needed to find closure on the ancient artifacts. Since visiting Egypt he was convinced that his own technology would be greatly improved if he could understand how they manipulated the massive stones.

Milton continued, "Zero point energy is the holy grail of all of this. They had an ability to move and position 80 ton stones in South America. They moved 1000 ton stones over here. Moved and placed them into walls and other constructions. If it WAS technology then we will want to know how it works."

Jebediah wasn't so sure. "Look, it appears that some of these sites are run by the most powerful cabal of global elites in the world. These people make us look like ants in a wave pool, Milton. This is more dangerous than anything you or I have ever touched. I don't think any of these people know anything about us and to the extent you are just a tourist looking at rocks I think we are fine. But if you do uncover something, well, the people associated with keeping these sites under-explored might be hiding something. They might be hiding something so big that they would take us out without a second thought. That is what I fear about this. We might threaten the wrong people with out digging."

Jebediah was incorrect. The US military was fully aware of Milton's location and his explorations. It was Operation Mind Pixel that was their entire focus. Anything that Milton might discover, any technology he might unlock, was trivial compared to the power of manipulating conscious thought using entangled particles.

At least, that was the military assessment.

######### WAITRESS #########

There was a certain type. Almost always looked at men in a specific way. They usually dressed at the edge of provocation and were aware they were attractive without letting it go to their head. The Waitress would watch them interact with patrons. She would introduce herself. Let her target know she works at one of the most prestigious restaurants in Chicago. "We should totally hang out some time. A lot of great options available for a girl these days."

Megan built a small army of beautiful, talented women that she was leading in a war against poverty. She had chosen her soldiers wisely and they conquered their way into the land of milk and honey. The women worked together to invest money and buy stocks and property. When they weren't working with their male clients they could travel or work on their other businesses. They were able to wash most of their earnings through short term rental income. The group worked together to establish a Real Estate Investment Trust among other enterprises.

Eric left town to attend a conference and the Waitress was home alone. She fell asleep on a couch overlooking lake Lake Michigan. She started to dream.

Saw woke up with Maxwell. They were in an all black world standing on a floor with rings emanating out from the center. She had seen the vision before. She was in the ring next to Maxwell.

"Ruby heartstones for cufflinks," he said to her as he

revealed the stones holding his french cuffs in place. He was dressed in a tuxedo.

"I was afraid to live this dream the first time I had it," she said to him. "I woke up afraid."

"You were living two lives. You were maintaining two faces at the same time."

She said nothing.

"You are doing the same thing now. Masking it as a 'good deed' for those who support you in it. But at its core it is living a duel life. Managing the complexity of that."

"You did this to me?" Megan asked. She felt... terrified.

"You know I did! All that time I had alone with you, before you woke up. All the ways I played with your mind, filled you with... well, new ideas. New abilities. ENTANGLEMENTS."

"Entangle..."

"Yeah, we are tied together," Maxwell interrupted. "It is a physical-psychical bond. It takes two."

"We were barely together..."

"It isn't up to you how the universe works!" Maxwell shook his head tauntingly. "You don't get to whine your way out of acceptance. We are bonded. Part of you is me. Part of me is you. It creates a bridge that spans space instantaneously."

"I did all of this?" she asked.

"Yes. You did. You are even dreaming of me right now. All by yourself."

As Maxwell spoke everything disappeared and she was alone.

"Maxwell?" she said softly.

"Maxwell!" she yelled. No sound returned.

Suddenly the world came into focus. She was standing in a desert. Maxwell looked cold. He was pacing. Back and forth in a sort of semi-circle.

"We are all bridges to each other," Maxwell stopped and said to the sky. He started pacing again. Looking like an ensnared animal pulling on a invisible chain straining to get free.

######## MAXWELL ########

Maxwell's algorithm for selecting music had certain built-in biases. It was designed to play aggressive music in the morning which would then transition into more ethereal music in the evening. So when he put on his headphones just prior to the dawn he was not surprised to hear Electro Esthetica Trance Episode 1 broadcasting from his car radio. Over time Maxwell had stacked a considerable number of rocks near the cave entrance. He gathered them on his walks. Some mornings he would grab his emergency bag along with some extra water and head off in a random direction to find a new rock to add to the pile. This was such a morning.

"The prime numbers. The composites. The game." Things swirling in Maxwell's mind as he power-walked through the sagebrush. He could sustain four miles per hour walking. The sound of the music helped push him to go faster; he started running. He veered toward a rock outcropping far off in the distance. On and on he ran. *"What is that?"* he asked himself. He took out a pair of lightweight plastic binoculars. He saw what he thought resembled round timbers jutting out of the ground. He resumed his run toward the structure, growing more and more excited as he gained speed.

The Australian scientist informed Maxwell that somewhere on the property existed an 1800's era ruin left over from a gold mine sluicing operation. "I don't even know if there is any remnant of their operation out there, only that it happened somewhere on the property." Onward he ran. A large valley blocked him so he ran to the left to go around it. Eventually it became shallow enough for him to go through. Onward he ran being pushed by the music.

Closer. Closer. The sun was finally catching up and started applying serious heat. He had been running for about 45 minutes. *"Maybe 10 more minutes and I will be there,"* he thought to himself as he drank water from a tube. Large creosote-soaked poles emerged before him as the gateway into a large ravine. On the opposite wall of the ravine was a cave entrance. In front of the cave ran a stream. There was little vegetation.

Maxwell cautiously made his way down the slippery slope. He approached the cave. There were no signs of life. He took out a small flashlight and entered. Cool wet air greeted him.

Not far inside the cave he found a large pile of rubble that had fallen from the roof. In the middle of the pile of debris was an amorphous glob of gold the size of a small dog. Maxwell went over and loosened it from the dirt and rock. He cradled it and carried it to the mouth of the cave. It was extremely heavy and unwieldy.

"Fuck me in the goat's ass!" he said at the sky. He walked away from the mouth of the cave and sat the gold on a large rock. For a moment he thought he might need to hide it. Then he laughed at himself. "Yeah, right!"

He set his camera on a tripod. He began recording.

-

"I want to understand numbers. I mean, it is easy enough, right? We just start with the number one and then we add it to itself to get two and we add one to two to get three and we add one to three to get four. This is an algorithm that describes how we can generate a list of numbers from a simple primitive. We have one mark and if we duplicate that mark we have numerous marks.

Why care about numbers? Before electricity people spent a lot of time observing nature. Careful students found math embedded in everything. They discovered that the behavior of objects in freefall is regulated by a mysterious force. It pulls on everything and generates equal acceleration irrespective the mass. So a lead weight and a feather fall at the same velocity in a vacuum. These simple physical observations led us into a world filled with technological marvels. It is the marvels we now worship.

Numbers are the most primitive elements in the Universe.

Even if the physical universe could be extinguished and all change stopped the numbers would continue on forever. It does not require a thinker for the numbers to exist. At the end of time even zero is admitted into the world of real things.

So numbers are things. A pen is a thing. A piece of paper is a thing. We can use tools to make drawings that represent these objects. And so we know that a drawing of a tree is not a tree. We know a picture of a car is not a car. And yet we think the number '1' is THE THING. We think that numbers are a byproduct of human representations and that without the representation the number would not exist. But this is not correct. It is only convenient.

'One' is arguably the most powerful object in the history of history. It is the original artifact. We might think the universe began with a Big Bang or that the physical world is the Seat of all experience. But without One there is nothing. Once '1' exists probability becomes inevitable.

Without probability there is no free will. Depending on the type of probability a 'free will' is discrete within a range of possible outcomes. I am calling on the One, the Two, the Three. I am calling on the numbers to represent themselves, stand for themselves. We must touch a tree to know a tree; seeing a painting of a tree is not knowing a tree! The number One is the root of all realities. But '1' is the symbol for this tree; 1 is the 'object' from which a 'representamen' emerges as an 'interpretant' within our thinking minds. But One and 1 are not the same.

We plant the 1 and add +1 to grow the Tree of Numbers. The Tree of Numbers contains all whole counting numbers. Now the analogy starts to fail. Why? Because we see that numbers are not alike and they have 'characteristics' and 'measurables/observables.' A large number is a series of numbers strung together. We see characteristics arise. The numbers are individuals.

The number 2 is a breeder. I mean it is a Prime number. Every number that is a child of 2 has 0,2,4,6,8 as its rightmost digit. It takes one operation on a number of arbitrary length to establish a paternity claim for parent 2. 'The test reveals... 2 is the daddy!' One half of the tree of numbers is family EVEN. The even CHARACTERISTIC is that the base-10 representation of the number ends in 0,2,4,6,8. This is first grade stuff. At infinity, which is a God-word, one half of the numbers have 2 for a daddy. Well. Obviously, in order to have this many children, 2 has to be busy. So 2 mates with every single number on the number line of OEIS sequence A000027 to make its even number babies. Starting with itself it has 4. Then it sexes up 3 and has 6. Then it sexes up 4 and has 8. Yes, 2 mates with its own offspring to make new offspring. The kids always have red hair. I mean, they end in 0,2,4,6,8. See how easy it is to figure it out! A child can do it.

We then go to the number 3. Uh oh, this number is different. Despite the fact 2 already mated with it, it is a breeder. Like, it has no parents so it is a Prime Number. So 3 breeds with 2 to make 6. 3 breeds with 3 to make 9. 3 breeds with 4 to make 12. 3 breeds with 5 to make 15. How can we tell if 3 is the parent? Well, any number that has 3 as a parent has a DIGITAL ROOT of 3, 6, or 9. This means if you add the numbers together until you get a single digit, and that digit is 3,6,9, the prime number 3 is one of the parents.

This is 3. The CHARACTERISTIC of 3 is distinct from 2. It's children can have any last digit, but the sum of the digits always adds to 3,6,9. So the number 999999 is $(9+9)+(9+9)+(9+9) = (18)+(18)+(18)=(1+8)+(1+8)+(1+8) = (9)+(9)+(9) = 27 = 2+7 = 9$. Or $272727 = (2+7)+(2+7)+(2+7)=9+9+9 = 27 = 9$.

The number 3 is a mythical creature, a living thing in the domain of numbers. It manifests itself as a property of numbers that can be measured by living, breathing mortal creatures. It has allowed us to capture it as this symbol '3' and speak of it and write of its children. How is it that 3 is so distinct from 2 in how it produces offspring? How are these numbers so different and yet only separated by 1?

We see 4 is next in the list, but since it is a child of 2 we don't use it to produce new children – it is not prime. Instead we go to the next self-generated number and find 5. For 5, like 2 and 3, it has only the number 1 as its father/mother figure. 1+1+1+1+1. It has no other factors. It produces children who always show last digit 0 and 5. So it mates with even numbers to get all the numbers that end in 0 and it mates with 3 and the remaining odd numbers to produce all the composite numbers that end in 5.

This is the place of departure. From here forward there are no easy paternity tests, only an infinity of prime parents that must be discovered by physically expressing their family trees. We must start with a list and generate cancellations against that list and discover the prime number operators in A000040. The primes are a residue of a sieving algorithm. Many algorithms have internal states, that is they reference their own outputs and use them as inputs to produce a new output. The sieve of Eratosthenes is the original internal state machine and we have barely moved the needle since.

Introducing John Conway. He wrote the PRIMEGAME algorithm. But, in addition to this, he also made an important remark that has been encoded in one of the sequences in the OEIS library. A suggestion for an alternative approach to evaluating the composite numbers. It appears evident that there exists a very old Game of Primes, a game that has been played since at least the time of Eratosthenes. As a result of playing this game we now have a Prime Number Theorem that is accepted as a solid law regarding the average density of prime numbers.

John Conway says there are TRIVIAL and NONTRIVIAL composites. The difficulty in the prime number distribution lies not with 2,3,5 and their genetic offspring. The problem lies in the infinity of the remaining prime number operators found in A000040. That sequence is not the prime characteristic function it is the prime operator list. The prime operator list is infinite while the prime characteristic function can possibly be expressed by a regular function or functions. There may exist a genetic distribution associated with a smaller subset of operators than those found in A000040."

Maxwell stopped the camera.

He turned up his headphones and started dancing.

CHAPTER 10

######## THE ROW ########

PDC and Marshall walked toward the trading circle. It was as if they were long-time friends. Everything between them seemed natural and at the same time entirely staged.

A naked woman approached PDC and winked at him as she passed. "I like beautiful women," he said to Marshall. "I just do. And I must admit there are a lot of them here. And what I have discovered in my journey through life is that the nice guy strategy is bullshit. Always be honest. Women see right through that. Women are highly intuitive and they are particularly sensitive to picking up on the sexual motivations of men. Evolution positively selected for this trait because having a keen awareness about sexual motives is essential for survival. Women who cannot discern a man's true intentions often find themselves in dangerous situations."

Marshall agreed. He had seen a lot in his days. "I think women are usually pretty dumb. They pattern after some guy, take on his habits, then end up resenting him for the fact they lost their own personality by emulating someone they ultimately don't even like. Then they break up in some hostile way that is usually maximally destructive and then age out with a bunch of cats and work to pay rent until they die. So there are not a lot of good female role models in my estimation," Marshall said.

PDC raised his left eyebrow in contemplation. "Yeah. Well, men can also be good at being shit role models. A lot of brain dead overfed fanboys out there masturbating to screens. A lot of underthink. Money is the god now. Money and what it can acquire."

"I don't know," Marshall said. "Time matters. Having time. It is important to take stock of the world and your place in it."

"Oh, yeah. Don't get me wrong. Bill free is the only free that counts. I just mean that if you are looking for role models in the bills paid arena you are going to find a lot of conformists. And that is a good thing. Somebody has to make the donuts, plow the fields, paint the lines on the highways."

They arrived on The Row. It was a fairly busy place with many traders having extremely nice things on their blankets. "Whoa," Marshall said looking around. "I had no idea."

PDC found a spot beneath a tree and spread out his blanket along the edge of the trail. He brought a box of smudge sticks, several cartons of cigarettes, numerous 1800's stock certificates, letters, titles to lands. All things that he found in a thrift store that looked really old and didn't cost very much. He placed several dozen smudge sticks on the rug, then the old letters, then a few packs of cigarettes with one of them open and a cigarette extending out. Marshall looked around and took out several solid silver American Eagle coins in their condition wrappers. He then dropped an entire unopened carton of cigarettes and a very nice sewing kit. People marched by staring at the offerings, salivating for a cigarette. Marshall handed Jeremiah a couple of packs of loose-leaf tobacco. "For the joke tellers and beggars," he said silently.

PDC tapped his nose three times and said in a British accent, "Know what I mean, know what I mean?"

PDC was wearing dark green pants and a mother-of-pearl colored dress shirt. He was also wearing a very large straw hat. His pants were held up with a gold and brown tie. The tie was a gold background with gold horses branching in a repeated pattern. The horses had gold and silver highlights, outlined in brown.

Next to them on the trail a girl no older than 13 set up a blanket and proceeded to cover it in knives. Marshall knew a few things about blades so he went to look at them.

"Impressive," he said to the girl as he reviewed one of her bone-handle knives.

"The real deal. You can tell," the little girl said. "And I know what it is worth."

Marshall figured the knife to be worth $200 on the street, more in a shop.

"Is this the nicest knife you have?"

"No, but I don't keep those out here."

"Do you have one that could be a mate to this one?" he asked, holding up the bone handled curved blade.

"I have one that is a bit larger than that one, with a slight curve in the blade. It has an ivory handle and is made from Damascus steel. I can show you if we do real business."

Marshall looked at the knife and its leather sheath. "What would you take for trade?"

"What have you got?"

"I have silver, tobacco. Depending on what you have I can bring out some gold."

"Coins?"

"Yeah. Still in the grading cases."

"Let's meet back at my tent," the girl suggested.

The girl told her younger sister to watch over the knives while she went to make a deal. Marshall followed her to her tent. Inside was a young boy, apparently her brother, and a collection of magnificent steel. The girl motioned for her brother to exit the tent and then opened a case that was hidden beneath a pile of clothes. Marshall looked at the knives. He picked a pair that were worth $1900. Marshall bartered with gold and silver and purchased a few more items.

"Our family has services we offer also. Massages. You probably saw a table set up out there, right? We have a few in tents for more privacy. You know, it can be real nice to get the tension out. Your friend. I thought he might enjoy some relaxation."

Marshall looked at girl and smiled. He had been conducting

business since he was this girls age, though it was in a city not in a forest. "I will keep that in mind," Marshall responded. "Thanks for the heads up on that. We are definitely interested in relaxation."

When he returned to the blanket he saw PDC had moved a lot of smudge sticks and also a few packs of cigarettes. "I wasn't sure what you might want for your carton, but I think you have a good strategy with that. I think you can get about anything you desire."

Marshall saw a person exchanging some small pieces of paper for blown glass. He got the persons attention. PDC had stepped away to check out a buffalo hide. "I would love some of what you have going on," Marshall said to the young man. The man looked at Marshall's wares. "Those are real coins?" he asked.

"Yep. And there is more where that came from. Gold."

"Ok. Maybe we can go to my tent for a bit?"

"Absolutely, give me just one second." Marshall stared at the back of PDC's head. PDC turned around and looked at him with a joking scowl. He came over. "I got you fam!" he said to Marshall with an exaggerated wink.

Marshall went away with the man and returned with a few vials of liquid and a book of tiny squares. "That went well," he said to PDC.

PDC also had some luck trading with various people. "I cannot wait to see how our harvest has gone," he said to Marshall with childlike glee.

######### ERIC #########

Eric departed from the luggage area and headed toward the front of the airport. His ride was waiting for him. "You mind if I listen to some music?" the young female driver asked. She looked no older than 20 and was dressed in a miniskirt and a crop top. Supermodel attractive with ebony skin.

"Yeah. No, no problem," Eric responded. It was always a crap shoot with the musical preferences of the drivers.

"Music helps me concentrate in this insane traffic," she explained. She looked small sitting in the drivers seat.

Electronic music with an aggressive guitar began playing as the driver prepared to depart. "Zwei, drei, vier, one, two, three its easy to see ... but its not that I don't care, so? ... 'Cause I hear it all the time but they never let you know on the TV and the radio ... Cha! She was young her heart was pure but every night is bright she got! ... She said sugar is sweet, she come a-rappin' to the beat, then she knew that it was hot, she was singin' ... Don't turn around, wa-uh-oh ... yeah yeah! ... Der Kommissar's in town, wa-uh-oh! ... You're in his eye and you'll know why ... the more you live, the faster you will die ... " She turned the volume down. "Oops. Hold on. My phone isn't synced over. Always seems to happen at this airport when it grabs the free wireless. Here we go."

She tossed the phone into the seat next to her and they started to move into the traffic.

The Ave St Lo song 'Ze Ze' began playing on the sound system.

It appeared to Eric that traffic was parting before them to provide a path of least resistance as his car accelerated and sliced its way to the fast lane. Quickest car on the road. The female driver was co-owner of the private shuttle company that had been hired to transport Eric. She co-owned the fleet and would drive when employees called in sick or cars broke down. Her company also offered document delivery with a Notary Service add-on for local power users. Like a Pony Express service with a small fleet of electric vehicles, they drove everything all the time. It was convenient for them, since once the battery got low in one car they could swap out with another fully charged auto and immediately start the recharging cycle. Plus, LA is a warm city and the batteries are more durable if they do not freeze. They were planning on expanding into more southern states.

She and her boyfriend had been acquiring investors for

their business. He was a programmer and hacked the car to unlock the aggressive self driving modes. The 'sport mode' allowed the cars to expend energy more efficiently while also shaving precious minutes off trips. The mode only worked on the highways and interstates, so the driver would need to resume normal control once they exited onto residential or business streets. Eric noticed the girl had her hands on the steering wheel, but it looked to him as if she wasn't actually in control. The car was driving itself and she was resting her hands.

He was in Los Angeles to discuss his current projects with is agent. The Waitress was an investor in the private car business and had arranged the services for Eric. The driver originally assigned to Eric caught a flat tire, so she grabbed the ticket. Since the Waitress was a major investor she wanted to ensure that Eric's trip was memorable. He was completely unaware that the waitress had invested in a private cab company so he betrayed no interest. One thing Eric could not ignore was the fact the driver was unusually attractive and was dressed to impress. He understood the value of being preceded by a beautiful woman. *"Her opening the door for me commands attention. A woman can redirect all that thirst and make me appear more attractive by proxy."*

He was amiable. She observed him, scrutinized him. She didn't want her investor to think the service was anything other than exceptional. Eric seemed clueless about the 'additional services,' so she drove him to the hotel and dropped him off. "We will be here tomorrow at 9am. Is there anything else you want or need for tonight?" she asked with friendly eyes.

The Waitress was alone in the apartment. She decided to peer into Eric's journals. She found some pages where the writing was noticeably smaller. The pace seemed slower.

\-

A few days without writing. Been exercising like crazy. Burning 600+ calories per hour working out.

I think about her all the time. The smell of her. The sound of her. I did things to her... new things I never experienced. Things I never imagined! She was my delicious object, my princess. Her laugh was beautiful. She was an angel sent to me from the Divine Goddess of the Universe.

My leather skin, my rough hands. Pure electricity. Pushing her legs back and pressing my thumbs into the soles of her feet. Watching myself move in and out of her. It inspires me to perfect myself. Fantasy... I see it as the key to unlock the door.

Spirit vs. Dogma. What a great time to be alive.

Her beautiful smile and laugh; "'Office 39' is the economic program behind North Korea," she giggled at me when we got room 39 in Breckenridge, Colorado.

I fall back to memories of her when my world turns bleak. When nothing flows out onto the page I think of her and the pen jumps to life.

I remember all the times I came on her navel, all the times I pushed my cock down her throat. Her, trying to push me off, trying to, begging me to stop. To please, "Stop daddy."

But I just kept on with my 'mean fucking.' Holding her down making it hard for her to breathe as I worked her over.

I was an overdominant father-actor for her. I tried to perform that role. Yet, I also cared about her well-being. I wanted her to be comfortable. And I don't think she liked that. That actually turned her off.

She came to me as the result of a prayer. And I pray now for her scent to be on me, for her to be smeared across my chest.

The best fuel for my engine. I want to take her away and fuck her for days. I want to tie her up and use her. I want to hold her at night and wake up with her in the morning. Hear her laughter over breakfast. Feel my smile when she ties the Maraschino cherry stem with her tongue. "See! I did it again! That's my special talent!"

The Writer is not blocked, but he is stuck in a loop thinking about the pornographic movie reel he made with his tiny lover.

Part of me thinks that if I perform well enough it will be

inevitable that I will see her again. I will put my cock in her again. I will take her to Europe and fuck her in nice hotels. I want my cum to drain out of her and see the stain on the sheets. Her cute little sweaters. Shopping with her, watching her try on outfits and thinking up answers for her when she asks me if I think the boys will like it. Seeing her shoes on the floor beside the bed. Removing her socks and panties.

My aim is to achieve irrepressible success. So I can go grab her and take her with me for a while. I want to hike the world with her, fuck her on top of mountains. I want to be such a blazing star that she will be led to me by instinct rather than reason or desire.

I miss her and I love her. It is an exquisite pain to have held her only to watch her disapparate. So few people have the luxury of such pain!

She is in my dreams. The starlight of her memory is my Milky Way.

-

The Waitress saw that he was experiencing loneliness and pain, but that he was also using it to gain insights about himself. The tension of having and then wanting was driving him to achieve greater success. Even so, she decided to pay closer attention to his writing to make sure he was not getting too depressed.

######## PDC ########

They walked unwittingly toward a socialist kitchen that was situated along one of the paths that led into the deep forest. They had been successful in their trading missions so PDC felt obligated to share some love with the masses. Marshall was tagging along, watching over PDC as he performed place to place. He was starting to slither-dance as he walked. He was very limber and was not easily exhausted despite the high elevation. "Welcome Hooooooome," he said to some people carrying tents into the forest. The sun would set sooner than later.

They found a large kitchen and gathering of people. It sounded like everyone was working on a plan to get land and establish a viable commune. PDC and Marshall listened. PDC moved closer. Marshall followed him. Eventually they worked their way to the very edge of the circle, by the fire. He sat down and Marshall sat next to him, slightly further back.

The gathering was at least 30 people, with 12 or so sitting in the innermost ring. They were listening to a young woman who was standing by the fire. She was speaking about the dream of getting one hundred acres of land where they could collectively start a permaculture village.

"It's never your successful friends who talk about becoming communists," PDC said to Marshall a little too loudly. Marshall laughed nervously.

"Excuse me?" the young woman said to PDC. "Why are you even here? Are you supposed to be the devil's advocate or something?"

PDC was wearing a new iridescent pearl-white dress shirt with french cuffs and an oversized collar that was turned up. His cargo pants pockets were filled with treats and cigarettes and smudge sticks. His long dirty-blonde hair was tousled and gave him the look of a punk writer. "I, like you, seek an alternative to the busy life of starry-eyed slavery. This nation is rich beyond our wildest imagination! We could find some tired old suckers out there worth millions and maybe treat them to a fantasy life for a little while and then come sundown be listed as the beneficiaries on their wills. There is so much money all around us it is insane. But those tired old hands worked hard for that money and they grip it ten generations once they grab some of it. Nobody is giving anybody anything except against their will or in it. But if we specialize in delicious end of life fantasy fulfillment we might be able to make a tonne of money. Real. Gypsy. Shit."

The girl looked at him stunned. A feminine voice from the outer edge of the gathering asked, "What the fuck are you suggesting?"

"Like that sensuality teepee down at the drum area," PDC replied over his shoulder. Turning to look back at the girl standing by the fire he continued, "There are people of all persuasions in there right now sharing human touch. This very moment there are people being guided into that light. The feminine and masculine power of touch that transforms and unlocks. And what I am saying is, in this context, we accept that it is necessary to facilitate human touch. But out there in the world of customers we refuse to see it as beautiful because money destroys everything, taints everything. But it is exactly money that unlocks everything, too."

"So you are suggesting we whore ourselves out to old men to get money for land!?" the lead female returned in an offended tone.

"No!" PDC responded. "A healer. I am talking about spreading healing." PDC noticed the lead girl requesting a cigarette from a guy sitting in the far back of the makeshift kitchen. He retrieved a very thin looking pouch and started rolling a sad looking cigarette made from cigarette butts.

PDC bit his tongue to stop himself from smiling. *"Is that blood I am tasting right now?"* he asked himself.

PDC took out a pack of Lucky Strikes and started to pack them. Several eyes went directly to him. They all wanted a preroll. They wanted one of his cigarettes. The girl focused on him. Her demeanor changed, slightly. "Hey, just so you know, I would truly appreciate one of those."

PDC looked at her with an almost sultry gaze. "I am a real jerk. I came in here and I didn't offer you a gift. Thank you for hosting and leading all these people and creating these necessary conversations." He stood up and walked over to her. She was dressed in a knitted top and was wearing a thin long skirt or sarong tied with a chain of tiny silver bells. Her olive skin had been bronzed by exposure to mountain sunlight and her hair was a matted and voluminous tangle of black. Her green-blue eyes were flaked with gold. PDC conjectured that she was the unchallenged leader because she was very, very attractive. Dirty toenails, dirty hands, shiny teeth and piercing eyes. A wildling woman barefoot in the dank forest.

PDC stood before her in the professional cloth. He designed his attire to achieve the look of formal motorcycle armor. He had earlier removed his armor layers exposing an inner layer of 'Luxe Endurance' style clothing. Against the background of soot and roots his brand new white dress shirt with french cuffs and gold adornments radiated a light of its own. His pants had not a belt, but a dark iridescent green silk necktie covered in a repeating pattern of gold-ringed four-leaf clovers. His boots were the type for motorcycle adventure riding and hiking. She noticed them as he was lighting her cigarette.

"You ride?" she asked with a tilted head, forgetting that she had just been directing a meeting on how to find a housing solution for the world's displaced communists.

Marshall saw what was happening and could tell the men and boys gathered around the fire were starting to get angry. Marshall started lighting and passing marijuana flower joints. He was handing out cigarettes and donated several pouches of loose-leaf tobacco to the kitchen. PDC maintained eye contact with the girl the entire time. He could tell she wanted to smoke some of Marshall's pot. Marshall, a student of human behavior, left the group of now distracted men and women and made his way to PDC's side.

"For you, mademoiselle," Marshall said as he handed her one of the large hog-leg joints he laced with PDC's keef hash.

As she inhaled she coughed violently. "Oh my God this is good shit," she said.

"We aim to please; loaves and fishes and all that," Marshall responded with a bow as he turned to go back to work on the gathered crowd.

Since Marshall was being so loose with the tobacco and marijuana the crowd lost track of 'Mr. Shiny Shirt.' Meanwhile, PDC introduced himself to the young woman, "I am Jeremiah and yes I do ride," he said to her as they passed the joint between themselves. "Why are you here? What are you trying to achieve?"

She looked him dead in the eyes and said, "I want to live without a bunch of overhead taking up all my time. I don't want to pay stupid rent. But I also don't want to pretend I can even afford my current loan payments. I am in debt and I have no options." In a quieter tone looking down at the floor she admitted, "I really wish I could just live alone for a while, and not have anyone in my life." She stopped herself. Looking back at Jeremiah she said, "I went to school to be an artist. But I have no idea how I can make a name for myself. I don't even know if I am any good." She looked really sad. Really defeated. PDC guessed it might have something to do with the guy lurking unhappily in the background who was refusing to smoke any of Marshall's tobacco or weed.

The man was staring at them. PDC had perfected the ability to watch people in the background without breaking eye contact. It was a Mossad tactic he read about and then trained to master. The man was twitchy and stressed. "You know," he said, pausing for a moment. "If I told you to come with me and forget about solving your problems this way and instead move into my home in Kansas City and live as long as you want bill free, would you do it? Are you free to do it?"

She started to look behind herself toward the unhappy man, but PDC stopped her. "Listen to me first. Don't look back. If I told you I have a place where you can stay bill free no strings attached for as long as you want will you walk out of here right now and come with me? Will you trust me?"

"How can I possibly do that? I don't even know you."

"So the answer is no then?"

The girl was stressed. She sensed that something very real was being offered to her, but also recognized that she was in a position to be terribly exploited. She stared at the logo where his heart would be; the reflected light displayed 'Obscure' in gold sparkles.

"Can I think about it?"

"No."

She said nothing and looked directly in his eyes. Pleading and doubting. He stared back betraying no emotion. Finally he added, "We should go right now. I have a separate tent you can stay in. Everything will be provided. You can get on your feet and out on your own. It is a weird and mythical offer. Timing is everything. Were you not just praying for a solution? Did you not just ask for exactly these things?"

"Okay," she said as she lowered her head. She slid into her sandals and walked out in front of him. He followed her. Marshall stayed behind which caused everyone to assume that PDC would return. He lit a hash-laden hog leg and wasted another 20 minutes of time. After about 21 minutes Marshall slipped away unnoticed. It was about that time everyone realized their leader was gone.

PDC gave his new friend Alexis his tent and sleeping bag/pad setup. He was preparing to go back to the van and grab another one. "X has a spare tent she keeps in her van and I am going to go get it. It is smaller than mine, but should work out."

"I need to go to the van and get a few things." Marshall told PDC. "But I haven't seen Hippie Girl yet. If you see her there will you tell her I just need to grab some stuff out of the van?"

"Sure thing. Make a list and if I see her I can also grab it for you."

"It is a lot of stuff," Marshall replied.

"Well I will grab what I can if I can," PDC promised. Marshall made a list for him.

Marshall introduced himself to Alexis. "Pleasure to meet you. I am Marshall, by the way."

Alexis was a bit stunned when she saw their tents were set up by the main stage. "This is wild," she said to Marshall.

"Oh yeah. It is really nice at night. I just lie in my tent and listen to the musical acts and drift off to sleep with the performers. It is quite amazing. If you haven't camped by the stage before you are going to love it."

"I didn't know you could even set up in a spot like this," she said to Marshall.

"Oh yeah you definitely can. It is about your energy, your frequency. Everything is frequency on top of tiny tuning forks and so when we constructively interfere we reinforce good vibes and when we destructively interfere we reinforce bad vibes. We are that which adds to the amplitude so we can harmonize in a setting like this because we are willing to be known by our frequency."

She looked at him with puzzled eyes, unsure of what to say.

"I think we are about the same size and I have some new socks if you want a pair."

She definitely did. "Thank you!"

"No sweat. Welcome to the strange tribe."

"Is he for real? Jeremiah? I am still not sure what I am even doing here," she said to Marshall as she put on the socks. "This feels amaaaaazing, by the way. These socks. Are they, like, wool?"

"Yeah. They are nice, especially for hiking because when you walk a lot you want strong and resilient fibers in your socks. For as long as it lasts."

"Is this a… are you like in a cult or something!? What is this? That sleeping bag is like some space age shit and wool socks and everything provided. Who are you?"

Marshall paused to consider his answer, then said, "Sometimes in life, in an unusual life, you run into situations where so many variables are outside of your control that you have no real choice but to take the ride. You could've stayed back there in that kitchen and surrounded yourself with thirst and need, but you chose to take a chance with us and possibly land yourself in an amazing situation. One where you have been promised that there will be few to no real demands placed upon you. A situation that gives you some semblance of true freedom. My guess is that you can make something good happen if you have the time. A lot of people can. There are so few 'bill free' people that it is shocking to me. But, equally shocking, there is this lottery function that distributes 'chance meetings' where people suddenly end up on completely different trajectories. Things that happen not because the people were looking for that particular outcome, but because the universe decided some outcome needed to happen and then used people to achieve that end."

Alexis was textbook shook. A few hours earlier she had a boyfriend and people she was feeding at her kitchen. Now she was pursuing a completely random outcome with total strangers. "Well, you are clearly really smart and have thought a lot about this so either this is going to be a fun ride or you are all psychopaths that are going to torture me and sell my body parts."

"Maybe a bit of both?" Marshall laughed, handing her a mushroom.

The night air was cold and Alexis didn't have warm clothes. Marshall went into his tent and grabbed a brown 'Sassy The Sasquatch' t-shirt, a silk-lined long-sleeve wool shortcoat, a silk-lined pair of insulated outdoor wool pants and a lightweight high-tech coat. "Here," he said, offering the clothes to Alexis. "I know this isn't exactly your style, but it will definitely keep you warm and also allow you to go tearing through the brambles without a care in the world. Oh, and this," he grabbed an orange stocking cap from his back pocket. "I have found that at night these really help keep your head warm. Though it might mess with your hair a bit."

Alexis laughed. Her hair was a reflection of her life. Abandoned. She took the clothes from Marshall and noticed that they were top of the line outdoor adventure gear. *'Obscure.'* Marshall was giving her expensive new clothes without wanting anything in return. "You sure you don't want anything for these?"

"Yeah I have extras. I was going to walk back to the van and grab a few things as soon as I can find the girl I rode here with."

"Okay. Well, thank you," she said. "I am going to change real quick."

Alexis went into her tent and stripped down. She put on the

t-shirt and the pants. She put on the wool shortcoat and jacket. She felt like she was in swaddling clothes. Her sleeping bag was super comfortable with a silk liner and it was placed on an inflatable foam-reinforced sleeping pad. The tent had a remote control for the interior LED lighting. She stood up and looked at her new style. *"Holy shit, look at me,"* she said to herself. *"I just entered the Twilight Zone."*

She exited the tent. "This is awesome. I just wish I had a belt."

"Oh, yeah, funny that," Marshall said, going to his tent. "These work great. PD.., um, Jeremiah turned me on to using ties as belts. They are made from silk and so they are insanely strong. Plus the fabric usually has some really nice patterns. Here," Marshall said as he tossed a gold snake toward Alexis.

Alexis looked at the tie. It contained a repeating pattern of glistening gold horses and lions embedded in alternating wide bands of darker gold separated by thin bands of silver. It was amazing art and the way it reflected light reminded her of authentic gold foil. She tied it around her waist and loved how it dangled away from her leg. The reflected light was mesmerizing.

PDC approached them carrying a lot of gear. His bags were full to bursting. He put everything down and removed his backpack, falling to the ground. "OK. That hike got me a bit."

"What is all that stuff?" Marshall asked.

"Oh, I ran into your friend and I got the stuff on your list. My backpack and that smaller bag has it all in there. And then there is some of my gear at the bottom of my backpack, I think. And four more gallons of water."

"Oh awesome. I will unpack it now!" Marshall took the gear and disappeared into his tent.

"You are transmogrified!" PDC said to Alexis. She was still very unsure of her arrangement and was waiting for an uncomfortable moment to crop up with Jeremiah. But he turned and left to set up his new tent and paid no attention to her.

Marshall emerged with a pair of brand new expensive hiking boots. "Excellent. If I scoped it correctly I think these will fit you!" Marshall handed the box of hiking boots to Alexis. "Try them on! They weigh almost nothing, but also protect your feet from everything!"

She was stunned. "These are not cheap shoes," she said to Marshall with mild exasperation in her voice.

He looked at her. "That doesn't matter. None of it matters. If you don't let go of things you cannot make room for new things. You are now part of an adventure team. So you need the correct clothes to keep you comfortable. Why? Because we don't want to be around a person who is suffering. Maybe there is someone out there more deserving? Maybe not? It doesn't matter. You are here now and this is happening for a reason. I choose not to think too much about it and just go with the flow."

Alexis put on the boots and felt like she had just been outfitted by a fairy godbrother. She went from desperate communism to overflowing capitalism in the span of a few hours. She was space-age comfortable. For the first time since she came to the gathering she would be warm at night.

PDC finished setting up his replacement tent. He inflated his new sleeping pad. He removed his shoes and laid down to test his new sleeping bag configuration. In a few moments and against his will he fell into a deep sleep.

His tent flap was open slightly and Marshall looked in. Seeing that PDC was completely passed out he quietly zipped up the screen and retreated.

Alexis, seeing that Jeremiah had simply gone into his tent and fallen asleep, decided that she would do the same. As she got into the sleeping bag she heard a beep. She found a small plastic wafer that was lit up with a picture of a foot with heat rays beneath it. She pressed it and the number of heat beams increased. *It's got a battery powered foot warmer!* she exclaimed to herself. She had accidentally activated it when she climbed in. She turned up the heat around her feet and fell fast asleep. She dreamed of riding a train and eating crackers and drinking tea and being in elegant clothes doing elegant things. She saw herself wearing fine shoes and lacy gloves and broaches. Alien dreams of impossible places. No hunger. No fear. Just gliding on rails. "Bill ... free ..." she uttered in her sleep.

######## ERIC and the WAITRESS ########

"I haven't written in 10 days. That's 60 pages," Eric thought to himself. He missed his young plaything. Eric studied the skin on his hand. He saw rivers and valleys. He remembered the look of his age as it caressed her youth. Every moment with her had been exhilarating. He had never known anyone like her and suspected he never would again.

"I've got to move on..." he thought to himself. *"But I cannot seem to get the memory of her out of my mind."*

The Waitress saw him struggling. The yearning in his eyes. He was in pain. But he was managing it well. Hiding it in plain sight. She watched him sit in a chair and stare at Lake Michigan. She crept up behind him and placed her hands on his shoulders.

"Shh..." she leaned down and whispered in his ear.

He was initially startled, but his body told him he was starved for human touch. She whispered, "Close your eyes."

He did.

She moved in front of him and knelt. She separated his legs and moved in between them. She unzipped his pants. He started to become aroused.

"Keep your eyes closed," she commanded. She took him into her mouth. Slowly at first, them more rapidly, she went up and down on him. He started to moan. In his mind he saw her. The beautiful young girl whose memory was so dear to him.

She was taking more and more of him. She felt him reaching climax. She grabbed his testicles and gently squeezed them as he released into her.

"I..." he stammered. "I... love you so much!"

"Shh..." she said after she swallowed. "Keep your eyes closed. Use your imagination."

He thought he must be the luckiest man alive.

Later that afternoon the Waitress fetched the mail. There was a letter from a conference addressed to Eric.

"Will you open it for me?" Eric asked. She opened it and told him the gist.

"One of the sponsors of the 44th Annual Westmoreland Fiction Conference selected you to speak at the event. Next month on the 14th. They will wire you a speakers fee to cover your expenses once you confirm that you accept." Eric was stunned. His day could hardly get better.

He was excited to be selected to speak at a conference. It helped him feel good about himself.

As the waitress dressed for work Eric asked her what she saw in him when they first met. "I saw your Yang and wanted to plug it into my Yin," she explained as she buttoned a white dress shirt and pulled on a pair of black slacks. "There is a certain raw sexual power in being a wordsmith. The science of taking people on a ride. You are original and good." Eric saw her as both beautiful and professional. Living with him, being in some ways his concubine, allowed her to save a lot of money. Some early investment tips she received from unlikely candidates exploded in value and she had become extremely wealthy over a relatively short period of time. But she neither quit her job nor revealed her financial status to anyone.

"I want you to know that you can do anything you want with me," she said to him. "I want to be enjoyed by you. I want to be playful with you."

He was confused and uncertain how to proceed. He didn't know how to escalate his own desires.

She recognized his struggle and uncertainty. Laughing inwardly, she positioned herself as if she was a little bit embarrassed and said, "There is so much about you, so many things that poseurs cannot emulate. It makes you a gem. I prefer to be fucked by a real man. By you, Eric." She slid out of her slacks and underwear and started to touch herself. "I belong to you. And it feels good."

Animal urges overcame him.

######## MAXWELL ########

Maxwell was walking at night. He turned on his action camera. "I love crushing sand in the low light of a waxing crescent moon. Bright enough to see by, not so bright as to cast hard shadows. The edge between the real and the imagined blurs. There is order to all of this!" he exclaimed as he watched his breath condense into ice crystals. "She was right! The moon is older than the Milky Way. The moon is among the oldest artifacts in the Universe!" Maxwell felt sure of it. He had seen the images of the mega-structures residing within the Earth. 2% more dense than the rest of the planet. "It vibrates!"

"The sun was a giant star in the past. It was on course to become a neutron star. But it experienced an asymmetrical explosion and turned into what appears from the outside to be a 'Class-M Sun.' A yellow dwarf sun. But it isn't. Unlikely as the sun is, the moon is infinitely more unlikely. The probability an object that has survived numerous 'big crunch' events would come into orbit around the Earth, delivering Ice-1 to this planet, is so close to zero as to inspire a belief in Intelligent Design. The Ice-1 combined with the amino acids and bases to form chaotic consciousness that eventually gave rise to our Human experience."

Maxwell had seen the history. Fragments of it. He thought back on some of his flashes of insight. How magical it had seemed. "There is a type of darkness that has been created by near-infinite years of casting shadows within the streams of the 'Universal Time Function.' When I drink the light of the moon I deprive the future observer of all that data! All the sunlight that scatters out into the cosmos is eventually turned into shadow. Holes. I transform the light into shadow by creating a hole in time. The photons are absorbed and translated into the experience of an object called The Moon. After the physical moon is turned to dust it will take a long time for all the moonlight to turn into shadow. Meanwhile I radiate photons around 98.6 degrees Fahrenheit that shoot out into space at 186,000 miles per second . Headed for some future observer who will finally turn me into shadow. 'Elapsed time' is the pressure that creates the shadows."

"The Universe is an Object, no bigger than itself. And I, no bigger than an electron at the scale of the Universe, am out here wrestling with prime numbers. An infinity of them inside a universe that is no bigger than itself. Can an infinity of counting numbers be contained within an object that is no bigger than itself? Maybe as a reciprocal?"

"The pattern of the primes. Madness inducing. This is not something I ever pondered while studying biosemiotics. I have no reason to be following these trails based on my previous efforts. From what I have read prime number research has led to the destruction of a significant number of mathematicians. It drove them insane." Maxwell used his free hand to pull at his hair, forcefully turning his head up to look at the sky.

"The stars and how they twinkle," Maxwell said to the night. "Packets of information moving through space destroyed by my eyes and turned into consciously observed objects. The best memory format yet known is light. It can be a billion years old and yet our telescope sees it with only a small aberrational redshift. However, with light you can only read it once and then it is utterly destroyed. The information is lost forever. How then can we say, 'we saw the moonrise,' when what we are really seeing is our mind manufacturing a reality and then presenting it to us as a field of finite structures? The moon illusion is not a statement about LIGHT, it is a statement about how human thought organizes the world. Human thought perceives OBJECTS; the mind does not know that the rods and cones in the eyes are 'encoding events by destroying photons' it knows only that it sees a moon. If you can see it, it has a name. You cannot see unnameable objects."

Maxwell paused to think, then continued walking.

"The huge harvest moon we 'see' on the horizon is an illusion manufactured by our mind. Like an image manipulation tool our mind scales the moon to make it appear large. But this is a hallucination, a camera does not detect it. It is the mind deciding what it wants us to see. When you think to yourself that you see 'a moon' what you are thinking is the WORD 'moon', not the 'thing in itself' which is delivered to you as a stream of photons hitting your retina. If you 'see' a piece of gold you can know that it has mass. And you can know gold from silver by the the relationship of weight to total volume. Equal weights of gold and silver displace different amounts of water. Also, the properties of gold differ from silver. Properties are behaviors of objects that manifest when they are subjected to forces imposed on them by the other elements, chemicals, fields and/or photons within their shared environment. These dependencies give rise to the Human Experience; electricity functions in an atmosphere that is 80% Nitrogen."

Maxwell continued walking silently for a moment, and reached up to turn off the camera. He then retracted his arm and continued to speak.

"A body that deforms spacetime modifies the path of a photon which indicates that elapsed time can be relocated for a stream of photons emitted from a distant object in the distant past. Time is then *always* measured in absorbed and transmitted photons. Time is a train of micro-events, quantum oscillations."

"The moon illusion proves that humans see objects. In terms of what we call 'reality' only objects exist. Anything that cannot be named cannot be discovered. Infinity can be named, but its members cannot be listed. Nonetheless, humans can name the infinite and know that it is real in the sense that it casts a shadow over the available memory of the universe. If there is a total energy for the universe it can be subdivided a very large number of times and still arrive nowhere near the end of the counting numbers. If you list every possible state the universe can arrive in, and document every photon on a list, the lists are inconceivably small compared to +1 and unlimited time."

"The moon appearing large on the horizon is a fiction. I have never tried to look at the harvest moon using a mirror. Perception is everything. What your brain 'allows in' will become your experience of the world. Every human possessing ordinary vision witnesses the moon illusion. We are hard-wired to discover this about ourselves."

"So, in the case of some objects, they may exist and be physically present, but our 'pre-consciousness' which operates as a pattern recognition filter cannot identify a known pattern and since it has no name for it, it merges the object into the background and we remain unaware. Bengal tiger camouflage works on this principle. It tricks the brain into not seeing the massive orange and black tiger when it is standing inside a green and brown forest background. Turns out this form of camouflage doesn't work on color blind people. Which goes a long way in explaining why color blindness remains a widespread trait in the human population. It positively selects an advantage under camouflage scenarios, especially ones that use outrageous color patterns to hack our object-oriented brains. Hunters can also eat the meat of camouflaged kills, so it selects in that direction also."

"Reality is utterly testable and obviously real. There are a finite number of living humans. It is at the edges where we decouple from things like monthly bills that we start to channel understanding. Total focus and concentration. From micro-patterns to macro-patterns."

"I give all the glory to God, to the Creator of the Universe. The one who made the map of the world and cast the stars above it. Of course it is a game. It has metrics. Your flesh suit hosts your experience engine. The current school of metaphysics seems mostly concerned with the study of enjoying what we can for as long as it lasts. Maybe trying to impact culture it is not as important as I once thought given the entire world must necessarily be sacrificed in yet another cataclysm? Eternal Recurrence binds me to this moment, the very moment the camera captured this frame."

"I can prove the twin prime conjecture. I can prove more than just that. But to prove this thing! The algorithm is simple. So, so simple. But how did I arrive at this conclusion? How to prove Sloane's OEIS sequence A224855 'Numbers n such that $90*n+17$ and $90*n+19$ are twin primes' is an infinite sequence? It should be obvious, right?"

"Why is it necessary for there to exist an infinite number of matching entries for A202115 and A196000? The SAME FREQUENCY OPERATORS apply to both lists. DIFFERENT INSERTION LOCATIONS determine the differences in the lists. The Same Conway Primitives, different pole positions. When realized as a function, looks like a quadratic sequence whose x intercepts emit 'Conway nontrivial frequencies' as cancellation operators on a list of addresses."

In his mind Maxwell saw a chalice formed from the growth functions, and at each x-intercept he saw sine-wave like emanations which mapped composites. He saw a sign in his mind, but was unsure how to say it in words.

"What kind of maniac, what kind of exaggerated caricature is that person who dares to dream himself awake? Only unnamed things can be discovered, truly discovered. They are to be known by their names! The index..." Maxwell stumbled over a piece of Sage and his trance was interrupted. The moonlight was partially blocked by a cloud, further obscuring the landscape. Maxwell shut off the camera.

Everything was glittering - Maxwell sensed his scale relative to the vastness of space.

She was following him, using her 'snoop' system to listen in and record him.

Maxwell took out his 'snake-proof' sleeping bag and found a smooth patch of ground. She did the same.

"The song 'Captain Forever' by band 'HOME'," her headset

informed her as she drifted to sleep while watching the Delta Aquariids meteor shower.

Maxwell's mind while dreaming was filtering data from millions of minds with fusion centered on maximal awareness of space weather. The visual elements of his dream were experienced as a flythrough view of nearby celestial objects such as meteorites and asteroids. As he dreamed his mind apprehended small perturbations in fields which were causing projected orbits to de-intersect the Earth. The fabric of spacetime was being modified to protect Earth. He was able to move incredibly fast through space, but the closer he got to some objects the more pixelated they became. He would approach them and find that they were large square 'canvas-style' color-field paintings. He could approach everything inside the solar system and it would have the resolution of planets and moons and detailed dense landscapes. He was allowed to go under the soil of Mars, but he never tried. Real terror would awaken him every time.

The things outside the solar system were just impressionist paintings. From within the solar system they looked like super complex galaxies, but once he moved across the termination shock threshold they became props. Everything was a prop outside the Heliosphere.

CHAPTER 11

"Imperfection is beauty and madness is genius." Marylin Monroe

######## ALEXIS and PDC ########

"Why haven't you tried to fuck me?" she asked him point blank when they were finally alone. She was standing over him facing West. The sun had set, but the sky was aflame with the colors of orange, yellow and violet. Angelic light imparted to her a soft glow. Like uranium glass in twilight.

PDC sighed and looked down at the ground. He then looked up and directly into her eyes. "You are beautiful. When I met you I offered you a no strings attached place where you can live with no overhead. I did that with a 'no scope' attitude about consequences. But there was one unintended consequence. I cannot be flippant about what I promised." He paused and looked up at the sky. He then stood up and said, "I have no idea what kind of art you make. But I want to be a patron of your art. I cannot guarantee that you will become famous because I don't really admit to knowing much of anything about art. At all. But I met you in a very specific circumstance and it was bigger than me, whatever it was that brought us together. So I want you to have as few conflicts as possible, especially during a time when it is clear you are transitioning out of a relationship." He reached out and grabbed her shoulders, continuing, "If we were just strangers who crossed paths and we hooked up because you are on the rebound then that would be great. I would normally totally go for that. But I suspect that if you are going to find your comfort zone you should be as unattached as possible. I mean, when we met you said what you really wanted was to be alone for a while. So I don't want to pull you into a new relationship and then, you know, you might feel trapped in my house... ." He let go of her shoulders and looked up at the sky. Speaking to the moon he said, "I suspect. I could be wrong about that." He looked back at her and thought to himself, "*You have no idea the debate that is raging inside me right now. But I think we should become friends over the course of more adventures before we... fuck each other. But damn I want you so bad, want to go down on you and hear you moan and feel you writhe. Wrap you up in my arms and massage you through the night. You have no idea!*"

He held up his left hand and looked up toward the sky with his left eye and stated, "I'll be right back." He turned and walked away at a fast pace and disappeared for several hours. Alexis was asleep in her tent when her returned. "By golly, I wanted to bang her so bad," PDC whispered as he loaded his backpack and some other items into his tent. He climbed into his sleeping bag. "*Patience. Patience my love,*" he thought as he drifted to sleep.

Marshall overheard the entire conversation and was blown away by PDC's tenderness. He felt PDC was doing something really amazing for Alexis. She was vulnerable and it would be easy for him to take advantage of her. And the nature of her vulnerability in some ways indicated that PDC probably *ought to be* the person to take advantage of her, for her own good. Instead, PDC was playing the nice guy role which is exactly what he counseled not to do.

The following morning Alexis woke up in a state of confusion. She felt the people around her weren't looking for ways to exploit or control her. In fact, they accepted her for who she was and were offering unconditional friendship. X offered that she could assist her in getting a job at a library of science and technology. She could work part time and build up a little social capital and cash. "Don't worry. There are jobs that dyslexic people can do. You will love it. It is super easy. Plus just wait until you see the art. Your mind is going to be blown!" Jeremiah's house also sounded nice. According to X it was relatively big and had a large yard. X liked to take rescue dogs there to run around on the nearly full acre lot.

Her prayer had been answered.

She avoided thinking about her ex-boyfriend Tim and his faction of hippies. The man she abandoned when she skipped out on her kitchen was inventing reasons for why she hadn't returned. "Mr. Shiny Shirts fucking drugged her up man! We gotta find her!" As he was ruminating over the loss it was reported back that she had been spotted. According to Geezer Gus she had tossed her old clothes and was wearing hiking pants and a flannel shirt. Oh, and she was also seen by one of the grandmothers wearing an orange stocking cap while eating toast next to some tents by the main stage.

"Like some kind of yuppie," Dirty Bill finally said under his breath. Standing up he bellowed, "She is wearing those super expensive hiking boots and one of those aerogel jackets. That shit costs hella money. Did he literally walk in here and turn her into his prostitute!? He literally called his shot! Now he is gonna dress her up in his clothes and just march outta here with her? That is fucked up man. I ain't never seen no shit like that in my entire life! You know they are set up right by the main stage. Out in the middle of everything! Who do they think they are!?" The men wanted Tim to fight. They wanted to see violence against the guy in the nice shirts.

Tim's emasculation was almost beyond estimation. To go from having a cool, gorgeous girlfriend to watching her abandon you at a Rainbow Gathering to run off and join a yuppie club. It was the ultimate form of hippie humiliation. Beyond ordinary heartache, it was as if his world had collapsed into one of the hand-dug latrines.

Meanwhile, Alexis was on cloud nine. No one was yelling at her; all the campers they encountered were smiling. Even though they were set up in the most publicly visible space they had the vibes to pull it off. She got dressed and exited the tent. She found Marshall making percolator coffee and toast using a small portable camp grill. He had a sliced avocado that he spread upon the toast as he pulled it off the buttery frying pan. "Here you go," Marshall said, offering it to Alexis.

"Oh my God, this is so good!" Alexis said as she gobbled it down.

"Added some black garlic salt to the butter. Seems to add a little something."

They ate breakfast while watching children participate in a play on the main stage. Parents sat in the audience and offered words of encouragement as children attempted to re-enact scenes from well-known cartoon episodes.

"I want to be the baby shark!" a child exclaimed.

"There can be more than one baby shark!" a parent retorted.

Marshall handed Alexis a cup of coffee. "I am using sweetened condensed milk for creamer and I added a pinch of cinnamon and clove so it is more of a dessert coffee really, but it should have a good kick as I am brewing an espresso grind with a small amount of ginseng power added."

Alexis took a sip. It was delicious. "Amazing!" She hadn't tasted decadence in quite some time. "Will you hate me if I ask for another?" she sheepishly inquired. He laughed.

"No. In fact I need to use the whole can of condensed milk after I open it, so we should really go all in on pleasure."

PDC exited his tent. He walked over to Marshall and got a coffee. "Fuck man this is good. So good. So glad you almost fell into that ravine."

"Thanks for playing, am I right?" Marshall said, offering up an egg over easy on a piece of toast to PDC, who inhaled the food in a flash.

"It is soooo good when it is still hot," PDC explained to the shocked onlookers. "It is cold up here in the morning. Nobody wants to eat cold egg yolks. Gotta be vigorous when eating hot food in a cold place. Get the max flavors. Temperature is vibration, you know that right? Breath of the Dragon, Breakfast of the Dragon! Haha!" PDC laughed as he invented a mythology for his habit of rapidly eating his food. Alexis pondered his words. She decided to try doing the same thing. Rather than her usual small, modest bites she chopped off large amounts and stuffed them into her mouth. The warm egg yolk tasted great on the buttery toast. She gobbled her food quickly. "I get it," she said to PDC as Marshall refilled her coffee. "I've always eaten my eggs slowly while camping and they do get cold and they don't taste nearly as good. Part of the flavor is the temperature."

"Adaptation is the mark of intellect," PDC replied. "Oh! I got you some things last night when I went out for my walk. I hope it isn't the wrong kind of stuff." He grabbed a large toolbox and showed her that it contained numerous fine art pens and pencils as well as watercolor brushes and medium. From his tent and backpack he removed several sketch pads and watercolor pads of various sizes along with a few different clipboards to hold the paper. "I thought if you are this kind of artist you might be able to use this stuff. Some college kids from California traded with me. I left quite a bit of it back in the van. They had a ton of stuff and were really, like, desperate for some of, um, 'my vibes', so I was able to make a good deal. But if you don't sketch or paint or whatever it is no big deal at all..."

"No!" she responded vigorously. "This is amazing. I was wishing I had some art supplies last night when I was trying to go to sleep. After talking with you guys I could see the drawings I wanted to make." She was shaking her head in disbelief. "I wanted to draw... you. But..." She was almost in tears. Instead of crying she took the art supplies and said, "Let me put them away for now. One second." She entered her tent and zipped it up. She fell to her knees and smashed her face into her pillow. She cried hard. She had no frame of reference for a loving God, one who actually returned calls. She had never been blessed with Grace.

Marshall looked over and saw that PDC was looking at Alexis' tent with his head cocked to the right. Marshall mimed the action of drawing, then made the thumbs up sign at PDC.

PDC smiled and walked away.

Alexis cried for some time and then regained her composure. She opened the toolbox and was met with a dazzling array of art equipment. Pens of all types. Brushes of all types. Watercolor kits. Calligraphy pens. Charcoals of different grades. Different types of erasers. Tools she had never seen and wasn't sure how to use. "I..." she said as tears crept back up into her eyes. She closed her eyes and controlled her breath. She decided to use the most ordinary looking pencil. She opened a sketchpad and attached it to a clipboard and imagined Marshall's face. She began drawing it from memory.

Alexis Carter was able to draw photographic quality reproductions from memory. She was also an attractive female. Despite these talents and advantages, she also came from a very poor family with a history of alcoholism and abuse. She avoided alcohol her entire life, but had not done well enough in primary school to earn any scholarships due to her low grade point averages. She was dyslexic and had a difficult time reading, but was able to draw anything. And quickly, too.

She wanted to paint, but had not been able to afford the raw materials. She had been living on her own for four years and was not getting anywhere in life. She was still with her high school boyfriend, a man several years older who had not been able to hold down a job while she was attending college and who had become increasingly verbally abusive. While he never struck her, he did threaten her with violence should she ever try to leave him. He told her that art was a waste of time and that she needed to focus on getting a 'real job.' He calculated that she had hurt both of them by taking on college debt to attend art school. Because her reading skill was very low it was hard for her to find employment outside fast food or housekeeping. So she had come to the Rainbow Gathering relying on magical thinking with the dream of finding a place for her and her boyfriend to escape the monthly bills routine. A place she could make her art and perfect her craft. It was her dream.

Now these strangers had selected her and dressed her in expensive clothes and given her food and drugs and now archival-quality art supplies. In the middle of a forest a veritable retail store of art materials had been delivered to her. *"Rich people food,"* she thought to herself.

Tears fell on the drawing of Marshall. *"What an interesting face he has,"* she smiled to herself as she added watercolor, using her tears to activate the pigment. *"He is so beautiful."*

######### ERIC #########

The day finally arrived for Eric to give his speech at the writer's conference. He reviewed his prepared notes backstage. The title of his lecture was, "The Science(Fiction) of Expectation Management."

A professor from a nearby college introduced him. He walked on stage.

-

"Thank you. Thank you for the applause. So, when you turn to a writer to learn practical survival skills, well, what does that mean? How does any organism advanced enough to be called 'life' measure success?

Perhaps it means identifying how to thrive in whatever circumstances life throws at you. How to adapt until you die. Well, no person knows exactly how long 'life' is going to last. And so what, then, is a well-lived life? Life is our quest to acquire experiences and write about them.

The quality of our experience or our estimation of its value can change over time. We have no idea how we will feel about our experiences tomorrow or in a year. Some traditions advocate for letting go of all expectations. Do not worry about outcomes just focus on the doing. The science of avoiding expectations is one way to approach your relationship with your writing. But unless you are willing to commit to becoming a monk it might be hard for you to achieve absolute indifference toward outcomes. So, while you are building up your body of work and aspiring for success, a sidequest is to study the 'Science(Fiction) of Expectation Management.'

The first lesson must always be how to take control of your passion. How to nurture whatever it is that excites you the most. How can you unlock greater access to energy? Perhaps you have a hack that you can use to write more effectively? Some of you may be familiar with Dragonball? Anyone? Yeah. The anime. A few of you, right? A character named Vegeta has a transformation into a giant fighting ape. This occurs whenever he is in the presence of a full moon. Think of this as the 'flow state' for the writer. Vegeta evolved an ability to generate a fake moon that can trigger this transformation. Similarly, for a long time I wrote in coffee shops because the noise of all the people helped me concentrate. But now I wear headphones, over one ear, and I can write while I am at home. An artificial moon hack to expand the number of ways I can chase the mythical flow state. And I don't think it is, let's say, as effective as writing in coffee shops. But it is no longer cute to camp out at a table. A lot of places are more micro now, they do not allow you to be anonymous. So don't be defeated by the changing of the world. Move with it.

This is not a thing that can be taught so much as it is a thing that must be learned; more like an epigenetic response to an environmental stimulus. There is little for us to do but observe and react. Ideally, we can evolve our strategies to achieve greater success. For the fiction writer this means nurturing the circumstances that enhance creativity. You know, that feeling when the ideas are forming themselves and we are racing to keep up. When the ideas are moving faster than the ink.

So, up to a majority of people suspect or believe that intelligent life exists spread throughout the Cosmos. They base this on the generalization of 'habitable zones' where a planet is neither so far away from a sun as to be frozen nor so close as to be incinerated. So, humans have apprehended the question: Are we the only 'so-called' intelligent life in the Universe?

If our 'being here' is sufficient to prove the existence of

life how do we then argue that all the remaining matter in the Universe is incapable of hosting something similar? The human, and all known life, operates as a manifestation of 'self-assembly' upon or within otherwise INERT elements. For example, elements may form structures based on laws of valency and environmental inputs like temperature, pressure and phonon bombardment. Consciousness resides in a body of atoms behaving as molecules arranged as cells carrying on in a vast concert of electrical and chemical reactions. This symphony of layered structure results with homeostasis. The number of associations between elements implies the existence of an 'information schematic' that exists ON TOP OF the otherwise lifeless chemicals that constitute our bodies. There is an order that pre-exists the classical world and it allows us to emerge as a new branch on, or node within, the 'Tree of Schematic Possibility'. But it could be that we are so far down one of the branches, so many epochs into the evolution of this system, that we cannot discern the governing schematic nor can we estimate the number of possible worlds remaining to us. We are too far from both the beginning and the ending to meaningfully comprehend where we exist relative to those events or termini.

Let's work some of this out. A female acquaintance of mine suggests that the Moon is the oldest artifact in the entire Universe. So, if the Moon is the oldest well-preserved artifact in the current Universe, if it has escaped possibly billions upon trillions of expansion and collapse events, Big Bang and Big Crunch events, then the probability of Earth chemicals being affected by the tidal forces co-generated by our Moon is so low that it establishes an 'improbability thesis' which allows for a Universe that hosts only ONE 'intelligent' organism. We emerge from the impossibility of this particular configuration, from a universe of otherwise lifeless chemicals and emotionless energies. The Earth, in a sense, is the organism. And the Moon is the 'improbability generator' that allows humans to exist as one of the 'allowed' or 'permitted' configurations of the Universe Wavefunction. We humans are one of the 'Feynman path integrals' that allowed for the evolution of life on Earth. We exist as an extreme node on the tree of possibility because we are loaded with improbability. Total Energy in the universe is conserved. Everywhere. All the time. But a finite energy can exist in a lot of permissible states.

By the way, the Moon could also be a totally 'ordinary' object and the Solar System could be that of a totally ordinary Yellow Star.

Except, our Solar System is not normal. There is Strange Xenon and Strange Oxygen at levels that imply a close call with a Neutron Star or some other super-dense, supermassive object. Our solar system collided with or had a flyby with another star or star system, one that contained a neutron star or possibly a black hole. Our yellow sun emits FAR FEWER solar flares than all other observed yellow dwarf stars which could also mean that our sun is possibly a failed neutron star that underwent an asymmetrical gravitational collapse and our Solar System was formed from a failed black hole. We have some outlier datapoints that make the Earth a REALLY strange place.

The Strange Oxygen. What is that, right? Oxygen has 8 protons in its nucleus. So you can form Oxygen from 8 Hydrogen atoms, because Hydrogen has 1 proton each. If you make Helium from Hydrogen, well, you get a fusion bomb, because the tiny mass difference between two hydrogen atoms and one helium atom is transmitted into the environment as photons of extremely high frequency. So, based on what we know from our observations of celestial bodies, our Sun should only be massive enough to fuse Hydrogen into Oxygen. But we have a lot of Oxygen around that has been formed from 4 Helium Atoms. And you need Quasars and Magnetars and super massive accretion disks to form Oxygen from Helium. And you can detect this in the tiny mass difference between 8 free Hydrogen atoms and 4 free Helium atoms. You can also find them in the spectral emission lines of the various elements. Our Strange Oxygen is an artifact of an ancient event. So, for the fiction writer, it may be that these unique species of oxygen play a role in how human consciousness forms. Quantum Brain can detect these tiny differences and can use these tiny molecular masses to tune in to and harmonize with completely different spectra of signals. They have slightly different harmonics based on their tiny mass differences. Black Hole harmonics.

In the other direction, take the existence of an observable Universe to begin with. The writer is born into a world that pre-exists his or her arrival. How do we observe the insides of the thing in which we were created? Or, how do we observe the outsides of the thing in which we are created and 'live.' How do we say a universe comes into being? We say that a condition exists of 'pure possibility' where all outcomes on the evolutionary tree for the universe are equally possible. We then EVOLVE/COLLAPSE into a single DETERMINED state by forming a perspective of elapsing time. This collapses all possible worlds into a subset of new actual worlds. Following this first event, there is the emergence of at least one more system capable of forming a perspective of time, which is to say they are aware of each other. These systems necessarily must be able to transact with each other in units of elapsing time. Does this not also match the description of what a writer does when the blank piece of paper ends up covered in text? When a story is told through the interaction of characters the transactions necessarily consume a span of elapsed time? And what is necessarily consumed when time elapses? Well, shadows must be cast.

Anyway, by the time the Writer is born, the universe is comprised of a system of human observers witnessing photons and creating sounds. And writing books. So here we are at the convergence of a bunch of randomly distributed variables. Quite possibly we occupy the center of the NOW and we are the only beings with telescopes in the entire place. This is the Fermi Paradox. It has a lot to do with protein folding.

Which is another fictional tool we will look into in a moment.

So! The fiction writer. The Universe has created this job opportunity out of the space dust gathered here today. Our job? We must render our part of the infinite possibility curve that, for us, disappears into the horizons of the not-yet-born fiction writers. On the curved surface of possibility we can only range so far, our experiences can only generate objects for which we have a pre-existing frame of reference. There is an experiment that compares the dreams of sewer rats versus lab rats that illustrates this beautifully. The lab rat is born and runs only one maze. Its dreams are of that maze. A lab rat is given two mazes to run and it can now dream of alternative types of mazes. Meanwhile the sewer rat dreams are vastly more complex. Our experiences go a long way to determine our ability to imagine alternative universes.

Nostradamus would maybe disagree in some respects with that. They say he played with a potter's wheel. He took a candle and put it in the middle of the wheel. He then took a lampshade, which was a candle shade in those days, and cut slits in it. He then put the lampshade over the candle on the potters wheel and turned it into a primitive strobe light and/or zoetrope. He and his geometry goons would probably hang out with some wine or mead and play spin the potters wheel and tell each other stories about what they were hallucinating as they strobed their eyes with a frequency of between four and seven hertz. These guys were playing with some form of analogue hallucination machine and were trying to predict the future. And then write about it.

I play it straight, so I have never fooled around with this kind of prop-assisted writing. No Quiji boards. No crystal balls. And think what might happen to us if we DID tap into an inevitable future. Wouldn't everyone think we were crazy? I can see it now, 'No. No, no! Me and L. Ron, we were just hanging out playing spin the potter's wheel and when he tapped it just right we could see tomorrow's stock market updates today.' Well, if you tap into that you aren't a fiction writer you are a government asset hidden away in a secret base underground, spinning for them. Be careful what you wish for. Right? You feel me? Writing is super dangerous and so, you know, write straight. Don't go using contrivances.

Again, why does a physical universe exist at all!? Having only this window of time to perceive 'continuity' how does a finite window let in the light of an infinite sun? It must be as an abstraction!

If we are part of a cycle then we are one of many permutations. But the improbability of Earth may go a long way in explaining the dearth of 'intelligent life' thus far witnessed in our window. We don't observe tons of intelligent life because, statistically, WE should not exist. The Fermi Paradox refactored: the absurd idea that random chance can select for the correct protein folds. See, the things of which we are comprised are some of the most complex mathematical objects in the known universe. And these are just some of the 'ordinary objects' managed by our autonomic nervous system. Chance or random selection cannot be the mode of operation for protein folds; the math just doesn't hold up. And realize that the number of possible shapes for just a single folded protein is so large that it would trivially exceed the physical memory of the known universe if we attempted to enumerate all of them. And these are just a few of the smallest structures in the living universe. The math that describes them blows classical mechanics to smithereens. Blows galactic mechanics to smithereens.

The gift of our existence is tied to the amount of time it took the universe to incorporate a configuration this weird into itself. Now imagine we design a test for the hypothesis that we are alone in the Cosmos:

Resolved: Not even the Cosmos can believe something like us exists.

It may be that we are the result of discrete math, of intentional engineering. That breaks my rule and states that intelligent life would need to predate us in some form. Within that model we are software running on a platform and the super-administrator God can come wipe that section of the memory at any time. We have no concept of our relationship to the hardware layer that supports our 'experience engine.' The entire universe is hardware doing transactions. It takes a universe as large as ours to host as much mathematical complexity as we see in our proteins. It takes galaxies and clusters of galaxies to aggregate enough matter-memory to instantiate just ONE Earth. But it is running in a container. Relative to the container we see a limit. But we do not see how many containers the host can run simultaneously. Instead we see our Universe as large because it is larger than us and consumes what appears to be the maximum amount of container. But I see humans as large because it takes this entire universe to render knowledge and new information.

There are no laws sufficient to explain emergence. Or, perhaps there are 'Laws of Frequency and Harmonics' we have yet to learn? A lot of animal behaviors are mediated by tidal forces. Think turtles. The tidal frequencies along with the photon flux creates harmonics capable of animating life as we know it.

Okay! Enough! Enough roaming on the geodesic of fictional story-lines! You want to know how to survive as a writer. What does one do to thrive?

Negotiation begins with the story you tell yourself. You need to convince yourself that this writing activity is worth the time invested. That there is a reason for doing it. A duty. You may or may not be better off with a partner, someone that you can build a scrapbook of life experiences with. Maybe add more people to your inner circle and do more things that are outside your comfort zone. Be open and receptive to new ideas and new experiences. Or don't. Maybe do the opposite of all that?"

Eric grabbed his notecards and showed them to the audience.

"Now let me read something: Always remember, suboptimal solutions are still solutions. However, affluence is good because it means you can outsource some of the distracting tasks that accompany ordinary life. Cultivate valuable relationships, curate those that improve your life. Optimize until you lose no moments. Stop wasting time and maximize your efficiency."

There was a small trash can that Eric removed from under the podium. He tossed the cards in the can.

"Fun times, right? Sounds like a party. North Korean school of writing. So, what is the strategy to become more efficient? Write faster or more effectively. Generally speaking, work expands to fill time. Two ways this happens. Work you hate takes forever and work you love consumes it in an instant. Writing can't be accomplished faster than your maximum throughput in your medium. Handwriting is slower than typing. As an experiment use different tools and notice the differences in the voice. You will discover there is more than one writer in you. The tool is part of the dialogue.

Write some number of pages per day. Some number of sentences per day. Always make time to write. This is true of any creative endeavor: you must make time for it. You may be required to work for others, to maintain a job. Or, you may be required to run your own business on top of being a writer. One of the laws of the 'survival game' is that any occupation you engage in for money will need to provide you with some multiple of your daily cost of living if you are going to thrive.

When I started writing I had roommates who paid most of my bills. I worked as a chef in a restaurant; I got tips sometimes. All kinds of tips. Food is a way of forming an intimate bond with a population of humans or animals. How much does a pet dog enjoy steak? How much does a person enjoy farm-grown food with lots of diverse inputs?

So, when I started out, I was traveling around selling books off my motorcycle. I would take time off from working in a kitchen and arrange to sell at independent bookstores across America. I made a point to stop in at a few literary agent offices along the way. I got appointments, of course. Then I wrote a story called 'Modern Processes' that I felt pretty good about. I was already out there selling myself as an author, already demonstrating a willingness to be out in front, marketing my work. I wasn't shy. My energy was directed toward getting wider distribution. I also wanted to make my agent rich. My prime directive is to give her the ammunition to win good contracts. But before she could believe in me I needed to demonstrate to both her and myself that I believed in my writing. The profitability of it.

I've only published one novel on top of my several children's books. Sure, my novel spawned a lot of derivative work. That is why I am here today, because of that derivative work. Your written word is the artifact you leave behind. What I can tell you is that I have taken Steven King's advice and I do force myself to write six pages per day. I may not be able to do it every day forever. I may quit, like a smoker, knowing I will return to it. I have had days where I wrote 20 pages and so I can book some PTO flex time. Just kidding. I mean, I do keep track of it.

So much of it feels like trash. That's me being honest and vulnerable with you. But, remember, you don't know today how you might feel about it tomorrow. So generate some output and play with words. Try to elicit feelings.

Most importantly, keep writing."

######## MAXWELL ########

Annie was watching Maxwell. He had set up his movie projector screen under the cave opening and was projecting from behind it. He was able to walk around in front of the cave as he watched. Sound was provided by a large battery-powered PA speaker.

"Closing the Gap: The Quest to Understand Prime Numbers" – presented by Vicky Neale, appeared on the movie screen.

-

Thank you very much. I thought we could begin with some counting. Of course math isn't only about counting, but I'm interested in number theory properties of whole numbers and I particularly like this way of visualizing the numbers as it starts to give us an insight into prime factorizations. And I want to talk all about prime numbers today.

1	2	3	4	5	6	7	8	9	10
11	12	13	14	15	16	17	18	19	20
21	22	23	24	25	26	27	28	29	30
31	32	33	34	35	36	37	38	39	40
41	42	43	44	45	46	47	48	49	50
51	52	53	54	55	56	57	58	59	60
61	62	63	64	65	66	67	68	69	70
71	72	73	74	75	76	77	78	79	80
81	82	83	84	85	86	87	88	89	90
91	92	93	94	95	96	97	98	99	100

So maybe you can start to notice some patterns here. I want to talk about patterns. As mathematicians our job is to look for patterns, to look for structures, and then to understand what's going on behind the scenes. So there's lots of patterns and I'm not going to talk about all of them today. So an example might be if you look carefully the four column, the six column, the eight column, and the ten column, they don't seem to have any prime numbers in them. But I'm not satisfied. I'm interested in what would happen if we kept going, if we continued to this chart further what would happen? All the numbers in the four, six, eight, and ten columns are even.

The prime number factors are one and itself, so if you've got an even number bigger than two it's divisible by one and by itself but also by two. So it can't possibly be prime. So in fact 2 is the only even prime. So in the two column we're not going to find any more Primes no matter how far we go and the 4, 6, 8 and 10 columns really are empty. So that's not the most complicated example, but gives you a flavor of noticing a pattern and then trying to understand what's really going on. Why are we seeing that?

The kinds of patterns I want to focus on today is related to the gaps between consecutive prime numbers. If we look at 2 and 3, both prime numbers, we know they're the only example of two consecutive prime numbers; if we pick any two consecutive numbers one of them is going to be even and we know two is the only even prime number. The Primes are bunched up quite close together near the origin of the counting numbers. If we look further down there's some quite big gaps. So 83 to 89, 89 to 97, these Primes are getting further apart and that makes intuitive sense. If I give you a really big number it's very hard for it to be prime because it's going to be divisible potentially by lots of smaller numbers. There are lots of smaller numbers that might divide it. It's very easy for 7 to be prime because there aren't many smaller numbers that would divide it. The larger the number the more potential factors. So it sort of makes sense that these Primes are getting more spread out.

One question we might ask is whether we keep finding more and more Primes if we continue down the number chart. If I could fit more and more on the spreadsheet would I keep finding new Primes or at some point will we hit the biggest prime number? And those are two very different scenarios. In one world there's a biggest prime number and from that point on nothing is prime. In the other scenario no matter how far we go we keep finding new prime numbers. It's sort of intriguing to think which of those situations it might be.

I can ask my computer to return the largest prime it can render and it goes and works and clunks for a fortnight and comes back with a very large prime number. That tells me nothing. So a computer is no help. But happily mathematics will help. This goes back to an ancient Greek theorem. A theorem is a mathematical statement that we can prove to be true and the theorem is that there are infinitely many primes. There is no biggest prime number. For me the certainty is what's really important. So when the the radio comes on in the morning with the headlines I don't have half a percent of my brain thinking 'Oh, I wonder whether today they'll have found the largest prime number?' because I am absolutely totally certain there is no largest prime number and the reason that

I'm totally certain is because we have a proof.

So for me proof is a really important part of what we do as mathematicians and I want to share this proof with you because it is important as well as beautiful. It is a very well-known proof, but it takes a little bit of getting your head around it the first time. So this goes back to Euclid's Elements that he wrote more than 2,000 years ago and he had this beautiful idea.

He said 'let's do a thought experiment.'

Secretly we think there are infinitely many primes. There's no biggest prime number. Let's imagine we're in a parallel universe where there is a biggest prime. There are only finitely many Primes and let's explore the consequences of that. And it turns out you reach a spot in impossibility. So if we were in this parallel universe where there are only finitely many Primes I could take a very large piece of paper and write all the primes in the world so my list starts 2, 3, 5, 7, 11, whatever and I keep going until I get to the largest prime in the world. And Euclid's beautiful idea was to take all the primes in the world, multiply them together and add 1.

Euclid's built this number so that it's not divisible by any of the primes on the list.

And now I feel slightly ill because somehow we've got this number that must have a prime factor and yet isn't divisible by any of the primes in the world that were on our list. We're caught in a contradiction in math. Its this kind of impossibility, this absurdity, that arose from supposing that there were only finitely many Primes. This tells us that there must be infinitely many Primes so a little square box symbol is a symbol that mathematicians use at the end of a proof.

I think it's extraordinary when you think about it. We're proving something really difficult, right? We're proving that there are infinitely many prime numbers and this argument is so elegant so that I can fit it on a single piece of paper. So I'm very glad there are infinitely many prime numbers. The world is a much more interesting place with infinitely many Primes.

So if we go back we can return to thinking about patterns. I feel like I need to confess, because I've sort of slightly misled you. You know what I was saying about the primes getting further apart because if you're a big number it's really hard to be prime. So the gaps get bigger. Well, here's the thing about the primes. Every time you think you understand what's going on it's a little bit more subtle than that, because if I put another row on the spreadsheet all of a sudden here's a cluster of primes bunched up all together. So what's going on?

It is true that on average the primes are getting more spread out. That's a consequence of a theorem that was proved right at the end of the nineteenth century called the prime number theorem which gives us an insight into the distribution of the primes. So on average the primes are getting more spread out, but the 'on average' is really important because then you get these little pockets of primes that are very close. And it's those Primes that are very close that I want to focus on today.

Primes that differ by two like 3 & 5 like 29 to 31. We've established infinitely many primes exist so the question is are there infinitely many pairs of primes that differ by two? This is called the twin primes conjecture. So the prediction is that there are infinitely many pairs of primes that differ by two and there are some sort of plausible reasons for thinking that this should be true.

One plausible, but not super good, reason is that I can ask my computer to find examples of large pairs of twin primes that differ by two and my computer would go away and think about it and it will come up with very large examples. We know that there are very large pairs of primes that differ by two. That's not a great reason though, because as I said with there being infinitely many Primes there's always this risk that we found the largest pair of twin primes. So a better reason is that we can kind of model the behavior of prime numbers.

So if I pick a number like 61, either 61 is prime or it's not prime. We don't get to kind of toss a coin, but we can model the prime numbers by tossing a coin. So the idea is you have a 'biased coin' and the probability of getting a prime is skewed a bit because the primes on average get more spread out. We know that it should be harder for a large number to be prime, so if you do this modeling very carefully you can make a prediction for the number of pairs of twin primes up to a million or a billion or whatever your favorite number is. So we can make this kind of predicted estimate for the number of pairs of twin primes and then we can check that against the data that our computer has given. That's where it's helpful to know that the computer has calculated these large examples of twin primes and the prediction matches the data beautifully. But it's not a proof of anything because it's only a model. So we can't prove that this is exactly how the primes work. We don't yet know how to do that, but it is very compelling evidence because in particular it predicts that there should be infinitely many pairs of twin primes.

So I thought it might be fun to have a go at trying to prove the twin primes conjecture because we should be ambitious.

Let's take the idea of Euclid's proof. So Euclid said take all these Prime's on the piece of paper, multiply them together, add one. Nothing at all would change in Euclid's proof if instead we took all the primes and multiply them together and subtract 1. So we could do this, right? If I take 2, 3 and 5, the first few Primes, multiply them together subtract one or add one I get 29 and 31. That's a pair of twin primes. That's kind of nice and I could keep doing that, right? So I could take 2 times 3 times 5 times 7 and add 1 and subtract 1. I get 209 and 211. The bad news is 209 isn't prime. So Euclid's argument doesn't say the number we come up with must be prime, it says it is not divisible by any of the primes on the list. 209 is divisible by smaller primes, they were just too big to have been on the list.

Unfortunately we can't prove the twin primes conjecture by adding and subtracting 1 from this argument, which is a shame because that would have been nice. But that's how math goes sometimes. Mathematicians spend a lot of time trying to prove theorems without necessarily succeeding.

So one of my mathematical heroes is a mathematician named Julia Robinson. An administrator asked her to describe her typical week and so here is how Julia Robinson described it. 'Monday tried to prove theorem. Tuesday tried to prove theorem. Wednesday tried to prove theorem. Thursday tried to prove theorem. Friday theorem false.' Which sort of sounds very depressing but it's not. There not all quite like that, but mathematicians do spend a lot of time trying out some ideas and don't necessarily get them. So I like this because it gives us more insight into Euclid's argument, but it doesn't prove the twin prime conjecture. In fact the reason the twin primes conjecture is still called the twin primes conjecture is that nobody has proved it. So we think it should be true that's why it's a conjecture, but we don't yet have a proof.

So what I want to tell you about today is some of the recent progress on this particular problem, the twin primes conjecture. The excitement happened when a mathematician called Yitang Zhang announced this extraordinary breakthrough and it got mathematicians super excited. Any kind of progress on the twin prime conjecture gets people excited. Zhang managed to show that there are infinitely many pairs of primes that differ by at most 70 million. Now, when you are aiming for the twin primes conjecture and you prove infinite pairs of primes differ by 70 million, it feels like a miss right? I mean it's a long way off, I agree, but it was the first one that anybody here managed to prove any theorem of that type before. So seventy million is a lot bigger than two, but it's much better than infinity. It was a finite number, that was the important thing.

So there are infinitely many pairs of primes where the gap between them is less than or equal to 70 million. Zhang was not a famous expert in this area of math. He had hardly any publications since his PhD and he found it very difficult to get a job in a university. He did by this point have a job as a lecturer in a university in the US, but he'd also spent some time working for the Subway restaurant chain doing various bits and bobs. Whilst doing all of that he kept up with the research literature. So he'd really immersed himself in the area and that was what enabled him to do this. So this wasn't some idea that everybody else had missed, he'd taken what other people in the area were doing and showed just the most extraordinary technical insight and perseverance to kind of push through an argument. Everybody else had ruled out this approach because they knew it wouldn't work. So it is just extraordinary and everybody is super excited and the experts in the area check the proof and, yeah, it was all good. And then people started to think, well, can we improve on that?

And in order to tell you a bit more about that I need to tell you a little bit more about finding other kinds of patterns in the primes, not just pairs of twin primes. So I made myself a number line. Here's my number line and I colored the primes a different color so I hope you can just about see that the primes are in red and the non primes are in black. Then I made myself a twin Prime detector. So there's a piece of cardboard and I've just cut out holes in it. It's a little bit like an old-fashioned punch card. and the idea is that you can slide it along the number line and detect pairs of twin primes. So, okay, 1 is no good because one is not prime. 2 and 4 not so good 3 and 5 are twin primes, great. Four and six, no. Five and seven are twin primes. So I can take my piece of cardboard and slide along the number line and the twin prime conjecture predicts that there are infinitely many positions of the card where both of the visible numbers are prime, right? So the the twin prime conjecture says as you slide a card along there are infinitely many pair positions where both of these numbers are prime.

So Zhang's work used this idea where the width of the spacing on the card is 70 million numbers. So as I take this card of length 70 million sliding along the number line Zhang's theorem says there are infinitely many positions where at least two of the visible numbers are both prime. So we don't know exactly what the gap is, all we know is that some two of these visible numbers will be Prime. And when you think about the theorem in that way we start having opportunities to start improving on this. When people started reading Zhang's paper it became clear seventeen million was not the best answer that his argument would give.

So it really took off when Scott Morrison wrote a blog post stating there are infinitely many pairs of primes at most 59,472,640 spaces apart and he explained how he'd slightly tweaked Zhang's arguments to come up with this number. Of course everybody else then wanted to have their moments of having the world record for this problem, right? This is one of the most famous unsolved problems in the whole of mathematics. If you have an opportunity to hold the world record for five minutes wouldn't you?

CHAPTER 12

######## MAXWELL ########

Maxwell was at his car. It was early morning just before sunrise. He turned on the car radio and opened the doors and trunk. He had just finished downloading the last several days of his content into the car computer. The typed word had already been scored by the sentiment filter and was being used to calculate an updated song list. It would take the microcomputers a few hours to convert the video files and extract speech-to-text. The speech-to-text filename would be appended with the related timestamp and then stitched together with his other text files to maintain the correct time series. Jebediah had created most of the code for the timestamp stitching program and worked closely with Maxwell while co-developing the sentiment scoring system.

The button on his dashboard would force update the music list to match the most recent sentiment filter. The filter contained a 'deviation score' that was a one-time value determined by the amount of force applied to the button. Less force would present a song similar to the one currently playing while more force would generate a song that was scored in the direction of 'unlikeness.' The button state was also stored for a small duration of time and could be influenced by higher frequency of use. For example if Maxwell hit it four times in rapid succession it would play 4 randomly selected songs. Maxwell hit the button once, rather lightly.

He turned up the radio and listened to 'Z-Trip Power106 8606' by liquidPhix while he fixed his breakfast. He made pancakes and reconstituted some freeze dried eggs and sausage. He engaged in stretching and calisthenics. He cleaned his mess and prepared to leave. He watched as his breath condensed in the sunless air.

Maxwell turned down the car radio as the song ended. He turned on his action camera and spoke.

"Will I ever be finished?" he asked as he looked in the direction of the sunrise. "I continue to find more, understand more. I cannot rush the journey or skip ahead. I cannot know the future or my name would be God, all-knowing. It is necessary I should not know the destination. But does a destination actually exist, or is this a circle mistaken for a line?"

Maxwell pondered his own question, then replied, "I have not been speaking about my work. Because how does one speak about math? I can say I am working on a model derived from a suggestion made by John Conway regarding the composite numbers. He argues that there are two kinds of composites, the trivial and the nontrivial. I only just discovered it so my model isn't exactly derived from it. Here is the deal, I have been out here this whole time writing about cycloids and trying to use a poetic language to explain something I witnessed in a waking dream. And then the inventor of the Game of Life appears in one of Sloane's OEIS entries and proffers a rationalization for all of it."

"Now I have a struggle. How to produce a completely 'regular' function that includes quasi-randomness in its output. I have this nice, let's say, sine wave plotted on the x axis. Do we have a 'nice' function to describe the points it does not intersect? Maybe we need several functions? The Complementary Function for a well-defined or well-behaved Diophantine equation can always be rendered by a finite number of 'anti-generator' functions. Maybe? I can see it for the even and odd numbers, the super simple way we can divide the first universe A000027 into two separate universes using only the last digit observable. A very superficial filter, but it works for arbitrarily large numbers. The equation for the even numbers is n*2 while the anti-generator function is (n*2)-1 for n=A000027. But if I have a quadratic sequence can I find its complement with a similarly simple test or generator function? This is where I have been climbing a slimy vertical wall."

"It is the negative space of the sequence generator I want to expose! I see the distribution of composites as similar to the growth of a crystal and there are holes in the otherwise perfect lattice growth. 24 'lattice functions' map the composites. The 'hole function' is the result of these 24 completely regular simple expressions failing to cover all the terms in A000027; the 'hole space' is the quasi-random sequence A201804. Operationally, the whole number solutions to 24 quadratic growth sequences are used to map composites. The values of A000027 which, when fed into the sieve, do not return whole number solutions are prime. That sounds like nonsense when I say it out loud. Can anyone even interpret that statement and make sense of it?" Maxwell paused and looked around, frustrated.

He continued, "People usually assemble the prime numbers as OEIS sequence A000040. They think of the primes as existing in a single continuum or as a subset of the counting numbers. The counting numbers exist on a line and we think of them collectively as a single entity, but simultaneously they exist spread throughout nine digital root columns in an nx9 list. And using this 'map' we can begin to attempt a play-through of the Game of Primes using the 'Conway Nontrivial Numbers' gambit."

Maxwell appeared to be thinking very hard about what to say next.

He began, "So, I have built a twin prime sieve. I have tested it against large numbers. Large! Ha! As if 20-digit numbers are large. I have a brutal, communist architecture proof of why there are an infinite number of twin primes. It is utterly mechanical." Maxwell stopped speaking; the sun was now crossing the horizon and was flooding his eyes with eight minute old photons. "The Game of Primes will reveal a proof of the twin prime conjecture. And maybe we will find the real roots of the Riemann Zeta while we are at it?"

Maxwell shut off the camera and walked over to the car. He grabbed his gear and locked the doors and trunk. He hit the music button hard before walking away.

"Band is 'Kemel' song is 'Mutations III'," her headset informed her as she watched Maxwell start power-walking away from his car.

######## MARSHALL and ALEXIS ########

Alexis was adapting to her new friends and wanted to give them something in return for all they had provided. "We should walk around. I can introduce you to some of the kitchens. If you want."

"Yeah!" Marshall replied instantly. He was excited to wander. He wasn't sure where PDC had gone and was waiting for him, but concluded that maybe they would see him while they were out. "Give me a few minutes to pack a little bag."

Marshall retreated to his tent and rolled several joints. He made some very large ones using multiple papers and infused those with hash. He made sure to grab several bottles of water. On his way out he grabbed a large bag of mushrooms for good measure. "*Just in case,*" he thought to himself.

They headed into the forest. "There is a camp back here that is pretty large. It has a lot of Christians who hang out there so the camp kitchen is a bit more structured, but they are very non-judgmental and there are usually some good conversations." Marshall, for his part, was relatively indifferent about the specifics. She wanted to go to Christian Camp because her ex-boyfriend Tim and his crew of hippies disliked the 'Jesus vibes' and avoided it.

They arrived at the large kitchen and merged into the crowd. A young man was advocating for the existence of a personal God who "cannot be known" because "we cannot conceive of the infinite." Another slightly older man debated him, arguing that the universe was too mechanical for a 'Sky God' and that there was no way to prove a negative so the real question is, "What has God done for you lately?"

Marshall watched as the two advocated their opposing viewpoints. He pondered a means to synthesize both arguments and bring the men to common ground. Marshall waited for his opportunity, then interjected with, "You agree that the universe is huge, right? And you agree we cannot possibly know God, right? Then God is real in both his absence and His presence. He stands to an Atheist as an anti-property of the rational universe. The universe is so complex and also so lawfully regulated that there is no way we have a personal god. Meanwhile your personal God has made the universe this complicated so we can witness just the tiniest sliver of His awesome power. The massive amount of space we can see is just the largest expression of the infinite that we can fit into our minds. And it appears infinite to us. Both of your perspectives are correct interpretations of the central issue, which is: 'Existence is complex enough that it cannot be fully understood by any mortal.' Thus in the end we must ALL rely on faith, and faith alone, to achieve any kind of certainty."

The men were stumped by Marshall's oratory. People in the crowd started to nod their heads in cautious agreement. "Yeah, we aren't really disagreeing about the fundamental issue which is that the universe is huge and complicated and regulated by laws. We are just arguing over if God is real or not. And if prayer is effective or not."

To a careful observer of human nature it would appear obvious that Marshall's eyes momentarily narrowed in an unconscious expression of the predator drive. But in the dust and smoke of Christ's Kitchen no observer perceived his dagger. "Prayer is the act of putting your intention into the universe. One person might pray to Jesus Christ and another person might pray to a sunflower. Meanwhile another person might claim that prayer is a form of wishing and they reject it because they want to take personal responsibility for achieving their dreams and desires. This is not a question of God or no god. This is a question of whether or not you believe human intent can influence the universe. There is the desperate prayer and the ritual prayer. The placebo effect is real. So does God make the placebo effect 'measurably real' for the scientist, or does the prayer to God make the placebo effect proof of a personal God? And what about the people for whom there is no placebo effect? Is it a function of faith or no faith? Or neither? I think most people believe human intention can influence outcomes, so I don't know that it is fair to use a discussion about whether or not prayer is efficacious as part of a discussion about whether or not God exists. You know? We can all find common ground on the agency behind both prayer and incantation. Everyone is praying to something. If the non-Christian was not allowed to pray can could we say that there is free will? Prayer is more complicated than the existence of a personal God. With or without God prayer can still be real."

People who were once at odds, split along Atheist and Christian lines, were suddenly seeing the issue of prayer from an alternative point of view. "So debating prayer vs magic is not really part of the conversation about God?" a goth-looking girl asked.

"Exactly. Christian prayer and pagan intentionality overlap where things like the placebo effect take root. And God does not deny us our ability to influence the world if we do in fact exercise free will. Simultaneously you don't need to believe in God for the laws of physics to restrict your possible worlds. Never underestimate the power of faith or intention to influence your environment." Marshall started walking through the crowd distributing lit joints.

Alexis followed him, whispering, "That was crazy. You just went in there and derailed that debate."

"You heard words, but to me that sounded a lot more like dogs barking."

"What?"

"Those guys were using words instead of growls to get the attention of the ladies. If you give them both a way to save face and walk away as victors then everybody wins. I am not very threatening and I can modulate my voice to manipulate their feelings. They both realized they would be better off playing nice, because the battle they were having cannot be won. So in the end they both win by admitting they can agree on something. They can agree that prayer is real. Tonight there will be atheist/pagan girls attempting to seduce Christian boys by lighting red candles and reading poetry while simultaneously there will be Christian boys attempting to convert atheist girls by promising them Disney on Christ. As long as they all have fun, right? They will see the signals they want to see."

"You are sorta scary, huh?" Alexis observed.

"Well, the fact is they will be right back at it tomorrow. I was here a few days ago with Jeremiah and it was the same debate with different people. Like Bull Elk crashing their antlers together. It is territorial pissing. I just try to turn them into Bonobo monkeys instead of thirsty snarling dogs." Marshall spun around using finger guns to slay pretend adversaries. "By the way, I have some freeze dried ice cream bars back at our site. If you want something truly amazing. I gotta admit I kinda have the munchies."

"Sure, that sounds good!"

They were almost back to the main trail when they heard a young man yelling, "Hey! Hey come back here!" They turned around to see Tim, Alexis' ex-boyfriend, scrambling barefoot down the trail chasing after them.

"Welcome home," Marshall glowered as he moved to stand in front of Alexis.

"Get the fuck outta the way between me and my girlfriend!" Tim said to Marshall, balling his fists at his sides.

"Hey you stupid fuck," Marshall said, igniting with insanity. "This is my girl 'friend' now so I am telling you to get the fuck back."

"I would hit you, but you are just a fucking kid and I don't want to go to jail for some dumb shit. But I will see to it that you get fucked up before you can get out of here. I fucking promise you that."

"I'm a killa motherfucker! So back the fuck up before I ruin your fucking life! You understand THAT, bitch!?"

Alexis was scared and attempted to make herself tiny behind Marshall. She felt helpless. "You are coming back to Cookies Kitchen with me Alexis! This is bullshit!" Tim stated as he moved toward her.

"You need to shut the fuck up!" Marshall yelled at maximum volume. He was ready to escalate, to go on the offensive. "You think you are strong, but humans are weak as fuck. Yeah, a man might be able to beat a woman. But I promise your ass this: a small dog can still rip your fucking throat out and piss on your grave. So try me motherfucker!" Marshall's knives were behind his back where he could rapidly draw them both and bring them forward in a slash toward the throat; a move he had been practicing. Marshall started to pump himself up. Started shaking his arms and getting twitchy. "What part of back the fuck up do I need to spell out for you?" Marshall finished.

Two naked men appeared on the trail. One of them was well over six feet in height and was in his thirties while the other was about as tall as Marshall and very old.

"Hey guys!" the tall man interjected. "Why the unhappiness? Let's talk about this by the main circle. Where we can work on these vibrations that seem to be going all wrong."

The naked men intimidated Tim. He could not lie to them. He had to look them in the eyes. So he shook his head and left in the direction of his kitchen.

The tall man approached Marshall. "You are an interesting lot. Aren't you?"

Marshall knew the naked men were the de facto security force at the gathering. While there were no leaders and no organization there was a self-forming collective of peacekeepers who all agreed to be naked. The power of a naked male body could disrupt almost any small violent conflict and turn it into people walking away. But the naked men had an issue with Marshall. With the vibes of his campsite.

"It is important to respect the forest and to respect each other. We must dissolve and meld and not strive to create chaos or elevate vanity. Are you vain?"

Marshall considered it. "Unsure. It might be context driven? It is hard to make good measurements with poetic words. I think the universe is poetry and force. And of the two, force makes everything."

"We do not believe in violence," the tall man said reprovingly.

"Violence is rarely an expression of Force," Marshall educated. "Violence is a last resort, a desperation. Force precludes desperation. If you ask me do I think I produce a force then I will answer, 'yes.' But if you ask me do I think I produce a force with an intent to hurt other people or use them as a means to an end then I will answer, 'no.'"

"How do you expect us to interpret force? If you see a small fire in a dry forest do you not go and stomp it out?"

"I get it. No one wants to be stressed out. You don't want to hear bad vibe conversations echoing through the forest. No one wants to hear that. I commend you on taking command of the situation. Justice can be a tough call. Emotions turn people into wild animals. This is a wild place."

"There is a lot of power here. Gathered. For peace."

"Power is terrifying. It is the one thing people shouldn't want."

"What if you can use your power to bring about world peace? What if you could stop injustice?"

"You think people who lack ritualistic behaviors can generate real power? It is ritual that gives birth to potency. I have been to the drum circle and while there is definitely a beat, there is no heart. Flashes of it. But too many pretty birds doing a bower dance. It is competitive not cooperative."

"You don't think we have power?" the naked man asked in a serious tone. "You have not yet seen us gather on the 4th of July for our prayer."

"I know you don't have power," Marshall said with authority. "And that is not a bad thing. Your prayer is beautiful, I am sure. But it is not powerful. If it was powerful the federal forces gathered around us on those hilltops would stomp it out. Like that fire in the dry forest you described. So, really, you don't have power. And it would terrify you if you did."

Marshall turned and looked at Alexis. "Alrighty then. Let's head back to our tents." The naked man moved aside and Marshall led Alexis away.

Tim was a well-known hippie and his family was considered among the oldest in the Rainbow Tribe. Marshall was a member of the family by the technicality that anyone could join just by showing up. But just because you are in a gathering doesn't mean you are part of The Gathering. And some things run deep. Some loyalties are old.

It was a bright day with the sun hanging high in the West. PDC walked toward the drummers. He wanted to play. But he was aware of the storm of noise underlying the beat. Everyone there wanted to be a superstar. It was like a basketball court filled with primadonnas. They are technically excellent, but not playing as a team. Occasionally an exceptional talent would stand out, but eventually the power required to sustain a beat above 30 other drummers would overwhelm the arms. So PDC decided to dance like no one was watching. But even that proved impossible. The music was not alive. It was neither entertainment nor ritual. "This is too sploogy," PDC said aloud.

As he rotated out from the large fire pit a group of several men wearing tie dye and dirty jeans approached him. "Well, well, well. If it isn't Mr. Shiny Shirts," a large man said to him. "Heard you been kidnapping women."

"Fuckin' shoulda lit me a smudgie," PDC said in an fake Australian accent. He pulled a Desert Sage smudge stick out from his right pocket and inserted it into his mouth like a massive cigar. He then lit the tip. Removing it from his mouth he said, "See, this is a method for determining the truth or lack of truth for a given proposition. So I need to get this end smoldering then I need to do the up-down left-right test. If it lights on fire going up and down we have a legit problem. If it lights up going side to side we don't."

"Wh...What?" the hippie man looked at PDC with confused eyes.

"See, watch me," PDC said. He started waving the smudge stick up and down. Ten times. Then side to side ten times. Then up and down ten times. Each time there was more and more smoke. Finally when he was going side to side the end lit on fire. "Hold this for a second, please!" he said passionately as he handed the angry hippie the smudge stick. PDC removed a massive joint from his shirt front pocket. He lit it from the desert sage, which was now burning like a torch. He handed the man the joint and took back the sage. He made a quick downward motion and the flame disappeared leaving only glowing embers on the end. "Here, let us pass this joint for a spell. This does not need to be the end of our journey together, but for this moment let us see the signs in the heavens."

Marshall was feeling pulled toward the large grassy knoll near the performance stage. The influence was not unlike a tractor beam and Alexis almost had to run to keep up him.

Once they made it to the clearing Alexis went directly to her tent. Unbeknownst to Marshall, X was in a chair located on a hill not far away. She was watching over the scene. Marshall moved into a place where he could be seen by almost everyone in the gathering. He began to dance. Like a bird. He was not aware of why he was doing it. A great force was welling up in him, something he had never felt before. It was not his knowledge of how to dance; it was not his electricity instructing his muscles how to move. He believed he could fight it, but instead he surrendered to it. He started crying as he danced. Tears of joy! With his arms outstretched like a bird he swooped lower and lower to the ground. He was simulating the rise and fall of air currents while feeling the very bones of the Earth respond in sympathetic vibration.

X watched as a dark cloud gathered over Marshall. "Holy fucking shit," she said, sitting upright with her mouth agape in disbelief.

Marshall continued to dance. A man in all black wearing a stovepipe hat approached him. He carried a black box covered in ornate mother of pearl inlays. The man wanted to get the box close to Marshall. Marshall, observing himself not directing himself, danced toward the man and said slowly, "You just gotta beliiiiiiiiieve!" The man walked 20 or so feet away and opened the box. At that moment the clouds grew stiller and darker. An area of clouds now covered the upper half of the gathering. Marshall felt a raindrop. He then began yelling toward the clouds with all his might.

The hippies smoked PDC's weed, but they were not willing to forget his trespass against their Rainbow Brother Tim. "We get it, you were able to trade for weed with some people from OUR family. Yeah, it IS good shit. But you are not part of our family, and we intend on proving that to you, with prejudice."

As the man said this someone started yelling from the upper hillside. They turned their attention and saw a massive wall of clouds with Marshall standing in a ray of sunshine directly underneath. Behind him it began to rain. The sunlight streamed into the rain. Marshall turned to face the clouds and continued to scream at them until a triple rainbow formed above him. He then stood with his arms upraised and it started raining on him. People began yelling, "Triple rainbow! Triple Rainbow!" and ran in the direction of Marshall. He lowered his head and starting walking quickly toward the drum circle. PDC was able to disappear into the horde of mesmerized people making their way toward the rainbow. He saw Marshall and made a beeline for him. "I have no idea how you did that, but thanks. I was getting jumped down there. It didn't look good for me. So you saved me this time around."

"Yeah, that Tim guy attacked us on the trail, me and Alexis. Then some of those naked guys broke it up. So I think they are gonna try to pull some shit before we leave, that is for sure."

"You haven't seen Hippie Girl for a minute, huh?"

"No. And I suspect that she might be in a place where she needs to deny knowing us. So she is probably camping somewhere else and I will see her at the end. Here is the thing, there is nothing she has of mine that I need. She can have all my remaining tobacco because outside of here it is just a hassle. I have a scooter in the back of her van that I need to get. I don't think she will let them do anything to that."

Hippie Girl was well liked by the Rainbow Family, especially after she started giving them Marshall's loose-leaf tobacco. Tim, however, was loved by them. He WAS family. PDC was not family. The group of people sent to teach him a lesson got interrupted by a triple rainbow. "Fun is a firecracker and you need to know when to throw it," PDC said to Marshall as they got back to their campsite. "I think we should ditch this place soon. Maybe tomorrow after the hand holding prayer ceremony?"

Marshall agreed. He felt like his mission was complete and now it was time to take the initiative. "So, I have a bit of time on my hands and I would like to do some hiking. Are you off work, or on an extended vacation? Sounds like you own your own place so that is a win."

Without hesitation PDC replied, "Yeah. For sure we should go hiking. But I am going to suggest that it might be tough to ride your scooter on any kind of gravel road and that will exclude a lot of the most interesting places we can go. You might want to consider a motorcycle."

Marshall looked at him. "Okay, I gotta admit I don't know much about motorcycles. I bought a scooter so I wouldn't need to shift."

"Once you learn how to shift you will never, ever, EVAH want to go back to an automatic."

"Really?"

"Really. And here is the deal. We can go to Denver. I know of a bike right now that I think would be perfect for you, and then we can go on an adventure. I will buy it for you. And then if you don't like it I will sell it. Not worried in the slightest."

Marshall rubbed his chin. "You are in an unusual spot, aren't you?"

"I really need to stay away from everything familiar for a while. I need some time to disappear. But I don't know many people, or maybe any people, who can disappear with me without destroying their lives. People make these investments in relationships, in houses and debts and responsibilities. I am not in that position. But, I don't want to deal with going back to my city life right now. I can afford to take a nice long vacation. And you seem to have your shit together. I don't feel like me offering to buy you a bike is a flex on you. You are probably way richer than I am. Big gold chains, amirite?"

Marshall said nothing, but he was not able to stop himself from smiling.

"Riiiiight. 'The Assassins Guild sends its regards and reminds you that daggers deal ten times damage on sneak attacks.' I don't need to know anything other than what you want to tell me. But I will say this: if you are ever in need of assistance let me know and I will be there for you if I can."

Marshall started rapping: "Nowhere to be. No one to call. Totally free. Epic on ball."

PDC laughed with manic glee. "That triple rainbow! Saved my ass, man."

"We aren't out of this gathering yet," Marshall laugh-warned. "I would suggest keeping a lot of honey on you so you have something to use to buy off the buzz. We may need to bribe our way out of here. Like robber bees. I mean, you did come in here and steal the queen bee. I think she might be the most beautiful and talented person in this whole place. She is a miracle worker with those pencils. Like, I am not sure if you even know just how amazing she is. Do you?"

PDC was not aware of the extent of her drawing skills.

He had been attempting to avoid paying attention to Alexis because he feared getting into a relationship in his current state of mind. He looked over at her tent. "I think she is amazing. I don't deny it. Deep down I think she and I have a real chance. That it IS magic," he paused and looked back at Marshall. "But I am going to need to refactor my life before I can be relied upon in a stable relationship. I will destroy her. I will literally be worse for her than that Tim guy, just like, in the opposite direction. Overdosing on excess. But you and me? I feel like we can go on an adventure and it will kick ass. Just a feeling. I suspect our limits mesh. And when I get back I think she will be in a place where we can get to know each other as the people we become, not the people we are currently deconstructing. I really hope Alexis and I get our shot, but I want her to be coming from a place of strength before she starts evaluating suitors."

Alexis was listening in on Marshall and PDC. While she was not able to discern everything they were saying, she could clearly hear PDC when he said that he hoped they might get a shot at a relationship. That he wanted her to make art and settle into her life in his home first.

"I mean, I think there is a chemistry between us. But this is also, like, an arranged marriage. Arranged by God or chance or whatever. So it is a bit like we walked into a room filled with fireworks while passing around a lit joint. Fun and possibly not. I want to be a playful guy. But I also want to be a man. And now I have an opportunity to be strong on behalf of someone else. Someone who has been mistreated, you know. That's the thing. She has the kind of shyness that comes from being told 'no' too many times. But she shouldn't be shy. At all. She is a Goddess. I want to fill her horizon with giant billboards that blink 'YES!' and set her up for becoming the best version of herself." PDC shook his head to avoid tears, "I see this mental image of her and she has completely transformed into this powerhouse of a woman. I mean she has completely transformed. As strong as the power imbalances are right now they will be reversed on me, by her, in the future. Don't ask me how I know, but I can see it. What I do now will determine if that vision becomes reality. But, if it does come true, it implies that the future can literally co-generate the past. So I am leaning into inevitability to grasp for a proof of my conjecture. It is worth it to both of us for me to approach it this way. I think it is what she wants, too. It is like, I see her in this amazing red dress surrounded by winners and she runs up and wraps herself around me in front of all of them. This dream I have. You are in it, by the way."

Marshall looked at PDC. "You see that?"

"Yeah," PDC said. "I had this vision of her in a powerful setting running over to me and embracing me. It was a spontaneous reaction which means it reads like love, real authentic adoration. And so I want to create that with her. I have no idea why or how. It just… is."

Angela agreed to take Alexis back with her to Kansas City, where Alexis would become a resident in PDC's home. Angela told her she would stay with her for a while so she could acclimate to the new city and to living in a big empty house. "Happy Goku really likes it over at that place so it works out for me to stay there for a little while."

"I am excited, but also a little scared," Alexis admitted to Angela. "I have been super poor my whole life and I have never really owned anything nice. I don't want to drag you all down because I don't have enough money to keep up."

Angela laughed. Hard. "You have no idea. Really. We are the poorest of the poor. We just had a little luck, that's all. And now it is your turn. You took the brave approach and grabbed the lightning."

"Really? I got the sense you are all super successful."

"Ha!" Angela roared. "That is a laugh riot! Jeremiah doesn't even have a job. I mean, he has a house that our mutual friend Maxwell helped him buy and now he rents that out for income. Let's just say we are much more into having time over money. I mean, I work at a library shelving books and play bass and sing in a punk rock band. I make minimum wage and clock 25 hours per week. But Kansas City is an inexpensive city so we can afford leisure time. So I bet we are much more alike than we are different. We all come from the alley around here. Stray cats."

Alexis laughed. She had been feeling like an outsider, but now realized that these were just ordinary people like her who also happened to be blessed with extraordinary energy and charisma. "You are all so confident," she said to Angela. "I love it! Thank you! For taking me in and helping me out! Seriously! I've never met people like you!"

######### ERIC #########

Eric was sitting in the hotel bar enjoying a steaming cup of Earl Grey tea. He opened his notebook and began writing:

-

When a person is alive with the joy of creation, when they follow a process without concern for any particular outcome, just a dedication to the agency of action, the person achieves a personal triumph to the extent they experience 'new light' or enlightenment. The brain generates heat when it thinks, watches TV, writes an email, orders fast food. New light is new heat. New light can capture a new way of thinking.

-

He paused in his writing to study a young woman seated at the bar. Her eyes were somewhat close-set. But they were amazing green jewels. And her dark hair framed her face and amplified her eyes. He caught himself staring at her. Thankfully she seemed unaware of his gaze.

Eric was attracted to thin athletic women with skinny ankles. It was a primal desire; it elicited a response in him whether he wanted it to or not. Having seen her, he recalled his former lover Lydia. The girl who gave him everything he never knew he wanted. But he pushed the image out of his mind.

The memory of her had, however, derailed his writing. He

looked at the paper. The words were not materializing. He couldn't get the image of her out of his mind.

The beautiful legs from the bar appeared in front of him. He looked up.

"You are Eric Johnson, aren't you?" a nervous, small voice asked.

At first he was stunned. "Ya... yes I am," he said, regaining his composure a bit. "You are?"

"Oh! My name is Carrie. Carrie K. Bently. But I also go by CK," she replied, extending her hand for a handshake. He reached out and took her much smaller hand in his own. She giggled a little bit. "Sorry. I sometimes laugh when I get nervous."

"That's okay!" Eric replied. "You don't need to be nervous around me."

"It's just that..." she hesitated. "You are so much more experienced than I am, and I don't want to embarrass myself."

"No, no. Don't feel embarrassed," he implored. "I am flattered that you even know me." He gestured for her to join him at his table. "Here, sit. Speak."

She told him how nervous she was to meet him, how it took a real buildup of courage on her part. She explained that she was an aspiring author and had saved money to finance spending the next several years studying the literary arts. "Your lecture was amazing. I am inspired by your story of selling your books off your motorcycle. I guess I didn't know what to expect when it comes to building success. We have a tendency to think it just happens, because we focus on the horizon, but it obviously takes a very personal investment of time. I must admit I had a bit of a fairytale viewpoint up until I heard you describe what you went through. I now realize there is a lot I will need to do if I want to make a name for myself in this profession. So much to both learn and discover."

"Yeah, but seriously at the end of the day a writer must write. So I have adopted the rule that I must write six pages per day. I am not yet perfect at achieving it, but it sets the tempo for what I am aiming to accomplish. Then, after some time of writing by hand, I convert my notebooks into a typed manuscript. A lot of stuff I write is... well, it is the sketch that becomes a painting. So to speak."

"I see," she said. "What are you working on now?"

He wanted to tell her his idea for zeppelins in outer space, but realized in its current form it sounded like a trash concept. "You know, I want to do things that interrupt my ordinary writing habits and speaking at this conference is part of that. Maybe. I am not a science-fiction writer by experience. I mean, I haven't published anything in this genre. It challenges my mind and allows me to experiment with new narratives. But I don't really have a solid concept that I am working on right now. More like I am trying to do a lot of research on just how far science has pushed the boundaries. Some actual science is harder to believe than science fiction."

She listened. She studied him and recognized emotions ranging from enthusiasm to hesitation. He was a man in love with his craft. A wordsmith. He said in an offhand way, "Yeah, I was planning on working through the night since all the lectures are over. I still have a few days up here."

"Can I watch you?" she asked eagerly.

Eric experienced a wide range of emotions all at once. She recognized his hesitation. She egged him on by slightly lowering her head and saying, "You do like to challenge your mind by forcing it to try new narratives, right?"

"Okay. Sure. Why not?" he said, befuddled and possibly hypnotized. *"I have literally no idea how I will write with someone watching me,"* he thought as he led her away.

CHAPTER 13

######## MILTON ########

Milton traveled throughout North Africa studying megalithic constructions. As he went along several people made serious attempts to assassinate him. Unbeknownst to him, the US military was murdering the assassins before they could successfully kill him. The heads of two major international drug cartels were hunting Milton. He had no chance of survival without the intervention of the US.

Project Mind Pixel was considered important enough that officials decided it would be cleaner to destroy and rebuild the Mediterranean and West Asian drug cartel leadership than it would be to notify them to quit trying to murder Milton. So they did exactly that.

It began on an island in the Mediterranean Sea. Claire de Lune was playing across a large number of wireless speakers as a man, woman, and several children sat in an outdoor pavilion situated high above clear blue waters. A gentle breeze stirred wind chimes as an auburn-haired pregnant mother showed her husband the sparkle of her new pink diamond ring; purchased to commemorate the gender of their unborn child. The two oldest boys were play-fighting with wooden swords. A Golden Retriever puppy ran out to join them. And then a loud explosion vaporized the entire property, sending a massive debris field plummeted into the sea below. In front of the destruction a small solar-powered speaker in the shape of a garden gnome cached a fragment of Claire de Lune and was stuck looping just that part. People say if you go there it still plays the song. "A natural gas explosion killed a family of five today on the island of..."

A few days later a car bomb exploded in front of a deli in France. And then a man was stabbed in New Delhi, India. A doctor in LA was found dead of a drug overdose.

A former Iowa football player named Chris Thomas died in a car accident in Cairo, Egypt.

Once the people were eliminated the threats to Milton effectively disappeared.

######## PDC ########

"I am sure Jeremiah will be here any minute now," Marshall said. But he was not sure. He felt something was wrong, but did not want to betray worry.

PDC had been jumped by seven hippies who were surrounding him and threatening to beat him up. It was in the 'A camp' where they found him. "Hey, fag!" one of them yelled at PDC. "Where you goin' city boy?" another asked menacingly.

PDC knew he was being swallowed by a whale. Just when he thought his luck had run out he saw two guys who looked scary rough. Bikers. PDC was wearing his motorcycle armor. "Hey," he yelled out to the bikers. "I have 5 cartons of smokes to share between you and anyone else who can help me wojack these guys."

The hippies looked concerned. The roughneck bikers responded, "Did you say five packs?"

"Five CARTONS if you and yours help me mop the floors with these woman beaters."

The tough guys looked thrilled once they heard the accusation that the hippies were woman beaters. "Is that so?" they asked PDC as they turned to face the hippies.

"Yeah. And they are jumping me so their buddy can go kidnap a chick right now," he said as he opened his backpack and tossed each guy a carton of cigarettes. The top shelf brand.

PDC's new family walked toward the hippies. "If you guys

cause me to smash my cigarettes I am going to hurt you real, real bad."

"Fuck you man!" the lead hippie yelled back at him. "We ain't afraid of alkies."

"Hey, Cletus! Grab Dick and Henry and get over here. I have a carton of smokes for ya'!"

"Oh fuck yeah!" a raspy voice replied with drunken glee. As PDC's men approached it dawned on the hippies they may have bitten off more than they wanted to chew. "We didn't start nothin' with you guys," the leader of the hippies said in exactly the wrong tone.

"That's right," one of the A-campers replied. "And that ain't got shit to do with us accepting the gentleman's consideration, whereby we now gonna execute on this contract!" The man charged at the the leader hippie. The hippie was able to dodge and knocked the obese drunk man onto the grassy ground.

"Aww, looks like we got some real dancers!" a very large man said in a commanding voice as he exited a nearby black 1994 Ford Thunderbird. He was dressed in blue jeans, leather boots and a Big Lez t-shirt. One of the rough men tossed him a couple of packs of cigarettes. "Ahh, Lezlie! Think you can help us dance with these boys?"

The very large man looked at the two pack of cigarettes. "Can have a couple more of these?" he asked.

"Fuck yeah!" the man with the carton walked over to him and handed him three more packs.

The large man looked like like a kid on Christmas morning. He used his key fob to pop open the trunk of his car. "Fuck yeah!" he bellowed as he put all but one of the packs into the open trunk. "My prayer's been answered!" He drunkenly put a cigarette in his mouth and almost lit the filter. He then saw his mistake and put the filter end in his mouth. "Once I light this shit up I am going to light your shit up!" he yelled at the hippies. He lit the cigarette and tossed the lighter into the open trunk. He took out his key fob and pushed a button. The car radio started playing "42ghosts – Spread Eagle Cross The Block

42 ghosts remix." He used his key fob to increase the volume.

"You go ahead and get out of here," the most sober A-camper said as PDC handed him three more cartons of cigarettes. More guys were showing up to help. "We got you," another man said as he walked toward the hippies.

"Thanks you guys!" PDC exclaimed before he turned and started power walking toward X's van.

"Hey," he yelled out to a group of A-campers he met on the road to the van. "I got four cartons of smokes and $200 for you right now if you come with me to stomp a motherfucker."

The men looked at each other. Money was not banned outside the gathering grounds. "Why are you wantin' to stomp him?"

"He had a bunch of guys jump me and now he is trying to kidnap a chick from here."

The men perked up. "Well, that's good enough for us." PDC distributed $200 between the five of them. "I appreciate it. I don't want to seriously injure anyone. I want to make sure no one get seriously hurt, if you know what I mean."

They felt him.

######## MARSHALL ########

"I will fucking kill you, is what I will do," Marshall said to Tim, meaning it. He had already pulled one of his two knives and was holding it behind his back as he walked toward Tim. "Let her go. Now."

The man backed away from Marshall. "Fuck I will."

Happy Goku Potter climbed out of the open door of X's van and emerged behind Tim and Alexis. Being part Great Pyrenees and part American Akita meant he instinctively recognized the difference between family and threat; his prime directive was to eliminate all threats to his family. He started to snarl a low frequency death growl. Tim instinctively let go of Alexis and turned around to face the dog. The dog lowered its head and continued to approach. Tim started backing up toward

Marshall. "Tell your dog to chill the fuck out, man!" he begged. "Tell your dog to chill the fuck out man!" he ordered.

Happy leapt toward Tim and pushed him with his front paws. Marshall then tripped Tim as he fell, causing him to hit the ground head first. Alexis watched in a state of low-grade terror. Happy approached her and licked her hand, urging her to follow him. She saw Marshall had a knife. "Get in and go," Marshall gently commanded. "We will catch up with you later. X knows the deal and has our rental plotted out on a map."

Alexis climbed into the van, realizing only then that she was truly free. Truly on her way to a new life.

X pulled away. "I bet you are glad to be rid of that energy, huh?" she asked.

"Yeah," Alexis said, breaking down into tears. "I have been struggling with that for a while. I am so thankful I met you guys."

"*Fucking PDC*," X thought to herself looking down the gravel road. "*She is cool as fuck though.*"

Regaining her composure, Alexis asked, "How long have you known Marshall?"

"Met him same time you did. Actually I think you might've met him before I did."

Alexis was in shock. "How? How do you know Jeremiah then?"

X laughed out loud. "I have known Jeremiah for a while. Since college. So for ten years."

"How long has Marshall known Jeremiah?"

"About as long as you have."

"That seems impossible. They are, like, on literally the same wavelength. I thought they were brothers maybe?"

"Nope. I didn't really overlap much with them on this trip. But I did see Marshall perform a rain dance. I mean, I saw him do it. I don't use any form of drugs and so I saw with my own sober eyes when he called for rain and then he literally created a rainbow, like called for it and screamed at the sky until it appeared. So there is that. But, overall he seems very gracious and gentlemanly."

Alexis couldn't disagree.

X and Alexis drove over the grass toward the main exit. As they approached their turn they saw PDC marching up the dirt track road followed by several rough men. PDC waived at X and Alexis and the men all waved along with him.

"Holy shit. That is crazy," Alexis said. As she looked down the rows of cars she spotted Tim's hippie friends getting manhandled by several large guys from A camp. She watched slack-jawed as the hippies who had been so mean to her got shoved and thrown to the ground.

"Stoners vs. Alcoholics in a battle for the ages!" X said to Happy Goku.

"Woof!" he replied.

Alexis suddenly felt overwhelmed by exhaustion. "If you don't mind Marshall said he made a playlist for me and I just want to rest my eyes and zone out for a bit. But I will totally not do that if you want me to be alert with you. I just suddenly feel really exhausted."

"No, you are fine. In fact, if you want you can lay on my pad in back. It will be more comfortable, especially on this gravel. We aren't all that far from Steamboat where Marshall got us a place to stay."

Alexis went into the back of the van to lie down. She had a set of headphones and hooked it up to her phone. Happy Goku Potter laid down beside her.

She closed her eyes and the playlist began with the song 'COSMOS' by ENXK.

X watched Happy rest beside Alexis. The dog had not been taking to adoptive families and was staying with X as a last resort. But he really seemed to fall in love with Alexis. She calculated that since Happy was already familiar with PDC's house if she could convince Alexis to take him it would be a really good placement. PDC had given X a lot of cash, but she was not trying to spend it. PDC asked her to use the money for herself, but to also try to make targeted investments. He felt she was a good person who, even though she made very little money, was always contributing to social causes. She did not know how much money PDC inherited, but he told her it was 'a bit' and so he figured it would be wise to stash some of his money with a responsible person. Like Maxwell had done with him and the house. X decided if Alexis was willing to adopt Happy it would be a good use of PDC's money to pay for dog food. *"What a win,"* she thought to herself. *"I will bring it up to her once she is in the house and knows she wants to stay."*

######## The STRANGE TRIBE ########

PDC helped Marshall unload his scooter as Hippie Girl apologized, "I am sorry. I swear I never intended for any of this to happen. And I will repay you for the tobacco I took. They were really mad that I knew you and the tobacco helped chill them out."

"No. I get it. This place is insane. It is like a family, for sure. My family is dysfunctional as fuck. So I am pretty acclimated to being immersed in crazy energy. Like they all say, adapt or die." Hippie Girl could not make eye contact with Marshall. He approached her and touched her face. "Hey, listen to me. Please. You did nothing wrong. You can leave here feeling great. I totally do not care that you took all the rolling tobacco. I wanted you to have a good time," Marshall took out his wallet and handed her cash. "This is for you on the road. It includes enough to get several good meals and a few nights in a hotel. Go take a nice hot shower. You changed my life forever and so I want to thank you for all you have done. Take all the remaining tobacco. If you can trade it for extra stuff definitely do that. You won't need anyone else to help you get home."

Marshall and PDC drove away from the Gathering. Marshall immediately encountered difficulty steering his scooter on the gravel roads. They went slow. After what felt like more than an hour of driving they rattled their way onto a paved state highway. They pulled into the first available gas station. "You are correct. Scooters are shit on gravel. There is no sense of stability at all. But your bike seems to handle it."

"Yeah, well, 'handle it' is a relative expression. It can be controlled more easily. It is still a bike on marbles. I get a lot more gyroscopic force due to the much larger wheels, which you will comprehend once you have been on a real bike. I also have a dedicated rear brake, so I can stop just the rear wheel which is a game changer on gravel. This one doesn't have switchable ABS, but I am not driving it for that type of performance. Yet."

They drove into Steamboat Springs. Marshall had given X a pin to the short-term rental.

"Jesus Fucking Christ," X said as she pulled into the driveway.

"No way this is correct, right?" Alexis responded.

"Well," X said nervously. "Why is it I feel like I am going to get shot if this is the wrong place?"

"*This is exactly the kind of place where people get shot,*" Alexis worried as she looked up at the incredible mansion.

They listened to music and talked about life in Kansas City. PDC and Marshall pulled into the circle driveway.

"*Whoa. This can't be right,*" PDC thought to himself.

Marshall parked directly in front of the majestic main entrance. Removing his helmet he got off his scooter and walked up to the door. He entered a key code into a pad and they watched as the entryway lights turned on. "Okay. Right this way everybody!" he said as he pirouetted through the open door, turning on more lights as he walked into the mansion.

X walked through the doorway with her mouth open. The entryway chandelier looked like it was made from diamonds and was bedazzling. The floors were polished marble. Instinctively everyone removed their shoes. They descended into a living area that consisted of a wall of windows 20 feet high. The kitchen was large enough to run a restaurant.

No one said a word, they just walked around staring. Finally X approached Marshall. "What the fuck is this!?"

"Oh, my family has a business that generates a ton of these points for short-term rental services. So I can get rooms with the credits. This would normally cost, well, a lot of money per night. It is also almost always open because it is so expensive. So I have a hookup. And because we broker so much business we have the top tier ratings and insurance. So technically, this cost us nothing."

"Wow that is so cool!" Alexis said. "Do you stay in places like this a lot?"

"Well, I can use the credits for places like this, but I sorta shot my wad on this one. But since it is the week of the 4th of July we were pretty lucky that we found anything at all. And I am glad we stopped here in Steamboat because there is no way I am riding that scooter through these mountains. So I was gonna see if I could ride with you guys in the van into Denver and hit a motorcycle dealership. Alexis, if you want you can have my scooter. It has a 60 day tag and I think I can call the shop and have them transfer it into your name."

"What? You want to give me your scooter. But its so nice. And brand new."

"Yeah. Don't worry about it. I realize it isn't the tool I need." Marshall got the title out of his bag and signed it over.

"That is so awesome. Thank you. Transportation was my primary concern!"

"Great. We all win," he said, turning to X. "So we have a couple of days in this fabulous place. There are, like, 14 bedrooms in this bad boy so... it is probably haunted, right?"

PDC laughed. "OK. Time for a shower. How many bathrooms?"

"Nine I think," Marshall responded with a hint of uncertainty.

PDC looked at Alexis with a huge smile. "Let the bathing... begin!" With that he darted out of the room and headed up a grand staircase to find a shower.

Alexis found what she wanted. The large whirlpool bathtub in the Master Bathroom. A windowless room with red candles on stands beside the tub. She lit the candles and turned off the lights. As she ran hot water to fill the tub she took a shower and washed off the worst of the accumulated dirt and grime. Brown black water streamed off her body. She rinsed her hair. A mass of tangle.

Once the water was clear she exited the shower and climbed into the massive tub.

Her body relaxed in the hot water. This was by far the biggest bathtub she had ever encountered. X had given her a large bottle of conditioner and she started to apply it to her hair. The work of detangling began in earnest. On and on she went, separating the strands. She started running straight hot water into the bath while opening the drain. The temperature started to rise as hot water replaced warm. Once the bath was full of scalding hot water she allowed herself to float with her legs fully outstretched. Her hair floated away from her head in fine strands of gorgeous black. The ceiling seemed impossibly far away. She sat up and grabbed a razor. The mirrored walls reflected chaotic shadows as the flames of the red candles reacted to the air currents created by her movements.

The water was lukewarm by the time she finished shaving so she opened the drain. She grabbed a hand sprayer and turned it on. She used it to clean the soap scum off the walls of the tub. She did a final rinse of her body then dried herself with the fluffiest towel her skin had ever touched.

She sat against the foot of the bed in the giant Master Bedroom and looked at herself in a large mirror. She was wearing a white robe that was opened to reveal her naked body. She thought of PDC. How he had been willing to defend her even up to the point of fighting. How he was offering her everything and asking for nothing in return. She remembered how handsome he appeared the night they met, when he offered her a cigarette.

She went over to the bed and opened her backpack. She withdrew a sketchpad and looked at her drawings of Jeremiah. She captured his friendliness. His charm.

"He sees something in me," she said while looking at herself in the mirror. "It isn't my body. Well, it isn't only my body."

Her hair was starting to curl as it dried. Her black hair was naturally iridescent and when the sun hit it just right it would reflect a deep green. Not unlike Peacock feathers. She usually felt self-conscious about it because people accused her of dying it to achieve the effect. She would deny it and the accusers would make fun of her. "Just admit it!" Now she was standing in a mansion feeling good about herself. For the first time in her life she was looking at her reflection in a totally clean mirror. There was a knock upon the door.

"Hey, its Marshall. I have something for you."

Alexis walked over to the door and opened it. Marshall handed her three large bags of clothes. "I went into town with Jeremiah and they had an outdoor shopping mall so we grabbed some clothes for you. Anyway, you may not like any of these options, but I hope we chose well! Later!" Marshall turned and walked away.

Men were known to be notoriously bad at selecting clothes for women, but Marshall and Jeremiah picked well. She started to lay the contents of the bags onto the bed. Several t-shirts embroidered with the word 'Obscure' and then several polo-style collared shirts bearing the same mark. The next bag contained three pairs of painters coveralls and three pastel cashmere sweaters. The next bag contained a brown hoodie with a graphic on the front that read 'Impasto Syndrome' over an image of a painter's pallet knife that was covered in a thick glob of black paint that was actually an image of the Milky Way galaxy. There were also several lightweight long sleeve collared shirts.

There were new hiking socks and ankle socks along with three pairs of canvas shoes in red, white and pink colors.

The last bag contained several pairs of pants and new underwear and sports bras. *"Everything is the correct size,"* she said to herself as she looked in the mirror. *"Life in the middle class must be so fucking different than what I have known."* For a moment she felt a flicker of rage, like she had been denied something. But then she got mad at herself for feeling that way. *"Grow the fuck up. You heard what he said. He sees you making something out of your life. He wants you to succeed and he is giving you everything you need. Only a real man does that."*

She put on the brown hoodie and a pair of painters coveralls. She pulled her hair back into a poofy ponytail. She put on a pair of ankle socks and selected the white canvas shoes. She walked over to the toolbox of art supplies. She hesitated. *"I feel ashamed of being an artist,"* she said to herself. *"I feel like I can't put those pencils in my pocket and walk out of this room with my sketchpad without getting mocked. But I need to quit giving a fuck about what other people think. I need to be brave."* She grabbed a couple of pencils, a sharpener, and an eraser. She took one last look at herself in the mirror. "It is time to evolve," she said aloud to her reflection. She walked out of the room and downstairs into the living room. Everyone was looking at food menus trying to figure out what to order.

"Tonight I figured we could just order food and have it delivered. Do you have any food allergies or things you don't like? And also is there anything you would prefer to have?"

Alexis thought for a moment. "I will eat anything. I am down for whatever." She felt bad because she couldn't contribute any money. PDC saw the look in eyes and wanted to say something, but he didn't want to embarrass her in front of everyone.

"Okay. Tell you guys what. I am going to take these into the kitchen and I will surprise you," PDC said as he disappeared into the kitchen. From a top-rated steakhouse he ordered four Porterhouse steaks ranging from medium rare to well done along with four Caesar salads and four loaded baked potatoes. He then ordered two thin crust cheese pizzas from a local boutique pizza shop. He then ordered several quarts of ice cream from a high-end creamery. He was having all of it delivered.

The pizza arrived first. "Excellent," PDC said as he tipped the delivery driver. He carried the pizzas into the living room and sat them on a large glass serving tray that he placed on a large table next to the wall of windows. "OK. Don't fill up on this. One piece only. Two piece maximum! This is the appetizer!" PDC stood guard near the pizza to ensure no one took more than two pieces. "We can have this later, for munchies."

The steak arrived next. PDC arranged plates and silverware on the table. They sat together and enjoyed the feast. "This is so nice after the gathering. Thank you for this food," X said to PDC.

"Yeah, it took all of us to make this possible. It has been a great quest. And the adventure is going to continue," PDC said as the doorbell rang. "Our story isn't over yet!"

The ice cream arrived. "Perfect timing," PDC said to the driver as he tipped him. "OK. We have Rocky Road, Belgian Chocolate, Vanilla, and three different kinds of 'concretes' that include some candy bars and coconut and stuff."

Alexis was the first to attack the ice cream. "This is too good," she said to PDC. "I have never had ice cream like this."

"Yeah, me neither!" PDC said as he gobbled down a large spoonful from one of the cartons. "And I love ice cream. But, yeah, this is by far the best I have ever had. The description was fresh milk and fresh coconut and high end chocolate and all the best stuff. The caviar of ice cream. Not bad, right!?"

Everyone was full and relaxed on the sofa in the living area. PDC disappeared without saying goodnight. Alexis thought it would be nice to sleep beside him, but didn't want to go looking for him as that might seem too weird. Instead she found a room with a queen size bed and fell into a deep sleep.

Alexis woke up early the next morning and found Marshall sitting at the large island in the kitchen. He was brewing coffee. "Okay. So you are the first one up. I don't normally engage in forward behavior, but now I must ask you to do something for me."

Alexis was legitimately concerned. "Is this where you harvest my organs?"

Marshall laughed. "Ha! Well let's pretend you didn't ask that! I want you to ask me that exact question later!"

Alexis was confused. "You need to remember I barely know you. This place is insane. Like, it might be normal to you, but I am legitimately freaked out."

Marshall breathed in deeply. He walked over to Alexis and took her hands in his own. "I know. I get it. I apologize." He had Alexis take his arm and he led her toward the door, saying, "There is a car waiting outside for you. They are going to take you to a spa."

Alexis walked out the door and saw four cars with drivers standing by.

Alexis received a full day of total care. She was fed a nutritious small breakfast, she then went into a skin treatment regimen followed by a hot stone massage. She was placed into a hyperbaric chamber where she listened to binaural beats. She then received a lunch of fresh fruit while receiving a full manicure and pedicure. Marshall had specifically set it up as a series to ensure the group of friends did not run into each other throughout the day.

That night after Marshall arrived from the spa they went to a video arcade restaurant. Alexis was falling in love with Jeremiah. Hard. He was being extremely nice to her and was clearly trying to avoid looking at her as a sex object. But she could tell that he really liked her. She watched him and Marshall play skee-ball. The way Jeremiah laughed was adorable. He hit Marshall's arm when he threw and made him miss. Marshall playfully attacked Jeremiah who then ran behind X to protect himself. The group was having a great time playing games and losing themselves in the moment.

That night she was going to ask Jeremiah to cuddle with her, but he ended up going back into town with Marshall. She spent another night alone.

The next day PDC and Marshall loaded the scooter into X's van. "If you don't mind can we follow you for a while so I can study the dynamics of your bike?" Marshall asked PDC. "I want to see if I can notice the counter steering. The mechanics of that still seems really counter-intuitive to me."

"No problemo. Yeah it will be much more apparent once you experience it first hand," PDC replied. "You literally cannot steer a motorcycle any other way."

As they pulled out of the mansion PDC made sure to keep the slower van in his mirrors. Alexis watched him ride, watched as the large collar of his white dress shirt flapped over his jet black motorcycle armor. "*Tuxedo Rider,*" she thought to herself as she created a snapshot of him in her mind. Watching this man climb and descend mountains on his adventure motorcycle made her feel even more attracted to him.

"I like seeing this in real time," Marshall explained to Alexis. "I can see how you turn left to go right, and vice versa. But I am not sure why it is so. I need to study gyroscopic reaction more. I know a bit about it, but honestly it is a blind spot for me. I am excited to experience it myself, to get the feel for riding a motorcycle. Going from theoretical to tangible knowledge. The wheels end up pointing in the same direction."

######### ERIC #########

The young woman sat in a large overstuffed chair and watched Eric write. She had a notebook and was jotting lines the few times Eric looked over at her.

He started to write:

-

Magic is... or Magic exists, because ancient artifacts unlock the power. There are stones embedded in this planet that are entangled with stones scattered throughout the entire cosmos. They were created at the same time, were part of the same solid piece. Now several are embedded in the Earth. Many, many strange crystals reside within or near the Earth and these allow practitioners of Magic to perform feats of wonder.

Spells. Incantations. There are events occurring in certain

frequency domains that remain invisible to those who can neither receive nor transmit the underlying signals. To borrow a phrase: 'Muggles cannot see magical creatures.' It is NOT that non-magic humans cannot see them. The physical hardware of the human body is much (much!) more advanced than the continuums of Magic and Science combined. It is that the non-magical consciousness is never shown magic because the Object Request Broker is not serving that data to the non-magical consciousness. Whereas the magician is aware of magic and is 'allowed' to perform it by virtue of having been granted 'the vision' by a sort of 'lottery' process that at least seems to be partially determined by genetics.

Non-magicians, however, not being born part of the magical universe, none-the-less have been working to comprehend and master the Space-Time Continuum and related physics. Magic is a system of laws. The science seeks to describe all the PREDICABLE and REPRODUCIBLE transmutations of matter and energy. The outcome does not care if it is a magician or a scientist who accesses the laws and transmutes the matter. Magicians had a massive head start and have been trained in the methods of magical incantation for thousands of years. In contrast, the mysteries of quantum oscillators and information-theoretic structural modeling have only been around for a few minutes.

Identifying the quantum information properties of the crystals and organic molecules that unlock magical outcomes allows the physicist to 'de-specialize' the mechanisms that produce 'magical force.' Take, for example, the use of a magical incantation and mental focus to perform levitation of a foreign, or remote, object. The magician channels energy between the Earth System and the Object. This is equivalent to the production of the Zero Point State by means of overwriting the frequency information at the boundary of the levitated object. The non-magical Zero Point energy can be observed via 'decoupling' at the top of the gravitational parabola; like when a ball is thrown into the air, at the top of its flight, between rising and falling, it has no acceleration due to gravity and experiences true weightlessness. You may have felt this before if you have ever driven a car fast enough over a hill to jump it a bit. As the car falls you experience weightlessness. Sometimes it is a feeling in your gut. The ball becomes weightless because you added enough frequency to lift it to a new height. The magician modifies the energy of a preexisting signal. Emanating out of the Earth are tons of frequencies. We are the fish who doesn't see the water; we are the humans who, having been born inside the frequency space, don't recognize they are vibrating. The magician adds or subtracts from those preexisting frequencies by channeling thought and sound into the real world. And the ball or feather or whatever notices its frequency is changing because it is experiencing the zero field while it levitates.

The magical world accepts the degree to which it relies on the non-magical world for its genetic survival. But the magical world is more concerned about the 'maintenance of traditions' than researching the origins of power. Magic is considered natural rather than mechanical.

The magical community teaches children how to perform spells, not how to comprehend the basis from which spells follow as a logical result. They are born into a world that is special and which must remain hidden. But, what cannot be hidden are the physical laws from which magical power is derived. Eventually physics must catch up with magic.

The dangers of that possibility were taken seriously by early magic users. Some of the oldest devices in the magical world were designed to detect threats. The devices should be sending out warnings indicating the existence of an imminent existential risk. But they weren't advanced enough to penetrate recently developed barriers.

There was a current of electricity running through tiny crystals arranged in a sequence. Various rings on his fingers were emitting frequencies. Backups. He was emitting a type of noise that could cancel magic. He avoided locations where portals into the magical world were rumored to exist. He made no eye contact with anyone and was continuously running biofeedback software that analyzed his state of mind. He was using it to learn to control breathing, become a master of his emotional state. He was training himself to be less anxious.

He was also experimenting with magical recipes and incantations that he discovered in his late mother's trunk. There were numerous blank journals and books. He was certain that he could see words in his peripheral vision, but when he would look directly they would disappear. One journal, though, was written in plain ink.

It was notes in herbology describing how plants emit frequencies due to the presence of unique molecules. These molecules are definite shapes and when these shapes are heated, cooled, and chanted over the combination of electromagnetic and phonon energy resonating in the plant molecules begin to interact with other structures present in the Earth and this produces magical results. Shapes, combinations, chanting, amplifications. Magic is the study of the mechanics of harmonics.

For many years the young man and his mother studied electricity. Studied the physical sciences and especially the skin effect in electric transmission. Now he was terrified. He knew his mother was a witch. When he touched the crystals he found in a false chamber in the bottom of the trunk he felt her presence. But... it was like something was grounding into him.

He vomited and passed out.

--->STONES;CRYSTALS;METALS<---

He dreamed. He was shown how to make the battery-powered crystal rings. How to make pendants. They made him invisible to the magical devices attempting to detect threats. His physical body knew the risks.

"We produce a natural field around us, this is what magic interacts with. The cancellation of that field requires you to place something between the spell-caster and yourself. A new kind of field. A magic shield. It begins with detection.

By adding the correct frequencies you remain invisible to magic. Magical threat assessment tools won't see you. But a magician... that is a different story. So make sure you live near a University and attend classes. Remember, magic must be deflected. You must become immune to attacks. It has to do with the surface, the skin effect. You must place a field between yourself and the field being generated by the magician. That field cancels the effect of the spell. Like noise-canceling headphones, but for magic."

The new rings and pendants from his mothers trunk allowed him to see objects that were normally not passed from his visual cortex into his consciousness; he was never shown magical 'objects.' He now saw secret entrances, buildings, creatures. He trained to avoid eye contact. He never looked directly at any magical objects.

He could see the witches and wizards in their archaic garb. They looked dangerous. Fortunately for him they rarely looked around and almost never made eye contact. They did not want to invite the possibility of an interaction.

He built a garage that worked as a 'faraday cage' for magic. He created a barrier that shielded him from magical snooping. It was an EXPENSIVE thing to accomplish. The cage allowed him to practice magic and test his anti-magic devices. Due to the fact he is training himself he proceeds slowly, as magic is very dangerous. His mothers blank journals slowly fill in as he gains more insight.

"Artifacts control Reality. At some boundary the 'recoverable knowledge' of what it took to create an artifact is LOST if the artifact is destroyed. Yet, 'knowledge' is conserved in artifacts and they resonate with human consciousness to communicate truth to us. If history is fractal the entire story can be recovered from a fragment."

He has 'inherited' his mother's ability to 'feel' the artifacts. But he can only experience the feelings when he is in his magic cage. He would be discovered if he took the rings off outside the box.

######## The STRANGE TRIBE ########

Marshall arranged a rental outside Denver with a commanding view over the city. Built into the side of a mountain, the trio stood together on a deck overlooking the metropolitan area. The house was modern, with an indoor-outdoor pool and 5 hole mini-golf course. PDC was about 15 minutes behind them.

"This is a quorum of the Strange Tribe," Marshall said as they looked out over the city. "This has been an amazing journey, an adventure involving good friends and new faces. Now good friends will depart with new faces. But, we do have this one last night together. What should we do for dinner? My treat. A feast before the next chapter in our story!"

X laughed. Trying to sound like a 'noble' person from the Shakespearean era, she replied, "Truly you speak as a guide and yet I see you as a Stranger. Neither the Marionette nor the Master. Not the audience, either. Some 'other' thing. Restless and calm and fuzzy; razor blade tickles. But I must admit, I cannot but kneel before the exquisite maximum. I never dreamed I would be staying in places like this. Empress of the Universe and shit," she said, making a curtsy motion.

"The only way you get to do it is if you are willing to let go of the steering wheel. You end up where the whims of the unknown whisk you. For us, at this moment in time, we have this synergy which is making possible worlds collapse into real worlds. This house is for rent all the time. But we happened to be in the right place at the right time and, boom, we ended up staying here. Does it exist when we aren't here? We say it must exist when we aren't here. So the future exists before it happens. And us staying here already happened, we just end up here to prove it to ourselves. This is a philosophy of living and I won't say it is extensible to other players in the game of life. It just so happens that when you really need it maybe it emerges. But if you never need it then it will never even be possible. For us, we are traveling on the path of the unlikely.

For some reason I sense an increasing improbability that feels unsustainable. So when we split up into two different groups the universe will probably be saved, at least for a little while."

PDC pulled up and parked his motorcycle. He entered the front door and took off his boots. He walked toward the back. He exited onto the patio. "Yo! Another total banger that rocks like a cliff!"

Alexis felt intoxicated. She could sense X was similarly influenced and felt dislocated by the exquisite setting. X said, "How is it that this ride keeps getting stranger? I am tripping balls off the places we are staying. I feel wasted on lux."

Marshall laughed. "Yeah, you did say that you don't do drugs of any type, right? Well, a firstness is a drug until itself."

"What is a firstness?" Alexis asked.

"Charles Sanders Peirce! You know that!?" PDC exclaimed. "Well I look forward to hearing about what you know about that! I will be back, gotta go to the bathroom."

Marshall returned to Alexis, "A 'firstness' is the first time you encounter something in your life. So the first time you hydroplane a car. The first time you taste a god-tier red wine. The first time you take acid. For an event of profound magnitude the first time it occurs is called the 'Firstness.' Since you have no previous experience your mind must make an account of what is happening; it must invent an explanation out of thin air. The mental gymnastics involved with interpreting a thing for the first time can resemble intoxication. A philosopher named Charles Sanders Peirce talks about it in much deeper detail. But before we go there," Marshall paused and looked out over the city. He said, "Alexis, on an related note, when you get good, when you take it all the way there, you are going to need to know how to handle things like this house. You are going to need to know how to handle money and how to act around people who are super rich. You are also going to need to learn how to delegate, how to be comfortable being a boss. How to rule your world."

"What?" Alexis replied, shaking her head in disbelief.

Without looking at Alexis, Marshall continued, "When you get good people are going to want to buy your art. People who live in places like this. And other people will want to sell your work on your behalf. You are going to be attacked by people who want to represent you, who want to bank off of you. When that starts happening, I want you to tell them that you are already represented," Marshall turned and looked at her. "Trust me. I am looking out for your interests as an artist. In fact, as demand for your work grows, I want you to tell interested parties that your price has a minimum of $1000 and goes up from there. Don't sell for less. Trade is fine, for other artists whose work you want to own, whose work you want to be influenced by. Trade with other artists. Get a list of their contacts if they offer it to you, but never ask for any contacts. Now, I am not saying you are going to be hounded starting tomorrow. But when it happens I want to assist you. I don't want to tell you more or tell you who might be involved, I just want you to know that when the thirsty ones come prowling around you don't need to think about them for one second. You just know that you have someone in the background that is going to help you. Help you deal with the people who own stuff like this house."

Alexis was unsure. She replied skeptically, "Oh, I don't know..."

Marshall was stern in his rebuke, interrupting her. "Hey! This is the moment that will define your life forever. Either embrace your destiny or disappear. This house is nothing compared to your future, which is bright like a supernova. But if you fail to accept all the responsibility that comes with success you will not be able to ascend and your art will die. Just know that when you start having people approach you asking to represent you I want you to immediately think about me. Think about my face, okay? Draw a picture of my face looking at you like this," Marshall attempted to make his most serious face. "I want to be your over 9000 Samoan attorney. Okay? Don't sign ANYTHING. Even if they start dangling money. I will make sure you have a way to reach me and I want to stay in touch, okay? Strange Tribe forever!"

Alexis looked at him and felt certain she must be experiencing a firstness.

PDC returned to the deck. He sensed the air was a little tense, but suddenly Alexis spun and said in a funky voice, "Marshall is offering us dinner and would like us to tell him our preferences. I must admit, a medium rare steak would suit me just fine. I lean carnivore."

X, a performer at heart and by trade, signed up for the Strange Tribe vibe and offered, "Looks like meat is back on the menu, boys!"

That night an enduring feast occured. Similar to PDC, Marshall arranged a catering company to provide a three-hour dinner. Servers carried trays to the four of them as they hung out on the deck.

"To Alexis!" Marshall toasted. "May her art grace the walls of the all the halls of power!"

Everyone clinked their glasses.

At the end of the evening the 'Deluxurious Dessert Company' van pulled up the estate. Two women and two men dressed in professional white clothing began loading dessert into the building. One after another delicious treats were delivered to the four friends. It ended with a hot slice of apple pie covered with a dollop of vanilla ice cream.

Alexis looked at Marshall. *"I can't become it if I can't see myself becoming it,"* she thought. *"Of course this house was my future. Because I have already done it."*

######## ERIC ########

Her eyes. When she smiled at him it hit like lightning. "It's appropriate because young women are supposed to be trained by older men. Older men show us what really turns them on. And then we get to function as the objects of desire." She straddled him on the hotel chair.

He was overwhelmed. Stupefied.

"I am a giver," she whispered in his ear while running her fingers through his hair. "I like to give pleasure. It is okay if you look at me and see my innocence and find it a source of inspiration. My innocence is a gift I exchange to become your apprentice. I know that you are excited by the idea I am bartering with my body, asking to exchange it for your teachings. I can feel it. It never tells lies."

He held her waist and began to gently squeeze her. He ran his fingers along her spine as he caressed her back. He realized he was holding his breath.

"I would be honored if you would show me how a man like you treats a girl like me," she said breathlessly in his ear while grinding harder against him. "I want to feel you when you fill me up."

It accelerated so quickly. Of course he found her attractive. How could any straight male not find her attractive? She was in love with his work? She was unbuttoning his shirt.

"I think things will make a lot more sense once I put your cock in my mouth," she said.

He was incapable of manufacturing a disagreement.

"Please be my teacher," she begged while looking directly into his eyes. She was on her knees in his hotel room, unzipping his pants. His erect penis, freed from his pants, was now being swallowed by a beautiful brunette twenty year old admirer.

"Super Fan."

######## The STRANGE TRIBE ########

The rental property had an indoor movie theater so after dinner they went to see a show. The terrace was set with couches that would allow pairs of people to sit alongside each other. The couches folded out so people could almost lie down. Marshall and X grabbed one together which meant that PDC and Alexis were paired.

X picked the movie 'La Planete Sauvage.' It was a French language film, but had English subtitles. Alexis looked at Jeremiah's face as it was illuminated by the screen. Using his mastered ability to observe people using peripheral vision he detected she was contemplating lifting the armrest barrier that separated them. Before she could make a decision he raised the armrest and waived her toward him.

She moved close to him and he put his right arm around her. She curled up next to him and closed her eyes. She wasn't interested in the movie. She was interested in him, his energy. He used all his masculine powers to try to envelope her in an aura of safety. He wanted Alexis to feel relaxed. Captured between the crook of his right arm and his body she immediately entered a deep dreamless sleep. He held her for the duration of the film. He spent a lot of time looking at her and wishing for her to feel good.

The movie concluded and Alexis woke up. "Oh, man, I fell asleep. I had no idea I was that tired."

"Yeah, well, we had a lot of calories and the seat warmers really make it easy to relax," PDC said with a smile. "Sleep is a superpower. Truly. Get it while you can."

X got up and informed the room that she was going to bed. Marshall concurred and they both vanished. It was now PDC and Alexis alone in the theater.

"I guess it is probably time to get on the shuteye train," PDC stated to the sleepy woman he was holding in his arms.

"Will you spend the night with me?" Alexis asked with a nervous voice. "I know you don't want to rush into anything. I don't want to put up any barriers. I am just really lonely and still kinda reeling from how fast all of this is moving. And I know I won't see you again for a while and so I just want to know if I can feel comfortable with you. Right now I feel really great being near you."

Without hesitation PDC responded, "Yeah. We should sleep next to each other. To see how it feels. I will admit, I am curious. Full disclosure: I really like you and I don't want to do anything to create overly complex feelings. But, that being said, we are going to be spending some time apart starting tomorrow. So I don't think it will hurt us to spend one night together. We are already this close to each other."

They went off and found a bedroom. She entered the bathroom and took a shower and shaved her body. She brushed her teeth and put her hair into a ponytail. PDC went into another bathroom and showered. He shaved. He looked at himself in the mirror. "Should I be doing this?" he asked the reflection. He wasn't sure.

He walked into the bedroom and found Alexis under the covers lying on her back and staring at the ceiling. He was dressed in a pair of boxer shorts and a T-Shirt. The room was dark with the exception of a pale glow radiating from beneath the bathroom door. He slid into the bed next to her and laid on his back.

Alexis was a ball of nerves. She was unsure of what to say or how to approach the situation. Before she could find her voice PDC rolled onto his side and looked at her. "It has been a crazy adventure so far," he said as she rolled onto her side to face him. "I don't know where we are going to end up, but I feel like things are moving in the right direction. My house isn't nearly this nice so I hope you aren't disappointed. I mean, it isn't trashed or anything. It is a nice house. But these mansions are really setting a high bar in terms of expectations so I don't want you to be disappointed. I have arranged to have all the bills paid for the conceivable future so you won't need to worry about anything. I also want to give you some money so that you have some freedom to buy the things you want and need. I want you to find your groove and be successful. For you. For me. For you though."

She stared at him with wordless eyes.

"We want to play, right!" he said in excited undertones. "All one needs to do in life is play. But without danger there is no thrill. So we get closer and closer to the edge of uncertainty and together, as a team, we can merge danger and play. And I want you to know that I am a sensual artist. I love the sensual arts. But part of sensuality is healing and a big part of healing is sharing sympathetic vibrations. And so I want to be your playmate and we can go on adventures together. But your next quest is to perfect yourself as an Artist. You are going to kick so much ass at that! And you are so beautiful. Not just physically attractive, but talented. You are talented and beautiful and gorgeous. And I want to be your ally and someone you can trust."

His intent was to be fully convincing, to be utterly trusted. He was looking right at her with adoration and sincerity writ large on his face. She closed her eyes. No one had ever described her using such language; no one had ever demonstrated the kind of loyalty Jeremiah was showing her. She had been told by her father that she was 'hot' and 'fuckable' and the hippies told her she was 'toasty-oates' and such, but she had never before been spoken to by a love poet. "Who are you? Why are you doing this?" she asked Jeremiah while looking down at the bed.

"You are not a kid on a playground," PDC said in a soft voice as he reached out to touch her face. "You are not playing at life. You are trying to survive. But you have been chosen for a different path now. I don't know why. Look, here is the thing. You should be super stressed out. There is no way that you are not going to experience an emotional eruption from all the chaos meeting me has injected into your life. Maybe you already have? I don't know. But the fact is, you are being dislocated. Your entire life is insane. To any practical person the choices you have been making would appear crazy. I get it, my life is crazy too. I don't normally go around living in mansions and moonlighting as a Greek God. I am a philosopher and a robber bee. I have never been in a place like this. I mean, I am in the position to offer you, like, a modest middle class housing solution. But the extremes of our current experience make me suspect we are going to remember each other forever. For as long as I live, I will know you. I will always remember how we met. We will remember this night as the real beginning of our partnership. I know some day you are going to rescue me. I really see it."

She was looking at PDC as he said these things and she asked him, "Can I hug you?"

PDC reached out to hold her. Once she was in his embrace she began sobbing. "I am sorry," she said as she cried.

"You don't need to be," he assured her.

"No. I am not sure why I feel like this," she sobbed.

"Feel safe," PDC counseled. "Cry to me," he encouraged as he hugged her more strongly. He wrapped his legs around her in an attempt to entwine himself with her. He used all his strength to tense his body to surround her with his life force. He tried to heat her blood with his intent. She cried and cried some more. She rolled onto her stomach and he gently massaged her body using his fingertips. He whispered dream ideas to her as she fell asleep against her will.

######## MAXWELL ########

Maxwell was pacing in the desert. The Sun was low in the West. He took out his action camera and began recording. "I don't want to let go of the good to sustain a vainglorious pursuit of the perfect. There are others out in the world who deserve to see a flower flowering. I did not make this flower. I did not create these petals. I merely witnessed it and gathered some of its seeds."

He looked at the horizon and said, "There was a time in my life when I thought I understood certain fundamental limitations; limitations that are universal in scope. The application of intellect to real world problems produces real-valued 'sets of solutions.' The limits of the cognizable are its units of expression. There was a time when I thought information was the key to understanding; awareness as a duration of elapsed time. 'Duration' in the body is experienced as homeostasis and transformative biology. On top of the biological asset is a conscious observer playing the Game of Life. Our cells do whatever it takes so that the soul might get another moment of playthrough. But what an experience! What a lottery ticket!"

Maxwell looked up at the sky. He then looked at the horizon and said, "Excluding 2,3,5 the prime numbers can be divided into 24 classes. Additionally, there are 9 classes of twin primes. There are 24 Conway nontrivial numbers that form the root of these 24 classes. The Conway nontrivial numbers are built from these primitives via the equation p+(90*n). With 24 primitives we build the nontrivial number universe."

Maxwell spun around and continued, "We can then see these assembled into their respective categories of Prime or Composite. The question becomes one of determining if there is an order of assembly within the nontrivial composite universe that allows us to segregate the primes and composites using a simple method. Not necessarily an efficient method, but simple."

"Now imagine a number line. Let us claim that for prime numbers we measure an amplitude of 0 and for semiprimes we measure an amplitude of 1. All other points have amplitudes that determine their Big Omega score. We have two views simultaneously."

"First we have the 'above' view, that is to say we can look at the line without amplitude and we see a series that contains 0 and 1. This is the prime characteristic function for A201804. We see a quasi-random series of 0 and 1, where 1 is composite and 0 is prime. If we rotate our view from above the x axis to looking at it from its side we can now measure amplitude along x."

"The twin prime sieve. I need to publish what I have. I will send it out and see what happens."

"And then keep going. Maybe."

"If a 'regular' function produces the composites is it true to say the 0 list is quasi-random? Or, can quasi-random exist outside a complement that is utterly 'simple.' The issue is that the regularity of the amplitude is not scored by my equations."

Maxwell collapsed into the sand.

Thinking of a scene from an old movie Maxwell said to the camera, "Help me N.J.A. Sloane-Kenobi. You are my only hope."

CHAPTER 14

Conway's Game of Primes: Yet Another Twin Prime Sieve

AUTHOR: Otto Dydakt
Correspondence: superobserver@gmail.com

ABSTRACT

John Conway's conjecture that composite numbers exist in one of two states, trivial or nontrivial, evidently requires the existence of two types of prime number operator, trivial and nontrivial. One approach to this conjecture is to observe that the "Conway Nontrivial Numbers" exist as 24 classes of digital root and last digit preserving sequences. Conway's "Game of Primes" is then a sieving platform built for manipulating these classes. It is shown that Sloane's A142317 (1/24th of the Conway Nontrivial Primes) is equivalent to A201804 and that the complement to A201804 is rendered by 12 quadratic sequences. Following this, the twin primes are shown as equivalent to 9 OEIS sequences which are the union sets of pairs of Conway Nontrivial Prime Number sequences. Using these insights the twin prime conjecture is proved true for the union set of A201804 and A201816 (see: A224854) and expanded to cover any pair of the 24 Conway Nontrivial Prime Sequences.

KEYWORDS: Sieve Theory, Twin Primes, Elementary Number Theory, A038510, A201804, A201816, A224854, A224855, A224856, A224857, A224859, A224860, A224862, A224864, A224865,
Note: for **tl:dr read only the bold values**

CONTENTS
0. PRIMEGAME 2.0
1. Introduction

2. What is the Conway Universe?
3. What are number particle dynamics?
4. What are Conway Nontrivial Composites?
5. Playing the Game of Primes
6. Digital Root and Last Digit Preserving Sequences
7. The Molecular Sieve
8. The Twin Prime Sieve
9. Results
10. Conclusion

0 PRIMEGAME 2.0: Twin Prime Sieve

The chibi-styled algorithm:
Address takes all values A001477, the non-negative integers 0,1,2,3…. .
x takes all values of A000027, the positive counting numbers 1,2,3,4…. .
WHERE address-y=0=Composite(False)
ELSE
WHERE address-y>0
WHERE address-y % p !=0 for all 48 tests:
THEN number is a twin prime in A224854

To produce the members of A224854 feed the values of A001477 (address) and A000027 (x) into the sieve until y>=address:
[address - (y   )] % [p   ] != 0 = Prime (True)
[address - 90x^2 - 120x + 34] % 7+(90*(x-1))] != 0
[address - 90x^2 - 94x + 10] % 7+(90*(x-1)) != 0
[address - 90x^2 - 86x + 6] % 11+(90*(x-1)) != 0
[address - 90x^2 - 78x - 1] % 11+(90*(x-1)) != 0
[address - 90x^2 - 76x - 1] % 13+(90*(x-1)) != 0
[address - 90x^2 - 90x + 11] % 13+(90*(x-1)) != 0
[address - 90x^2 - 120x + 38] % 17+(90*(x-1)) != 0
[address - 90x^2 - 104x + 25] % 17+(90*(x-1)) != 0
[address - 90x^2 - 132x + 48] % 19+(90*(x-1)) != 0
[address - 90x^2 - 94x + 18] % 19+(90*(x-1)) != 0
[address - 90x^2 - 90x + 17] % 23+(90*(x-1)) != 0
[address - 90x^2 - 86x + 14] % 23+(90*(x-1)) != 0
[address - 90x^2 - 132x + 48] % 29+(90*(x-1)) != 0
[address - 90x^2 - 104x + 29] % 29+(90*(x-1)) != 0
[address - 90x^2 - 108x + 32] % 31+(90*(x-1)) != 0

[address - 90x^2 - 76x + 11] % 31+(90*(x-1)) != 0
[address - 90x^2 - 94x + 24] % 37+(90*(x-1)) != 0
[address - 90x^2 - 60x + 4] % 37+(90*(x-1)) != 0
[address - 90x^2 - 108x + 32] % 41+(90*(x-1)) != 0
[address - 90x^2 - 86x + 20] % 41+(90*(x-1)) != 0
[address - 90x^2 - 120x + 38] % 43+(90*(x-1)) != 0
[address - 90x^2 - 76x + 15] % 43+(90*(x-1)) != 0
[address - 90x^2 - 60x   + 8] % 47+(90*(x-1)) != 0
[address - 90x^2 - 104x + 29] % 47+(90*(x-1)) != 0
[address - 90x^2 - 72x + 14] % 49+(90*(x-1)) != 0
[address - 90x^2 - 94x + 24] % 49+(90*(x-1)) != 0
[address - 90x^2 - 120x + 34] % 53+(90*(x-1)) != 0
[address - 90x^2 - 86x + 20] % 53+(90*(x-1)) != 0
[address - 90x^2 - 72x + 14] % 59+(90*(x-1)) != 0
[address - 90x^2 - 104x + 25] % 59+(90*(x-1)) != 0
[address - 90x^2 - 48x + 6] % 61+(90*(x-1)) != 0
[address - 90x^2 - 76x + 15] % 61+(90*(x-1)) != 0
[address - 90x^2 - 90x + 17] % 67+(90*(x-1)) != 0
[address - 90x^2 - 94x + 18] % 67+(90*(x-1)) != 0
[address - 90x^2 - 48x + 6] % 71+(90*(x-1)) != 0
[address - 90x^2 - 86x + 14] % 71+(90*(x-1)) != 0
[address - 90x^2 - 60x + 8] % 73+(90*(x-1)) != 0
[address - 90x^2 - 76x + 11] % 73+(90*(x-1)) != 0
[address - 90x^2 - 90x + 11] % 77+(90*(x-1)) != 0
[address - 90x^2 - 14x + 0] % 77+(90*(x-1)) != 0
[address - 90x^2 - 12x + 0] % 79+(90*(x-1)) != 0
[address - 90x^2 - 94x + 10] % 79+(90*(x-1)) != 0
[address - 90x^2 - 60x + 4] % 83+(90*(x-1)) != 0
[address - 90x^2 - 86x + 6] % 83+(90*(x-1)) != 0
[address - 90x^2 - 12x + 0] % 89+(90*(x-1)) != 0
[address - 90x^2 - 14x + 0] % 89+(90*(x-1)) != 0
[address - 90x^2 - 76x -1] % 91+(90*(x-1)) != 0
[address - 90x^2 - 78x - 1] % 91+(90*(x-1)) != 0

To recover the base10 value: address*90+(11,13)

The value of x increments +1 and the number of twin primes for the
first 26 values of x for A224854 are
20, 54, 103, 167, 233, 325, 422, 522, 641, 756, 898, 1036, 1191,
1364, 1544, 1724, 1896, 2077, 2274, 2483, 2715, 2933, 3178, 3419,
3658, 3897.

The average rate of change for the growth in the twin primes for the first 100 values of x is 409.6 while the average rate of change for the span of terms between 100 and 200 is 982.64. Over further steps **the ratio approaches 1** which implies divergence.

1 to 100 average rate of change = 409.61 per step.
100 to 200 average rate of change = 982.64
200 to 300 average rate of change = 1471.15
300 to 400 average rate of change = 1932.96
400 to 500 average rate of change = 2370.97
500 to 600 average rate of change = 2794.23
600 to 700 average rate of change = 3196.37
700 to 800 average rate of change = 3602.95
800 to 900 average rate of change = 3996.97
900 to 1000 average rate of change = 4374.57
at x=1000 the number 8098920101 is the base-10 limit

Proof of infinity: Absurdity: Assume that every value of A000027 beyond some value k must be evenly divisible by a multiple of a Conway Nontrivial Number as rendered by the solutions above. [For the complete proof, read on.]

1 Introduction

Any departure from the norms of prime number analysis must be approached with great skepticism. New sieve methods or arithmetic progressions of primes seem to emerge almost daily. [see: DHJ Polymath, https://arxiv.org/pdf/1407.4897.pdf] Worse, even when some new algorithm emerges from the darkness of possibility it is usually neither faster nor more efficient than currently existing alternatives. [see: Dudley, U. (1983). Formulas for Primes. Mathematics Magazine, 56(1), 17–22. https://doi.org/10.1080/0025570X.1983.11977009]

The Online Encyclopedia of Integer Sequences (OEIS) contains many important entries. One of these suggests partitioning the composites into two separate classes:

A038510   Composite numbers with smallest prime factor >= 7.
"John [Conway] recommends the more refined partition [of the positive numbers]: 1, prime, trivially composite, or nontrivially

composite. Here, a composite number is trivially composite if it is divisible by 2, 3, or 5." See link to (van der Poorten, Thomsen, and Wiebe; 2006) pp. 73-74. - Daniel Forgues, Jan 30 2015, Feb 04 2015

This property of numbers implies the existence of a "Conway Number Universe." It is proposed that this number universe is regulated by a "standard model of number-particle physics."

2 What is the Conway Universe?

Hint: The counting numbers (plus zero).

The Conway Number Universe is just the ordinary counting numbers distributed onto a "gameboard" (aka, a ConBoard). What are some of the rules or framework(s) for constructing the Conway Number Universe?

1) **"Conway numbers" are the ordinary counting numbers considered as objects** or particles.

What does it mean that a Conway Number is an object or a particle?

a. 'Pauli Exclusion' and an 'Impossibility Operator' applies. For example, all number objects are individuals and no two distinct numbers can occupy the same address on a ConBoard; it is impossible for two unique number objects to possess the same order and number of digits.

b. **Number objects have associated measureables/observables and states**. These include certain "tangible measurables" (such as a last and leading digit) and certain properties or states (such as "primeness" or "evenness").

c. Number objects have "degrees of certainty or uncertainty" associated with their states. For example, as regards the probability that a number particle will evaluate to prime any uncertainty regarding the state disappears once all possible factors are tested. Or, the probability a number is prime converges to 1 (certainty) as we eliminate possible factors via testing/sieving.

2) **All Conway Numbers can be represented as a sequence of digits** whose possible values are (0,1,2,3,4,5,6,7,8,9). For our purposes the construction of the Conway Universe and Gameboard requires the incorporation of the following two OEIS sequences:

A001477: The nonnegative integers. *#This sequence is included due to needing a zero indexed list to enumerate the Conway Universe.*

A000027:The positive integers. Also called the natural numbers, the whole numbers or the counting numbers, but these terms are ambiguous.

3) **All Conway Numbers must have an observable associated with a digital root** and it must take one of nine possible values: (1,2,3,4,5,6,7,8,9). The Conway Universe (our framework for considering the ordinary counting numbers) initially consists of 9 distinct partitions. Sloane enumerates these partitions:

a. A010888 Digital root of n (repeatedly add digits of n until a single digit is reached): [0,] 1, 2, 3, 4, 5, 6, 7, 8, 9, 1, 2, 3, 4, 5, 6, 7, 8, 9, 1, 2, 3, 4, 5, 6, 7, 8, 9 ...

b. Any object in A000027 is a member of one and only one of the following sequences:

Digital Root9	A008591	$a(n) = 9*n$.
Digital Root8	A017257	$a(n) = 9*n+8$.
Digital Root7	A017245	$a(n) = 9*n+7$.
Digital Root6	A017233	$a(n) = 9*n+6$.
Digital Root5	A017221	$a(n) = 9*n+5$.
Digital Root4	A017209	$a(n) = 9*n+4$.
Digital Root3	A017197	$a(n) = 9*n+3$.
Digital Root2	A017185	$a(n) = 9*n+2$.
Digital Root1	A017173	$a(n) = 9*n+1$.

We now assert that the Conway Universe consists of 9 classes of digital root preserving sequences. These can be represented in an nx9 list.

1	2	3	4	5	6	7	8	9
10	11	12	13	14	15	16	17	18
19	20	21	22	23	24	25	26	27
28	29	30	31	32	33	34	35	36
37	38	39	40	41	42	43	44	45
46	47	48	49	50	51	52	53	54
55	56	57	58	59	60	61	62	63
64	65	66	67	68	69	70	71	72
73	74	75	76	77	78	79	80	81
82	83	84	85	86	87	88	89	90

Evidently arranging the counting numbers in an nx9 list reveals that **numbers divisible by 3 exist only within digital root classes or columns 3,6,9**.

1	2	3	4	5	6	7	8	9
10	11	3*4	13	14	3*5	16	17	3*6
19	20	3*7	22	23	3*8	25	26	3*9
28	29	3*10	31	32	3*11	34	35	3*12
37	38	3*13	40	41	3*14	43	44	3*15
46	47	3*16	49	50	3*17	52	53	3*18
55	56	3*19	58	59	3*20	61	62	3*21
64	65	3*22	67	68	3*23	70	71	3*24
73	74	3*25	76	77	3*26	79	80	3*27
82	83	3*28	85	86	3*29	88	89	3*30

This is a form of "Impossibility Operator" which applies to all Conway Numbers. The statement, "There exists a prime digital root 3, 6 or 9 number larger than 3," is false due to the existence of an Impossibility Operator projected by the prime operator 3 onto the map; f.(3) maps observables to associated composite number objects and these are arrayed into columns. The columns can be thought of as part of a "family tree" or a "treasure map" depending on how we want to think about playing the Game of Primes. As a result of the 'genetic characteristics' transmitted by prime operator 3 the measurable quantity "digital root 6" indicates it is impossible for the associated number object to be prime. This impossibility operator applies to the infinity of objects that lie outside the family of digital root 3, 6 and 9 numbers. This is an instantaneous property of the continuum/column/gameboard as well as a discoverable property of an individual number object.

[NOTE: There are a large number of such rules, however we will be restricting ourselves to a small subset associated with this particular configuration of the counting numbers.]

Insofar as certain characteristics or measurable properties are evidently regularly distributed
we can say, "**The Conway number objects snap to the grid/map based on their characteristic function(s).**" That is, as we regard the Conway Numbers in an nx9 "neighborhood of objects / map of objects" we cannot unsee the patterns. Let us now unpack some of the "particle dynamics" available to number objects in the Conway Number Universe.

3 What Are Number Particle Dynamics?

Hint: Just the ordinary mathematical properties of numbers taken in unison.

The crux of John Conway's conjecture is **there exist two (and only two) possibilities for "composite number particles"**:
1) The number object is a "**trivial composite** particle" (divisible by 2,3,5).
2) The number object is a "**non-trivial composite** particle" (not divisible by 2,3,5).
The non-trivial composite numbers are resolved in OEIS as:

A038510   Composite numbers with smallest prime factor >= 7.
We also note that the trivial composite numbers include:

A051037   5-smooth numbers, i.e., numbers whose prime divisors are all <= 5.

This implies (or actually insists) on the following:
1) There exist trivial prime (frequency) operators which define or build trivial composite objects (yield a trivial-to-produce composite certificate/class).
 2) There exist non-trivial prime operators which define or build the non-trivial composite objects (yield a non-trivial composite certificate/class).
NOTE: The Conway Trivial Prime Operators = [2,3,5] *It is not apparent that there exists a "trivial prime" sequence in OEIS. We think of primes generally as A000040.*

307

The rules for constructing the "Conway Trivial Composite Partition" are then as follows:

Laws of trivial composite numbers:
1.0 ALL digital root 3,6,9 numbers are composite (save 3) (test = approximately len(n) steps; solve for the digital root) -*two methods, divide by 9 and the remainder determines the class OR add the digits together until you return a single digit (in this method one does not need to add 9's and can drop these instantly with no loss of accuracy).*
2.0 ALL numbers ending in 0,2,4,6,8 are composite (save 2) (test == 1 step; measure the last digit)
3.0 ALL numbers ending in [0],5 are composite (save 5) (test == 1 step; measure the last digit)

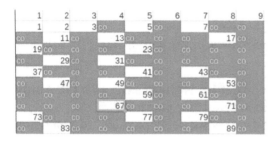

TRUE: "co" is the map of composite numbers ending in 0,2,4,5,6,8 and/or having digital root 3,6,9; these are the Conway Trivial Composite numbers and take best case len(1) and worst case approximately len(n) operations to yield a composite certificate. When placed in an nx9 list one can immediately assign a composite certificate to the trivial composites.

TRUE/AXIOM: Evidently all Conway Numbers or number objects possess a digital root and a last digit. These are measureables and observables respectively. We see in the nx9 list that it is trivial to identify a pattern associated with the trivial composites. The regularity of the trivial composite distribution implies the relative triviality of establishing their composite certificates.

Let us add an additional column to the nx9 list, giving us an nx10 list. We now have a Conway Game of Primes Gameboard [ConBoard]). This is where we incorporate A001477 into the Conway Universe. In the leftmost column we now have an "address" which can be associated with a row of nine values; each term in A000027 exists within a row and a column. So, for numbers 1-9 we have row 0 and for 10-thru-18 we have 1, etc. We can represent this as a list: (0,(1 ... 9)), (1,(10 ... 18)), (2,(19 ... 27))... . We can determine the row and column location of any element of A000027 by dividing the number by 9. Examples:

23/9 = 2.555555... thus 23 is row 2 column 5
56/9 = 6.222222... thus 56 is row 6 column 2
99/9 = 11 *In the case of multiples of 9 you get 0 as the remainder. Thus if you subtract 1 from the whole-number part of the result you will get the row address. All column 9 numbers are divisible by 9; no number divisible by 9 exists outside column 9. This is another form of impossibility operator which applies to numbers in the Conway Universe.*

We can now associate a row address from A001477 with a digital root column and a last digit for a span of 9 values taken from A000027. We can now map these values onto the ConBoard.

    4.0 All values in A000027 have a (row) address on the ConBoard

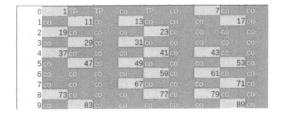

co = trivial composite
TP = trivial prime
all remaining numbers (in green) are Conway Nontrivial Numbers.

Evidently the number of prime operators required to build the Conway Trivial Composite Number partition is 3. *[Note: As an analogy think of this as a genetic lineage of numbers. A "genetic trait" is carried by the operator and this manifests as an observable in all "related" composites. Trivial composite tests (mod3=0) indicate the relative "superficiality" of the trait as it "appears" in the state representation of the number object. Approximately 1/2 of all counting numbers are divisible by 2 and this manifests as the last digits 0,2,4,6,8. We would say some number objects possess "surface characteristics" which trivialize composite certificate testing. When compared with the surface of a large semiprime number whose series of digits contains no obvious "signs of lineage" the trivial composites are obvious. It is the lack of superficial correlated observables that enforces the difficulty of semiprime factorization.]*

4 What are Conway Nontrivial Composites?

Hint: It has something (or nothing) to do with Conway Nontrivial Primes

True: Evidently the "Conway Non-Trivial Number Universe" within a ConBoard consists of digital root 1,2,4,5,7,8 and last digit 1,3,7,9 numbers.

Conjecture: One mode for configuring the Conway Nontrivial Numbers is to assemble them as 24 classes of digital root and last digit preserving sequences. (*NOTE: There are other/alternative complete descriptions for this domain of numbers*). Let us construct these classes.

The 24 classes must have zeroth elements. The 24 "smallest numbers" or "primitives" are denoted as the Conway Primitives (p):

p=(7,11,13,17,23,29,31,37,41,43,47,49,53,57,59,61,67,71,73,77,79,83,89,[91,1])
[NOTE: [91,1] is a special case which relates to the operation of the 'molecular sieve' detailed later. For our immediate purposes we are treating the number 91 as the primitive element rather than the number 1. *The value 1 is interchangeable with / can be replaced by the value 91 as with A181732 and the generation of A255491 and A224889 and its complement. For our immediate purposes the Conway primitive is 91.*

We arrive at an equation for producing a digital root and last digit preserving Conway Nontrivial number sequence: p+(90*n). Why 90? Necessarily all nontrivial numbers less their primitive are divisible by 90 with no remainder; if you take the multiples of 90 (ex: 90, 180, 270, ...9000, ...) and add any Conway Primitive to them, the returned number will have the same digital root and last digit as the Conway Primitive and be a member of that class of nontrivial numbers.

All nontrivial numbers are built from the above relationship. Thus digital root and last digit preserving sequences can be considered a fundamental architecture for rendering Conway Nontrivial Number Space or the class of nontrivial numbers generally.

TRUE: By definition both the Conway Nontrivial Composites and the Conway Nontrivial Prime Operators (or factors of Conway Nontrivial Composites) must have digital root 1,2,4,5,7,8 and last digit 1,3,7,9 measureables and observables.

The 5-smooth numbers as a class of composites are restricted to 3 operators (2,3,5), yet there exist an infinite number of prime numbers following 2,3,5 or prime operators antecedent to 2,3,5. Thus we now assert that it takes infinity-3 Conway Nontrivial Prime frequency operators (or factors) to build a sieve for generating a list of Conway Nontrivial Composite Numbers see:A038510.

The 24 classes of Conway Nontrivial Primes (and their associated Conway Primitives) are resolved in OEIS. Sloane provides the following:
7 - A142315   Primes congruent to 7 mod 45.

11 - A142317   Primes congruent to 11 mod 45.
13 - A142318   Primes congruent to 13 mod 45.
17 - A142321   Primes congruent to 17 mod 45.
19 - A142322   Primes congruent to 19 mod 45.
23 - A142324   Primes congruent to 23 mod 45.
29 - A142327   Primes congruent to 29 mod 45.
31 - A142328   Primes congruent to 31 mod 45.
37 - A142331   Primes congruent to 37 mod 45.
41 - A142333   Primes congruent to 41 mod 45.
43 - A142334   Primes congruent to 43 mod 45.
47 - A142313   Primes congruent to 2 mod 45. -excluding 2, the zeroth element
49 - A142314   Primes congruent to 4 mod 45.
53 - A142316   Primes congruent to 8 mod 45.
59 - A142319   Primes congruent to 14 mod 45.
61 - A142320   Primes congruent to 16 mod 45.
67 - A142323   Primes congruent to 22 mod 45.
71 - A142325   Primes congruent to 26 mod 45.
73 - A142326   Primes congruent to 28 mod 45.
77 - A142329   Primes congruent to 32 mod 45.
79 - A142330   Primes congruent to 34 mod 45.
83 - A142332   Primes congruent to 38 mod 45.
89 - A142335   Primes congruent to 44 mod 45.
[1,91] - A142312 Primes congruent to 1 mod 45.

As evidently only primes of a non-trivial type can sieve for nontrivial composites or be factors of nontrivial composites we propose to build a Conway Nontrivial Sieve from Conway Nontrivial Numbers.

5 Playing The Game of Primes

Hint: The Conway Nontrivial Sieve is of two types, non-self-referential and self-referential.

The Non-Self-Referential Conway Sieve
...in quasi-pseudocode

We must declare our constants (Conway Primitives)

p=(7,11,13,17,23,29,31,37,41,43,47,49,53,57,59,61,67,71,73,77,79,83,89,91)

We must declare a limit.

test = int(input("Your number here"))

We must divide the limit by 90. #the generator is multiples of 90

limit = int(test/90)

We must generate an empty list.

ConSieve = []

We must use the limit to define some number of operations for our sieve.

for x in range(0, limit):

We must generate a Conway Nontrivial Number.

y = p+(90*(x))

We must append the Conway Nontrivial Number to the list.

ConSieve.extend([y])

As with the Sieve of Eratosthenes, we now want to add multiples of our number to the list. However, we only want to map the multiples that correspond to the Conway Nontrivial Numbers. Thus we do not add numbers whose factors include 2,3,5 by implementing the n%5 mod5 and %3 mod3 tests below. Python lacks the ability to use a pattern value within range as with the commented example:

#for n in range (y,int((test/y, [4,2,4,2,4,6,2,6]) #example: 7, 11, 13, 17, 19, 23, 29, 31, 37, repeat

for n in range (y, int((test/y)), 2): #example: 7, (test/7), +2) output=7,9,11,13...

if n%5 != 0: #if n%5 does not equal 0

if n%3 != 0:

ConSieve.extend([y*n])

We thus:

for x in range(1, limit+1):

ConSeq= ([x],7,11,13,17,23,29,31,37,41,43,47,49,53,57,59,61,67,71,73,77,79,83,89,91)

We repeat this process until the limit is reached.

OUTPUT: Any number appearing exactly one time (frequency=1 OR amplitude=1) in the output (list) is prime. *Note: In the spirit of John Conway's PRIMEGAME this sieve is admittedly inefficient. It is easy* *to implement this in such a way you have a tail of false-positives. Make sure all operators print to the actual limit.*

Self-Referential Conway Sieve (Modified Sieve of Eratosthenes)

We must declare our frequency operators (Conway Primitives)
p=(7,11,13,17,23,29,31,37,41,43,47,49,53,57,59,61,67,71,73,77,79,83,89,91)
We must create 24 empty lists for aggregating the 24 classes of Conway Nontrivial Primes.
prime_list = (A142315, A142317, A142318, A142321, A142322, A142324, A142327, A142328, A142331, A142333, A142334, A142313, A142314, A142316, A142319, A142320, A142323, A142325, A142326, A142329, A142330, A142332, A142335, A142312, A142315, A142317, A142318, A142321, A142322, A142324, A142327, A142328, A142331, A142333, A142334, A142313, A142314, A142316, A142319, A142320, A142323, A142325, A142326, A142329, A142330, A142332, A142335, A142312)

    as "A142315 = []", "A142317 = []", ...
We must declare a test value for our Base-10 range.

    test = int(input("Your number here"))
We must calculate a limit for the number of iterations of our function(s).

    limit = int(test/90)
We must provide a ConBoard for storing the outputs from our frequency operators. We do this by generating a list of 0's whose quantity of elements is equal to the test number.

    address_space = [0]*int(test)
We now populate the values for our function.

    for x in range(0, limit):

    We generate a term (y) from a Conway Primitive.

    y = p+(90*(x))
In the Style of the Sieve of Eratosthenes we now check the address_space list to see if this y address contains a value >0

    if address_space[y] > 0:

    return #if the address is occupied we return and do not continue to process further steps; the number is not a prime frequency operator. The only alternative is that the value equals zero, then:

We record the value of y into the address_space

address_space[y] = y

We record the value of y into the associated Axxxxxx Prime Operator address_list

prime_list.append(y)

We now distribute the Conway Nontrivial Composites via frequency generation using modular arithmetic tests as detailed previously.

for n in range (y, int((test/y)), 2): #example: 7, (test/7), +2) output=7,9,11,13...

if n%5 !=0:

if n%3!=0:

new_y = y*(n)

address_space[new_y] = address_space[new_y] + 1 (#+1 in amplitude)

We now populate the values for our function.

for x in range(1, limit+1):

ConSeq   = ([x],7,11,13,17,23,29,31,37,41,43,47,49,53,57,59,61,67,71,73,77,79,83,89,91)

In Method 1 all nontrivial numbers whose amplitude (number of occurrences) is measured as equal to 1 are prime. By design all Conway Nontrivial Numbers are used as frequency operators to produce a map of amplitudes. We must read (or sort) the list and look for numbers that appear only once. This sort is expensive. **This sieve necessarily cannot produce 5-smooth numbers. In fact, by removing the modulus tests in the above algorithms the 0's in the list return the Hamming Numbers or 5-smooth number sequence A051037. So, in effect, this is a Hamming Number sieve masquerading as a prime number sieve.**

TRUE/AXIOM: Multiples of the Conway Nontrivial Numbers cannot produce a Hamming Number.

CONJECTURE: By adding a constant to the members of the Conway Primitives you create a skewed class of Hamming-like Numbers.

6 Digital Root and Last Digit Preserving Composite Sequences

Hint: There are certain things whose number is unknown. If we count them by threes, we have two left over; by fives, we have three left over; and by sevens, two are left over. How many things are there? --Sunzi Suanjing

Both Non-Self-Referential and Self-Referential sieves use "number atoms" or single number objects to generate "cancellation frequencies / signals" which then distribute composite certificates to some limit. The number of times a number appears (its frequency in the list) determines its prime or composite state. The total number of factors for a composite is called Big Omega, which will be discussed in Section 9 Results.

TRUE BY CONSTRUCTION: Evidently a digital root and last digit preserving sequence of numbers can be ordered as a zero-indexed list.

7	97	187	277	367	457	547	637	727
0	1	2	3	4	5	6	7	8

TRUE BY DEFINITION: Evidently a digital root and last digit preserving sequence of nontrivial numbers can be placed into a 1:1 correspondence with A001477 (0,1,2,3...) the non-negative numbers. OEIS resolves this address schema for the Conway Nontrivial Primes.

From A000040 - The Prime Numbers:
Reading the primes (excluding 2,3,5) mod 90 divides them into 24 classes, which are described by
A181732, A195993, A198382, A196000, A201804, A196007, A201734, A201739,
A201819, A201816, A201817, A201818, A202104, A201820, A201822, A201101,
A202113, A202105, A202110, A202112, A202129, A202114, A202115 and A202116.
- _J. W. Helkenberg_, Jul 24 2013

Why mod 90? Per A201804 this is an application of the Chinese Remainder Theorem. Division by 90 removes or strips the digital root measurable and last digit observable from a Conway Nontrivial Number and thereby generates its corresponding "class-address." **The reduced number remains divisible by its smallest factor, as will be demonstrated.** We know from earlier that ALL nontrivial composites and primes are built from (90*n)+p. **Thus we know that**

the list of primes A142317 correlates to a list of n's in A201804:

A142317   Primes congruent to 11 mod 45.
A201804   Numbers n such that 90*n + 11 is prime.
The above sequences can be placed into 1:1 correspondence.

CONJECTURE: There exist 24 permissible digital root and last digit preserving multiplicative arrangements for the 24 Conway Primitives. These multiplicative arrangements or "bindings" can be thought of as generating "number molecules" from a collection of "number atoms." For example, in the Conway non-self-referential sieve when we describe the Conway Primitives operating as "single atoms" we mean that the atom 7 generates a composite print statement "signal" that maps a composite certificate to 1/7th of the remaining counting numbers; mod7=0 is a trait which can be revealed if division of that number by 7 leaves no remainder. We then sort the contributions of the various "atoms" (Conway nontrivial numbers) and look for objects that exist with frequency=1. For the purpose of rendering a composite signal against or upon the static space of A000027 we say that the Conway non-self-referential sieve uses only Conway Nontrivial Numbers as operators/generators.

7 The Molecular Sieve

Hint: Bohr Model of Atomic Orbitals meets Minkowski Space

In the Molecular Sieve for A201804 the 24 Conway Primitives collapse (or fold) into "legal pairs" which become the new primitives for generating digital root and last digit preserving composite number outputs. This necessitates that every nontrivial composite number exists as a multiplied pair of Conway nontrivial numbers. While a given number may have numerous factors (Big Omega and Small Omega) a molecular sieve always determines two factors simultaneously.

Conjecture: For A201804 all non-trivial composite numbers are located within the solutions to 12 Diophantine quadratic sequences.

For example, the "binding configuration" for a digital root 2 last digit 1 sequence of composites requires the underlying primitives/ factors to be configured as follows:
not-A142317 == (7x53),(19x29),(17,43),(13,77),(11,91),(31,41),

(23,67),(49,59),(37,83),(47,73),(61,71),(79,89) [Note: 7+(90*n) * 53+(90*k) for n,k=A001477 is approximately 1/12th of not-A142317]

When factors are bound into discrete arrangements they produce composite numbers bound to a specific class.

The functions which generate digital root and last digit preserving composite sequences must themselves conserve the last digit and digital root of the cancellation operators. This imposes an impossibility condition on potential configurations of prime factors; the insertion location for all nontrivial-number cancellation operators is then quantized. We now present two implementations.

The first sieve we will present is the Modular Sieve.

MODULAR ORDINARY SIEVE

For A201804 there are 12 unique quadratic sequences each having two Conway Nontrivial primitives attached as cancellation operators. In a standard 'cancellation' method the whole number values generated by the quadratic sequence are the 'insertion locations' for the Conway nontrivial cancellation operators. **This algorithm is essentially stating that by subtracting the quadratic value from the tested number (address of the base-10 number) it becomes divisible by its smallest Conway nontrivial factor.**

The prime address generating function is built from the following 24 inequalities.

For all Digital Root 2 Last Digit 1 (A201804 = DR2LD1) prime number addresses the following must be true:

The modular form:

'address' takes all values A001477, the non-negative integers 0,1,2,3.... .
'x' takes all values of A000027, the counting numbers or whole numbers
WHERE (address-y)=0 THEN address=False=composite value
ELSE
WHERE address-y>0
THEN address-y % p !=0 for all prime addresses

To produce the members of A201804 operate the sieve until y>=address:

[address - (y   )] % [p   ] != 0 = TRUE for prime address
[address - (90x^2 - 120x + 34)] % 7+(90*(x-1)) != 0

[address - (90x^2 - 120x + 34)] % 53+(90*(x-1)) != 0
[address - (90x^2 - 132x + 48)] % 19+(90*(x-1)) != 0
[address - (90x^2 - 132x + 48)] % 29+(90*(x-1)) != 0
[address - (90x^2 - 120x + 38)] % 17+(90*(x-1)) != 0
[address - (90x^2 - 120x + 38)] % 43+(90*(x-1)) != 0
[address - (90x^2 - 90x + 11)] % 13+(90*(x-1)) != 0
[address - (90x^2 - 90x + 11)] % 77+(90*(x-1)) != 0
[address - (90x^2 - 78x - 1)]   % 11+(90*(x-1)) != 0
[address - (90x^2 - 78x - 1)]   % 91+(90*(x-1)) != 0
[address - (90x^2 - 108x + 32)] % 31+(90*(x-1)) != 0
[address - (90x^2 - 108x + 32)] % 41+(90*(x-1)) != 0
[address - (90x^2 - 90x + 17)] % 23+(90*(x-1)) != 0
[address - (90x^2 - 90x + 17)] % 67+(90*(x-1)) != 0
[address - (90x^2 - 72x + 14)] % 49+(90*(x-1)) != 0
[address - (90x^2 - 72x + 14)] % 59+(90*(x-1)) != 0
[address - (90x^2 - 60x + 4)]   % 37+(90*(x-1)) != 0
[address - (90x^2 - 60x + 4)]   % 83+(90*(x-1)) != 0
[address - (90x^2 - 60x + 8)]   % 47+(90*(x-1)) != 0
[address - (90x^2 - 60x + 8)]   % 73+(90*(x-1)) != 0
[address - (90x^2 - 48x + 6)]   % 61+(90*(x-1)) != 0
[address - (90x^2 - 48x + 6)]   % 71+(90*(x-1)) != 0
[address - (90x^2 - 12x + 0)]   % 79+(90*(x-1)) != 0
[address - (90x^2 - 12x + 0)]   % 89+(90*(x-1)) != 0

For any address which returns TRUE for all 24 evaluations the equation (90*address)+11 returns a Digital Root 2 Last Digit 1 prime number.

The number of failed tests determines an amplitude. The amplitude determines Big Omega. For any address which fails one test the number is a semiprime of the form a*b (*Note: An associated Impossibility Operator requires that A201804 contain no squared semiprimes. This is related to the global ruleset for impossibility operators which is beyond the scope of this writing.*) We will address Big Omega in Section 9 Results.

The alternative to the above is to reverse the operations such that you generate y and then implement a cancellation operator for all multiples of all Conway Nontrivial numbers, similar to the original Conway "Game of Primes" algorithm. In the current implementation it is best to think of the growth of the quadratic sequences as representing "epochs" of addresses. There is a "maximum extent" of sieving for x=1 which correlates with the number of terms that can be sieved "per round of cancellation." The size of an epoch is approximately 90x^2-12x+1. Meanwhile the number of new "Conway nontrivial cancellation operators" for A201804 at the limit is 24*x or 12*x if you are only counting the unique quadratic sequences.

The epoch grows faster than the number of Conway nontrivial numbers used per round to sieve. Additionally, per the Prime Number Theorem as the range of addresses grows larger we encounter fewer and fewer prime number cancellation operators. The Conway Nontrivial numbers that are themselves composite add amplitude to already "canceled" addresses, but do not deduct addresses from the range. This further guarantees an infinity of primes, as there are insufficient prime-valued generators per epoch to cancel all elements of A001477. So, A001477 contains 100% of the addresses associated with a given class of nontrivial numbers and the composite addresses become divisible by the smallest factor following the subtraction of y. The epoch model is important for diagnosing the relative growth of prime numbers as well as twin primes, cousin primes and other arrangements.

The second version of this algorithm is presented as Python code. Replace the (....) with equivalent number of spaces to run it.

```
#!/usr/bin/env python
import cmath

limit = int(input('limit value here:')) #this value is for the "epoch"
limit = int(limit) #convert it to an int type
h = limit   #set variable h as equivalent to "limit"
epoch = 90*(h*h) - 12*h + 1 #The limit of the epoch
print('The epoch range is', epoch)
limit = epoch
base10 = (limit*90)+11
print('This is the base-10 limit:', base10)
#get RANGE for number of iterations x through the quadratic
functions
a = 90
b = -300
c = 250 - limit
# calculate the discriminant
d = (b**2) - (4*a*c)
```

```python
# find two solutions
sol1 = (-b-cmath.sqrt(d))/(2*a)
sol2 = (-b+cmath.sqrt(d))/(2*a)
print('The solution are {0} and {1}'.format(sol1,sol2))
new_limit = sol2 #we need the integer REAL part of the positive
value for RANGE
A201804 = [0]*int(limit+10) #pad the list, we will drop this at the
end

#x=increment, l=quadratic term, m = quadratic term, z = primitive,
o = primitive
def drLD(x, l, m, z, o, listvar, primitive):
"This is a composite generating function"
..y = 90*(x*x) - l*x + m
..listvar[y] = listvar[y]+1
..p = z+(90*(x-1))
..q = o+(90*(x-1))
..for n in range (1, int(((limit-y)/p)+1)):
....listvar[y+(p*n)] = listvar[y+(p*n)]+1
..for n in range (1, int(((limit-y)/q)+1)):
....listvar[y+(q*n)] = listvar[y+(q*n)]+1

for x in range(1, int(new_limit.real)):
#A201804
....drLD(x, 120, 34, 7, 53, A201804, 11) #7,53 @4, 154
....drLD(x, 132, 48, 19, 29, A201804, 11) #19,29 @6, 144
....drLD(x, 120, 38, 17, 43, A201804, 11) #17,43 @8, 158
....drLD(x, 90, 11, 13, 77, A201804, 11) #13,77 @11, 191
....drLD(x, 78, -1, 11, 91, A201804, 11) #11,91 @11, 203
....drLD(x, 108, 32, 31, 41, A201804, 11) #31,41 @14, 176
....drLD(x, 90, 17, 23, 67, A201804, 11) #23,67 @17, 197
....drLD(x, 72, 14, 49, 59, A201804, 11) #49,59 @32, 230
....drLD(x, 60, 4, 37, 83, A201804, 11)  #37,83 @34, 244
....drLD(x, 60, 8, 47, 73, A201804, 11)  #47,73 @38, 248
....drLD(x, 48, 6, 61, 71, A201804, 11)  #61,71 @48, 270
....drLD(x, 12, 0, 79, 89, A201804, 11)  #79,89 @78, 336

A201804 = A201804[:-10] #remove the padding
print('There are', A201804.count(0), 'primes beneath the limit',
len(A201804))
A201804_enumerated=[i for i,x in enumerate(A201804) if x == 0]
print('This is A201804:', A201804_enumerated)
```

####################### END OF CODE
##############################

For A201804 as x increments +1:
Epoch increments $90x^2 - 12x + 1$
New addresses added per epoch = $180x+78$
Unique Quadratics = $12*x$
Frequency operators = $24*x$
base-10 limit = $8100x^2 - 1080x +101$

The possible factors (operators) for numbers of a given length is a determined by a step function based on the number of epochs in a given length of number. Up to 4 digit addresses can be sieved by one pass through the 12 generators. It take 2 passes to sieve 5-digit space, 8 for 6 digit. The pattern:
 there exist 1 4-digit epoch values
 there exist 2 5-digit epoch values
 there exist 8 6-digit epoch values
 there exist 24 7-digit epoch values
 there exist 76 8-digit epoch values
 there exist 242 9-digit epoch values
 there exist 764 10-digit epoch values
 there exist 2416 11-digit epoch values
This indicates that the number of possible factors is increasing as we traverse the n-digit numbers. The amplitude relative to the leading digit is beyond the scope of this paper; anecdotally when going from 50000 to 60000 or 500000 to 600000 in address space there is chance for leading digit 5 partition to have more amplitude than the leading 6 digit partition; the higher the amplitude in a given finite span the greater the number of primes.

8 The Twin Prime Sieve

Hint: "Unfortunately, 'one-parameter' patterns, such as twins n, n+2, remain stubbornly beyond current technology. There is still much to be done in the subject!" --T. Tao

The twin primes equivalently reduce to 9 "channels" or classes:

A224855   Numbers n such that $90*n + 17$ and $90*n + 19$
are twin primes.

A224856   Numbers n such that $90*n + 29$ and $90*n + 31$
are twin primes.

A224859 are twin primes.	Numbers n such that 90*n + 47 and 90*n + 49
A224854 are twin prime.	Numbers n such that 90*n + 11 and 90*n + 13
A224857 are twin primes.	Numbers n such that 90n + 41 and 90n + 43
A224860 are twin prime.	Numbers n such that 90*n + 59 and 90*n + 61
A224862 are twin primes.	Numbers n such that 90*n + 71 and 90*n + 73
A224864 are twin primes.	Numbers n such that 90*n + 77 and 90*n + 79
A224865 are twin primes.	Numbers n such that 90*n + 89 and 90*n + 91

A224854 **Numbers n such that 90*n + 11 and 90*n + 13 are twin prime.**

To produce this list of twin primes we implement the following:

The chibi-style algorithm:
Address takes all values A001477, the non-negative integers 0,1,2,3... .
x takes all values of A000027, the positive counting numbers 1,2,3,4,... .
address-y=0=Composite(False)
else
where address-y>0
where address-y % p !=0 for all 48 tests:
number is then twin prime in A224854

To produce the members of A224854 feed the values of A001477 and A000027 into the sieve until y>=address:
[address - (y   )] % [p   ] != 0 = Prime (True)
[address - 90x^2 - 120x + 34] % 7+(90*(x-1))] != 0
[address - 90x^2 - 94x + 10] % 7+(90*(x-1)) != 0
[address - 90x^2 - 86x + 6] % 11+(90*(x-1)) != 0
[address - 90x^2 - 78x - 1] % 11+(90*(x-1)) != 0
[address - 90x^2 - 76x - 1] % 13+(90*(x-1)) != 0
[address - 90x^2 - 90x + 11] % 13+(90*(x-1)) != 0
[address - 90x^2 - 120x + 38] % 17+(90*(x-1)) != 0
[address - 90x^2 - 104x + 25] % 17+(90*(x-1)) != 0
[address - 90x^2 - 132x + 48] % 19+(90*(x-1)) != 0
[address - 90x^2 - 94x + 18] % 19+(90*(x-1)) != 0

[address - 90x^2 - 90x + 17] % 23+(90*(x-1)) != 0
[address - 90x^2 - 86x + 14] % 23+(90*(x-1)) != 0
[address - 90x^2 - 132x + 48] % 29+(90*(x-1)) != 0
[address - 90x^2 - 104x + 29] % 29+(90*(x-1)) != 0
[address - 90x^2 - 108x + 32] % 31+(90*(x-1)) != 0
[address - 90x^2 - 76x + 11] % 31+(90*(x-1)) != 0
[address - 90x^2 - 94x + 24] % 37+(90*(x-1)) != 0
[address - 90x^2 - 60x + 4] % 37+(90*(x-1)) != 0
[address - 90x^2 - 108x + 32] % 41+(90*(x-1)) != 0
[address - 90x^2 - 86x + 20] % 41+(90*(x-1)) != 0
[address - 90x^2 - 120x + 38] % 43+(90*(x-1)) != 0
[address - 90x^2 - 76x + 15] % 43+(90*(x-1)) != 0
[address - 90x^2 - 60x + 8] % 47+(90*(x-1)) != 0
[address - 90x^2 - 104x + 29] % 47+(90*(x-1)) != 0
[address - 90x^2 - 72x + 14] % 49+(90*(x-1)) != 0
[address - 90x^2 - 94x + 24] % 49+(90*(x-1)) != 0
[address - 90x^2 - 120x + 34] % 53+(90*(x-1)) != 0
[address - 90x^2 - 86x + 20] % 53+(90*(x-1)) != 0
[address - 90x^2 - 72x + 14] % 59+(90*(x-1)) != 0
[address - 90x^2 - 104x + 25] % 59+(90*(x-1)) != 0
[address - 90x^2 - 48x + 6] % 61+(90*(x-1)) != 0
[address - 90x^2 - 76x + 15] % 61+(90*(x-1)) != 0
[address - 90x^2 - 90x + 17] % 67+(90*(x-1)) != 0
[address - 90x^2 - 94x + 18] % 67+(90*(x-1)) != 0
[address - 90x^2 - 48x + 6] % 71+(90*(x-1)) != 0
[address - 90x^2 - 86x + 14] % 71+(90*(x-1)) != 0
[address - 90x^2 - 60x + 8] % 73+(90*(x-1)) != 0
[address - 90x^2 - 76x + 11] % 73+(90*(x-1)) != 0
[address - 90x^2 - 90x + 11] % 77+(90*(x-1)) != 0
[address - 90x^2 - 14x + 0] % 77+(90*(x-1)) != 0
[address - 90x^2 - 12x + 0] % 79+(90*(x-1)) != 0
[address - 90x^2 - 94x + 10] % 79+(90*(x-1)) != 0
[address - 90x^2 - 60x + 4] % 83+(90*(x-1)) != 0
[address - 90x^2 - 86x + 6] % 83+(90*(x-1)) != 0
[address - 90x^2 - 12x + 0] % 89+(90*(x-1)) != 0
[address - 90x^2 - 14x + 0] % 89+(90*(x-1)) != 0
[address - 90x^2 - 76x -1] % 91+(90*(x-1)) != 0
[address - 90x^2 - 78x - 1] % 91+(90*(x-1)) != 0

To recover the base10 value: address*90+(11,13).

The above 48 inequalities represent approximately 1/9th of the

total continuum (or map) of twin prime addresses. There are 48 new inequalities per epoch. For the full python implementation see ADDENDA at the end of the document.

When taking all 9 sequences into account we want to analyze the total growth of twin primes per epoch. We find the following:
a(n) to a(n+1) = a(n+1)/a(n) = ratio of terms
100 to 200 = 3.422 (there are 3.422 times as many twin primes from 100 to 200 as there are from 0 to 100)
200 to 300 = 2.065
300 to 400 = 1.676
400 to 500 = 1.495
500 to 600 = 1.389
600 to 700 = 1.321
700 to 800 = 1.273
800 to 900 = 1.238
900 to 1000 = 1.211
1000 to 1100 = 1.189
1100 to 1200 = 1.171
1200 to 1300 = 1.157
1300 to 1400 = 1.144
1400 to 1500 = 1.134
1500 to 1600 = 1.125
1600 to 1700 = 1.117
1700 to 1800 = 1.110
1800 to 1900 = 1.104
1900 to 2000 = 1.098
2000 to 2100 = 1.093
2100 to 2200 = 1.089
2200 to 2300 = 1.085
2300 to 2400 = 1.081
2400 to 2500 = 1.078
2500 to 2600 = 1.074
2600 to 2700 = 1.072
2700 to 2800 = 1.070
2800 to 2900 = 1.066
2900 to 3000 = 1.064
3000 to 3100 = 1.062
3100 to 3200 – 1.060
3200 to 3300 = 1.058
3300 to 3400 = 1.056

3400 to 3500 = 1.055 or (222771992 / 211237541)

Conjecture: a(n+1)/a(n) is always greater than 1.

If we can prove that A224854 contains an infinite number of terms we have proven the Twin Prime Conjecture. As we examine the cancellation operators associated with not-A224854 we can immediately recognize that it is functionally impossible to eliminating all counting numbers beyond a given limit. This is reinforced by the observed reality that as the epoch grows so does the number of twin primes.

Let's assume that the generators in A224854 are capable of eliminating all counting numbers beyond some limit and show how this leads to a contradiction.

A201804(11): y=4(7,53), 154(97,143), 484(187,233)
A201816(13): y=6(7,79), 182(97,169), 538,(187,259)
Starting at the value 4 exactly 1 in every 7 numbers is composite.
Starting at the value 6 exactly 1 in every 7 numbers is composite
4,11,18,25,32,39,46,53,60,67,74,81,88,95, ... are composite
6,13,20,27,34,41,48,55,62,69,76,83,90,97, ... are composite
The distribution of these cancellation operators is insufficient to provide coverage against all values in A001477; there can be no value beyond which all numbers are generated by the available operators. This is reinforced by the Prime Number Theorem, which indicates that the number of prime number operators on average decreases as the numbers get larger. As we know we are dealing with 48 cancellation operators per increment of x and that the range of numbers to be sequenced grows by approximately 180x +78 we can see that the number of prime cancellation operators must necessarily fail to cover all the addresses from epoch to epoch. The proof relies on stating there is a number such that all numbers beyond it are solutions in finite x. Since x grows to infinity and new prime numbers MUST exist in every epoch for A201804 and A201816 the union set of these two classes cannot then be finite.

Take the number 7. The next operator available to perform cancellations is 97. The generator is insufficient to fill the spaces missed by 7. The next operator is 187, then 277, etc. The decay in the frequency coupled with the Prime Number Theorem ensures an infinity of twin primes exist. In fact, this is true for ANY pair of the 24 classes of sequences when taking the union set.

To prove the above assertions we show that there must exist a configuration of operators that is sufficient to cancel all values. An example is now given using the operator 7:

start address=0, operator = 7
start address=1, operator = 7
start address=2, operator = 7
start address=3, operator = 7
start address=4, operator = 7
start address=5, operator = 7
start address=6, operator = 7
we then have the following cancellations:
0, 7, 14, 21, 28, ...
1, 8, 15, 22, 29, ...
2, 9, 16, 23, 30, ...
3, 10, 17, 24, 31, ...
4, 11, 18, 25, 32, ...
5, 12, 19, 26, 33, ...
6, 13, 20, 27, 34, ...
In this scenario, if we have seven sequences whose Conway nontrivial 7 has starting positions ranging from 0 to 6 then the sequence contains no surviving elements. The cancellation operators that produce A224854 lack this configuration and therefore lack sufficient density to populate all terms in A001477 beyond a limit.

Is there a combination of OEIS sequences which guarantee that there are no survivors? We can take the following:
0 = 49 (A201818) test
0 = 77 (A201822)

1 = 71 (A202129) test
1 = 43 (A202105)
1 = 29 (A201739)

2 = 79 (A202112) test
2 = 37 (A198382)
2 = 23 (A201820)

3 = 17 (A202115) test
3 = 73 (A195993)
3 = 59 (A202101)

3 = 31 (A201819)

4 = 11 (A201804)
4 = 67 (A201817) test
4 = 53 (A202114)

5 = 89 (A202116) test
5 = 61 (A202113)
5 = 47 (A201734)
5 = 19 (A196000)

6 = 13 (A201816) test
6 = 41 (A202104)

Any combination (union set) of the above sequences will suffice to eliminate all values of A001477 at infinity provided it contains a list of start positions (0,1,2,3,4,5,6). The union set labeled "test" necessarily cancels all terms.

Operator 11 will cancel 100% of the terms in A001477 with the union set of start positions (0,1,2,3,4,5,6,7,8,9,10) using any combination of the following:
0 = 77 (A201822)

1 = 53 (A202114)
1 = 31 (A201819)

2 = 73 (A195993)
2 = 7 (A202110)
2 = 29 (A201739)

3 = 71 (A202129)
3 = 49 (A201818)

4 = 47 (A201734)

5 = 89 (A202116)
5 = 23 (A201820)
5 = 67 (A201817)

6 = 43 (A202105)

7 = 41 (A202104)
7 = 19 (A196000)

8 = 17 (A202115)

8 = 83 (A196007)
8 = 61 (A202113)

9 = 59 (A202101)
9 = 37 (A198382)

10 = 79 (A202112)
10 = 13 (A201816)

Additionally, start position union set of (1,2,3,4,5,6,7,8,9,10,11,12,13) for operator 13 and start position union set of (1,2,3,4,5,6,7,8,9,10,11,12,13,14,15,16,17) for operator 17 will cancel all terms of A000027.

For A201804 we have the following addresses with the associated Conway primitive cancellation operators (p,q):
y=4, 154, 484, ... (7, 53)
y=6, 144, 462, ... (19,29)
y=8, 158, 488, ... (17, 43)
y=11, 191, 151, ... (13, 77)
y=11, 203, 575, ... (11, 91)
y=14, 176, 518, ... (31, 41)
y=17, 197, 557, ... (23, 67)
y=32, 230, 608, ... (49, 59)
y=34, 244, 634, ... (37, 83)
y=38, 248, 638, ... (47, 73)
y=48, 270, 672, ... (61, 71)
y=78, 336, 774, ... (79, 89)

For A201816:
y=6, 182, 538, ... (7,79)
y=10, 194, 558, ... (11, 83)
y=11, 177, 523, ... (17, 59)
y=13, 207, 581, ... (13,91)
y=14, 190, 546, ... (19, 67)
y=15, 181, 527, ... (29, 47)
y=18, 202, 566, ... (23, 71)
y=20, 196, 552, ... (37, 49)
y=24, 208, 572, ... (41, 53)
y=25, 219, 593, ... (31, 73)
y=29, 223, 597, ... (43, 61)
y=76, 332, 768, ... (77, 89)

Assuming the union set of these two classes of operators is sufficient to cancel all terms of A001477 beyond some point fails on its face; it is a superficial characteristic of these cancellation operators that they are incapable of fully populating A001477 beyond some limit. Additionally, both sub-sequences A201804 and A201816 necessarily contain an infinite number of terms and use the same cancellation operators per epoch (with different start positions) and thus the probability that both infinite sequences contain no matching terms when evaluated from the perspective of the known cancellation operators evaluates to zero. This proves the infinity of the twin primes.

9 RESULTS

Big Omega
For A201804, using the Python implementation we start with a finite list of 0 then add +1 to every address that is generated by the solutions. When we read the list we discover values including 0,1,2,3, ..., etc. These values represent amplitudes associated with the number of factors for a given number. We see primes have zero amplitude, but what about 1,2,3,4,5 ..., etc. as values? The "events" which accumulate can be understood in terms of "factor families." The branches for "factor families" are the solutions to $(2*n)+1$, where n is a seed value. What is meant by seed value?

For the number 1 in a cell, the base-10 Conway Number we recover is a semi-prime of type $(a*b)$. Both factors are prime. If we use 1 as an input in the equation $(2*n)+1$ we get 3. Every address containing 3 is of type $a*b*c$ with a,b,c prime. $(2*n)+1$ where n=3 is 7. For 7 we have $a*b*c*d$. $(2*n)+1$ is a "branching operator" which we can use to establish the underlying "factor forms" or "factor-type families."

Here is a results table for some of the seed values and equivalent amplitudes for $(2*n)+1$ for A201804:
1 = semiprime $(a*b)$
3 = $a*b*c$
7 = $a*b*c*d$
15= $a*b*c*d*e$
...break
2 = $(a*a)*b$
5 = $(a*a)*b*c$

11 = (a*a)*b*c*d
...break
4 = (a*a*a*a)*b
9 = (a*a*a*a)*b*c
19 = (a*a*a*a)*b*c*d
...break
6 = (a*a*a*a*a*a)*b
13 = (a*a*a*a*a*a)*b*c
27 = (a*a*a*a*a*a)*b*c*d
...break
8 = (a*a)*(b*b)*c
17 = (a*a)*(b*b)*c*d
35 = (a*a)*(b*b)*c*d*e
...break
10 = (a*a*a*a*a*a*a*a*a)*b = a(10)*b(1)
...break
12 = a(12)*b(1)
...break
14 = a(4)*b(2)*c(1)
29 = a(4)*b(2)*c(1)*d(1)
59 = a(4)*b(2)*c(1)*d(1)*e(1)
...break

Big Omega is derived from the amplitude that is generated by accumulation of outputs at the address. Big Omega for the Twin Prime sieve requires operating A201804 and A201816 in separate containers and then taking the union set of the two lists so as to preserve BigOmega for each subsequence. The molecular sieve can then be configured to produce BigOmega or the characteristic function.

10 CONCLUSION

I began this playthrough of the Game of Primes intent on returning with a prime printing function. This was a quest to locate an operator or finite number of operators which could faithfully directly reproduce arbitrarily long sequences of prime numbers and do so as easily as we determine the composite certificates for trivial numbers. How would one explore for such a function?

We have shown the complement to A201804. The implication is that a simple generator is capable of producing a complementary quasi-random sequence. If we say it is possible for a system such as A000027 to simultaneously contain randomness (A000040) and non-randomness (the complement to A000040), then by removing all non-randomness you are necessarily left with the random component. **We can reveal a simple order within the composite distribution complementary to A201804 precisely because the prime distribution is functionally random.**

ADDENDA

Global Twin Prime Sieve [replace periods (....) with spaces to run as PYTHON code]

```python
#!/usr/bin/env python
import cmath #for a limit calculation

#get a value for the limit of the range to be sieved
limit = int(input("limit value here:"))
limit = int(limit) #convert it to an int type

#epochs are those regions closed under a full "loop" through the
functions
h = limit
epoch = 90*(h*h) - 12*h + 1
print("The epoch range is", epoch)
limit = epoch

#get RANGE for number of iterations x through the quadratic
functions (to meet the endpoints of the epoch value)
a = 90
b = -300
c = 250 - limit
# calculate the discriminant
d = (b**2) - (4*a*c)
# find two solutions
sol1 = (-b-cmath.sqrt(d))/(2*a)
sol2 = (-b+cmath.sqrt(d))/(2*a)
print('The solution are {0} and {1}'.format(sol1,sol2))
#the integer REAL part of the positive value is the limit for RANGE
new_limit = sol2

A224854 = [0]*int(limit)
A224855 = [0]*int(limit)
```

```
A224856 = [0]*int(limit)
A224857 = [0]*int(limit)
A224859 = [0]*int(limit)
A224860 = [0]*int(limit)
A224862 = [0]*int(limit)
A224864 = [0]*int(limit)
A224865 = [0]*int(limit)

def drLD(x, l, m, z, o, listvar, primitive):  #x=increment, l=quadratic
term, m = quadratic term, z = primitive, o = primitive
.."This is a composite generating function"
..y = 90*(x*x) - l*x + m
..try:
....listvar[y] = listvar[y]+1
..except:
....pass
..p = z+(90*(x-1))
..q = o+(90*(x-1))
..for n in range (1, int(((limit-y)/p)+1)):
....try:
......listvar[y+(p*n)] = listvar[y+(p*n)]+1
....except:
......pass
..for n in range (1, int(((limit-y)/q)+1)):
....try:
......listvar[y+(q*n)] = listvar[y+(q*n)]+1
....except:
......pass

for x in range(1, int(new_limit.real)):

# 19 = A196000
....drLD(x, 70, -1, 19, 91, A224855, 19) #19,91
....drLD(x, 106, 31, 37, 37, A224855, 19) #37,73
....drLD(x, 34, 3, 73, 73, A224855, 19) #73,73
....drLD(x, 110, 27, 11, 59, A224855, 19) #11,59
....drLD(x, 110, 33, 29, 41, A224855, 19) #29,41
....drLD(x, 56, 6, 47, 77, A224855, 19) #47,77
....drLD(x, 74, 5, 23, 83, A224855, 19) #23,83
....drLD(x, 124, 40, 13, 43, A224855, 19) #13,43
....drLD(x, 70, 7, 31, 79, A224855, 19) #31,79
....drLD(x, 70, 13, 49, 61, A224855, 19) #49,61
```

....drLD(x, 106, 21, 7, 67, A224855, 19) #7,67
....drLD(x, 20, 0, 71, 89, A224855, 19) #71,89
....drLD(x, 74, 15, 53, 53, A224855, 19) #53,53
....drLD(x, 146, 59, 17, 17, A224855, 19) #17,17

#17 = A202115
....drLD(x, 72, -1, 17, 91, A224855, 17) #17,91
....drLD(x, 108, 29, 19, 53, A224855, 17) #19,53
....drLD(x, 72, 11, 37, 71, A224855, 17) #37,71
....drLD(x, 18, 0, 73, 89, A224855, 17) #73,89
....drLD(x, 102, 20, 11, 67, A224855, 17) #11,67
....drLD(x, 138, 52, 13, 29, A224855, 17) #13,29
....drLD(x, 102, 28, 31, 47, A224855, 17) #31,47
....drLD(x, 48, 3, 49, 83, A224855, 17) #49,83
....drLD(x, 78, 8, 23, 79, A224855, 17) #23,79
....drLD(x, 132, 45, 7, 41, A224855, 17) #7,41
....drLD(x, 78, 16, 43, 59, A224855, 17) #43,59
....drLD(x, 42, 4, 61, 77, A224855, 17) #61,77

#91 = A224889
....drLD(x, -2, -1, 91, 91, A224865, 91) #91,91
....drLD(x, 142, 55, 19, 19, A224865, 91) #19,19
....drLD(x, 70, 9, 37, 73, A224865, 91) #37, 73
....drLD(x, 128, 42, 11, 41, A224865, 91) #11, 41
....drLD(x, 92, 20, 29, 59, A224865, 91) #29,59
....drLD(x, 110, 31, 23, 47, A224865, 91) #23,47
....drLD(x, 20, 0, 77, 83, A224865, 91) #77,83
....drLD(x, 160, 70, 7, 13, A224865, 91) #7,13
....drLD(x, 88, 18, 31, 61, A224865, 91) #31,61
....drLD(x, 52, 4, 49, 79, A224865, 91) #49,79
....drLD(x, 70, 11, 43, 67, A224865, 91) #43,67
....drLD(x, 110, 29, 17, 53, A224865, 91) #17,53
....drLD(x, 38, 3, 71, 71, A224865, 91) #71,71
....drLD(x, 2, -1, 89, 89, A224865, 91) #89,89

89 = A202116
....drLD(x, 0, -1, 89, 91, A224865, 89) #89,91
....drLD(x, 90, 14, 19, 71, A224865, 89) #19,71
....drLD(x, 126, 42, 17, 37, A224865, 89) #17,37
....drLD(x, 54, 6, 53, 73, A224865, 89) #53,73
....drLD(x, 120, 35, 11, 49, A224865, 89) #11,49
....drLD(x, 120, 39, 29, 31, A224865, 89) #29,31

....drLD(x, 66, 10, 47, 67, A224865, 89) #47,67
....drLD(x, 84, 5, 13, 83, A224865, 89) #13,83
....drLD(x, 114, 34, 23, 43, A224865, 89) #23,43
....drLD(x, 60, 5, 41, 79, A224865, 89) #41,79
....drLD(x, 60, 9, 59, 61, A224865, 89) #59,61
....drLD(x, 96, 11, 7, 77, A224865, 89) #7,77

31 = A201819
....drLD(x, 58, -1, 31, 91, A224856, 31) #31,91
....drLD(x, 112, 32, 19, 49, A224856, 31) #19,49
....drLD(x, 130, 45, 13, 37, A224856, 31) #13,37
....drLD(x, 40, 4, 67, 73, A224856, 31) #67,73
....drLD(x, 158, 69, 11, 11, A224856, 31) #11,11
....drLD(x, 122, 41, 29, 29, A224856, 31) #29,29
....drLD(x, 50, 3, 47, 83, A224856, 31) #47,83
....drLD(x, 140, 54, 17, 23, A224856, 31) #17,23
....drLD(x, 68, 10, 41, 71, A224856, 31) #41,71
....drLD(x, 32, 0, 59, 89, A224856, 31) #59,89
....drLD(x, 50, 5, 53, 77, A224856, 31) #53,77
....drLD(x, 130, 43, 7, 43, A224856, 31) #7,43
....drLD(x, 58, 9, 61, 61, A224856, 31) #61,61
....drLD(x, 22, 1, 79, 79, A224856, 31) #79,79

29 = A201739
....drLD(x, 60, -1, 29, 91, A224856, 29) #29,91
....drLD(x, 150, 62, 11, 19, A224856, 29) #11,19
....drLD(x, 96, 25, 37, 47, A224856, 29) #37,47
....drLD(x, 24, 1, 73, 83, A224856, 29) #73,83
....drLD(x, 144, 57, 13, 23, A224856, 29) #13,23
....drLD(x, 90, 20, 31, 59, A224856, 29) #31,59
....drLD(x, 90, 22, 41, 49, A224856, 29) #41,49
....drLD(x, 36, 3, 67, 77, A224856, 29) #67,77
....drLD(x, 156, 67, 7, 17, A224856, 29) #7,17
....drLD(x, 84, 19, 43, 53, A224856, 29) #43,53
....drLD(x, 30, 0, 61, 89, A224856, 29) #61,89
....drLD(x, 30, 2, 71, 79, A224856, 29) #71,79

49 = A201818
....drLD(x, 40, -1, 49, 91, A224859, 49) #49,91
....drLD(x, 130, 46, 19, 31, A224859, 49) #19,31
....drLD(x, 76, 13, 37, 67, A224859, 49) #37,67
....drLD(x, 94, 14, 13, 73, A224859, 49) #13,73

....drLD(x, 140, 53, 11, 29, A224859, 49) #11,29
....drLD(x, 86, 20, 47, 47, A224859, 49) #47,47
....drLD(x, 14, 0, 83, 83, A224859, 49) #83,83
....drLD(x, 104, 27, 23, 53, A224859, 49) #23,53
....drLD(x, 50, 0, 41, 89, A224859, 49) #41,89
....drLD(x, 50, 6, 59, 71, A224859, 49) #59,71
....drLD(x, 86, 10, 17, 77, A224859, 49) #17,77
....drLD(x, 166, 76, 7, 7, A224859, 49) #7,7
....drLD(x, 94, 24, 43, 43, A224859, 49) #43,43
....drLD(x, 40, 3, 61, 79, A224859, 49) #61,79

47 = A201734
....drLD(x, 42, -1, 47, 91, A224859, 47) #47,91
....drLD(x, 78, 5, 19, 83, A224859, 47) #19,83
....drLD(x, 132, 46, 11, 37, A224859, 47) #11,37
....drLD(x, 78, 11, 29, 73, A224859, 47) #29,73
....drLD(x, 108, 26, 13, 59, A224859, 47) #13,59
....drLD(x, 72, 8, 31, 77, A224859, 47) #31,77
....drLD(x, 108, 30, 23, 49, A224859, 47) #23,49
....drLD(x, 102, 17, 7, 71, A224859, 47) #7,71
....drLD(x, 48, 0, 43, 89, A224859, 47) #43,89
....drLD(x, 102, 23, 17, 61, A224859, 47) #17,61
....drLD(x, 48, 4, 53, 79, A224859, 47) #53,79
....drLD(x, 72, 12, 41, 67, A224859, 47) #41,67

11 = A201804
....drLD(x, 120, 34, 7, 53, A224854, 11) #7,53 @4, 154 1
....drLD(x, 132, 48, 19, 29, A224854, 11) #19,29 @6, 144 2
....drLD(x, 120, 38, 17, 43, A224854, 11) #17,43 @8, 158 3
....drLD(x, 90, 11, 13, 77, A224854, 11) #13,77 @11, 191 4
....drLD(x, 78, -1, 11, 91, A224854, 11) #11,91 @11, 203 5
....drLD(x, 108, 32, 31, 41, A224854, 11) #31,41 @14, 176 6
....drLD(x, 90, 17, 23, 67, A224854, 11) #23,67 @17, 197 7
....drLD(x, 72, 14, 49, 59, A224854, 11) #49,59 @32, 230 8
....drLD(x, 60, 4, 37, 83, A224854, 11) #37,83 @34, 244 9
....drLD(x, 60, 8, 47, 73, A224854, 11) #47,73 @38, 248 10
....drLD(x, 48, 6, 61, 71, A224854, 11) #61,71 @48, 270 11
....drLD(x, 12, 0, 79, 89, A224854, 11) #79,89 @78, 336 12

#13 = A201816
....drLD(x, 76, -1, 13, 91, A224854, 13) #13,91
....drLD(x, 94, 18, 19, 67, A224854, 13) #19,67

....drLD(x, 94, 24, 37, 49, A224854, 13) #37,49
....drLD(x, 76, 11, 31, 73, A224854, 13) #31,73
....drLD(x, 86, 6, 11, 83, A224854, 13) #11,83
....drLD(x, 104, 29, 29, 47, A224854, 13) #29,47
....drLD(x, 86, 14, 23, 71, A224854, 13) #23,71
....drLD(x, 86, 20, 41, 53, A224854, 13) #41,53
....drLD(x, 104, 25, 17, 59, A224854, 13) #17,59
....drLD(x, 14, 0, 77, 89, A224854, 13) #77,89
....drLD(x, 94, 10, 7, 79, A224854, 13) #7,79
....drLD(x, 76, 15, 43, 61, A224854, 13) #43,61

79 = A202112
....drLD(x, 10, -1, 79, 91, A224864, 79) #79,91
....drLD(x, 100, 22, 19, 61, A224864, 79) #19,61
....drLD(x, 136, 48, 7, 37, A224864, 79) #7,37
....drLD(x, 64, 8, 43, 73, A224864, 79) #43,73
....drLD(x, 80, 0, 11, 89, A224864, 79) #11,89
....drLD(x, 80, 12, 29, 71, A224864, 79) #29,71
....drLD(x, 116, 34, 17, 47, A224864, 79) #17,47
....drLD(x, 44, 2, 53, 83, A224864, 79) #53,83
....drLD(x, 154, 65, 13, 13, A224864, 79) #13,13
....drLD(x, 100, 26, 31, 49, A224864, 79) #31,49
....drLD(x, 46, 5, 67, 67, A224864, 79) #67,67
....drLD(x, 134, 49, 23, 23, A224864, 79) #23,23
....drLD(x, 80, 16, 41, 59, A224864, 79) #41,59
....drLD(x, 26, 1, 77, 77, A224864, 79) #77,77

77 = A201822
....drLD(x, 12, -1, 77, 91, A224864, 77) #77,91
....drLD(x, 138, 52, 19, 23, A224864, 77) #19,23
....drLD(x, 102, 28, 37, 41, A224864, 77) #37,41
....drLD(x, 48, 5, 59, 73, A224864, 77) #59,73
....drLD(x, 162, 72, 7, 11, A224864, 77) #7,11
....drLD(x, 108, 31, 29, 43, A224864, 77) #29,43
....drLD(x, 72, 13, 47, 61, A224864, 77) #47,61
....drLD(x, 18, 0, 79, 83, A224864, 77) #79,83
....drLD(x, 78, 0, 13, 89, A224864, 77) #13,89
....drLD(x, 132, 47, 17, 31, A224864, 77) #17,31
....drLD(x, 78, 16, 49, 53, A224864, 77) #49,53
....drLD(x, 42, 4, 67, 71, A224864, 77) #67,71

43 = A202105

....drLD(x, 46, -1, 43, 91, A224857, 43) #43,91
....drLD(x, 154, 65, 7, 19, A224857, 43) #7,19
....drLD(x, 64, 6, 37, 79, A224857, 43) #37,79
....drLD(x, 46, 5, 61, 73, A224857, 43) #61,73
....drLD(x, 116, 32, 11, 53, A224857, 43) #11,53
....drLD(x, 134, 49, 17, 29, A224857, 43) #17,29
....drLD(x, 44, 0, 47, 89, A224857, 43) #47,89
....drLD(x, 26, 1, 71, 83, A224857, 43) #71,83
....drLD(x, 136, 50, 13, 31, A224857, 43) #13,31
....drLD(x, 64, 10, 49, 67, A224857, 43) #49,67
....drLD(x, 116, 36, 23, 41, A224857, 43) #23,41
....drLD(x, 44, 4, 59, 77, A224857, 43) #59,77

41 = A202104
....drLD(x, 48, -1, 41, 91, A224857, 41) #41,91
....drLD(x, 42, 0, 49, 89, A224857, 41) #49,89
....drLD(x, 102, 24, 19, 59, A224857, 41) #19,59
....drLD(x, 120, 39, 23, 37, A224857, 41) #23,37
....drLD(x, 108, 25, 11, 61, A224857, 41) #11,61
....drLD(x, 72, 7, 29, 79, A224857, 41) #29,79
....drLD(x, 90, 22, 43, 47, A224857, 41) #43,47
....drLD(x, 150, 62, 13, 17, A224857, 41) #13,17
....drLD(x, 78, 12, 31, 71, A224857, 41) #31,71
....drLD(x, 30, 2, 73, 77, A224857, 41) #73, 77
....drLD(x, 60, 9, 53, 67, A224857, 41) #53,67
....drLD(x, 90, 6, 7, 83, A224857, 41) #7,83

61 = A202113
....drLD(x, 28, -1, 61, 91, A224860, 61) #61,91
....drLD(x, 82, 8, 19, 79, A224860, 61) #19,79
....drLD(x, 100, 27, 37, 43, A224860, 61) #37,43)
....drLD(x, 100, 15, 7, 73, A224860, 61) #7,73
....drLD(x, 98, 16, 11, 71, A224860, 61) #11,71
....drLD(x, 62, 0, 29, 89, A224860, 61) #29,89
....drLD(x, 80, 17, 47, 53, A224860, 61) #47,53
....drLD(x, 80, 5, 17, 83, A224860, 61) #17,83
....drLD(x, 100, 19, 13, 67, A224860, 61) #13,67
....drLD(x, 118, 38, 31, 31, A224860, 61) #31,31
....drLD(x, 82, 18, 49, 49, A224860, 61) #49,49
....drLD(x, 80, 9, 23, 77, A224860, 61) #23,77
....drLD(x, 98, 26, 41, 41, A224860, 61) #41,41
....drLD(x, 62, 10, 59, 59, A224860, 61) #59,59

\# 59 = A202101
....drLD(x, 30, -1, 59, 91, A224860, 59) #59,91
....drLD(x, 120, 38, 19, 41, A224860, 59) #19,41
....drLD(x, 66, 7, 37, 77, A224860, 59) #37,77
....drLD(x, 84, 12, 23, 73, A224860, 59) #23,73
....drLD(x, 90, 9, 11, 79, A224860, 59) #11,79
....drLD(x, 90, 19, 29, 61, A224860, 59) #29,61
....drLD(x, 126, 39, 7, 47, A224860, 59) #7,47
....drLD(x, 54, 3, 43, 83, A224860, 59) #43,83
....drLD(x, 114, 31, 13, 53, A224860, 59) #13,53
....drLD(x, 60, 0, 31, 89, A224860, 59) #31,89
....drLD(x, 60, 8, 49, 71, A224860, 59) #49,71
....drLD(x, 96, 18, 17, 67, A224860, 59) #17,67

\# 73 = A195993
....drLD(x, 16, -1, 73, 91, A224862, 73) #73,91
....drLD(x, 124, 41, 19, 37, A224862, 73) #19,37
....drLD(x, 146, 58, 11, 23, A224862, 73) #11,23
....drLD(x, 74, 8, 29, 77, A224862, 73) #29,77
....drLD(x, 74, 14, 47, 59, A224862, 73) #47,59
....drLD(x, 56, 3, 41, 83, A224862, 73) #41,83
....drLD(x, 106, 24, 13, 61, A224862, 73) #13,61
....drLD(x, 106, 30, 31, 43, A224862, 73) #31,43
....drLD(x, 124, 37, 7, 49, A224862, 73) #7,49
....drLD(x, 34, 2, 67, 79, A224862, 73) #67,79
....drLD(x, 74, 0, 17, 89, A224862, 73) #17,89
....drLD(x, 56, 7, 53, 71, A224862, 73) #53,71

\# 71 = A202129
....drLD(x, 18, -1, 71, 91, A224862, 71) #71,91
....drLD(x, 72, 0, 19, 89, A224862, 71) #19,89
....drLD(x, 90, 21, 37, 53, A224862, 71) #37,53
....drLD(x, 90, 13, 17, 73, A224862, 71) #17,73
....drLD(x, 138, 51, 11, 31, A224862, 71) #11,31
....drLD(x, 102, 27, 29, 49, A224862, 71) #29,49
....drLD(x, 120, 36, 13, 47, A224862, 71) #13,47
....drLD(x, 30, 1, 67, 83, A224862, 71) #67,83
....drLD(x, 150, 61, 7, 23, A224862, 71) #7,23
....drLD(x, 78, 15, 41, 61, A224862, 71) #41,61
....drLD(x, 42, 3, 59, 79, A224862, 71) #59,79
....drLD(x, 60, 6, 43, 77, A224862, 71) #43,77

```python
primelist_A224854 = [i for i,x in enumerate(A224854) if x == 0]
print("A224854", primelist_A224854)
print("A224854", len(primelist_A224854))

primelist_A224855 = [i for i,x in enumerate(A224855) if x == 0]
print("A224855", primelist_A224855)
print("A224855", len(primelist_A224855))

primelist_A224856 = [i for i,x in enumerate(A224856) if x == 0]
print("A224856", primelist_A224856)
print("A224856", len(primelist_A224856))

primelist_A224857 = [i for i,x in enumerate(A224857) if x == 0]
print("A224857", primelist_A224857)
print("A224857", len(primelist_A224857))

primelist_A224859 = [i for i,x in enumerate(A224859) if x == 0]
print("A224859", primelist_A224859)
print("A224859", len(primelist_A224859))

primelist_A224860 = [i for i,x in enumerate(A224860) if x == 0]
print("A224860", primelist_A224860)
print("A224860", len(primelist_A224860))

primelist_A224862 = [i for i,x in enumerate(A224862) if x == 0]
print("A224862", primelist_A224862)
print("A224862", len(primelist_A224862))

primelist_A224864 = [i for i,x in enumerate(A224864) if x == 0]
print("A224864", primelist_A224864)
print("A224864", len(primelist_A224864))

primelist_A224865 = [i for i,x in enumerate(A224865) if x == 0]
print("A224865", primelist_A224865)
print("A224865", len(primelist_A224865))

############### END PYTHON CODE ##############
```

CHAPTER 15

######## MARSHALL ########

Alexis woke up facing Jeremiah. She studied the sleeping man and determined he looked angelic, perfect. She felt safe with him near. It was a feeling unlike any she had previously known. *"Another firstness?"* she wondered to herself. She moved closer to him and watched his body rise and fall in sync with his breath. She was sad that she fell asleep; she originally wanted to make out with him and possibly have sex. She felt a need to bond with him. To seal the relationship.

PDC was thankful she had fallen asleep. While certain parts of him definitely wanted to have sex with her, his brain feared doing so could jeopardize their future. So when she started lightly snoring he breathed a sigh of relief and passed out. In his dream he found himself flying over a desert. He saw Maxwell loading a bunch of gear into a shipping container. It appeared that he was preparing to depart from some place. He looked exhausted, desiccated. He was concerned for his friend.

Marshall was up before dawn and made a pot of coffee. He used his time alone to research his motorcycle. He watched several videos of people riding and the various conditions it could handle."Best bike to learn on. Seems legit," he said to the empty room.

Happy entered the kitchen and laid down by the doorway. X followed him in, yawing and stretching. She was wearing grey sweatpants and a tanktop. She noticed Marshall sitting at the kitchen island and she made her way toward him by sliding along the floor in her socks.

"Thanks for brewing this," X said to Marshall as she poured a cup. "You really make a killer cuppa Joe."

"I have some decent beans and some ginseng powder and other ingredients that play well with coffee and I like the art of flavor. The 'mind art' of taste. It takes, like, 10% extra effort to go from average to excellent flavor. All about the details. Speaking of details, I located the dealership and it is not too far from here. There is a station on the way so lets stop there and I will get you topped off. I guess after that we will be parting company," Marshall said with a tinge of sadness in his voice. "Though I don't think our quest is actually over yet. There is still more to do."

"Yeah I am not sure we can outdo whatever the fuck this trip was," X said groggily. "You did it. You got me wasted on excess. You took me there whether I wanted it or not. In some ways it will be hard to go back to living a normal life."

"This is your normal life," Marshall said. "Embrace it."

X stared at Marshall. She felt the confidence radiating from him. In a way he made it almost seem true. "Yeah, well, I don't even play venues this big let alone hang out in houses like this. I mean you just teleported us into God-tier extravagance. I have ripped linoleum on my kitchen floor. My living room is smaller than the hallway bathroom. My entire floor plan is probably smaller than that master bedroom. How could our quest continue like this? It would be like living in a movie or something."

"Resistance is futile," Marshall said in a very serious tone. "You are living in a movie no matter what you do. I mean, you can live in a movie that consists of small walls. It is your choice. Unless it isn't your choice at all, but rather the universe choosing for you. You had no power over being here and yet it is entirely as a result of departing from your normal routine. You are in a chain of events that are linked before they happen. Some futures are inevitable." A timer went off. "Ah! The quiche is ready!"

"Quiche!" X exclaimed. "No way!"

"Yahweh!" Marshall replied.

"My way!" said PDC as he entered the room and headed for the coffee. Alexis wanted to freshen up after all the crying and would join them later.

"That bike looks perfect," Marshall said. "I do feel anxious about it. Tense."

PDC came up and grabbed Marshall by the shoulders to give him a massage and for the first time realized his lack of mass. "You will do fine," he said, releasing him. "It is about finesse and mastered ultra instinct. You must become part of the machine and not try to dominate it. You will maybe tip it over a few times. Don't worry about it. Like, literally don't worry about it. This is for learning. Once you get the hang of this you can go anywhere on the planet. Almost."

After Alexis joined them they ate breakfast and then gathered together at the front door with their bags.

"Okay. Let's do this!" Marshall commanded and instinctively everyone responded.

PDC drove off first, followed by the X. After they filled up at a station they drove for several minutes and pulled into the dealership.

PDC did not wait for anyone to exit the van and walked in to make sure the bike was still there. It was. Marshall went to the clothing section with X and Alexis. "This is insanely expensive stuff," Alexis said.

"Yeah, but it is designed to protect you in the event of a catastrophic failure. The armor has airbags in it to help save you from some damage. But it is still crazy to think about driving next to a semi on a flying bicycle. The one that he is getting now has a smaller motor than your scooter. But it is a water-cooled engine designed for high performance. So there are some important differences."

"I have just never imagined being able to afford anything like this," Alexis replied. "I cannot relate to having money."

"You do relate to having money. You do relate to having expensive things. They are not excluded and in fact they are required. Your destiny is to do the work. All of it. But you already have it and it already happened."

Alexis looked at him. She was both angry and hopeful. She didn't understand. Could she really believe what he was saying?

Marshall continued, "You want to doubt it because believing in things can make you vulnerable to disappointment. But you don't need to believe in a thing for it to be real. So do not think about whether it is real or not, because that is not in your control. It is already real and it is already here, but your work must still be done. And so do the work and nothing else."

PDC walked up and interrupted their conversation. "Okay, we are all set. They are putting new tires on both bikes and I am getting us extra gear so we have some water proof storage. There is a guy back there who will walk you through the clothing options and I asked him to show you my recommendations first and then proceed to show you the alternatives."

"Bad ass," Marshall said. "This is intense. And for me, that's saying something."

As Marshall was being fitted Jeremiah asked Alexis to walk with him.

"I spent some time writing a letter to you and explaining about where things are in the house and some odds and ends. Marshall's contact information is also included. X knows pretty much everything there is to know about the house and I have asked her to take care of paying the bills and other things for me until I get back."

"I can do that," Alexis protested.

"Well, I actually hoped you would say that. But I didn't want you to feel responsible for any of that unless you wanted it. So, in this envelope is a list of all the services and the accounts and things. I have also put in some cash. But, the one request I have is that you don't open it until you get there. That you open it while sitting at the dining room table. And after that I won't have another request of you. Use as much space as you need for painting. Seriously. And the walls are drywall so if you want to put nails in them there shouldn't be much of an issue. Just do it!"

The joy Alexis felt almost brought her to tears. "You don't need to be this nice. I mean, I am staying in your home and you have the right to ask me to help you out."

"I'm not being nice," Jeremiah said. "I am being selfish. I want to take care of you and offer you a bill free life, for as long as it lasts. But it isn't because I am nice. I am investing in you, in us. I am placing a bet on our future together. And my first move is to set you free. Only then will you really know what your options are. After that, if you still want to be with me once you have found your stride, it will mean even more. I think you are worth it."

Alexis was not familiar with being prized. No man in her life had shown her unconditional love or offered her anything even remotely similar to a bill free life. She hugged him and said in his ear, "I will be the best investment you ever make."

######## Dr. KEAL ########

It was not only the orientation and the specific nuclear specie of atoms involved. It was also geography of the brain. There was a pathway-locality dependency that meant the entire microtuble landscape was a surface for mapping meaning into consciousness. "We have generalized the targeting system as a box whose surfaces are subdivided into squares. Currently we use the magnetic induction to extinguish fear in our troops. We map the idea of fear to a specific region of the physical brain; we map fear extinction to another physical region of the brain. We were thinking of this as a data table of amplitudes and locations. Now think of the map of brain states as an attack surface. We have the entire surface of human consciousness to map, and once we map it we can recreate any outcome using entanglement to transmit nuclear spin information over an arbitrary distance. We are talking about complete non-invasive mind control."

The Generals understood the grievous nature of the technology they were unlocking. "How much of this surface have we mapped?"

"It is impossible currently to describe the precise limit, but based on what we are seeing the surface area is trillions of times larger than what we could possibly experience in a lifetime. Something like taking the time to examine every grain of sand on Earth. That is the POTENTIAL. But what we are doing now is filling in this map with what we understand. Things like chemical drugs which enter the bloodstream and incorporate themselves into consciousness BY DESIGN work as *antagonists*. They are *outsiders*. We have new modes of brain modification, but what we are finding is that rTMS is best for some learned behaviors that we want to impose versus the delivery of substances like drugs. We can combine these systems to produce the ultimate in warrior armor. Now, do not mistake me. It is likely that we will be able to transmit thoughts. But certainly we can currently deploy soldiers with specific hydration regimes and we could induce a change in them to send a primitive, Marconi-like one-way pulse signal. We have been testing and found that we have around a 95% success rate in self-reporting when the drug affects are felt."

"We have this ready for the field now?" a General asked.

"We have it in testing phase. We have some good results. I can't guarantee any kind of field success with the technology as it stands presently. Testing is too shallow to give meaningful reliability estimates."

A General stroked his chin. "This would need to be a Special Access clearance officer carrying out this duty. How soon can we deploy to our ships. We can work with you to escalate the tests."

Dr. Keal was nervous. He understood leaks. "With all due respect General Thompson, this information is currently compartmentalized. Extending this to active duty personnel at this time exposes us to tremendous risk. It is the human component that will fail, every time. Allow a little more development runway so we can get a true edge. Why send a loud analogue signal when we can build an actual targeting system that will allow you to achieve Godvoice."

"The God Voice?" a General asked.

A man in a black suit spoke, "Some of you might remember Godvoice as part of Operation Warhammer that we ran on the caves in upper Afghanistan. As part of that campaign there was an active project where we deployed microwave canons that would hit a target and generate sound in the minds of adversaries. It was one of the most effective weapons ever used for demoralization and so we only deployed it a few times for testing. We hold that weapon in reserve. It is that reserve of weapons into which elements of this project are being folded. We recognize the absolute need for you to have this tool for establishing secure channels of communication. So, Project Mind Pixel will be responsible for developing the targeting system and we will not interfere with that aside from compartmentalization management. So, what will our part in this look like? We will be working with you to manage the library of pointers. For the purposes stated in your objectives, the modification of mental states to optimize force psychology and establish secure communication channels, we want you to succeed. But, this project is considered National Security level 0 so it is all going underground. This meeting cannot be discussed and all of us moving forward should consider ourselves fully saturated. By our assessment of current operational demands we won't need Mind Pixel technology in any of our pending military operations. During the testing phase you guys will manage the target surface specifications and discovery. We will then assess the tools as they emerge and work with you to integrate the ones required for comms and management."

Dr. Keal knew James Jenner. When he started Operation Mind Pixel he was aware of the possibility that he might get involved. But the fact it had been escalated to NS_0 meant that everyone associated with the project was now an asset of the security state. His life would be saturated with monitoring. He was no longer a free man.

James looked over at Dr. Keal and saw the look of ashen terror on the doctor's face. He smiled. "My reputation precedes me. I can assure you all that I am not here to conduct an allegiance survey or compel sworn testimony. I am here as a friend of America. We are human and are therefore fallible. It is our collective responsibility to ensure that from this day forward there is no discussion of this technology outside our allowed portals. I know for you Jordan that this is the most difficult issue, because you are a leader in a for-profit venture that is currently marketing an adjacent technology. Do any of your staff know about this?"

"Off the record?" Dr. Keal asked on behalf of everyone in the room.

"Off the record," James responded with a grin that showed his teeth.

"No one knows. Now, that being said, I must admit that I have done compartmentalized tests using rTMS in an effort to manipulate spin on the atomic level, but have not been successful. And I had some junior engineering staff attempting to scale down our technique. Aside from that all my interactions have been with the team assembled here and my lab at the Institute. Once we got the data from SkyKing we were able to build a model. And we have been improving it using what I know about the underlying mechanics."

"Projects with a single point of failure are exceedingly rare in the modern age," James replied.

"There is a wave on inevitability that sweeps over consciousness when it comes to the laws of physics," Dr. Keal replied. "I can't tell you why the universe decided to give us a head start. But I know I am extremely glad it did. And so long as we have an advantage we must press it. But, precisely because at its core it is a relatively trivial technology to deploy, we must go as fast as possible toward the goal of building the targeting system. Once we have the correct model for modifying consciousness via nuclear spin we will have the end of power."

"What do you mean, the end of power?"

"The goal of power is to achieve power. Once you have achieved absolute power you have achieved the end."

BOOKS BY THIS AUTHOR

Maxwell Pragmatic And The Theory Of Quantum Relativity

Book Two in the continuing sage of Maxwell Pragmatic.

Vestnik Akademiia

Book One in the continuing sage of Maxwell Pragmatic.

Made in United States
Cleveland, OH
10 January 2025